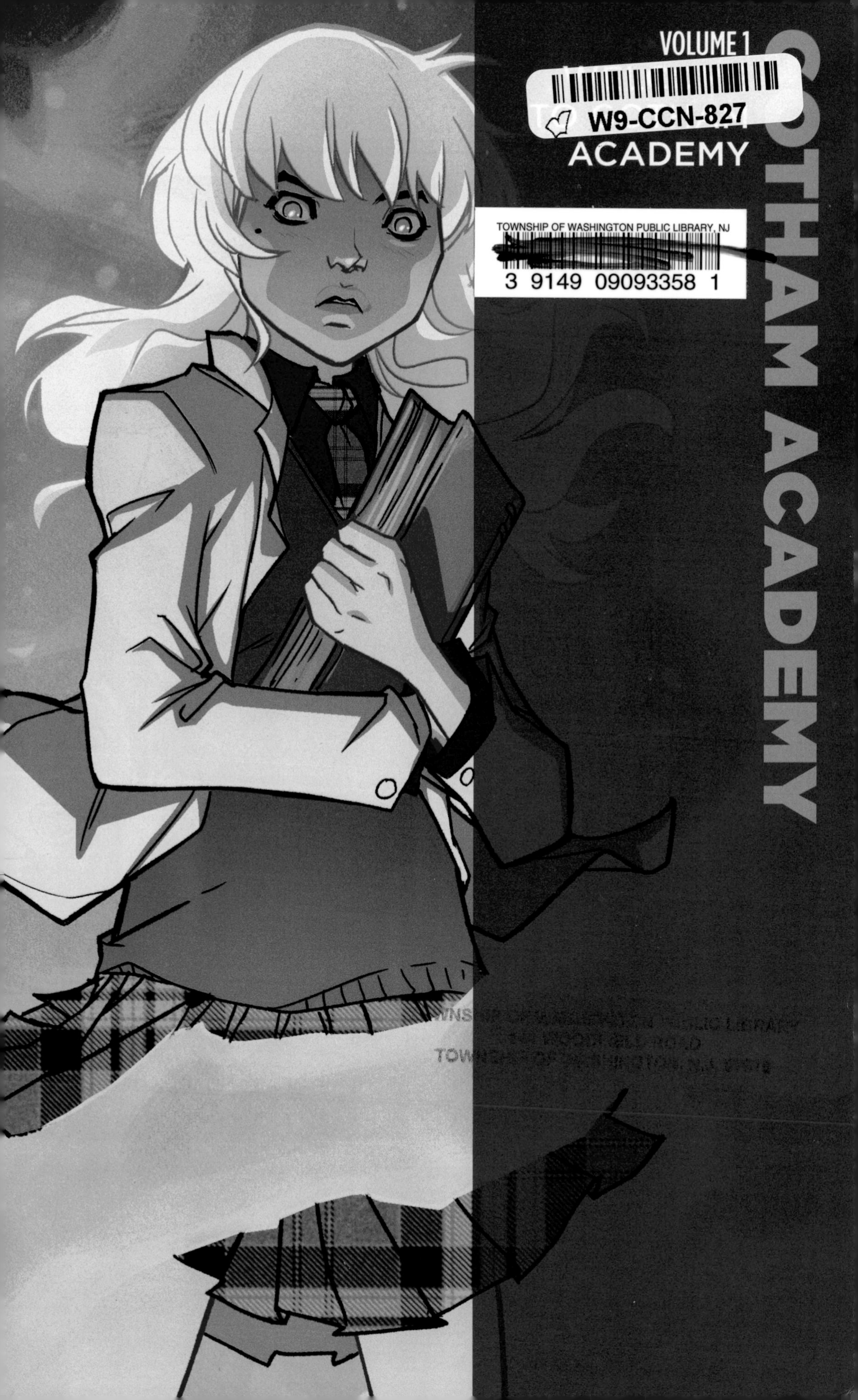
VOLUME 1
ACADEMY
GOTHAM ACADEMY

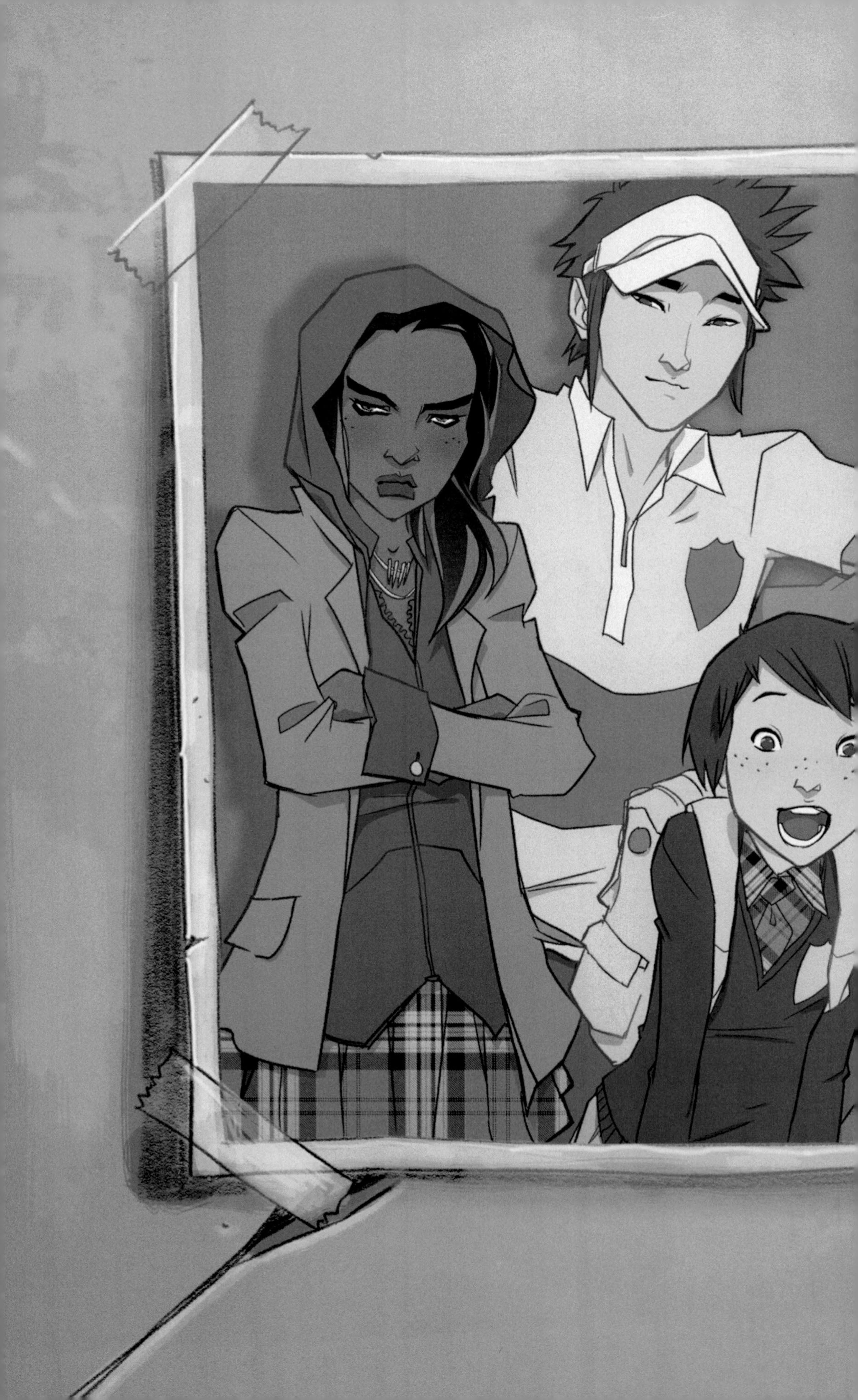

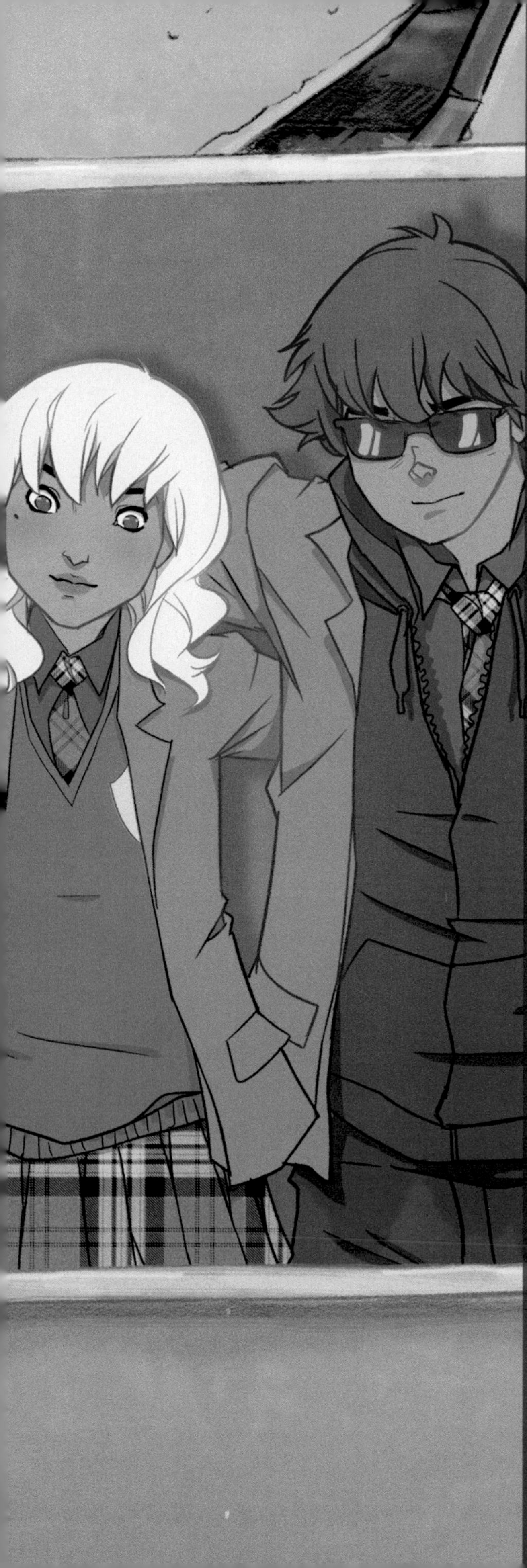

# GOTHAM ACADEMY

VOLUME 1

## WELCOME TO GOTHAM ACADEMY


WRITTEN BY
**BECKY CLOONAN**
**BRENDEN FLETCHER**

ART BY
**KARL KERSCHL**

EPILOGUE AND
ARKHAM FLASHBACK ART BY
**MINGJUE HELEN CHEN**

COLOR BY
**GEYSER**
**DAVE McCAIG**
**JOHN RAUCH**
**MSASSYK**
**SERGE LAPOINTE**
**MINGJUE HELEN CHEN**

LETTERS BY
**STEVE WANDS**

COLLECTION COVER ART BY
**KARL KERSCHL**

ORIGINAL SERIES COVER ART BY
**KARL KERSCHL**
**BECKY CLOONAN**

BATMAN CREATED BY
**BOB KANE**

MARK DOYLE Editor – Original Series
MATT HUMPHREYS Assistant Editor – Original Series
ROBIN WILDMAN Editor
ROBBIN BROSTERMAN Design Director – Books
CURTIS KING JR. Publication Design

BOB HARRAS Senior VP – Editor-in-Chief, DC Comics

DIANE NELSON President
DAN DIDIO and JIM LEE Co-Publishers
GEOFF JOHNS Chief Creative Officer
AMIT DESAI Senior VP – Marketing & Franchise Management
AMY GENKINS Senior VP – Business & Legal Affairs
NAIRI GARDINER Senior VP – Finance
JEFF BOISON VP – Publishing Planning
MARK CHIARELLO VP – Art Direction & Design
JOHN CUNNINGHAM VP – Marketing
TERRI CUNNINGHAM VP – Editorial Administration
LARRY GANEM VP – Talent Relations & Services
ALISON GILL Senior VP – Manufacturing & Operations
HANK KANALZ Senior VP – Vertigo & Integrated Publishing
JAY KOGAN VP – Business & Legal Affairs, Publishing
JACK MAHAN VP – Business Affairs, Talent
NICK NAPOLITANO VP – Manufacturing Administration
SUE POHJA VP – Book Sales
FRED RUIZ VP – Manufacturing Operations
COURTNEY SIMMONS Senior VP – Publicity
BOB WAYNE Senior VP – Sales

GOTHAM ACADEMY VOL. 1: WELCOME TO GOTHAM ACADEMY

DC Comics, 4000 Warner Blvd., Burbank, CA 91522
A Warner Bros. Entertainment Company
Printed by RR Donnelley, Owensville, MO, USA. 5/15/15.
ISBN: 978-1-4012-5472-8
First Printing.

Library of Congress Cataloging-in-Publication Data

Cloonan, Becky.
Gotham Academy. Volume 1, Welcome to Gotham Academy / Becky Cloonan,
Brenden Fletcher ; illustrated by Karl Kerschl.
    pages cm
ISBN 978-1-4012-5472-8 (paperback)
1. Graphic novels.  I. Fletcher, Brenden, illustrator. II. Kerschl, Karl, illustrator.
   III. Title. IV. Title: Welcome to Gotham Academy.
        PN6728.G64C57 2015
        741.5'973—dc23
                    2015007185

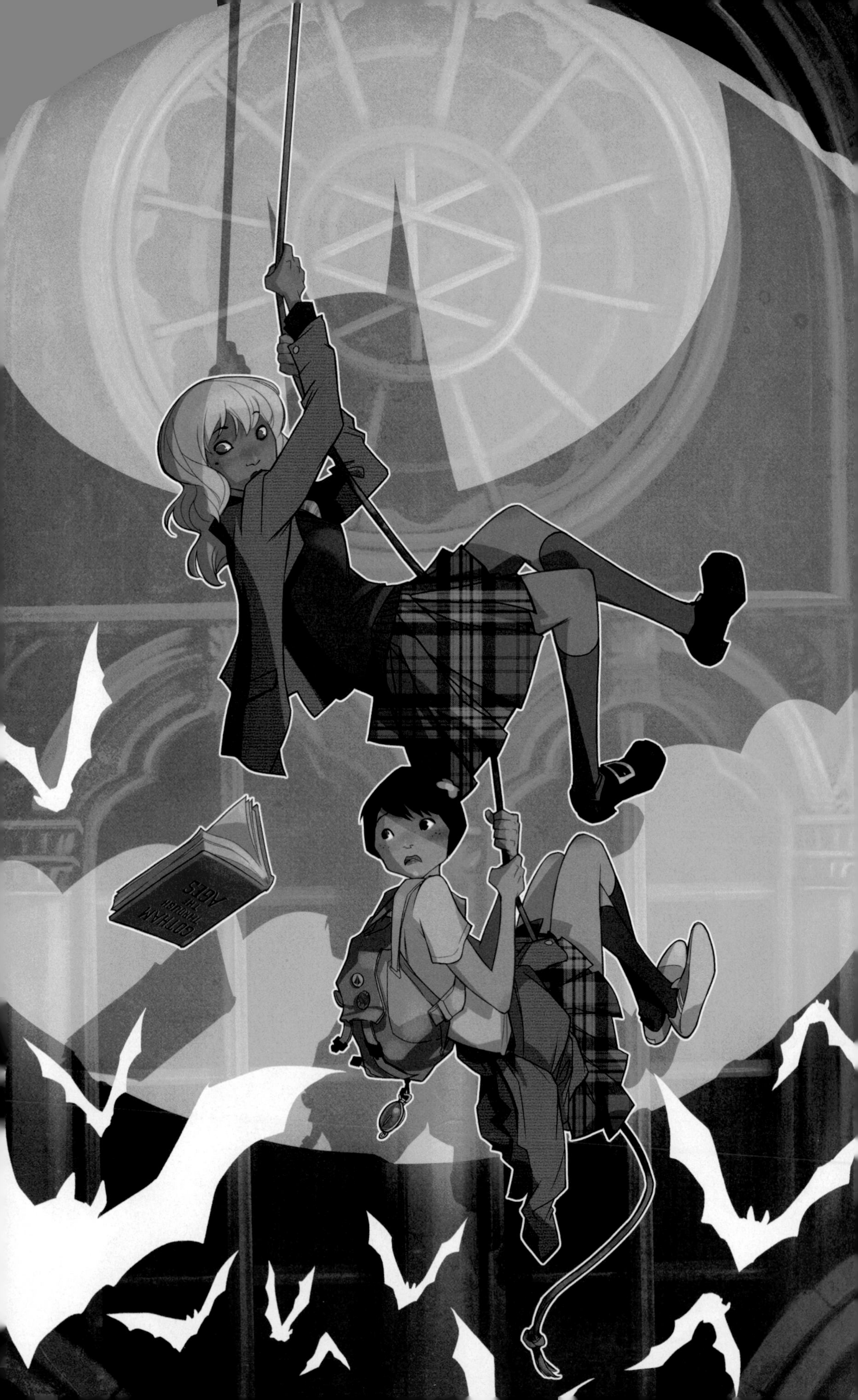
GOTHAM
THROUGH
THE
AGES

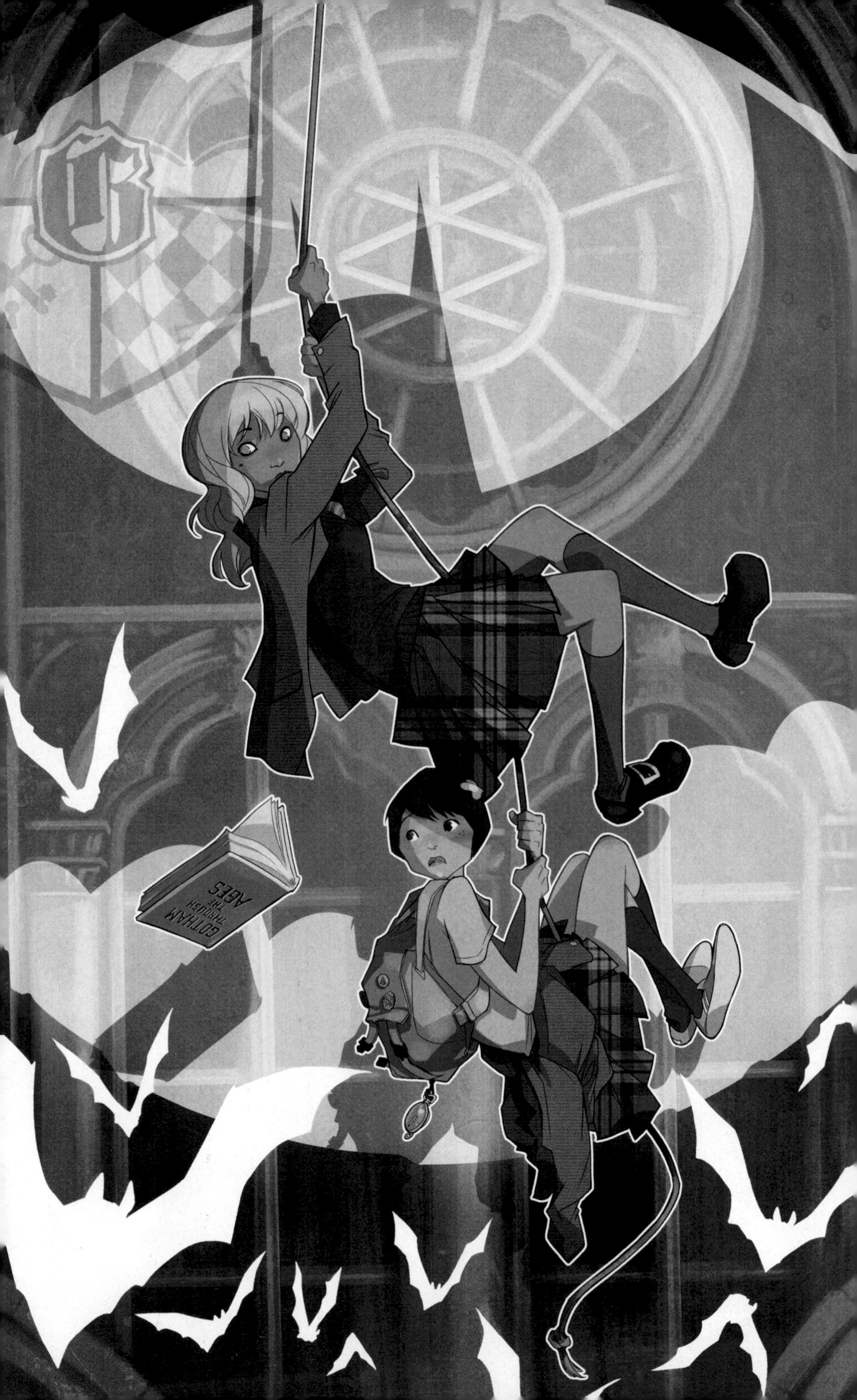
GOTHAM THROUGH THE AGES

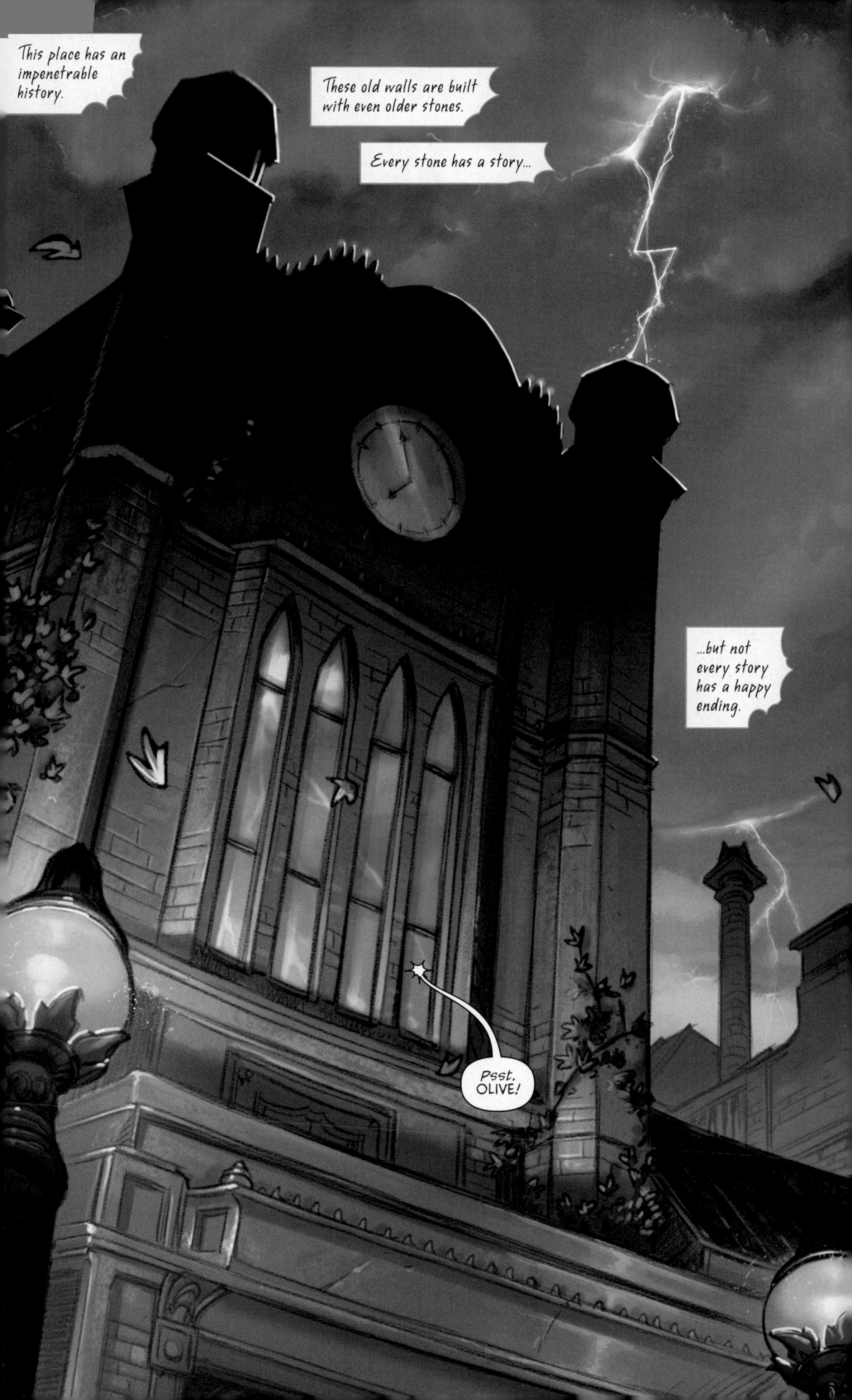
This place has an impenetrable history.
These old walls are built with even older stones.
Every stone has a story...
...but not every story has a happy ending.
Psst, OLIVE!

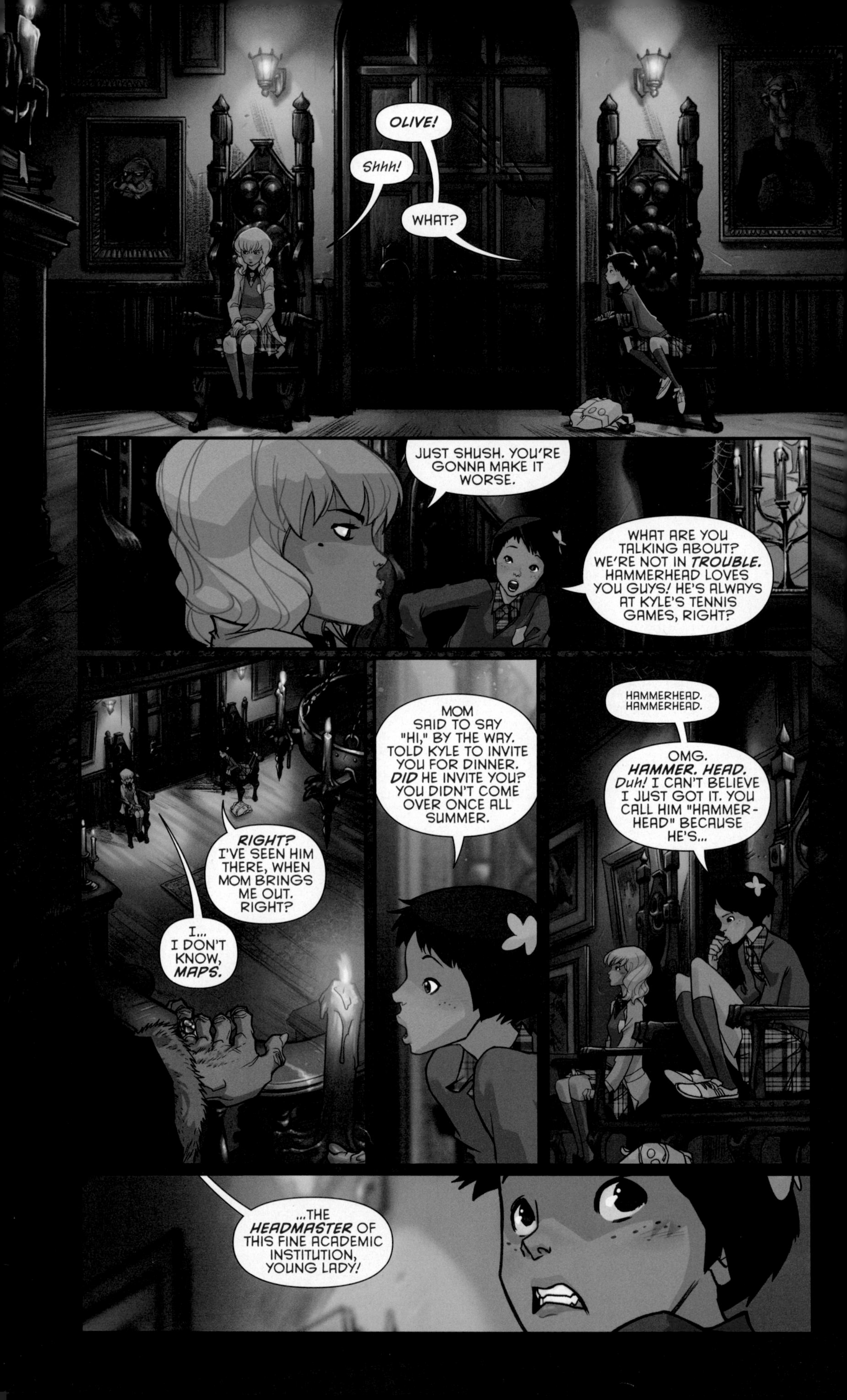
OLIVE!
Shhh!
WHAT?
JUST SHUSH. YOU'RE GONNA MAKE IT WORSE.
WHAT ARE YOU TALKING ABOUT? WE'RE NOT IN TROUBLE. HAMMERHEAD LOVES YOU GUYS! HE'S ALWAYS AT KYLE'S TENNIS GAMES, RIGHT?
RIGHT? I'VE SEEN HIM THERE, WHEN MOM BRINGS ME OUT. RIGHT?
I... I DON'T KNOW, MAPS.
MOM SAID TO SAY "HI," BY THE WAY. TOLD KYLE TO INVITE YOU FOR DINNER. DID HE INVITE YOU? YOU DIDN'T COME OVER ONCE ALL SUMMER.
HAMMERHEAD. HAMMERHEAD.
OMG. HAMMER. HEAD. Duh! I CAN'T BELIEVE I JUST GOT IT. YOU CALL HIM "HAMMER-HEAD" BECAUSE HE'S...
...THE HEADMASTER OF THIS FINE ACADEMIC INSTITUTION, YOUNG LADY!

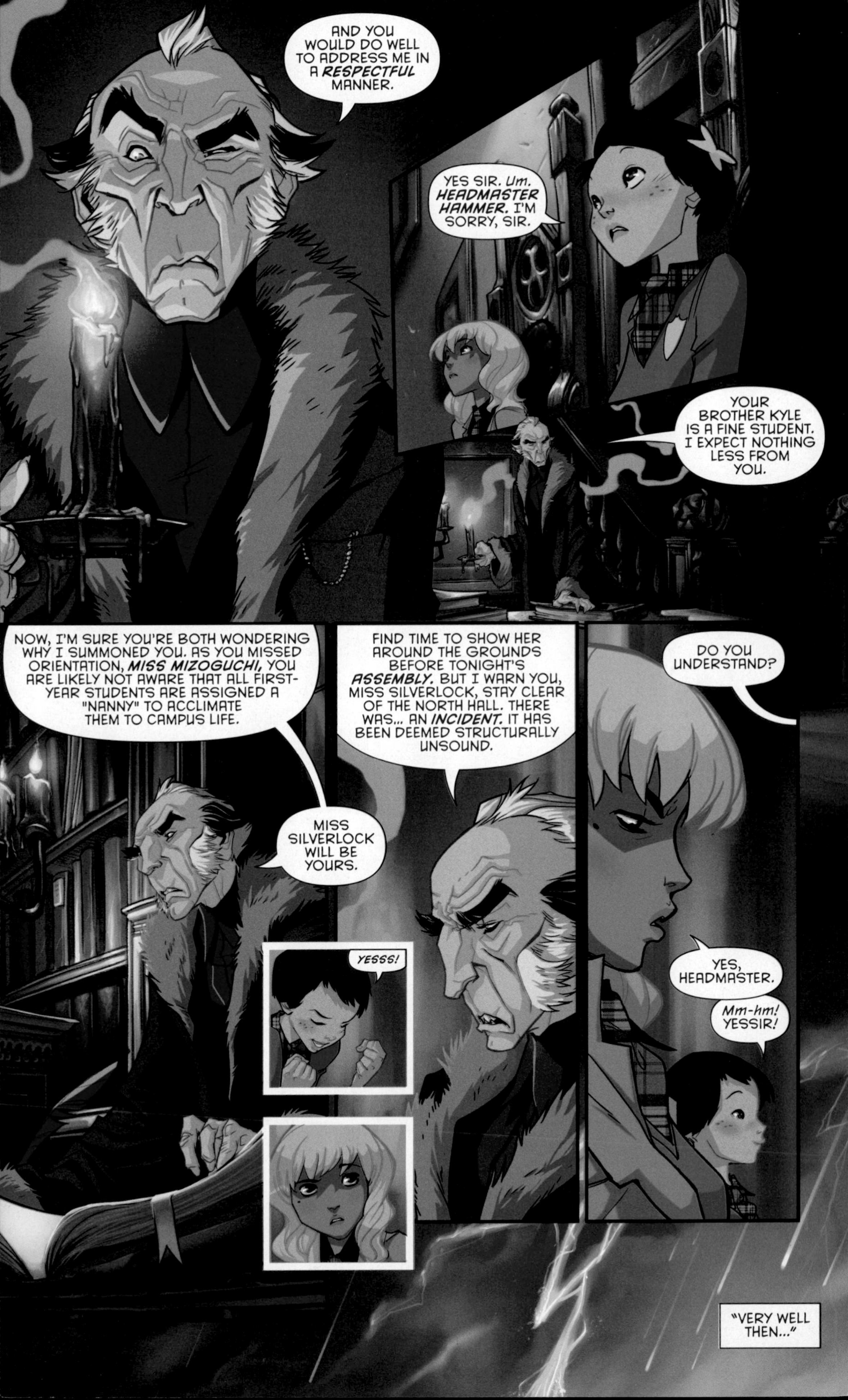
AND YOU WOULD DO WELL TO ADDRESS ME IN A RESPECTFUL MANNER.
YES SIR. Um. HEADMASTER HAMMER. I'M SORRY, SIR.
YOUR BROTHER KYLE IS A FINE STUDENT. I EXPECT NOTHING LESS FROM YOU.
NOW, I'M SURE YOU'RE BOTH WONDERING WHY I SUMMONED YOU. AS YOU MISSED ORIENTATION, MISS MIZOGUCHI, YOU ARE LIKELY NOT AWARE THAT ALL FIRST-YEAR STUDENTS ARE ASSIGNED A "NANNY" TO ACCLIMATE THEM TO CAMPUS LIFE.
MISS SILVERLOCK WILL BE YOURS.
YESSS!
FIND TIME TO SHOW HER AROUND THE GROUNDS BEFORE TONIGHT'S ASSEMBLY. BUT I WARN YOU, MISS SILVERLOCK, STAY CLEAR OF THE NORTH HALL. THERE WAS... AN INCIDENT. IT HAS BEEN DEEMED STRUCTURALLY UNSOUND.
DO YOU UNDERSTAND?
YES, HEADMASTER.
Mm-hm! YESSIR!
"VERY WELL THEN..."

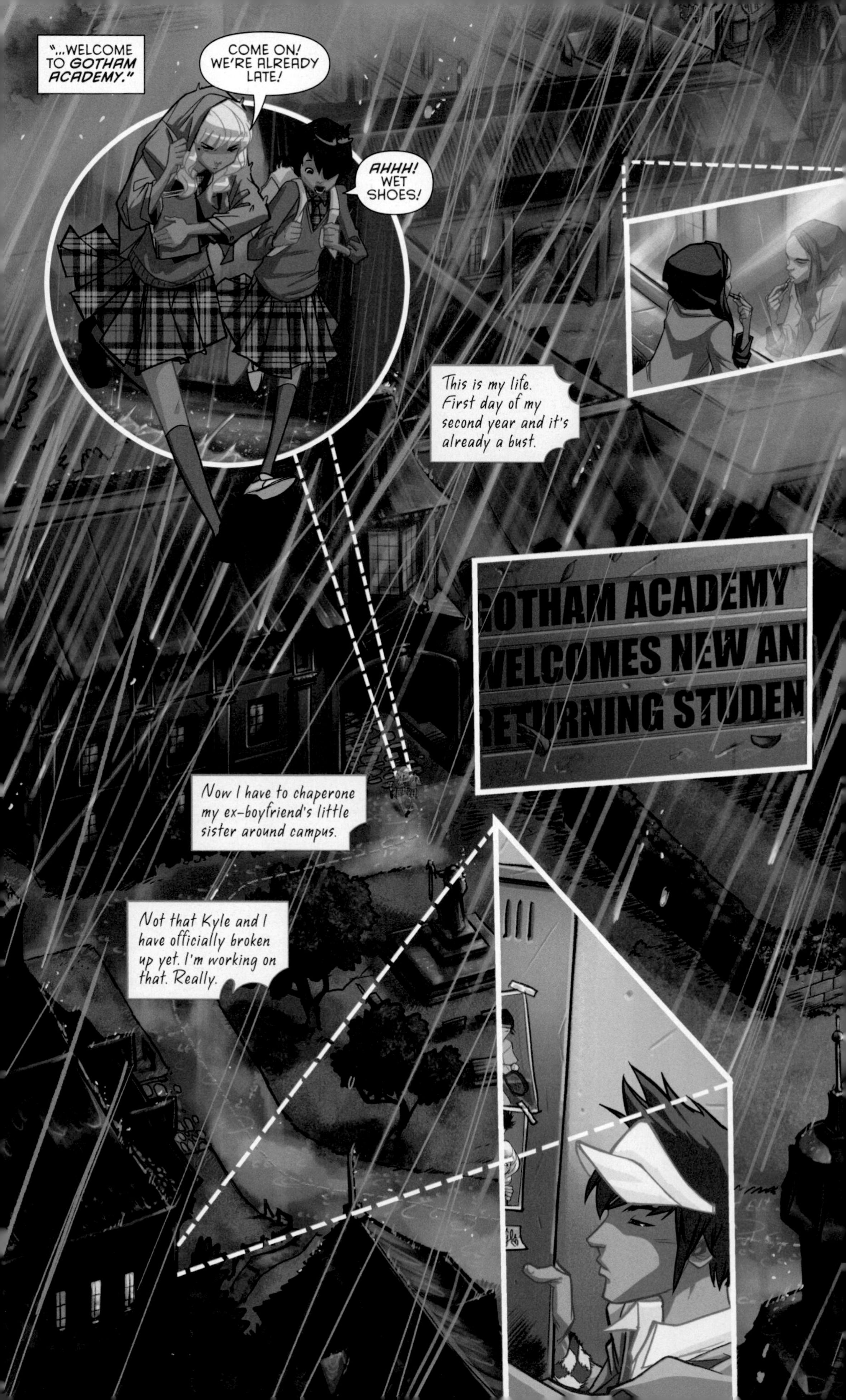
"...WELCOME TO GOTHAM ACADEMY."
COME ON! WE'RE ALREADY LATE!
AHHH! WET SHOES!
This is my life. First day of my second year and it's already a bust.
GOTHAM ACADEMY WELCOMES NEW AN RETURNING STUDEN
Now I have to chaperone my ex-boyfriend's little sister around campus.
Not that Kyle and I have officially broken up yet. I'm working on that. Really.

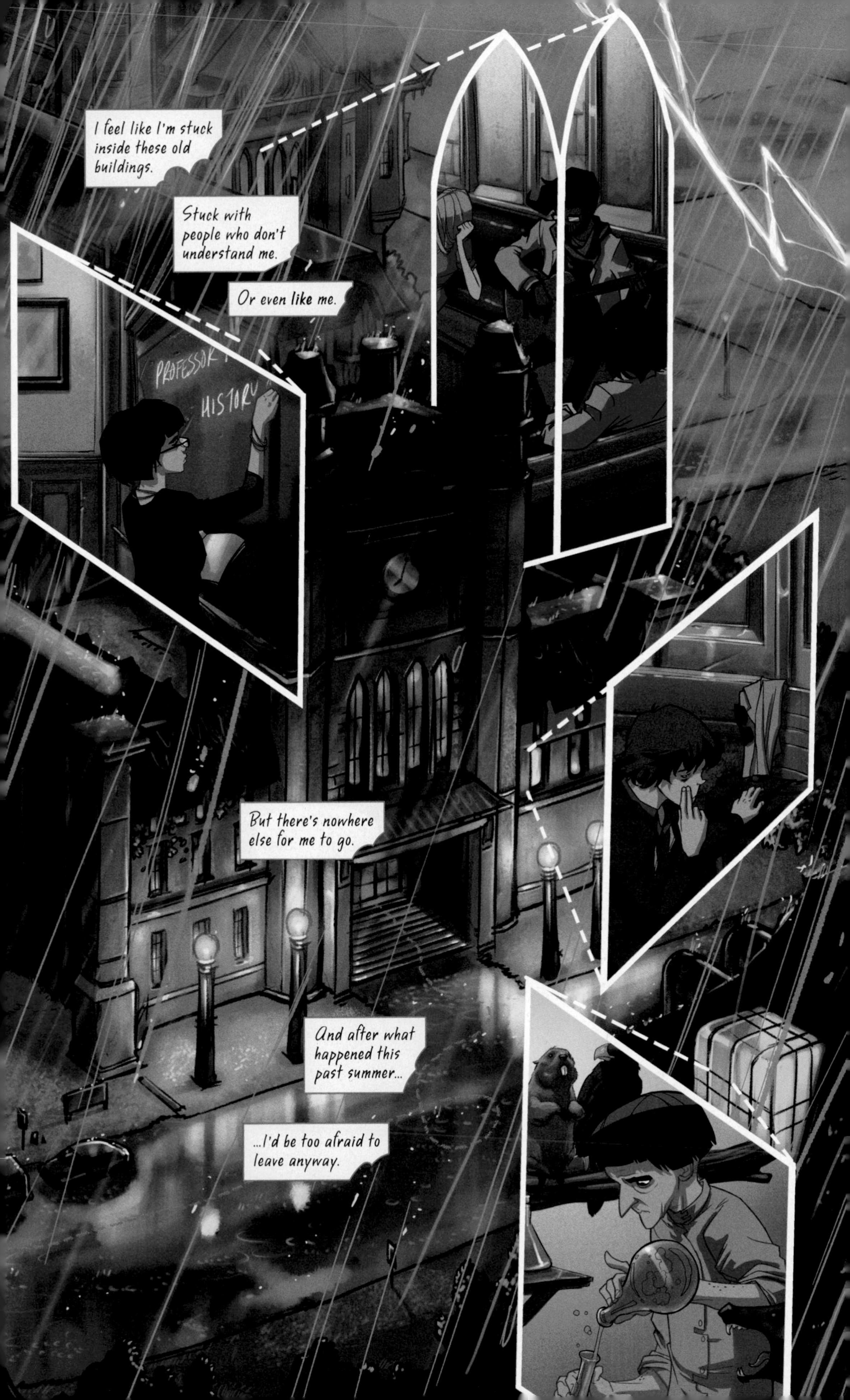
I feel like I'm stuck inside these old buildings.
Stuck with people who don't understand me.
Or even like me.
PROFESSOR
HISTORY
But there's nowhere else for me to go.
And after what happened this past summer...
...I'd be too afraid to leave anyway.

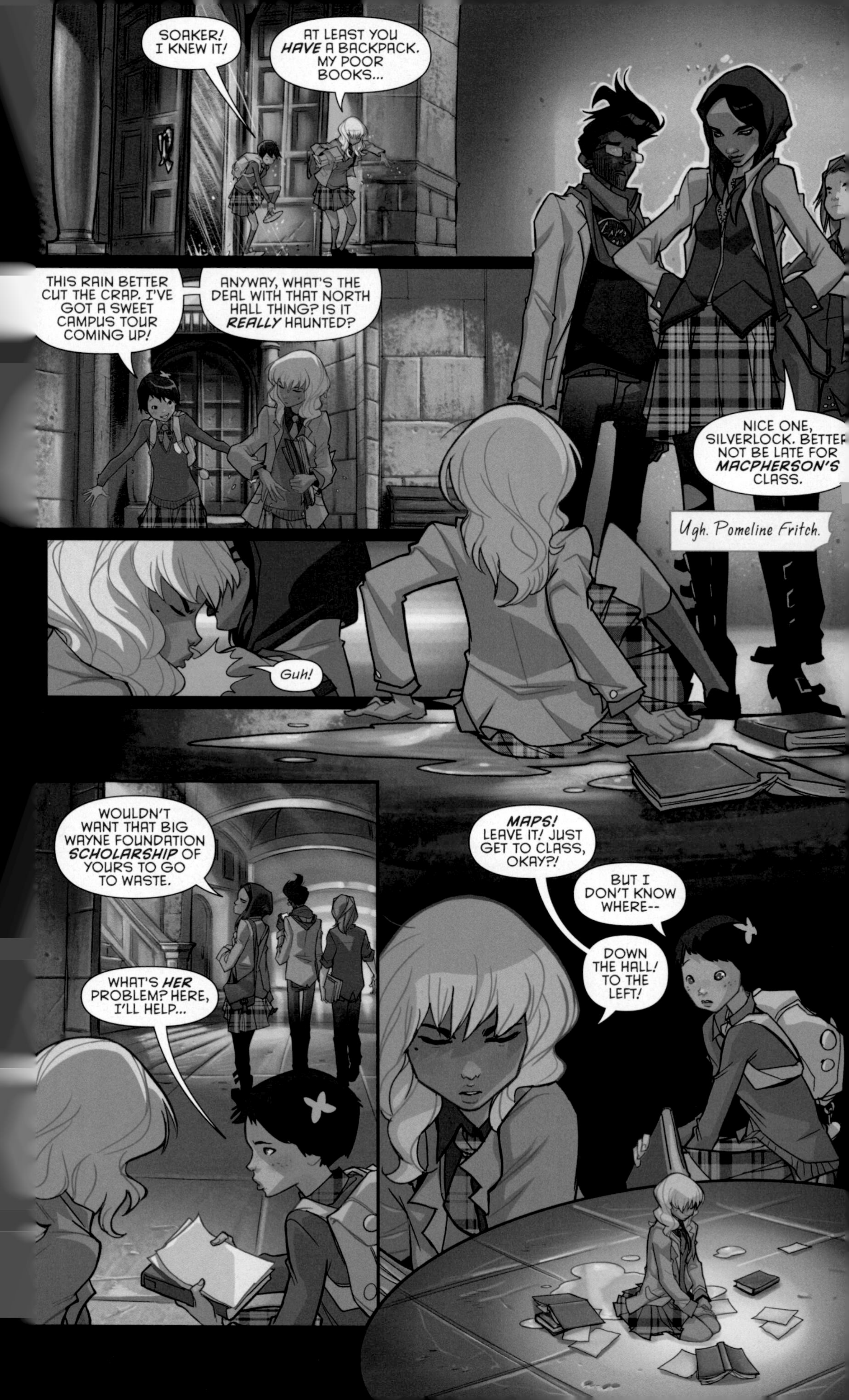
SOAKER! I KNEW IT!
AT LEAST YOU HAVE A BACKPACK. MY POOR BOOKS...
THIS RAIN BETTER CUT THE CRAP. I'VE GOT A SWEET CAMPUS TOUR COMING UP!
ANYWAY, WHAT'S THE DEAL WITH THAT NORTH HALL THING? IS IT REALLY HAUNTED?
Guh!
NICE ONE, SILVERLOCK. BETTER NOT BE LATE FOR MACPHERSON'S CLASS.
Ugh. Pomeline Fritch.
WOULDN'T WANT THAT BIG WAYNE FOUNDATION SCHOLARSHIP OF YOURS TO GO TO WASTE.
WHAT'S HER PROBLEM? HERE, I'LL HELP...
MAPS! LEAVE IT! JUST GET TO CLASS, OKAY?!
BUT I DON'T KNOW WHERE--
DOWN THE HALL! TO THE LEFT!

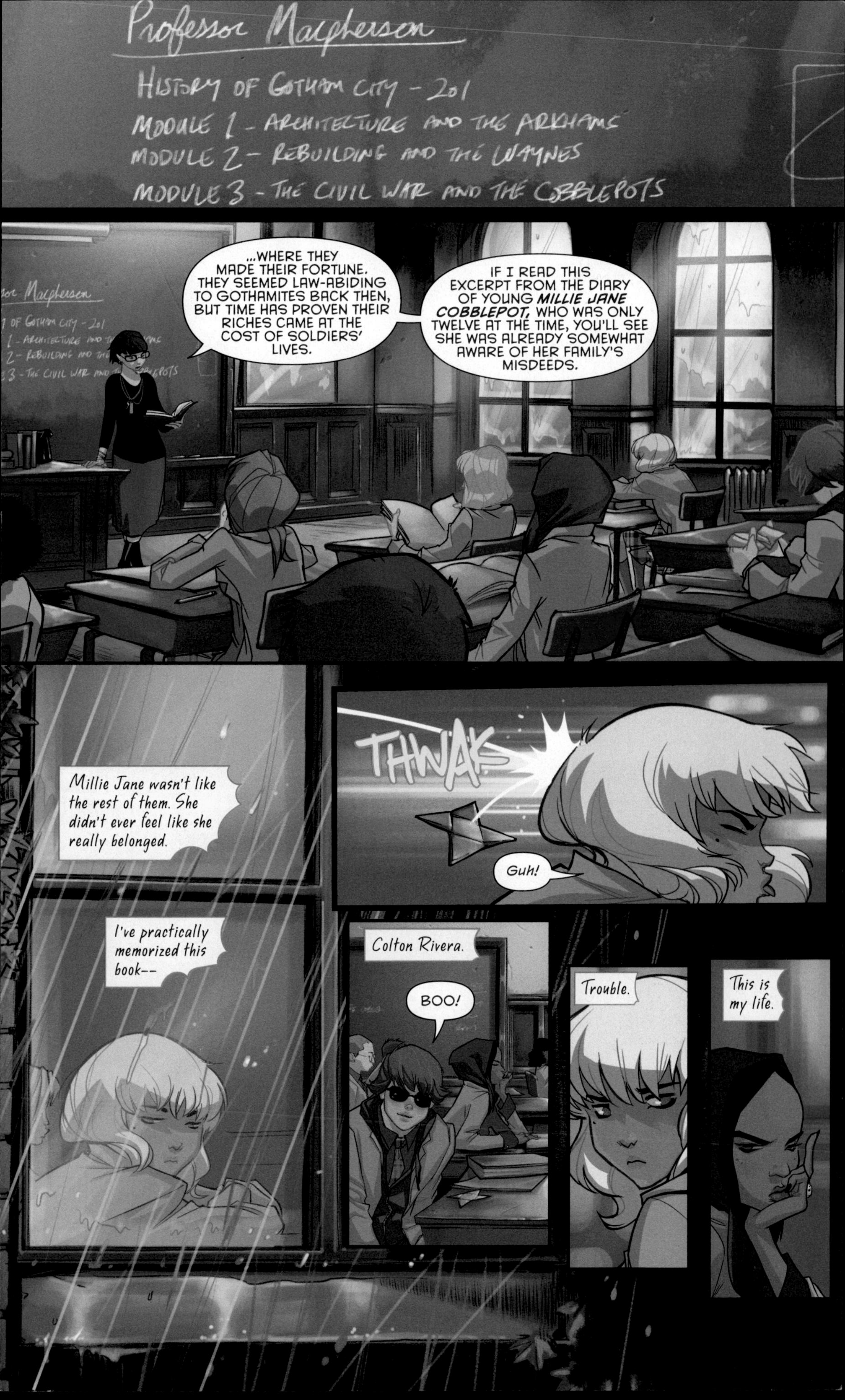
Professor Macpherson
HISTORY OF GOTHAM CITY - 201
MODULE 1 - ARCHITECTURE AND THE ARKHAMS
MODULE 2 - REBUILDING AND THE WAYNES
MODULE 3 - THE CIVIL WAR AND THE COBBLEPOTS
...WHERE THEY MADE THEIR FORTUNE. THEY SEEMED LAW-ABIDING TO GOTHAMITES BACK THEN, BUT TIME HAS PROVEN THEIR RICHES CAME AT THE COST OF SOLDIERS' LIVES.
IF I READ THIS EXCERPT FROM THE DIARY OF YOUNG MILLIE JANE COBBLEPOT, WHO WAS ONLY TWELVE AT THE TIME, YOU'LL SEE SHE WAS ALREADY SOMEWHAT AWARE OF HER FAMILY'S MISDEEDS.
Millie Jane wasn't like the rest of them. She didn't ever feel like she really belonged.
THWAK
Guh!
I've practically memorized this book--
Colton Rivera.
BOO!
Trouble.
This is my life.

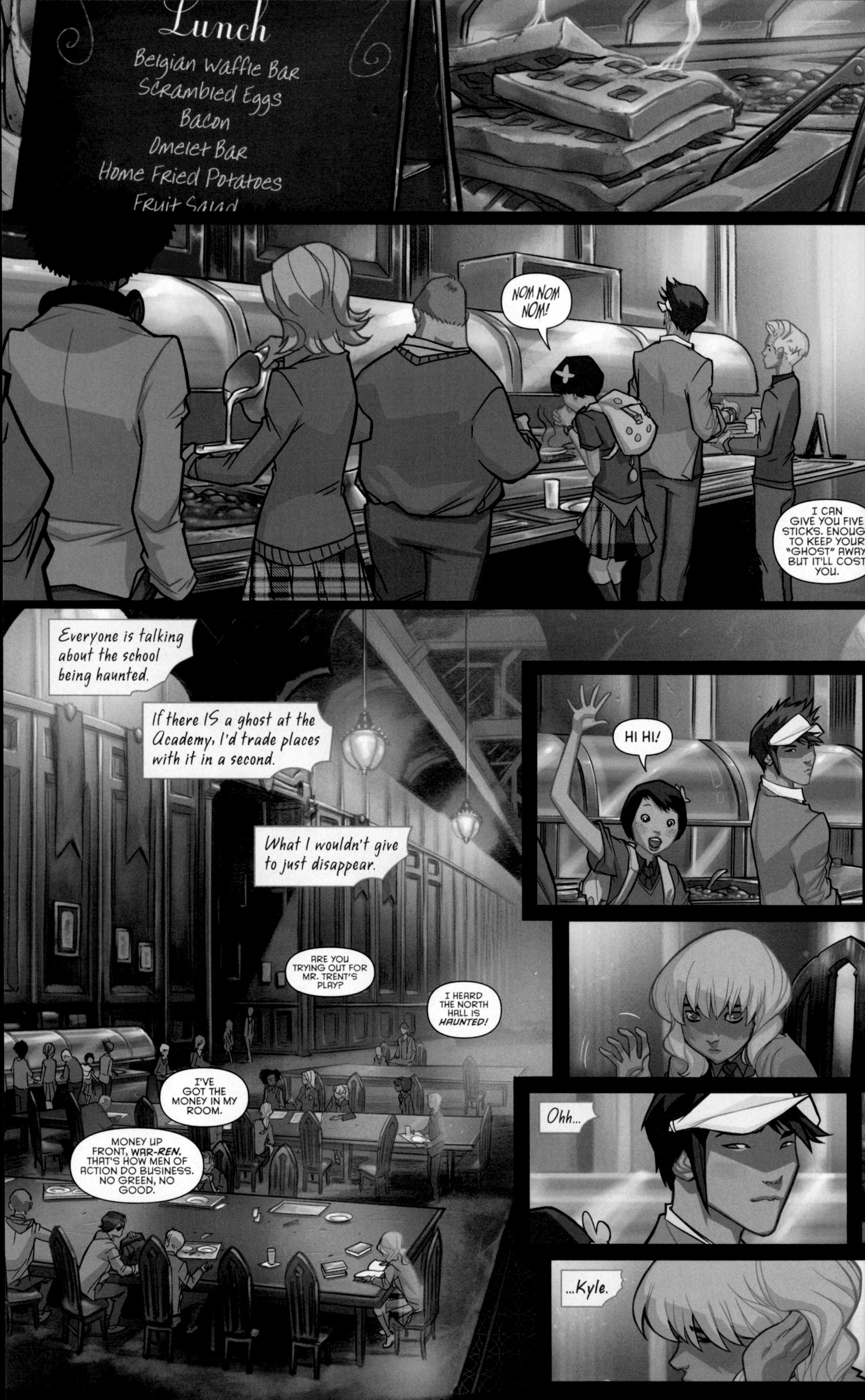
Lunch
Belgian Waffle Bar
Scrambled Eggs
Bacon
Omelet Bar
Home Fried Potatoes
Fruit Salad
NOM NOM NOM!
I CAN GIVE YOU FIVE STICKS. ENOUG TO KEEP YOUR "GHOST" AWAY BUT IT'LL COST YOU.
Everyone is talking about the school being haunted.
If there IS a ghost at the Academy, I'd trade places with it in a second.
What I wouldn't give to just disappear.
ARE YOU TRYING OUT FOR MR. TRENT'S PLAY?
I HEARD THE NORTH HALL IS HAUNTED!
I'VE GOT THE MONEY IN MY ROOM.
MONEY UP FRONT, WAR-REN. THAT'S HOW MEN OF ACTION DO BUSINESS. NO GREEN, NO GOOD.
HI HI!
Ohh...
...Kyle.

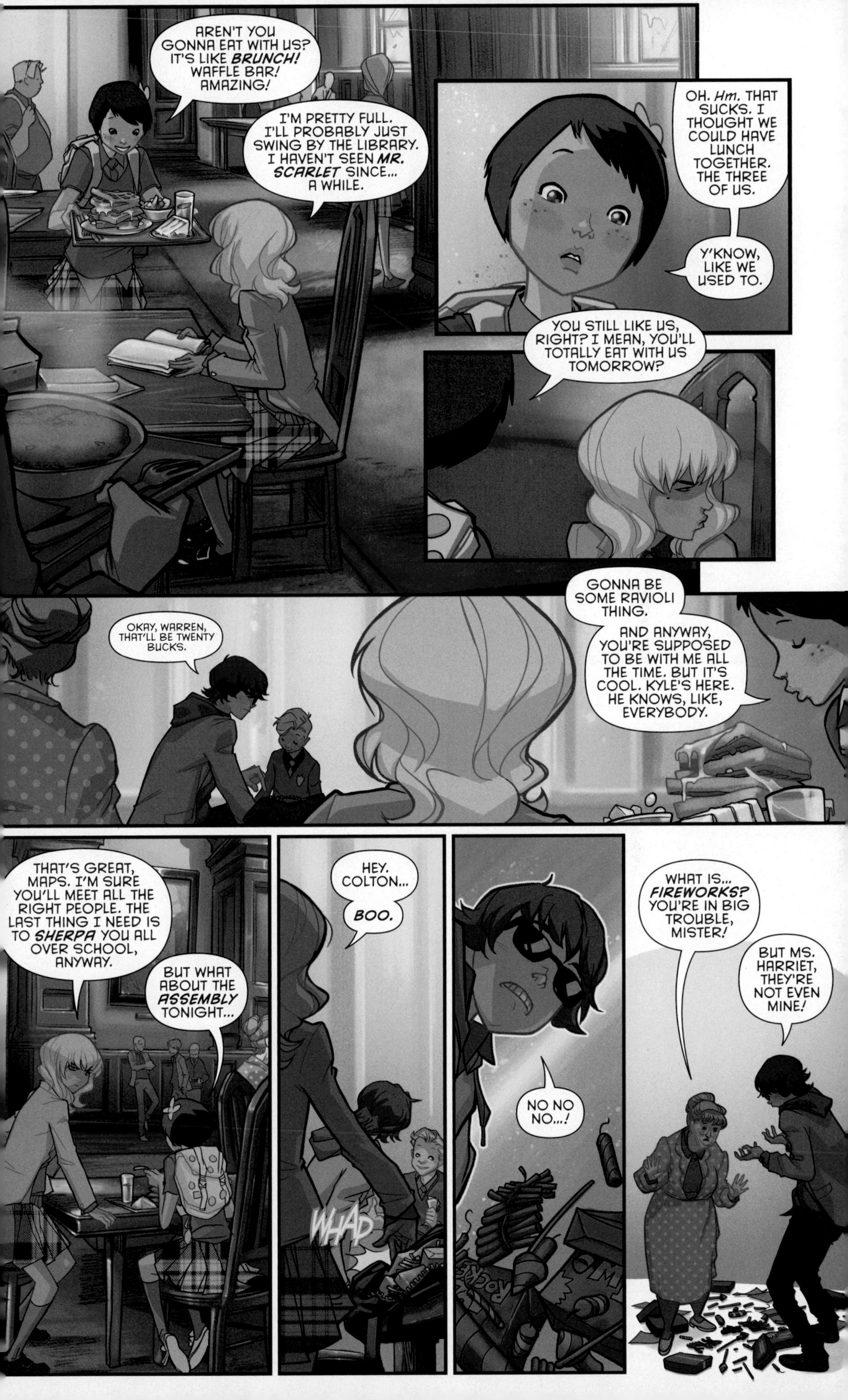
AREN'T YOU GONNA EAT WITH US? IT'S LIKE *BRUNCH!* WAFFLE BAR! AMAZING!
I'M PRETTY FULL. I'LL PROBABLY JUST SWING BY THE LIBRARY. I HAVEN'T SEEN *MR. SCARLET* SINCE... A WHILE.
OH. *Hm.* THAT SUCKS. I THOUGHT WE COULD HAVE LUNCH TOGETHER. THE THREE OF US.
Y'KNOW, LIKE WE USED TO.
YOU STILL LIKE US, RIGHT? I MEAN, YOU'LL TOTALLY EAT WITH US TOMORROW?
OKAY, WARREN, THAT'LL BE TWENTY BUCKS.
GONNA BE SOME RAVIOLI THING.
AND ANYWAY, YOU'RE SUPPOSED TO BE WITH ME ALL THE TIME. BUT IT'S COOL. KYLE'S HERE. HE KNOWS, LIKE, EVERYBODY.
THAT'S GREAT, MAPS. I'M SURE YOU'LL MEET ALL THE RIGHT PEOPLE. THE LAST THING I NEED IS TO *SHERPA* YOU ALL OVER SCHOOL, ANYWAY.
BUT WHAT ABOUT THE *ASSEMBLY* TONIGHT...
HEY. COLTON...
*BOO.*
WHAP
NO NO NO...!
WHAT IS... *FIREWORKS?* YOU'RE IN BIG TROUBLE, MISTER!
BUT MS. HARRIET, THEY'RE NOT EVEN MINE!

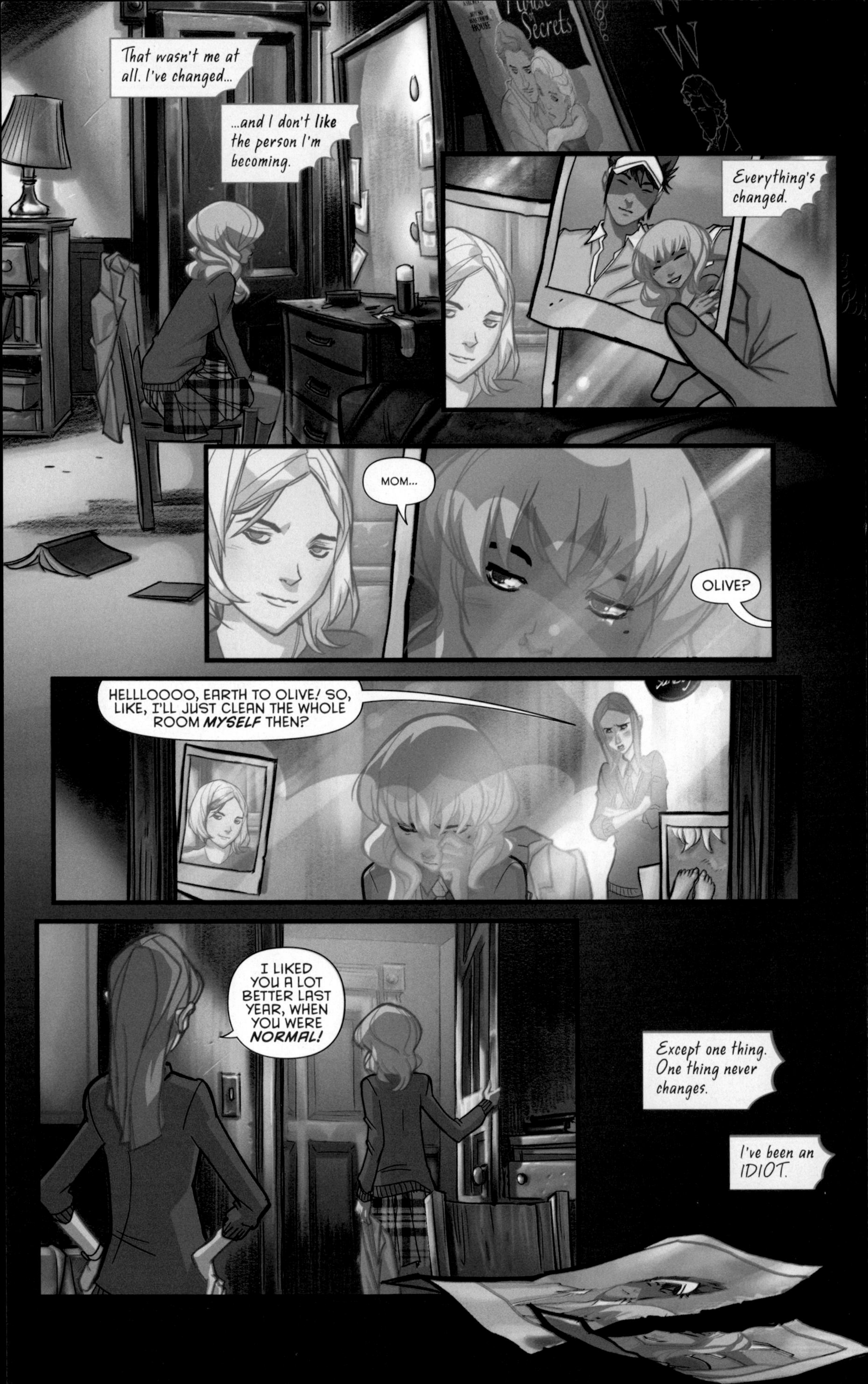
That wasn't me at all. I've changed...
...and I don't like the person I'm becoming.
Everything's changed.
MOM...
OLIVE?
HELLLOOOO, EARTH TO OLIVE! SO, LIKE, I'LL JUST CLEAN THE WHOLE ROOM MYSELF THEN?
I LIKED YOU A LOT BETTER LAST YEAR, WHEN YOU WERE NORMAL!
Except one thing. One thing never changes.
I've been an IDIOT.

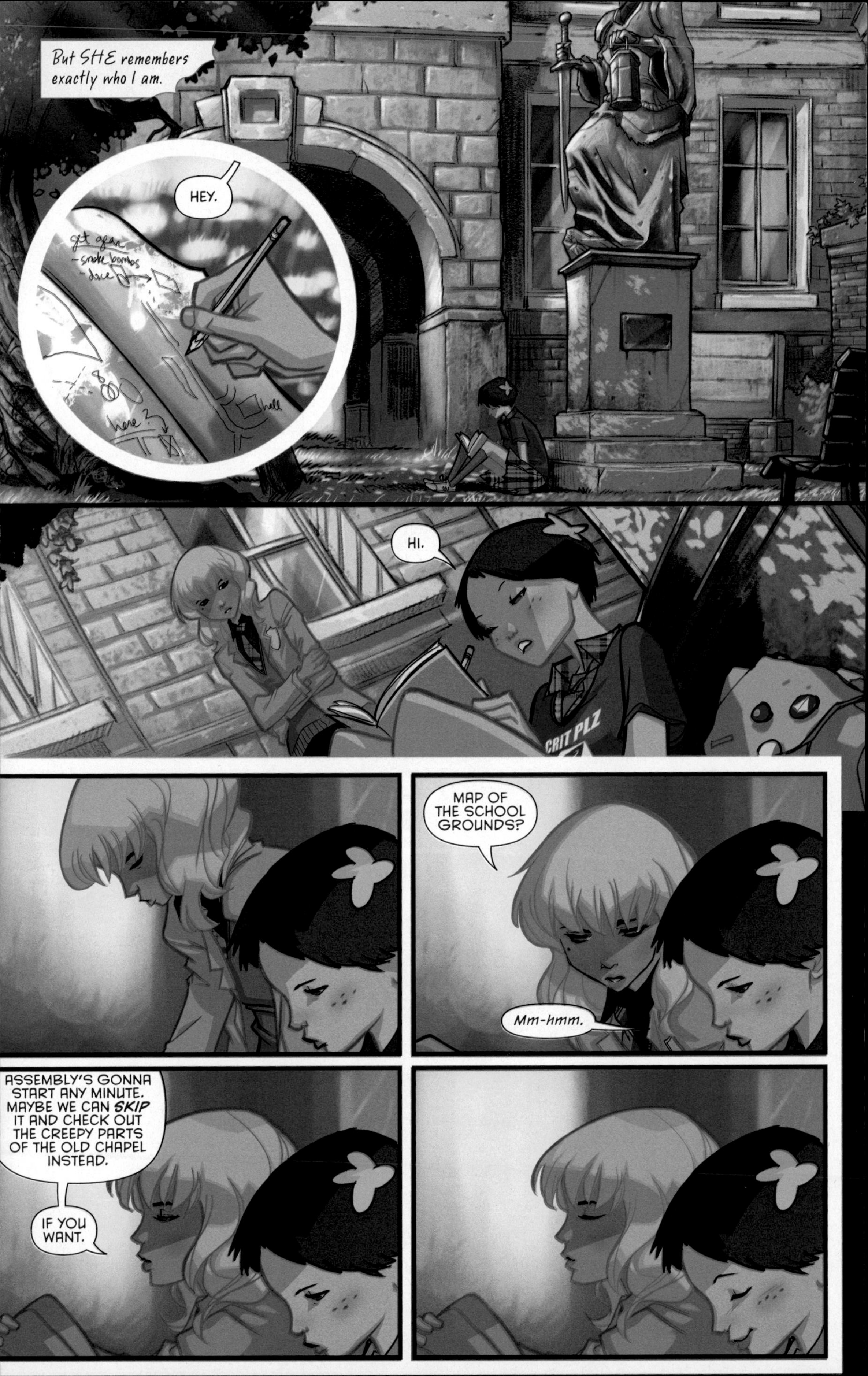
But SHE remembers exactly who I am.
HEY.
HI.
CRIT PLZ
MAP OF THE SCHOOL GROUNDS?
Mm-hmm.
ASSEMBLY'S GONNA START ANY MINUTE. MAYBE WE CAN SKIP IT AND CHECK OUT THE CREEPY PARTS OF THE OLD CHAPEL INSTEAD.
IF YOU WANT.

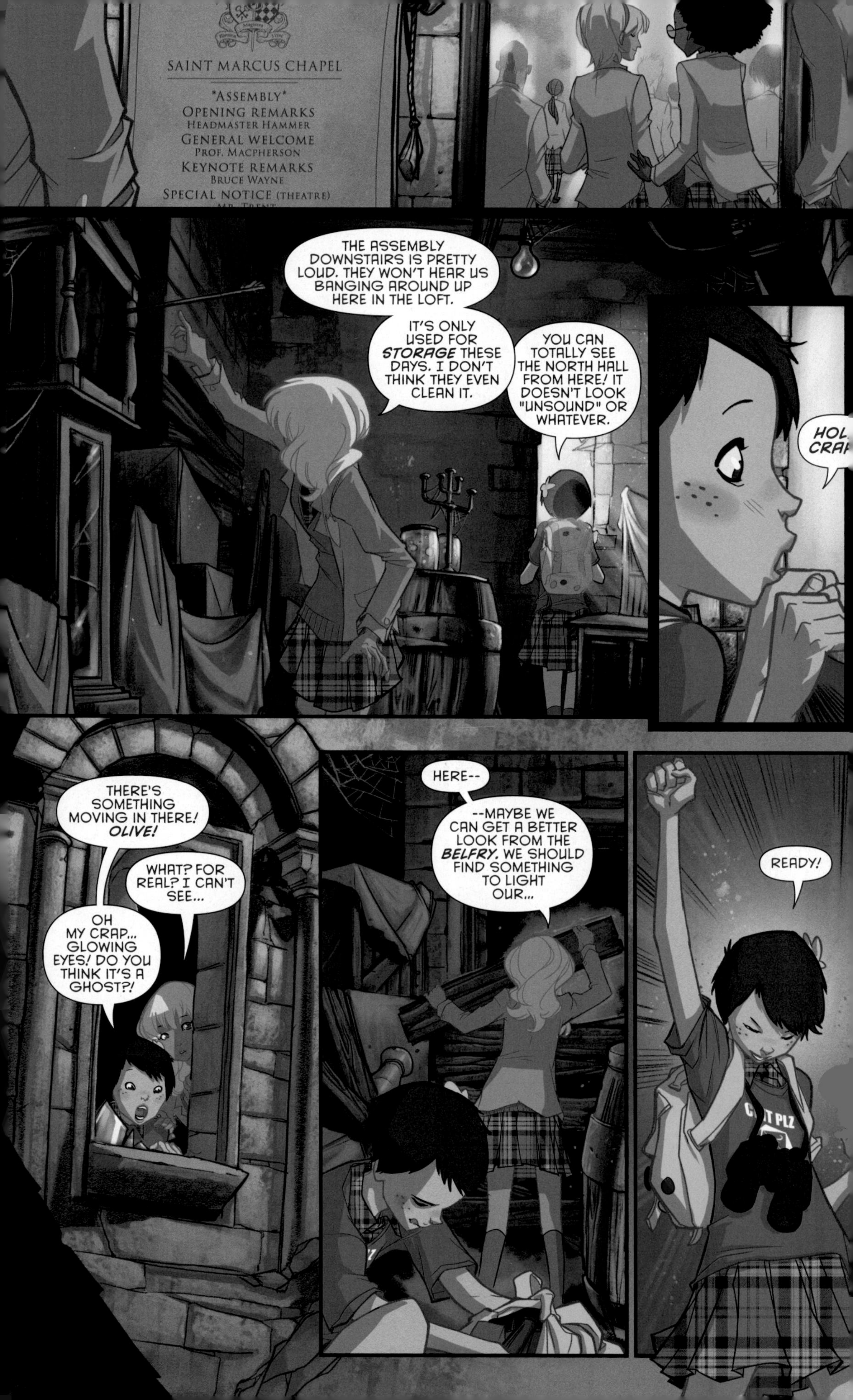
SAINT MARCUS CHAPEL
*Assembly*
Opening remarks
Headmaster Hammer
General welcome
Prof. Macpherson
Keynote remarks
Bruce Wayne
Special notice (theatre)
THE ASSEMBLY DOWNSTAIRS IS PRETTY LOUD. THEY WON'T HEAR US BANGING AROUND UP HERE IN THE LOFT.
IT'S ONLY USED FOR STORAGE THESE DAYS. I DON'T THINK THEY EVEN CLEAN IT.
YOU CAN TOTALLY SEE THE NORTH HALL FROM HERE! IT DOESN'T LOOK "UNSOUND" OR WHATEVER.
THERE'S SOMETHING MOVING IN THERE! OLIVE!
WHAT? FOR REAL? I CAN'T SEE...
OH MY CRAP... GLOWING EYES! DO YOU THINK IT'S A GHOST?!
HERE--
--MAYBE WE CAN GET A BETTER LOOK FROM THE BELFRY. WE SHOULD FIND SOMETHING TO LIGHT OUR...
READY!

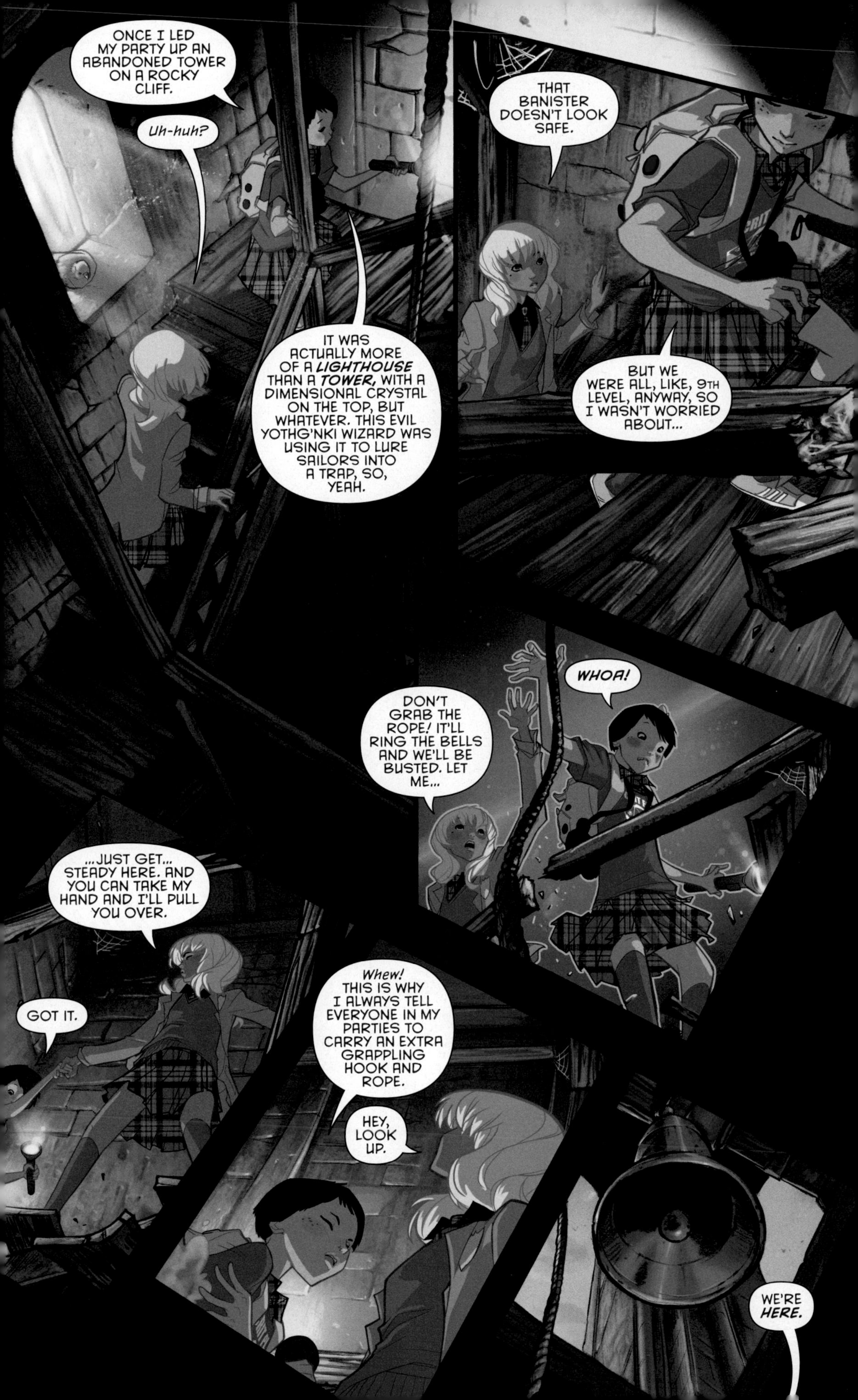
ONCE I LED MY PARTY UP AN ABANDONED TOWER ON A ROCKY CLIFF.
Uh-huh?
IT WAS ACTUALLY MORE OF A LIGHTHOUSE THAN A TOWER, WITH A DIMENSIONAL CRYSTAL ON THE TOP, BUT WHATEVER. THIS EVIL YOTHG'NKI WIZARD WAS USING IT TO LURE SAILORS INTO A TRAP, SO, YEAH.
THAT BANISTER DOESN'T LOOK SAFE.
BUT WE WERE ALL, LIKE, 9TH LEVEL, ANYWAY, SO I WASN'T WORRIED ABOUT...
WHOA!
DON'T GRAB THE ROPE! IT'LL RING THE BELLS AND WE'LL BE BUSTED. LET ME...
...JUST GET... STEADY HERE. AND YOU CAN TAKE MY HAND AND I'LL PULL YOU OVER.
GOT IT.
Whew! THIS IS WHY I ALWAYS TELL EVERYONE IN MY PARTIES TO CARRY AN EXTRA GRAPPLING HOOK AND ROPE.
HEY, LOOK UP.
WE'RE HERE.

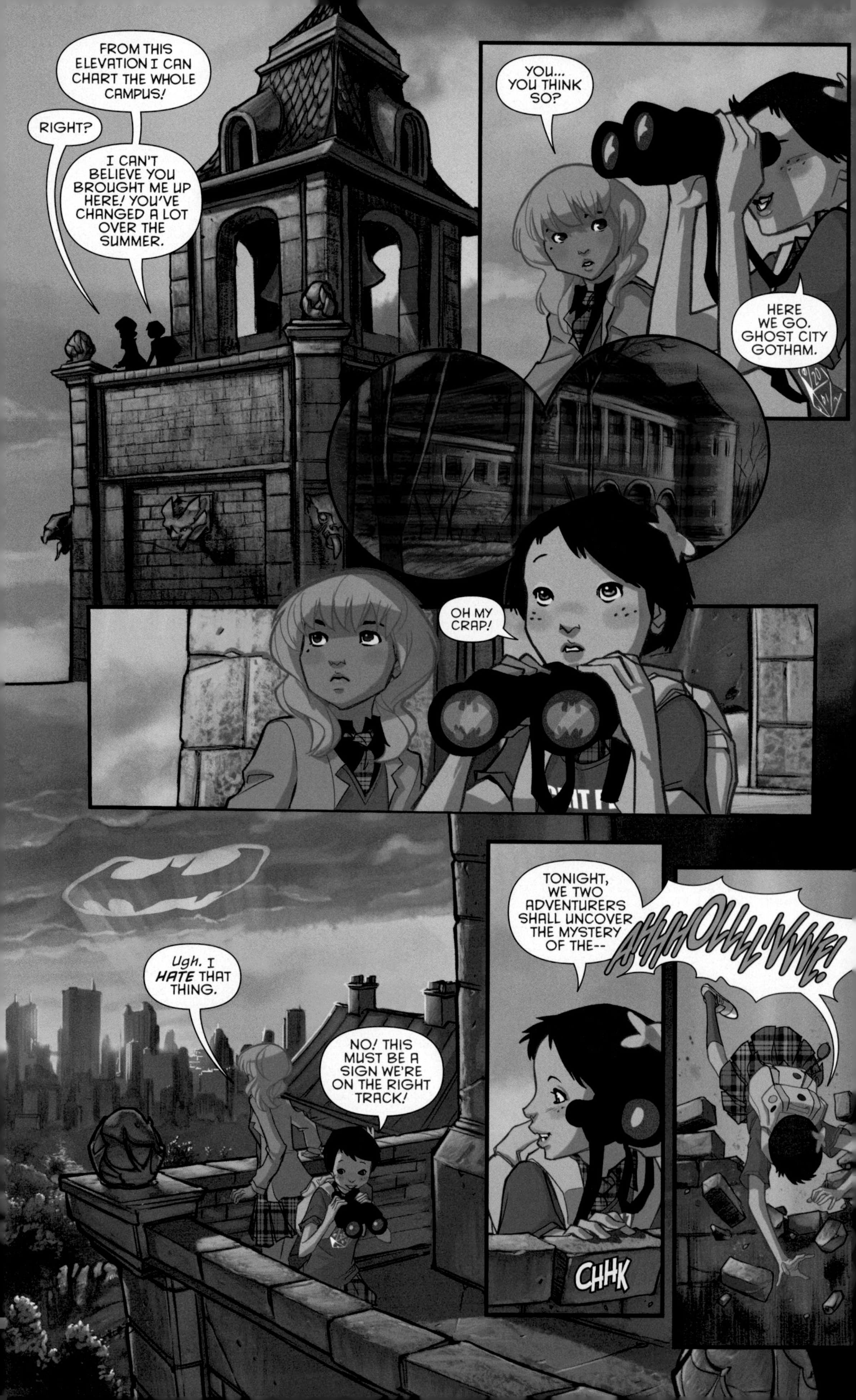

FROM THIS ELEVATION I CAN CHART THE WHOLE CAMPUS!
RIGHT?
I CAN'T BELIEVE YOU BROUGHT ME UP HERE! YOU'VE CHANGED A LOT OVER THE SUMMER.
YOU... YOU THINK SO?
HERE WE GO. GHOST CITY GOTHAM.
OH MY CRAP!
Ugh. I HATE THAT THING.
NO! THIS MUST BE A SIGN WE'RE ON THE RIGHT TRACK!
TONIGHT, WE TWO ADVENTURERS SHALL UNCOVER THE MYSTERY OF THE--
CHHK
AHHHOLLLLWWE!

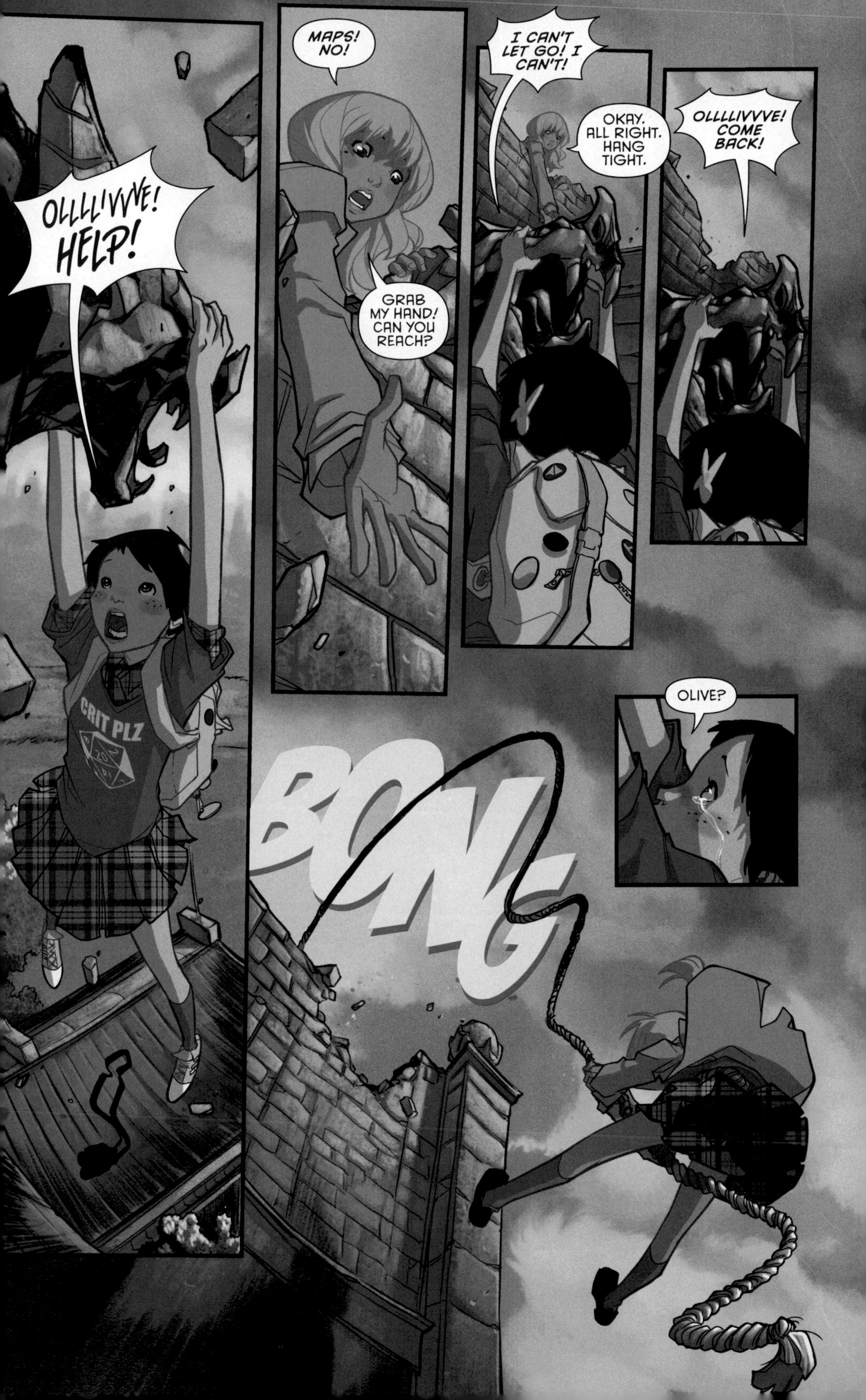
OLLLLIVVVE! HELP!
MAPS! NO!
GRAB MY HAND! CAN YOU REACH?
I CAN'T LET GO! I CAN'T!
OKAY. ALL RIGHT. HANG TIGHT.
OLLLLIVVVE! COME BACK!
OLIVE?
BONG

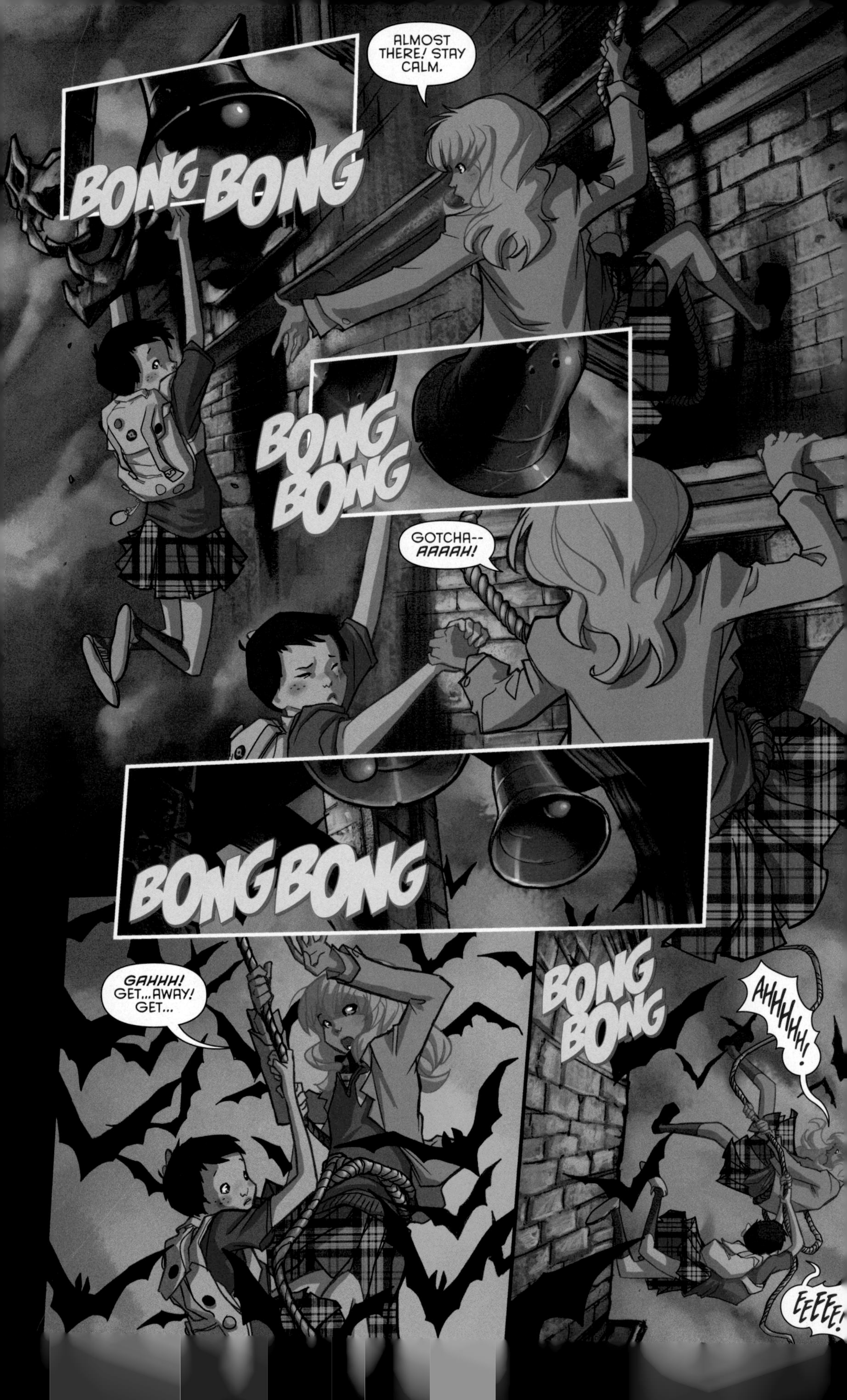

ALMOST THERE! STAY CALM.
BONG BONG
BONG BONG
GOTCHA-- AAAAH!
BONG BONG
GAHHH! GET...AWAY! GET...
BONG BONG
AHHHHH!
EEEEE!

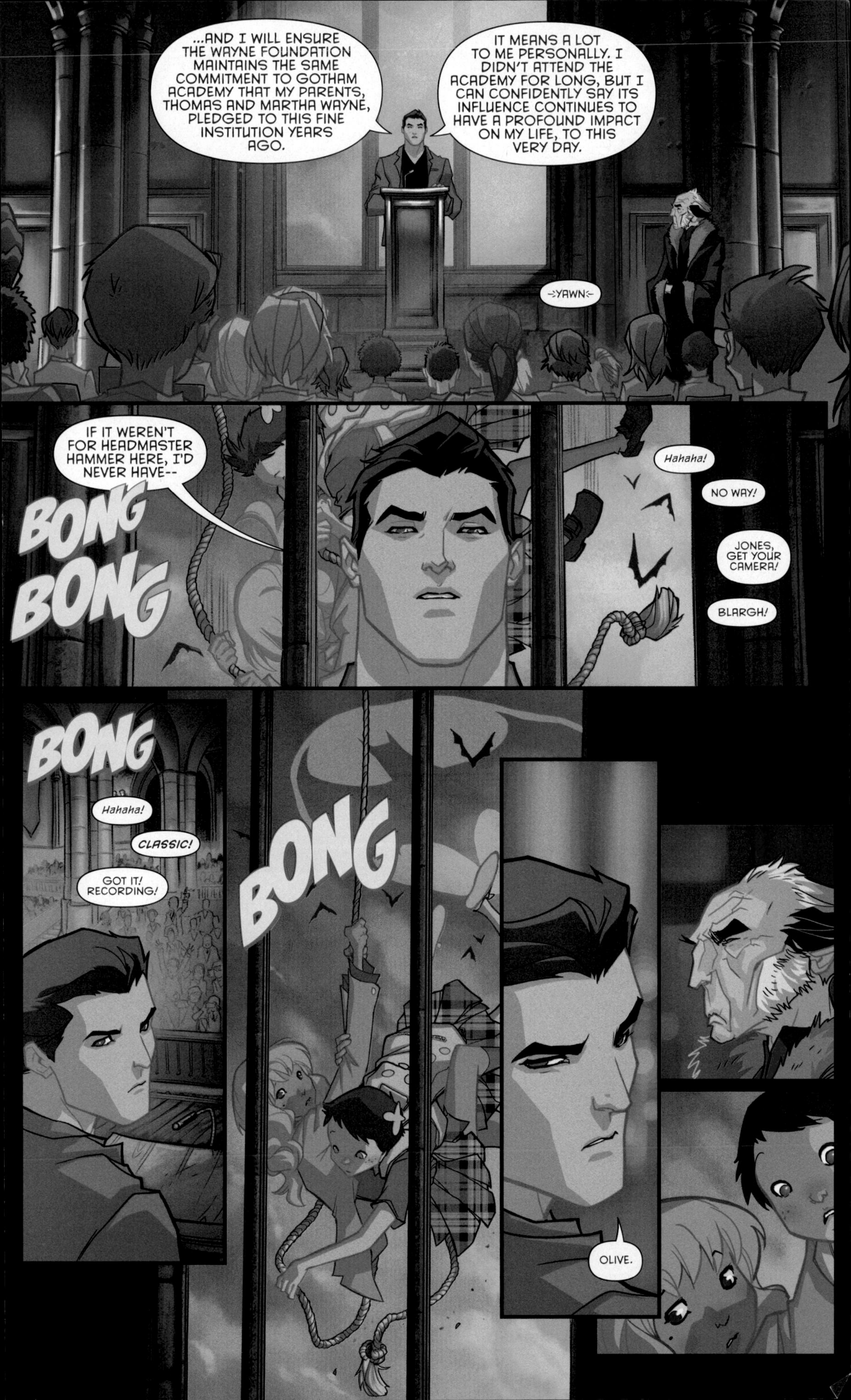
...AND I WILL ENSURE THE WAYNE FOUNDATION MAINTAINS THE SAME COMMITMENT TO GOTHAM ACADEMY THAT MY PARENTS, THOMAS AND MARTHA WAYNE, PLEDGED TO THIS FINE INSTITUTION YEARS AGO.
IT MEANS A LOT TO ME PERSONALLY. I DIDN'T ATTEND THE ACADEMY FOR LONG, BUT I CAN CONFIDENTLY SAY ITS INFLUENCE CONTINUES TO HAVE A PROFOUND IMPACT ON MY LIFE, TO THIS VERY DAY.
YAWN
IF IT WEREN'T FOR HEADMASTER HAMMER HERE, I'D NEVER HAVE--
BONG BONG
Hahaha!
NO WAY!
JONES, GET YOUR CAMERA!
BLARGH!
BONG
Hahaha!
CLASSIC!
GOT IT! RECORDING!
BONG
OLIVE.

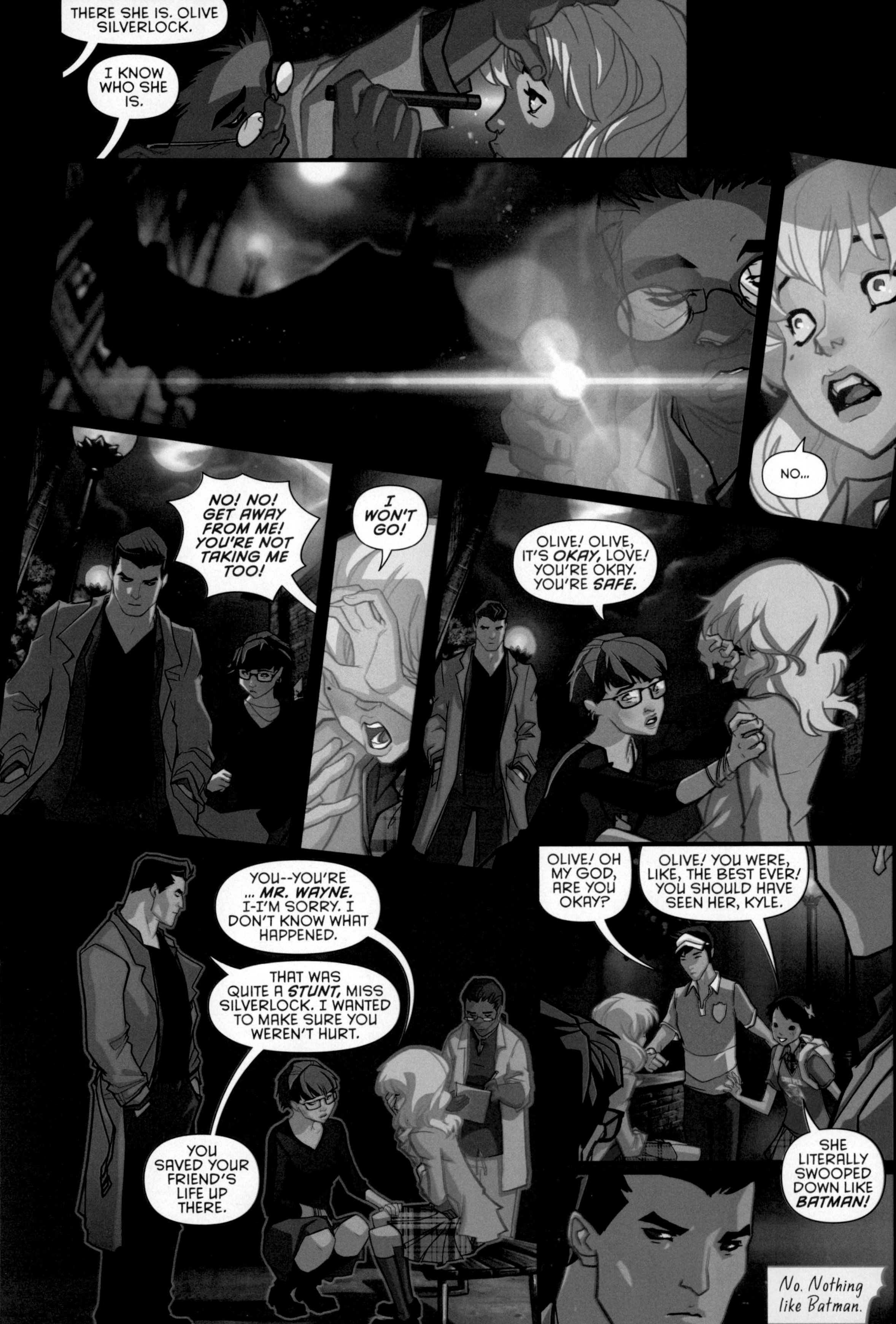
THERE SHE IS. OLIVE SILVERLOCK.
I KNOW WHO SHE IS.
NO...
NO! NO! GET AWAY FROM ME! YOU'RE NOT TAKING ME TOO!
I WON'T GO!
OLIVE! OLIVE, IT'S OKAY, LOVE! YOU'RE OKAY. YOU'RE SAFE.
YOU--YOU'RE ...MR. WAYNE. I-I'M SORRY. I DON'T KNOW WHAT HAPPENED.
THAT WAS QUITE A STUNT, MISS SILVERLOCK. I WANTED TO MAKE SURE YOU WEREN'T HURT.
YOU SAVED YOUR FRIEND'S LIFE UP THERE.
OLIVE! OH MY GOD, ARE YOU OKAY?
OLIVE! YOU WERE, LIKE, THE BEST EVER! YOU SHOULD HAVE SEEN HER, KYLE.
SHE LITERALLY SWOOPED DOWN LIKE BATMAN!
No. Nothing like Batman.

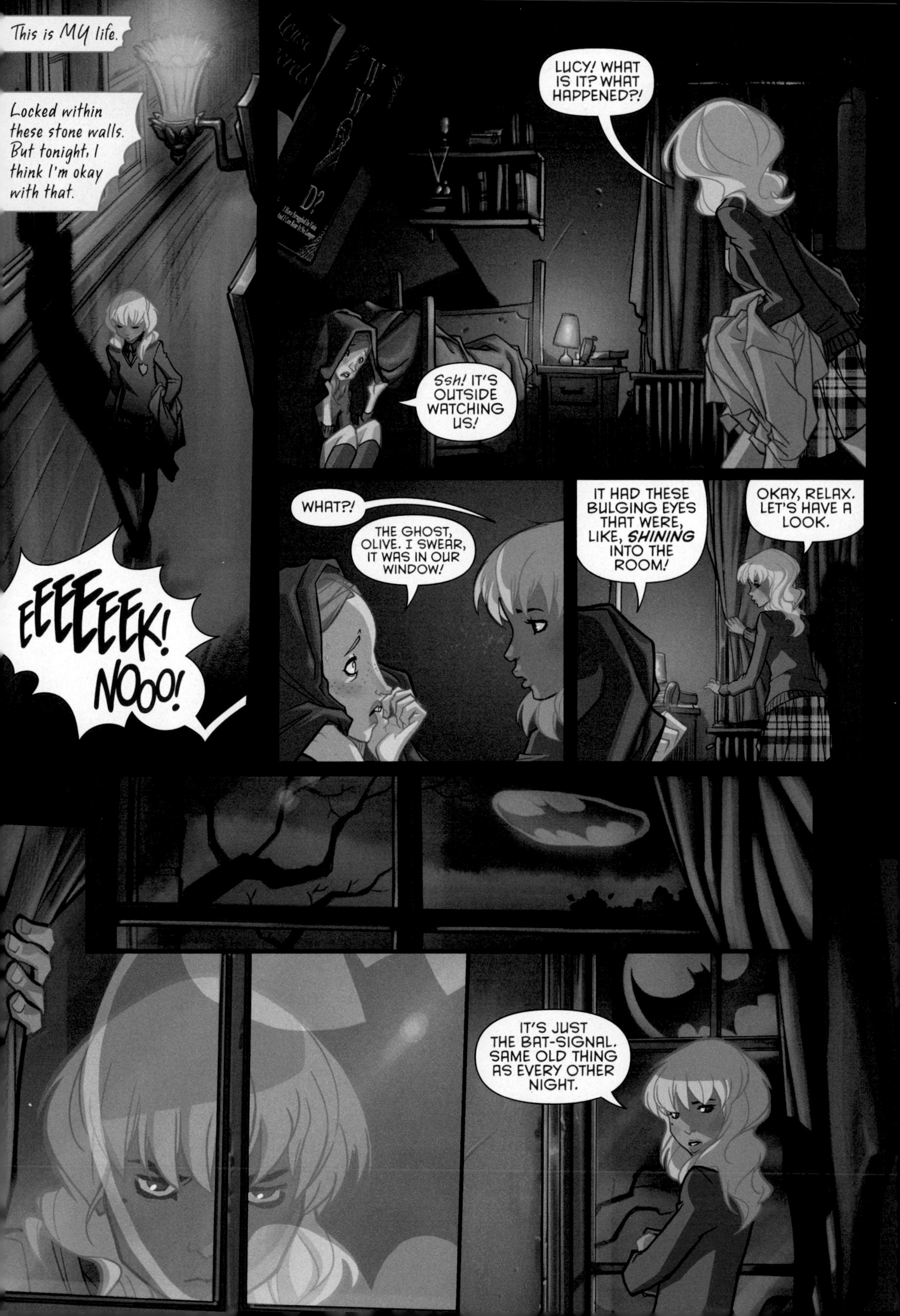
This is MY life.
Locked within these stone walls. But tonight, I think I'm okay with that.
LUCY! WHAT IS IT? WHAT HAPPENED?!
Ssh! IT'S OUTSIDE WATCHING US!
EEEEEEK! NOOO!
WHAT?!
THE GHOST, OLIVE. I SWEAR, IT WAS IN OUR WINDOW!
IT HAD THESE BULGING EYES THAT WERE, LIKE, SHINING INTO THE ROOM!
OKAY, RELAX. LET'S HAVE A LOOK.
IT'S JUST THE BAT-SIGNAL. SAME OLD THING AS EVERY OTHER NIGHT.

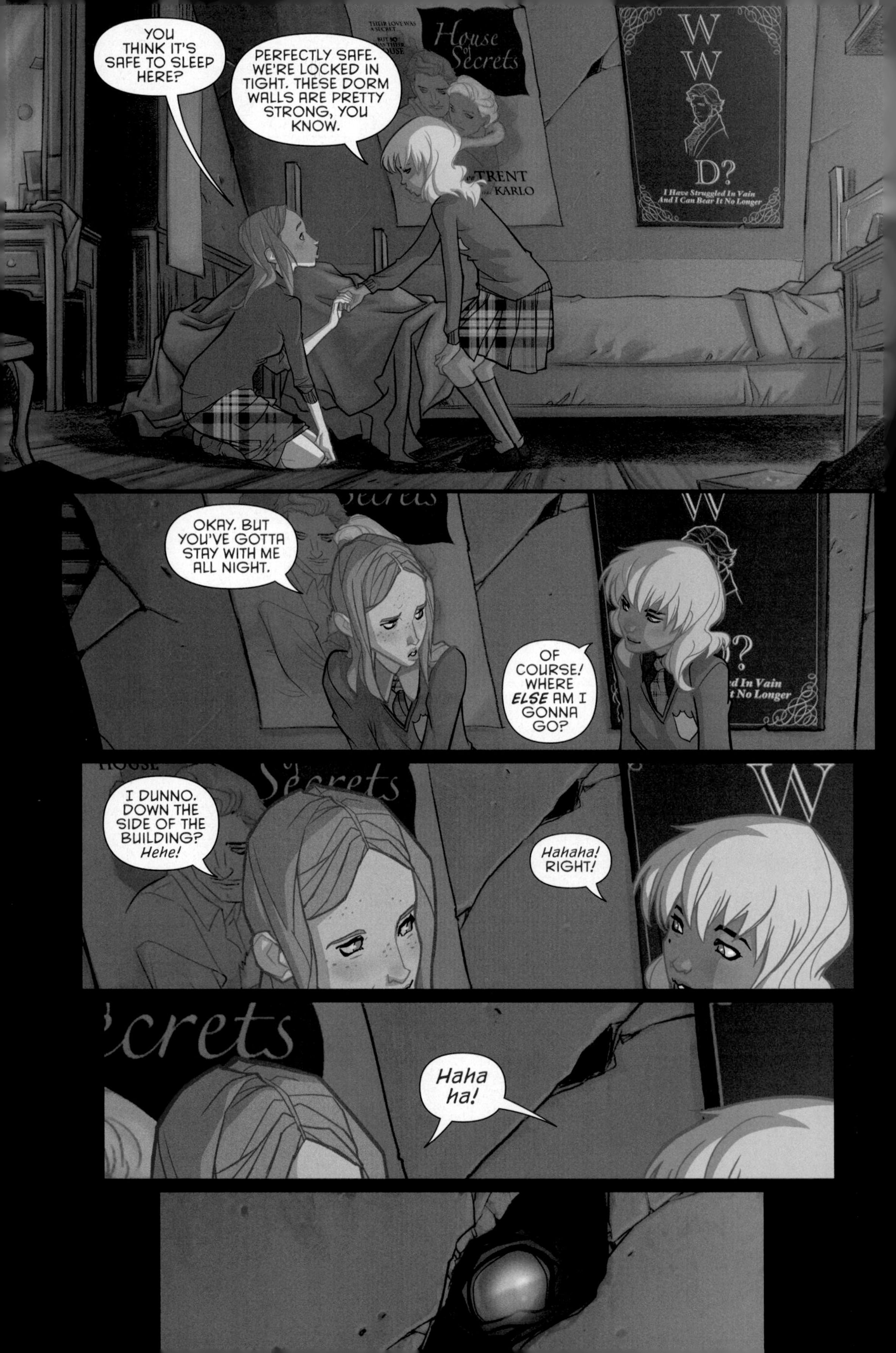
YOU THINK IT'S SAFE TO SLEEP HERE?
PERFECTLY SAFE. WE'RE LOCKED IN TIGHT. THESE DORM WALLS ARE PRETTY STRONG, YOU KNOW.
House of Secrets
TRENT
KARLO
W W D?
I Have Struggled In Vain
And I Can Bear It No Longer
OKAY. BUT YOU'VE GOTTA STAY WITH ME ALL NIGHT.
OF COURSE! WHERE *ELSE* AM I GONNA GO?
I DUNNO. DOWN THE SIDE OF THE BUILDING? *Hehe!*
*Hahaha!* RIGHT!
*Haha ha!*

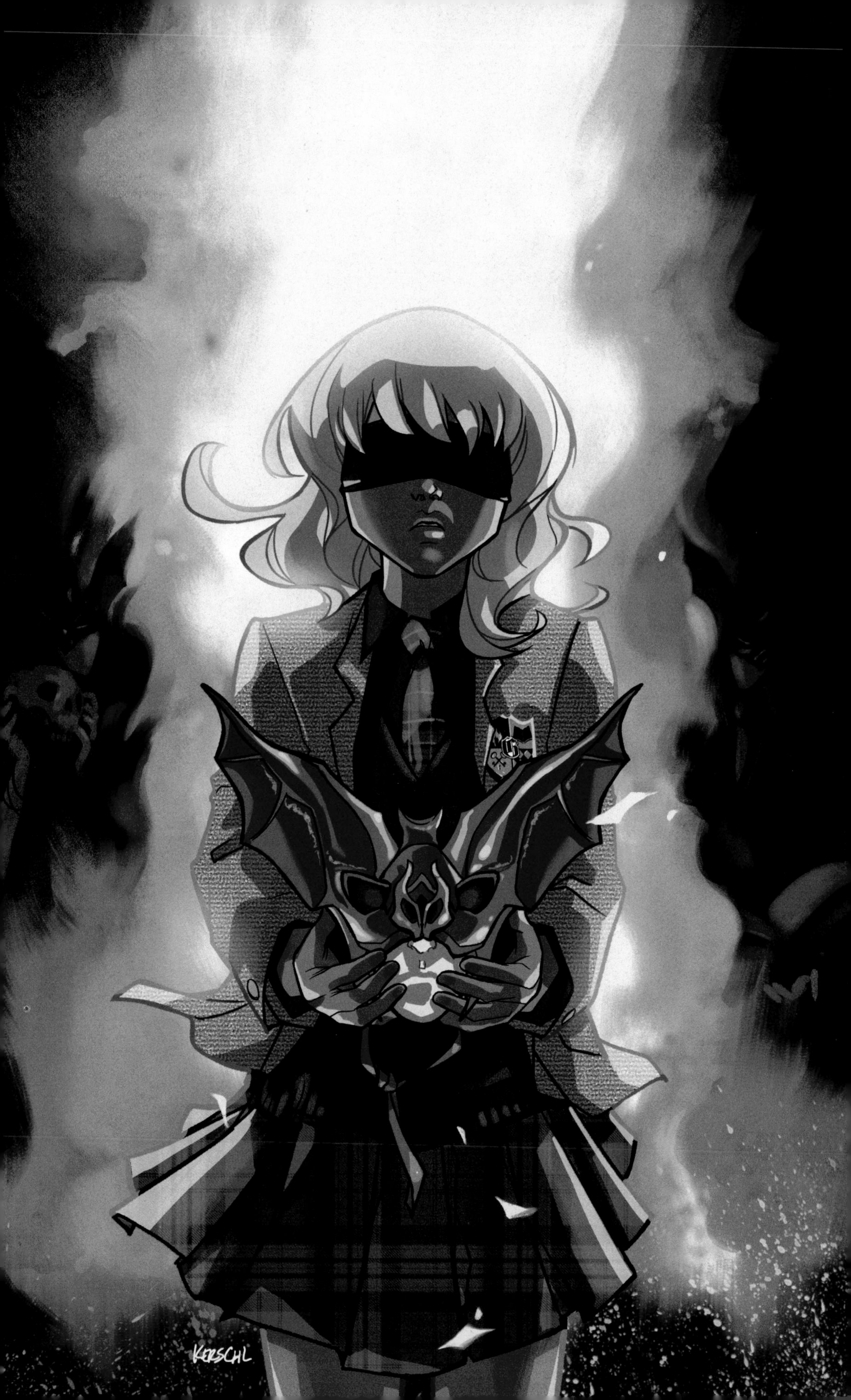
KERSCHL

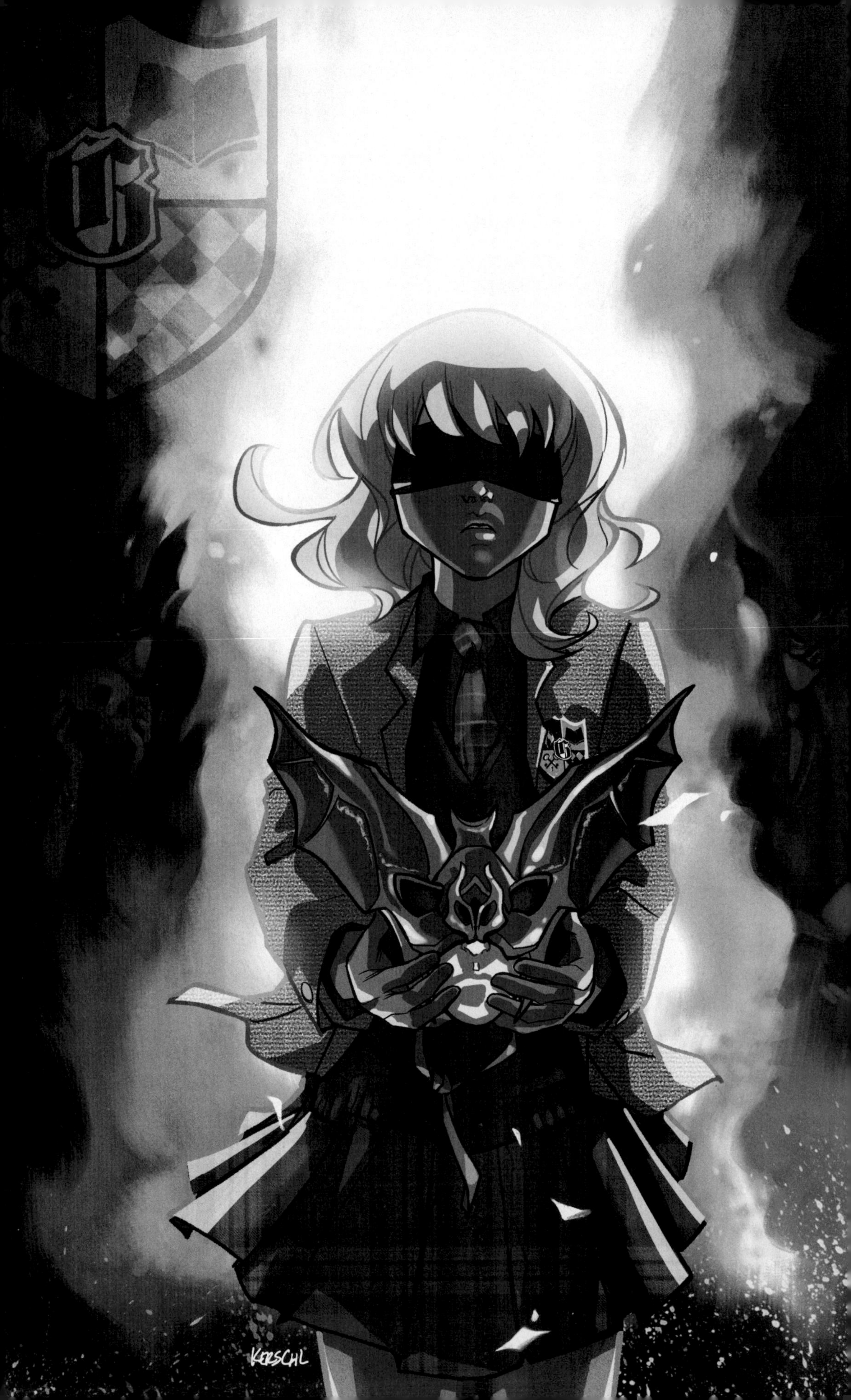
KERSCHL

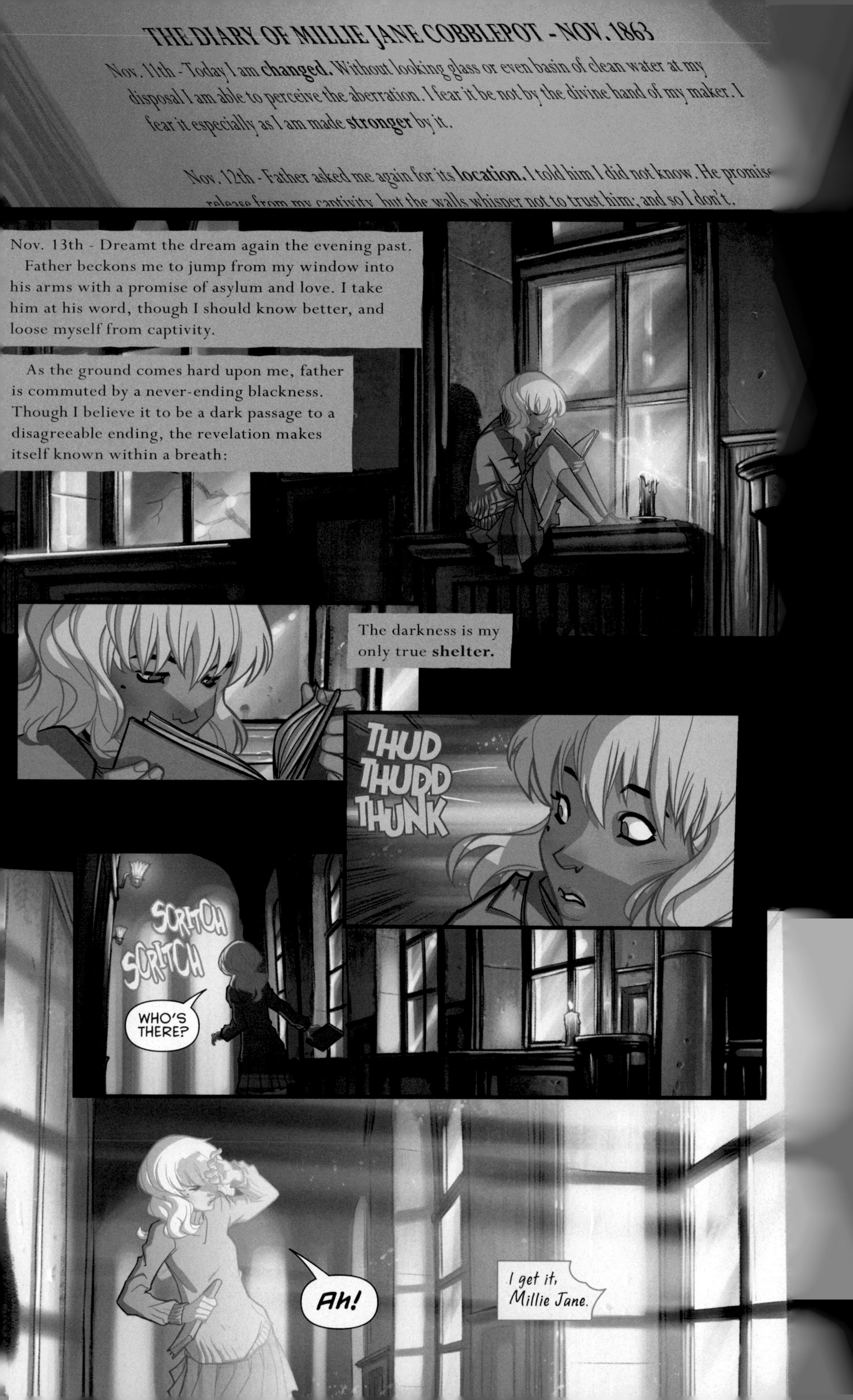
THE DIARY OF MILLIE JANE COBBLEPOT - NOV. 1863
Nov. 11th - Today I am **changed.** Without looking glass or even basin of clean water at my disposal I am able to perceive the aberration. I fear it be not by the divine hand of my maker. I fear it especially as I am made **stronger** by it.
Nov. 12th - Father asked me again for its **location.** I told him I did not know. He promise
release from my captivity, but the walls whisper not to trust him; and so I don't.
Nov. 13th - Dreamt the dream again the evening past. Father beckons me to jump from my window into his arms with a promise of asylum and love. I take him at his word, though I should know better, and loose myself from captivity.
As the ground comes hard upon me, father is commuted by a never-ending blackness. Though I believe it to be a dark passage to a disagreeable ending, the revelation makes itself known within a breath:
The darkness is my only true **shelter.**
THUD
THUDD
THUNK
SCRITCH
SCRITCH
WHO'S THERE?
Ah!
I get it, Millie Jane.

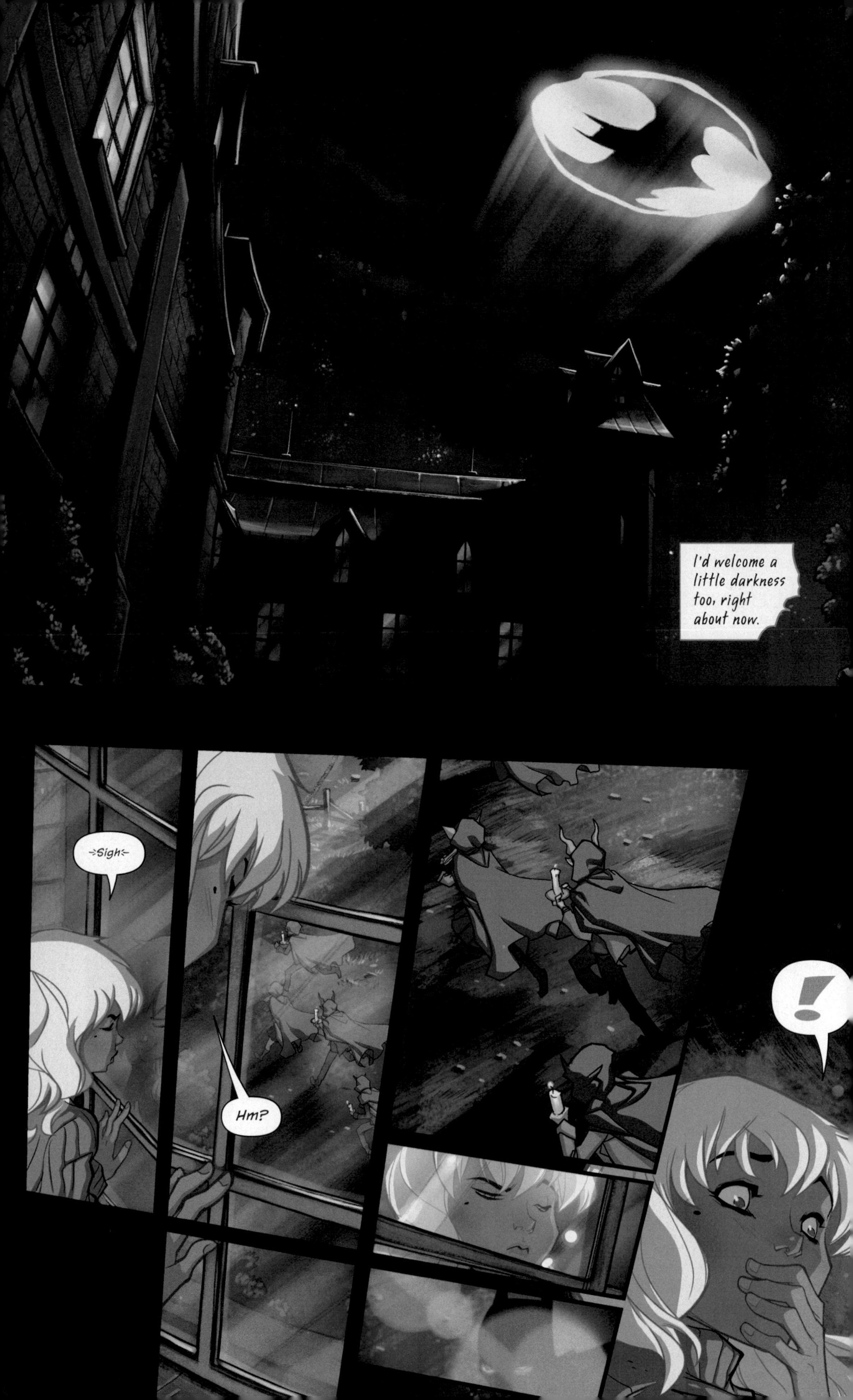
I'd welcome a little darkness too, right about now.
Sigh
Hm?
!

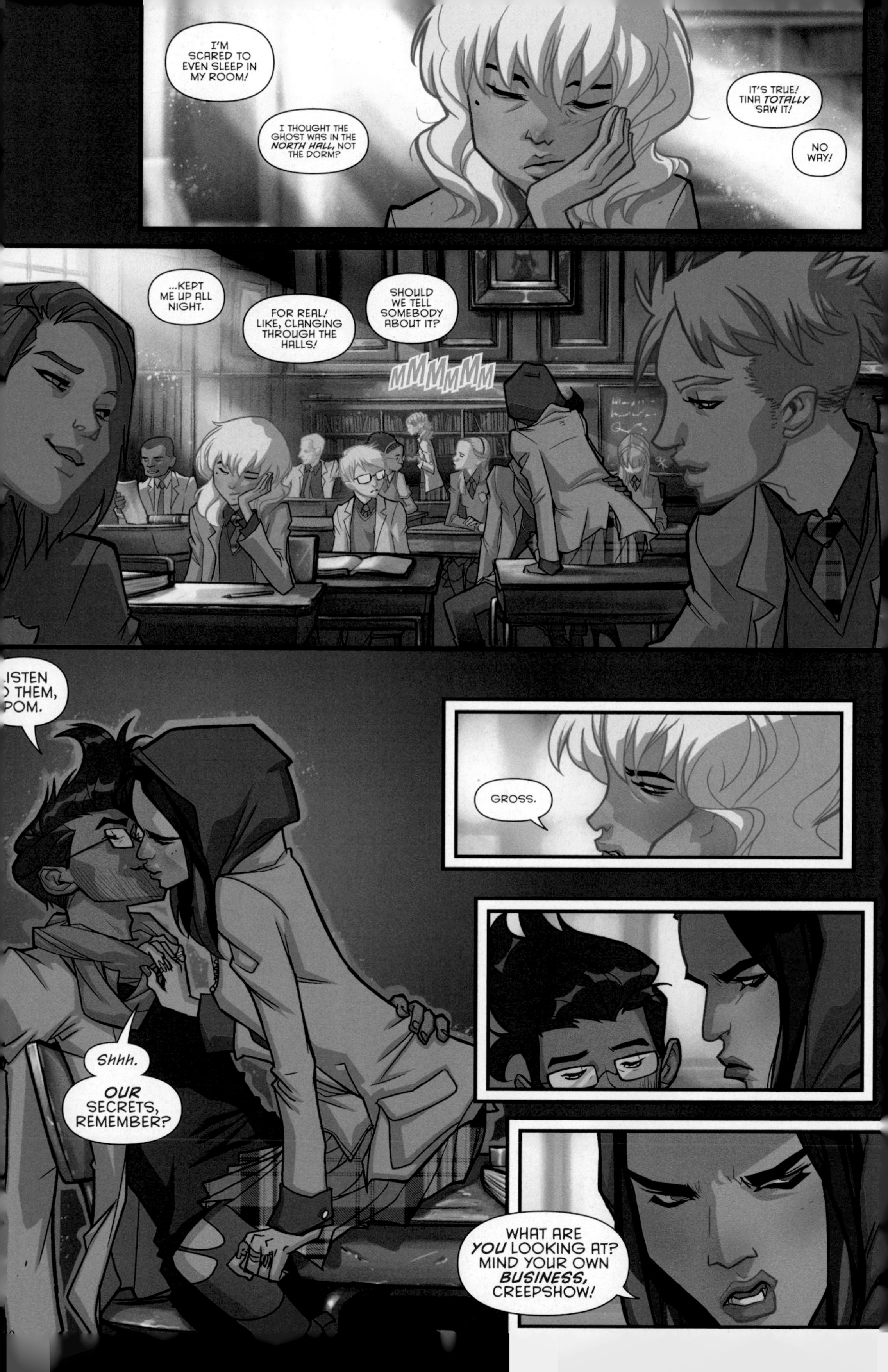
I'M SCARED TO EVEN SLEEP IN MY ROOM!
I THOUGHT THE GHOST WAS IN THE NORTH HALL, NOT THE DORM?
IT'S TRUE! TINA TOTALLY SAW IT!
NO WAY!
...KEPT ME UP ALL NIGHT.
FOR REAL! LIKE, CLANGING THROUGH THE HALLS!
SHOULD WE TELL SOMEBODY ABOUT IT?
MMMMMM
ISTEN
THEM,
POM.
Shhh.
OUR SECRETS, REMEMBER?
GROSS.
WHAT ARE YOU LOOKING AT? MIND YOUR OWN BUSINESS, CREEPSHOW!

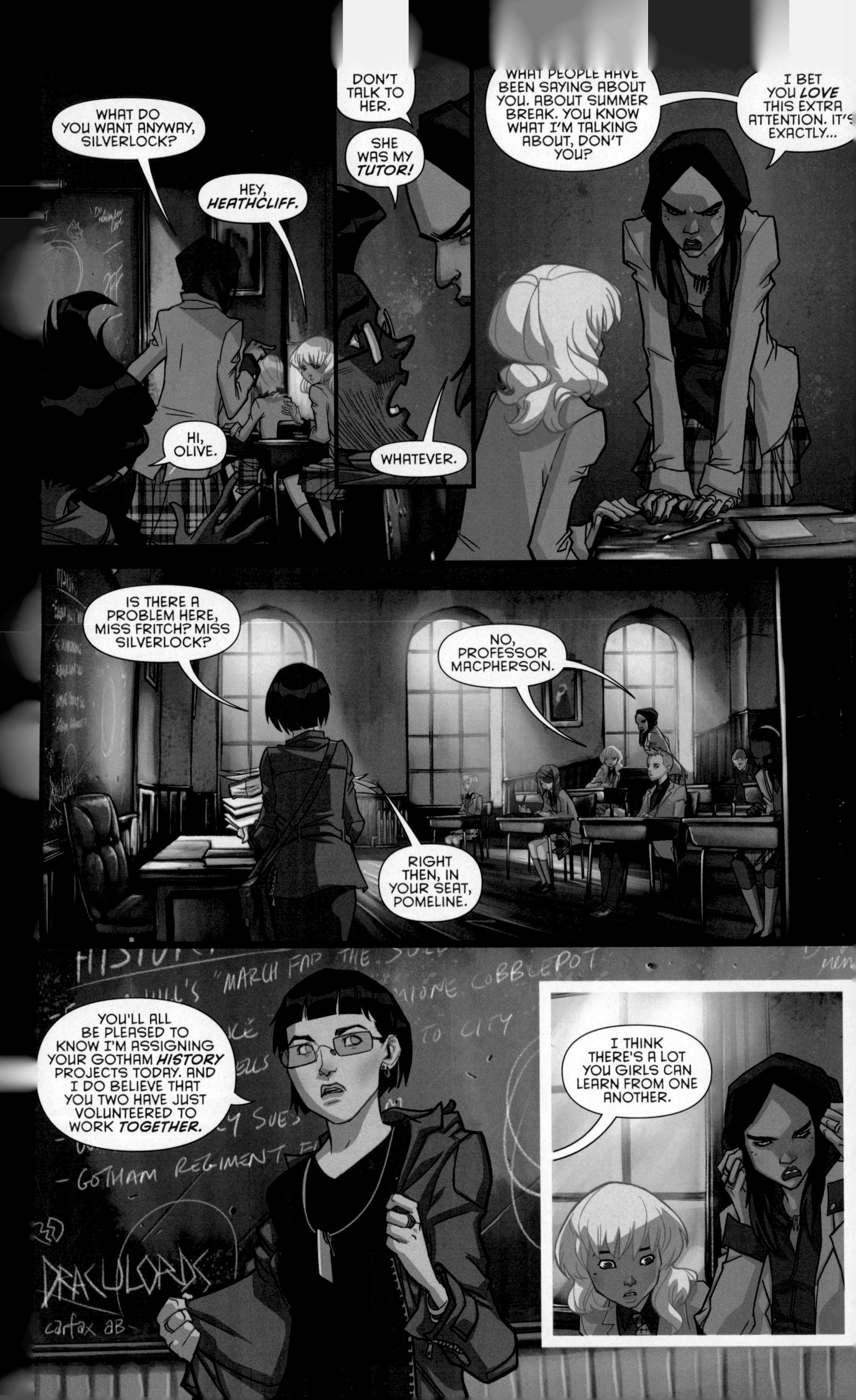
WHAT DO YOU WANT ANYWAY, SILVERLOCK?
HEY, HEATHCLIFF.
HI, OLIVE.
DON'T TALK TO HER.
SHE WAS MY TUTOR!
WHATEVER.
WHAT PEOPLE HAVE BEEN SAYING ABOUT YOU. ABOUT SUMMER BREAK. YOU KNOW WHAT I'M TALKING ABOUT, DON'T YOU?
I BET YOU LOVE THIS EXTRA ATTENTION. IT'S EXACTLY...
IS THERE A PROBLEM HERE, MISS FRITCH? MISS SILVERLOCK?
NO, PROFESSOR MACPHERSON.
RIGHT THEN, IN YOUR SEAT, POMELINE.
YOU'LL ALL BE PLEASED TO KNOW I'M ASSIGNING YOUR GOTHAM HISTORY PROJECTS TODAY. AND I DO BELIEVE THAT YOU TWO HAVE JUST VOLUNTEERED TO WORK TOGETHER.
I THINK THERE'S A LOT YOU GIRLS CAN LEARN FROM ONE ANOTHER.
- GOTHAM REGIMENT
DRACULORDS
carfax aB

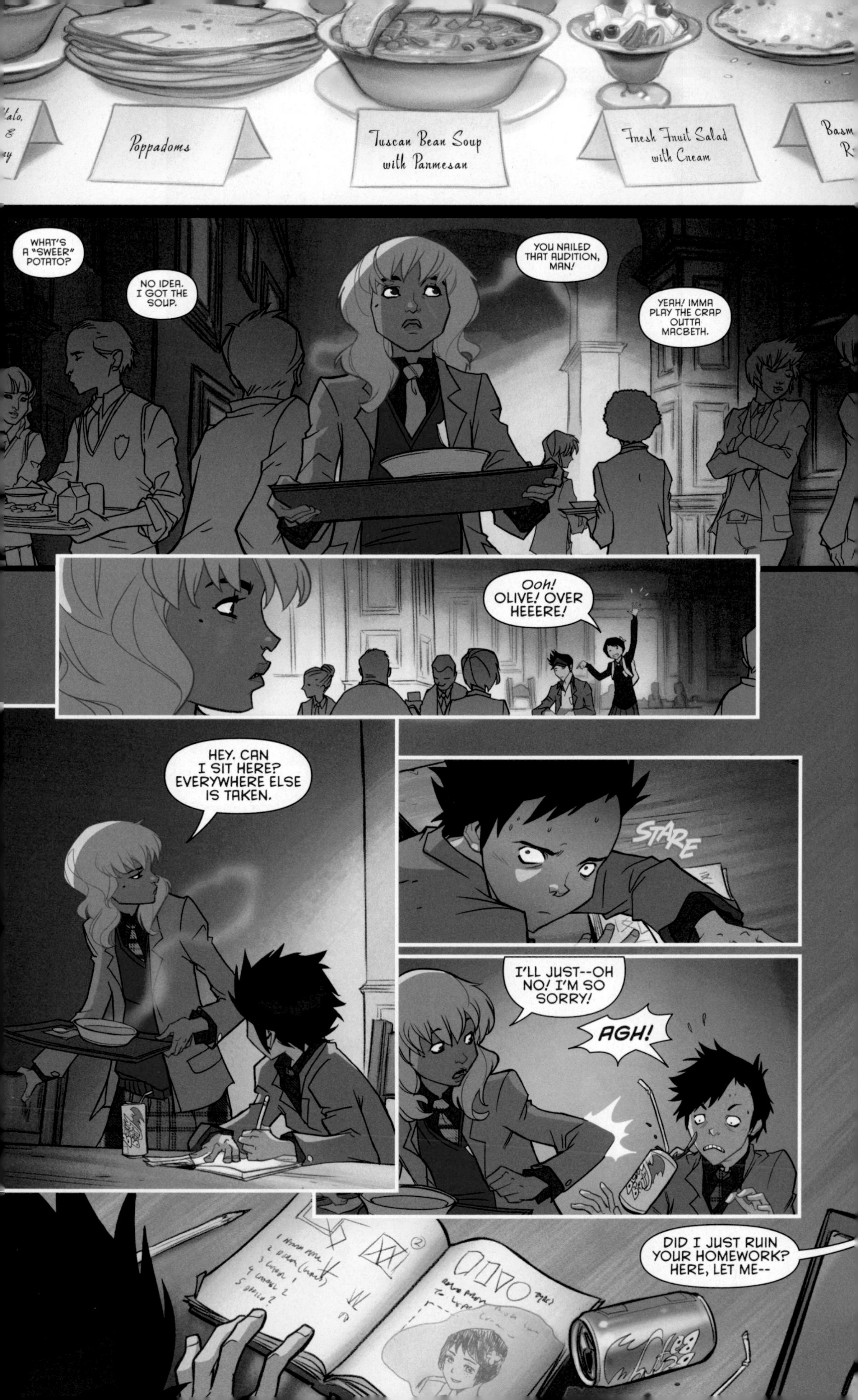
Poppadoms
Tuscan Bean Soup with Parmesan
Fresh Fruit Salad with Cream
WHAT'S A "SWEER" POTATO?
NO IDEA. I GOT THE SOUP.
YOU NAILED THAT AUDITION, MAN!
YEAH! IMMA PLAY THE CRAP OUTTA MACBETH.
Ooh! OLIVE! OVER HEEERE!
HEY. CAN I SIT HERE? EVERYWHERE ELSE IS TAKEN.
STARE
I'LL JUST--OH NO! I'M SO SORRY!
AGH!
DID I JUST RUIN YOUR HOMEWORK? HERE, LET ME--

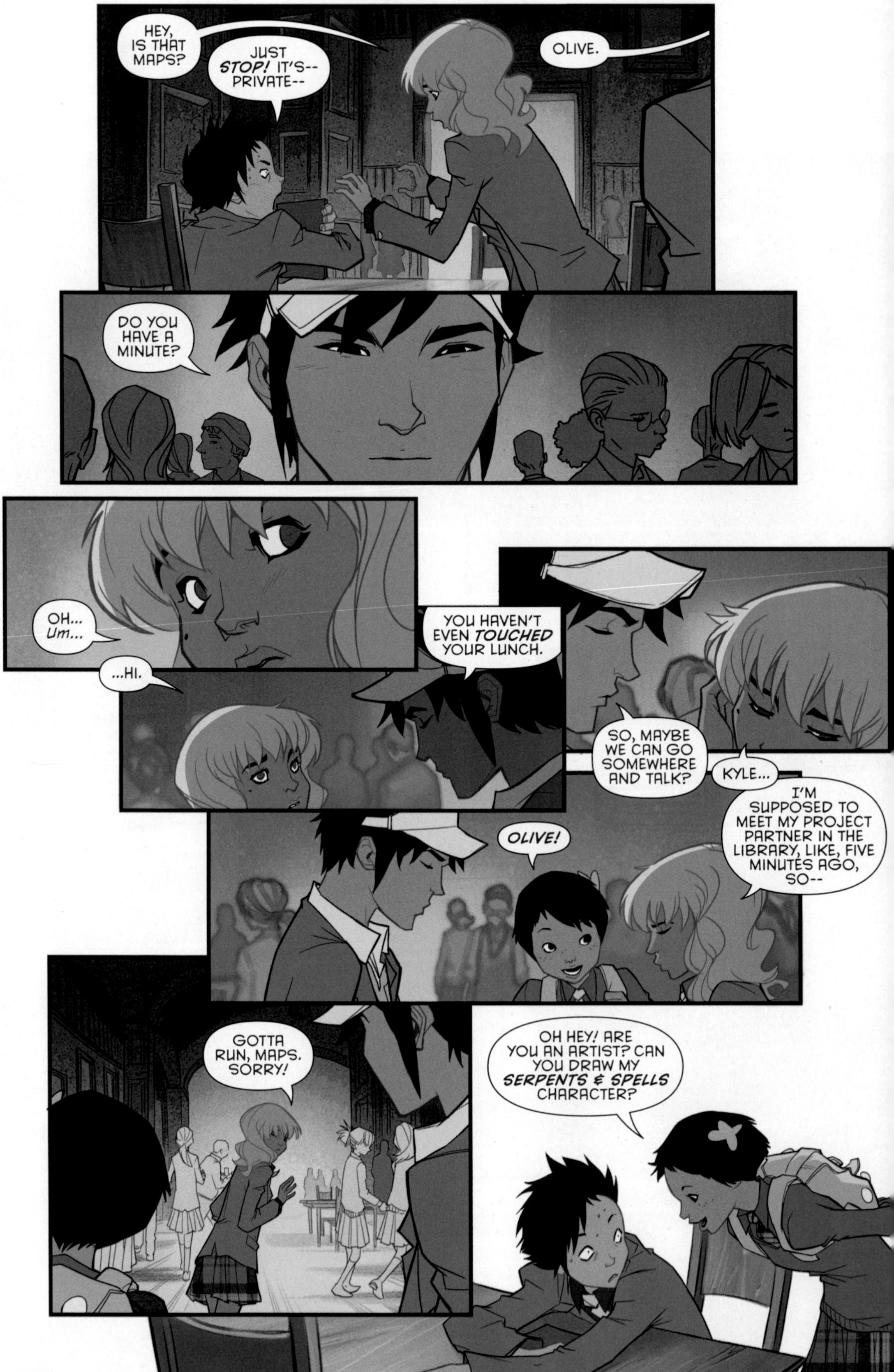
HEY, IS THAT MAPS?
JUST STOP! IT'S-- PRIVATE--
OLIVE.
DO YOU HAVE A MINUTE?
OH... UM...
...HI.
YOU HAVEN'T EVEN TOUCHED YOUR LUNCH.
SO, MAYBE WE CAN GO SOMEWHERE AND TALK?
KYLE...
I'M SUPPOSED TO MEET MY PROJECT PARTNER IN THE LIBRARY, LIKE, FIVE MINUTES AGO, SO--
OLIVE!
GOTTA RUN, MAPS. SORRY!
OH HEY! ARE YOU AN ARTIST? CAN YOU DRAW MY SERPENTS & SPELLS CHARACTER?

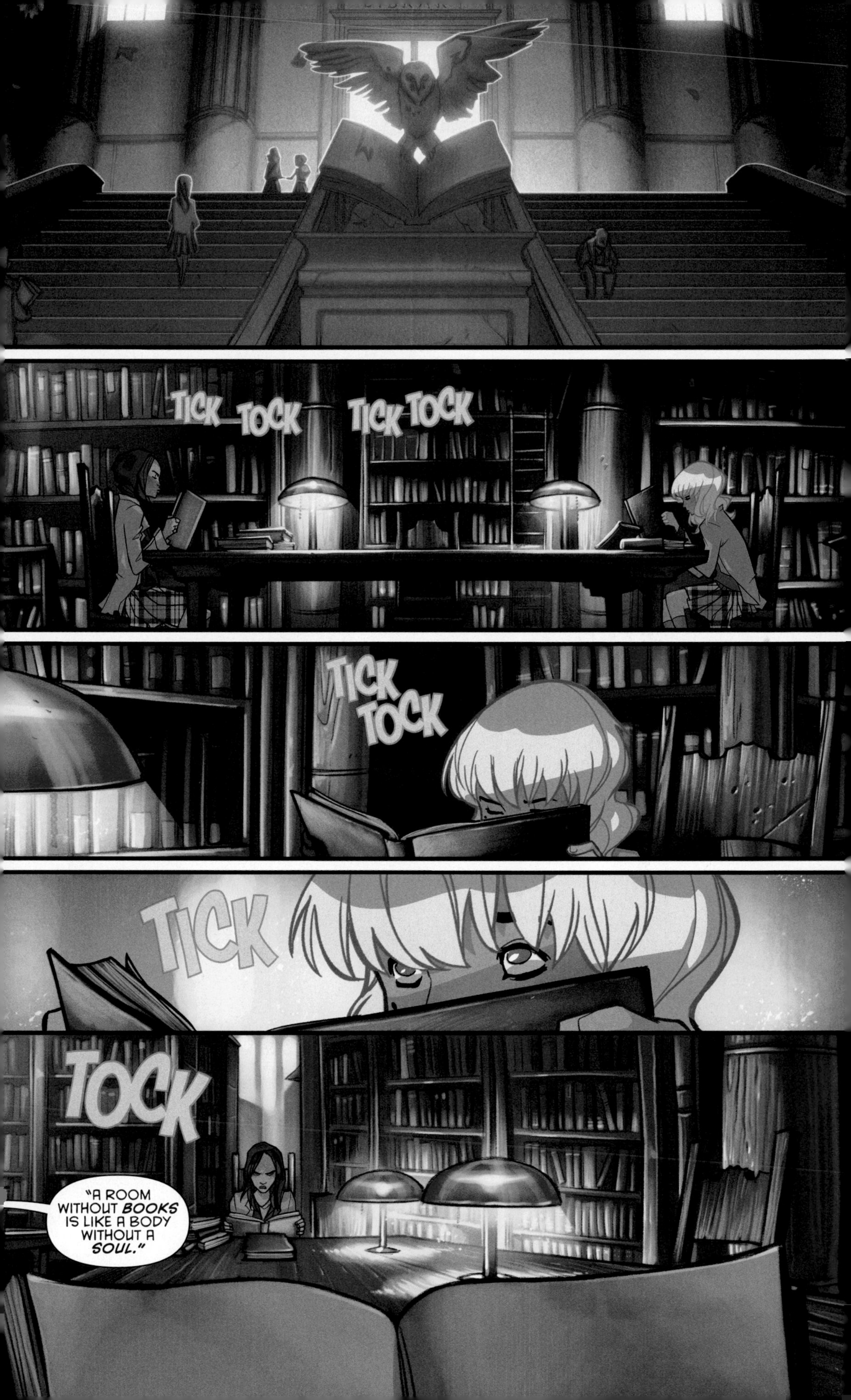
TICK
TOCK
TICK
TOCK
TICK
TOCK
TICK
TOCK
"A ROOM WITHOUT BOOKS IS LIKE A BODY WITHOUT A SOUL."

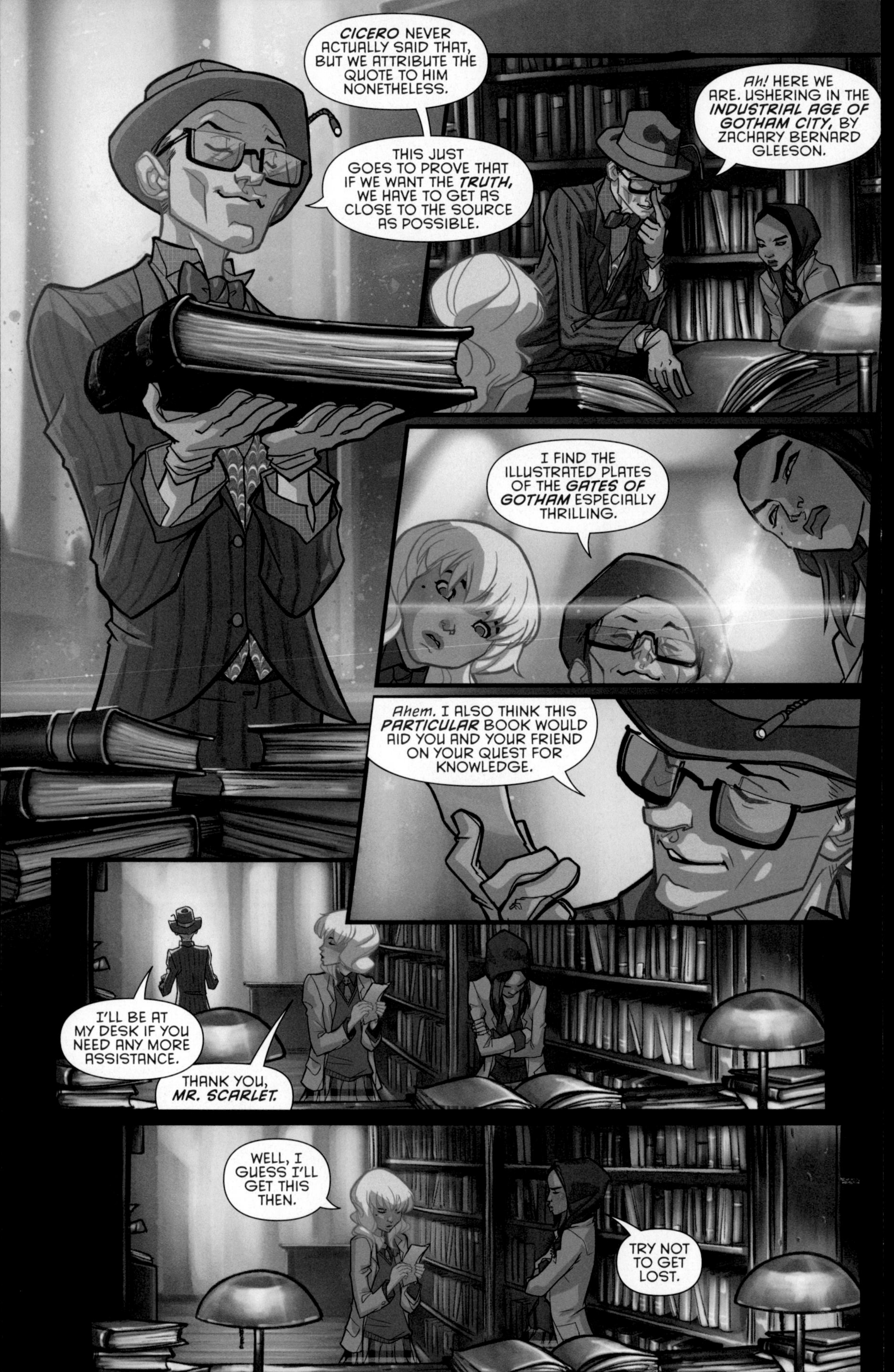
CICERO NEVER ACTUALLY SAID THAT, BUT WE ATTRIBUTE THE QUOTE TO HIM NONETHELESS.
THIS JUST GOES TO PROVE THAT IF WE WANT THE TRUTH, WE HAVE TO GET AS CLOSE TO THE SOURCE AS POSSIBLE.
Ah! HERE WE ARE. USHERING IN THE INDUSTRIAL AGE OF GOTHAM CITY, BY ZACHARY BERNARD GLEESON.
I FIND THE ILLUSTRATED PLATES OF THE GATES OF GOTHAM ESPECIALLY THRILLING.
Ahem. I ALSO THINK THIS PARTICULAR BOOK WOULD AID YOU AND YOUR FRIEND ON YOUR QUEST FOR KNOWLEDGE.
I'LL BE AT MY DESK IF YOU NEED ANY MORE ASSISTANCE.
THANK YOU, MR. SCARLET.
WELL, I GUESS I'LL GET THIS THEN.
TRY NOT TO GET LOST.

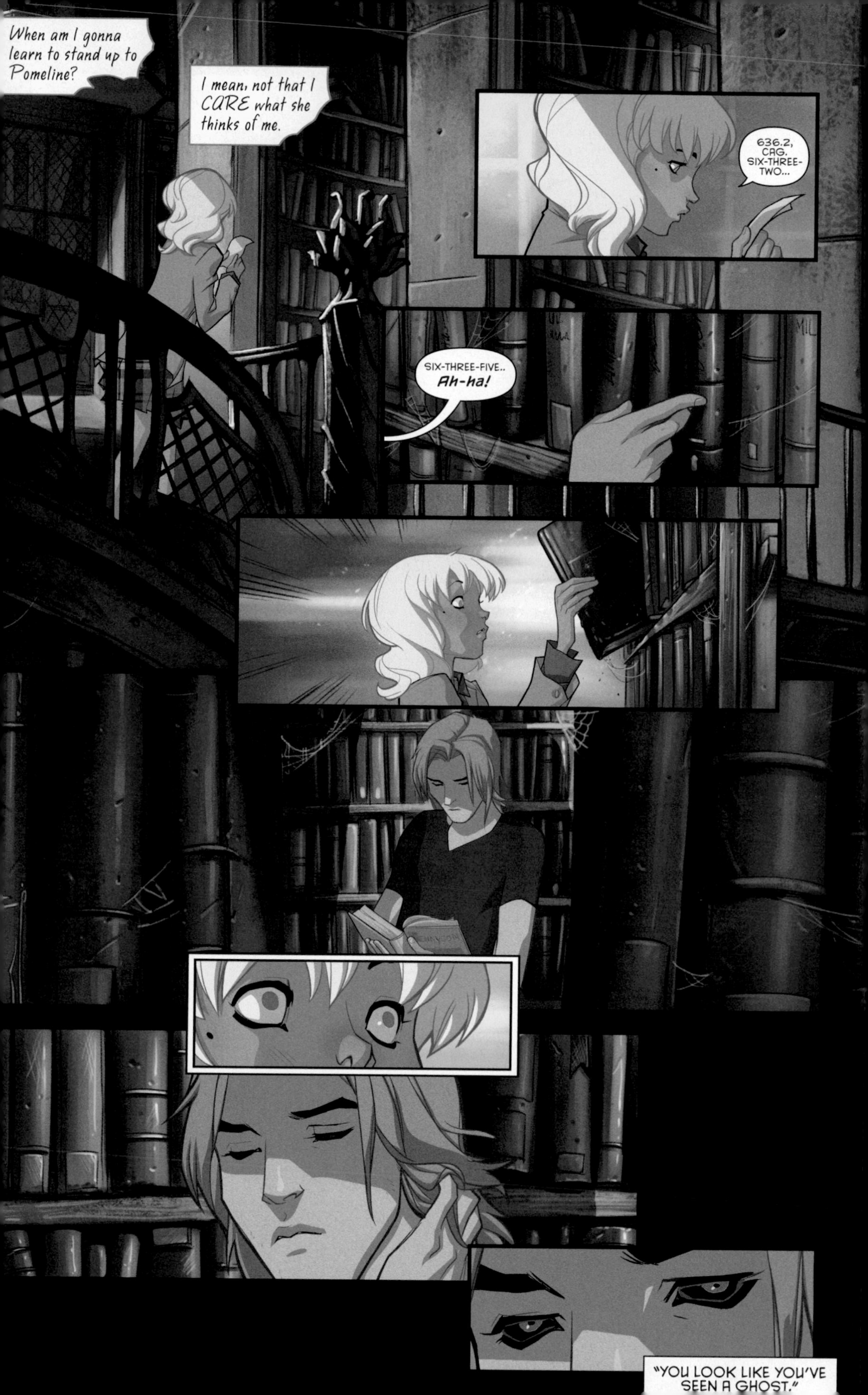
When am I gonna learn to stand up to Pomeline?
I mean, not that I CARE what she thinks of me.
636.2, CAG. SIX-THREE-TWO...
SIX-THREE-FIVE.. Ah-ha!
"YOU LOOK LIKE YOU'VE SEEN A GHOST."

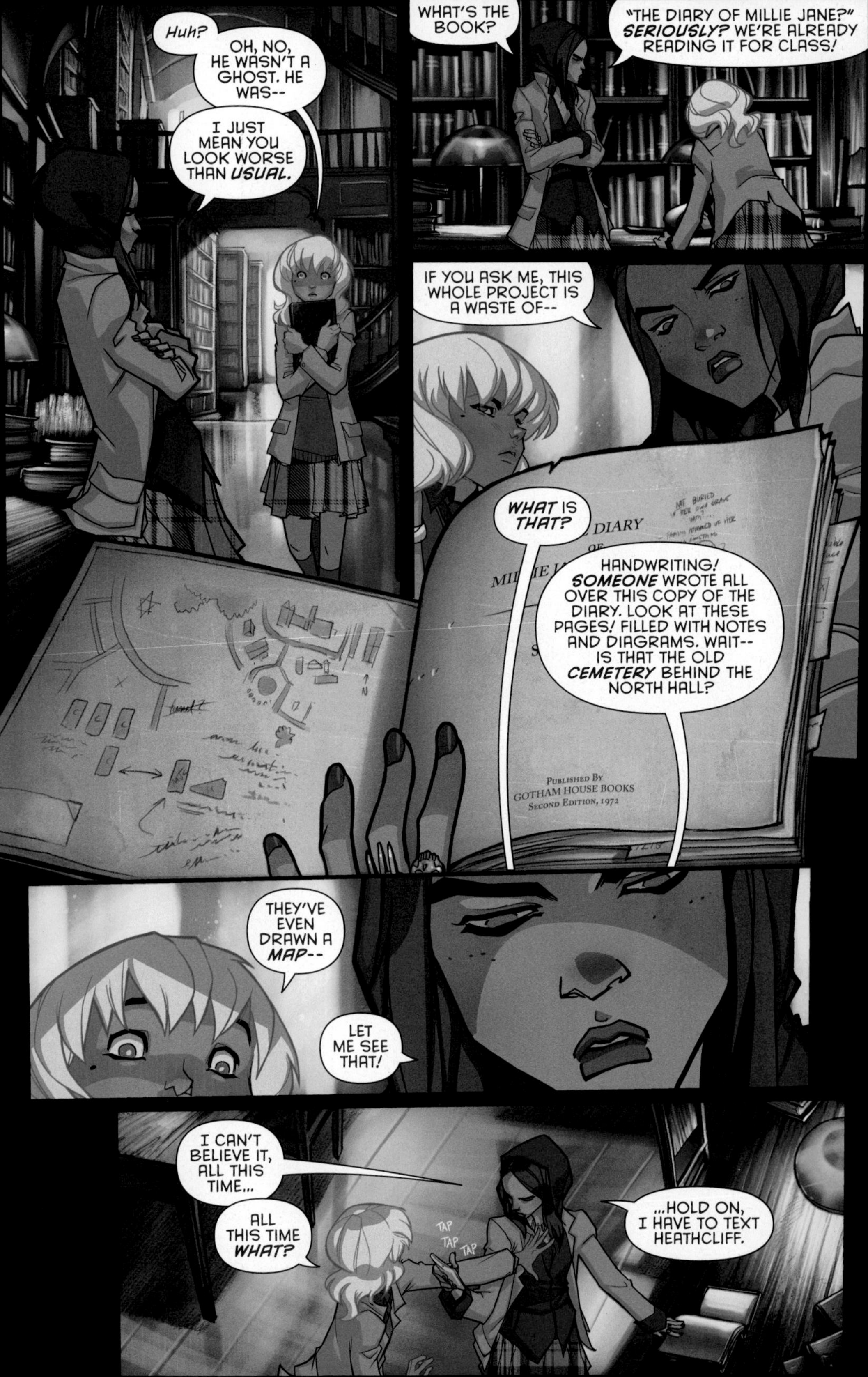
Huh?
OH, NO, HE WASN'T A GHOST. HE WAS--
I JUST MEAN YOU LOOK WORSE THAN USUAL.
WHAT'S THE BOOK?
"THE DIARY OF MILLIE JANE?" SERIOUSLY? WE'RE ALREADY READING IT FOR CLASS!
IF YOU ASK ME, THIS WHOLE PROJECT IS A WASTE OF--
WHAT IS THAT?
HANDWRITING! SOMEONE WROTE ALL OVER THIS COPY OF THE DIARY. LOOK AT THESE PAGES! FILLED WITH NOTES AND DIAGRAMS. WAIT-- IS THAT THE OLD CEMETERY BEHIND THE NORTH HALL?
PUBLISHED BY
GOTHAM HOUSE BOOKS
SECOND EDITION, 1972
THEY'VE EVEN DRAWN A MAP--
LET ME SEE THAT!
I CAN'T BELIEVE IT, ALL THIS TIME...
ALL THIS TIME WHAT?
TAP TAP TAP
...HOLD ON, I HAVE TO TEXT HEATHCLIFF.

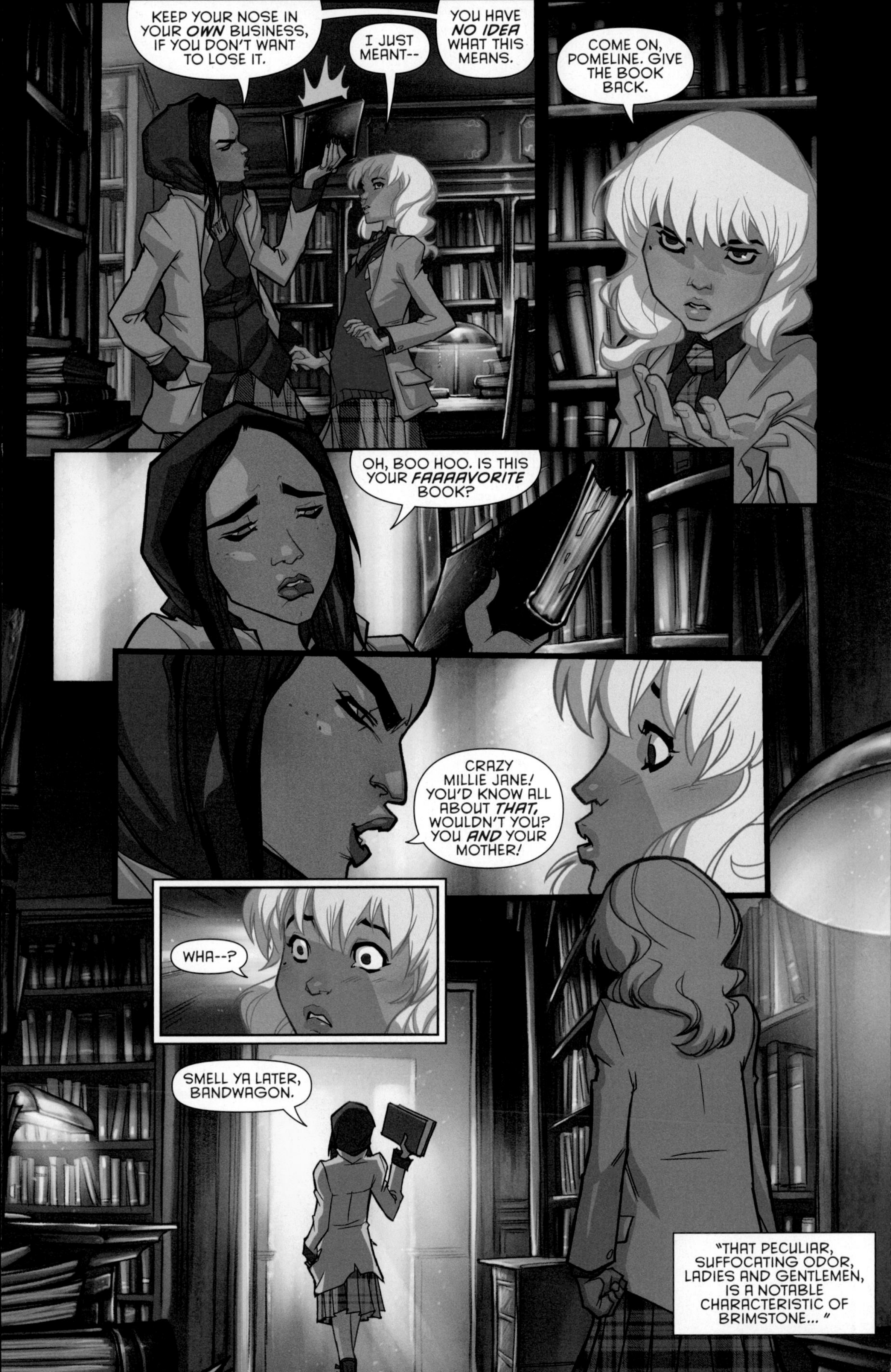
KEEP YOUR NOSE IN YOUR OWN BUSINESS, IF YOU DON'T WANT TO LOSE IT.
I JUST MEANT--
YOU HAVE NO IDEA WHAT THIS MEANS.
COME ON, POMELINE. GIVE THE BOOK BACK.
OH, BOO HOO. IS THIS YOUR FAAAAVORITE BOOK?
CRAZY MILLIE JANE! YOU'D KNOW ALL ABOUT THAT, WOULDN'T YOU? YOU AND YOUR MOTHER!
WHA--?
SMELL YA LATER, BANDWAGON.
"THAT PECULIAR, SUFFOCATING ODOR, LADIES AND GENTLEMEN, IS A NOTABLE CHARACTERISTIC OF BRIMSTONE..."

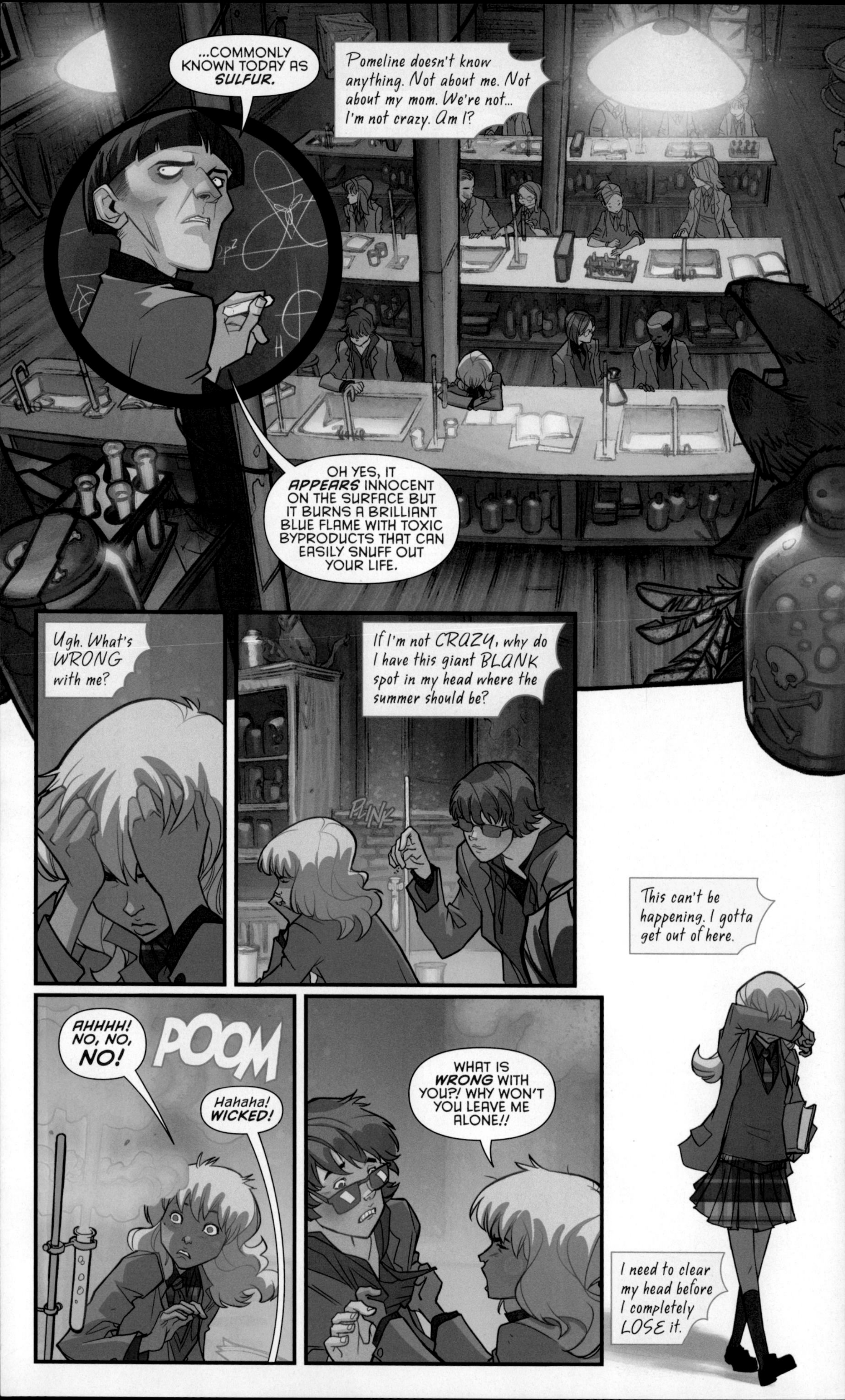
...COMMONLY KNOWN TODAY AS SULFUR.
Pomeline doesn't know anything. Not about me. Not about my mom. We're not... I'm not crazy. Am I?
OH YES, IT APPEARS INNOCENT ON THE SURFACE BUT IT BURNS A BRILLIANT BLUE FLAME WITH TOXIC BYPRODUCTS THAT CAN EASILY SNUFF OUT YOUR LIFE.
Ugh. What's WRONG with me?
If I'm not CRAZY, why do I have this giant BLANK spot in my head where the summer should be?
PLINK
This can't be happening. I gotta get out of here.
AHHHH! NO, NO, NO!
POOM
Hahaha! WICKED!
WHAT IS WRONG WITH YOU?! WHY WON'T YOU LEAVE ME ALONE!!
I need to clear my head before I completely LOSE it.

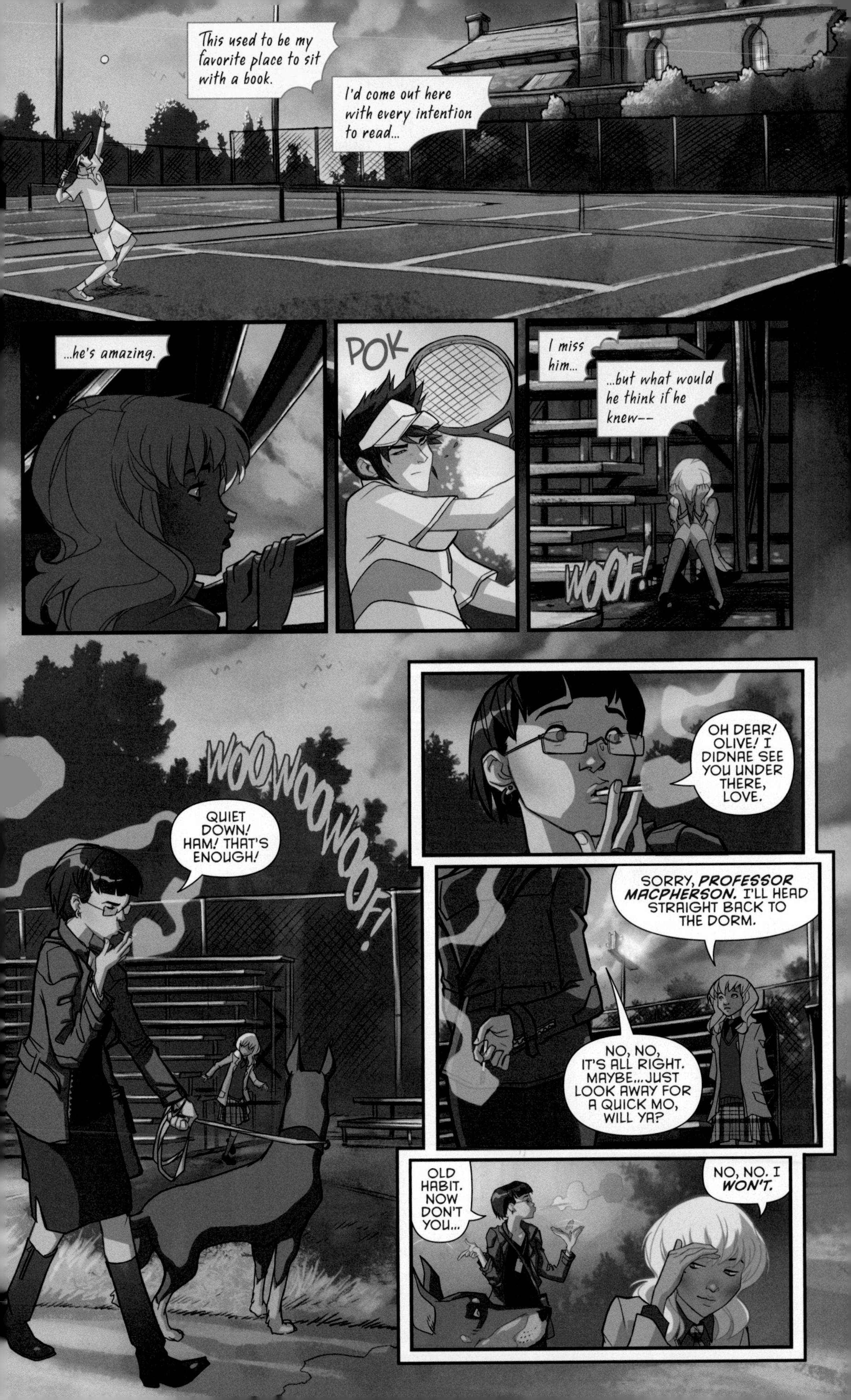
This used to be my favorite place to sit with a book.
I'd come out here with every intention to read...
...he's amazing.
POK
I miss him...
...but what would he think if he knew--
WOOF!
WOOWOOWOOWOOF!
QUIET DOWN! HAM! THAT'S ENOUGH!
OH DEAR! OLIVE! I DIDNAE SEE YOU UNDER THERE, LOVE.
SORRY, PROFESSOR MACPHERSON. I'LL HEAD STRAIGHT BACK TO THE DORM.
NO, NO, IT'S ALL RIGHT. MAYBE... JUST LOOK AWAY FOR A QUICK MO, WILL YA?
OLD HABIT. NOW DON'T YOU...
NO, NO. I WON'T.

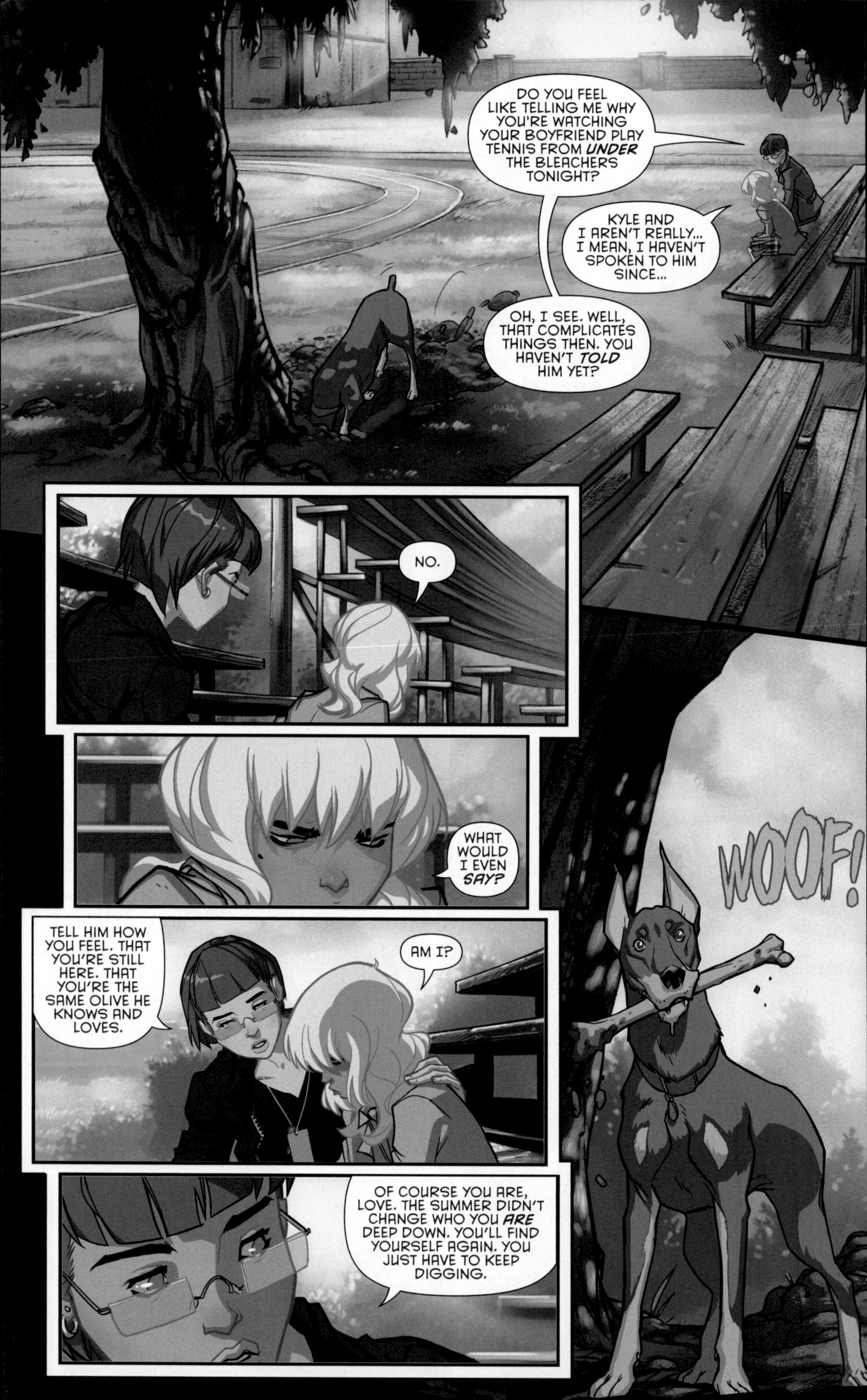
DO YOU FEEL LIKE TELLING ME WHY YOU'RE WATCHING YOUR BOYFRIEND PLAY TENNIS FROM UNDER THE BLEACHERS TONIGHT?
KYLE AND I AREN'T REALLY... I MEAN, I HAVEN'T SPOKEN TO HIM SINCE...
OH, I SEE. WELL, THAT COMPLICATES THINGS THEN. YOU HAVEN'T TOLD HIM YET?
NO.
WHAT WOULD I EVEN SAY?
TELL HIM HOW YOU FEEL. THAT YOU'RE STILL HERE. THAT YOU'RE THE SAME OLIVE HE KNOWS AND LOVES.
AM I?
WOOF!
OF COURSE YOU ARE, LOVE. THE SUMMER DIDN'T CHANGE WHO YOU ARE DEEP DOWN. YOU'LL FIND YOURSELF AGAIN. YOU JUST HAVE TO KEEP DIGGING.

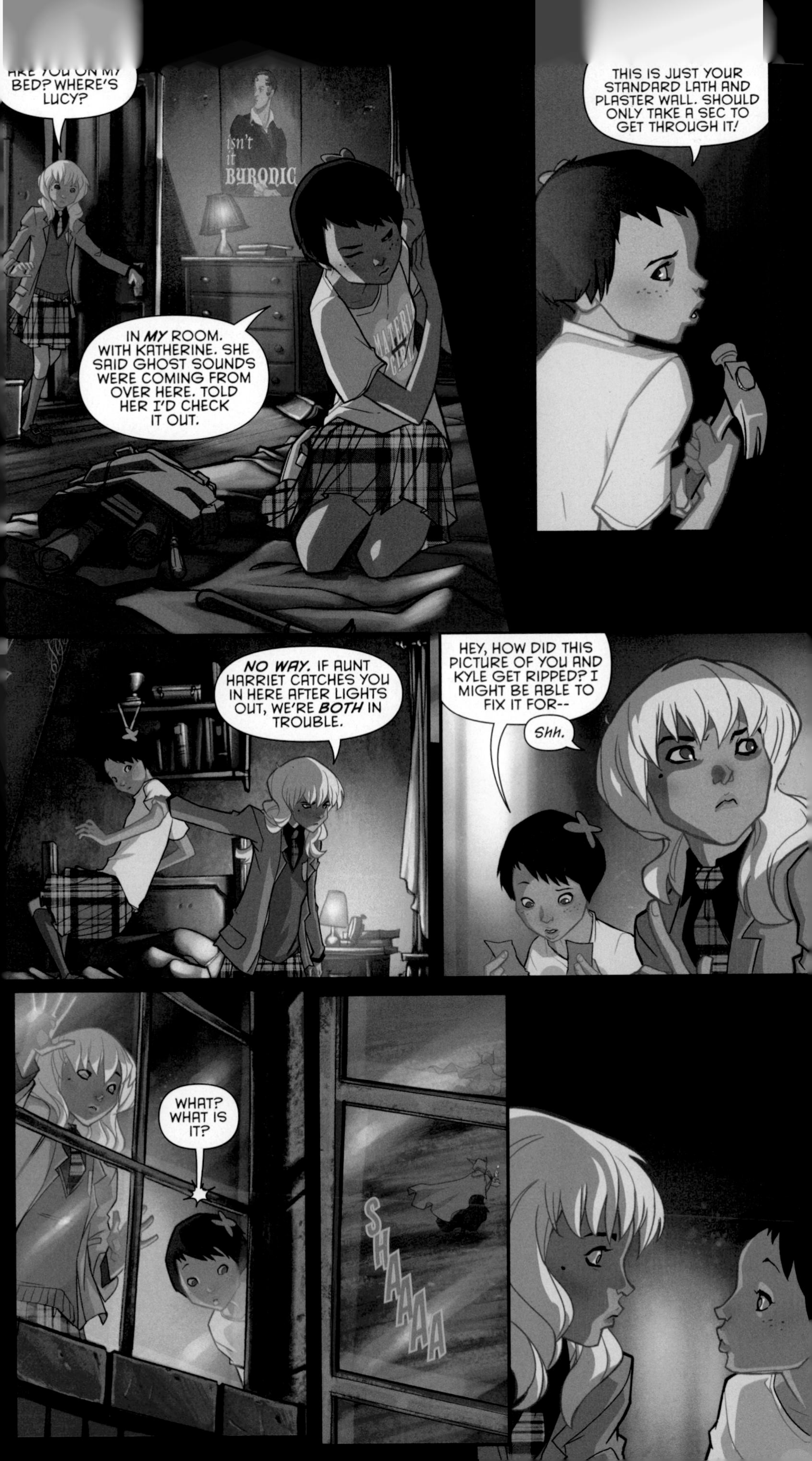

ARE YOU ON MY BED? WHERE'S LUCY?
isn't it BYRONIC
IN MY ROOM. WITH KATHERINE. SHE SAID GHOST SOUNDS WERE COMING FROM OVER HERE. TOLD HER I'D CHECK IT OUT.
THIS IS JUST YOUR STANDARD LATH AND PLASTER WALL. SHOULD ONLY TAKE A SEC TO GET THROUGH IT!
NO WAY. IF AUNT HARRIET CATCHES YOU IN HERE AFTER LIGHTS OUT, WE'RE BOTH IN TROUBLE.
HEY, HOW DID THIS PICTURE OF YOU AND KYLE GET RIPPED? I MIGHT BE ABLE TO FIX IT FOR--
Shh.
WHAT? WHAT IS IT?
SHAAAAA

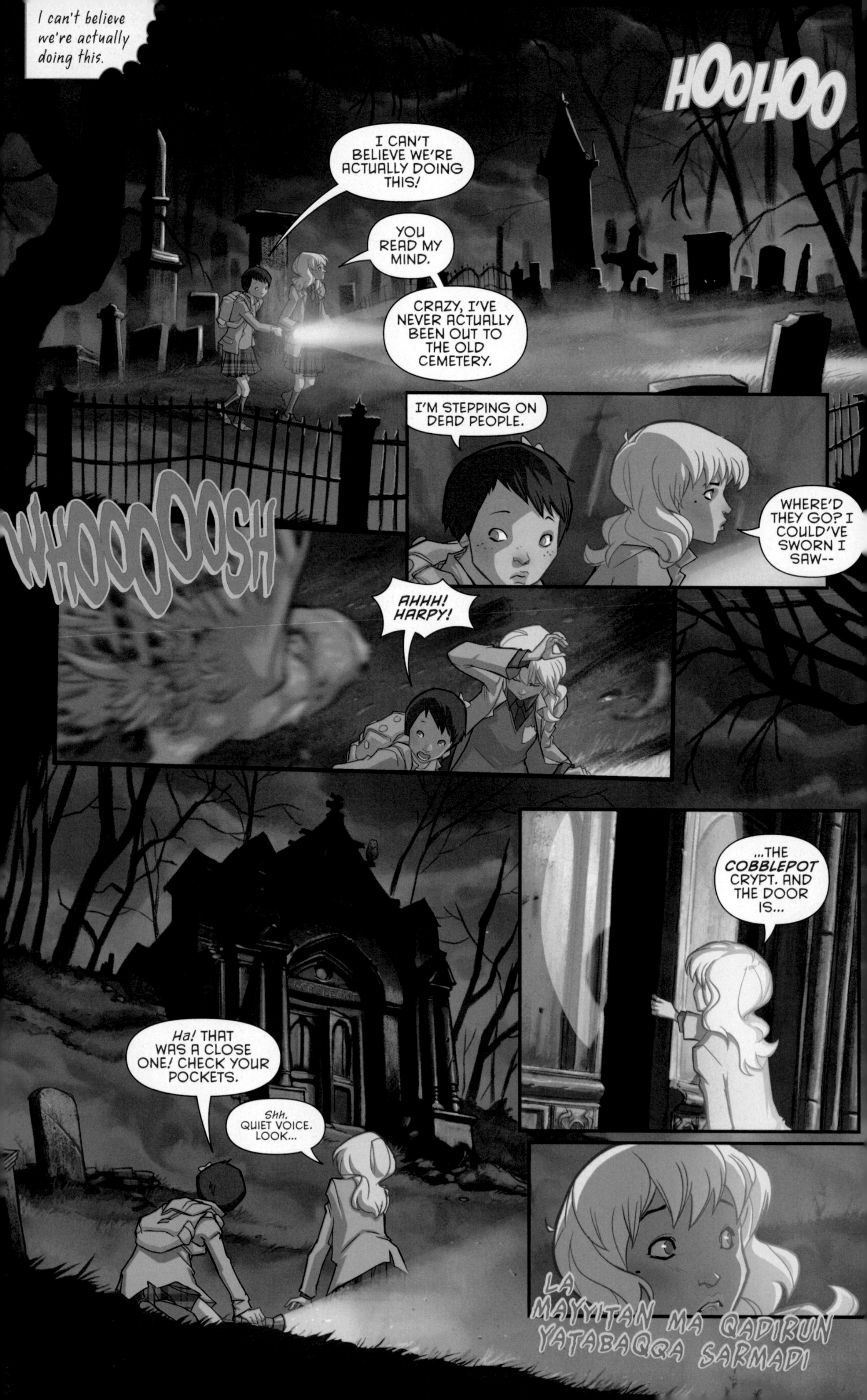
I can't believe we're actually doing this.
HOOHOO
I CAN'T BELIEVE WE'RE ACTUALLY DOING THIS!
YOU READ MY MIND.
CRAZY, I'VE NEVER ACTUALLY BEEN OUT TO THE OLD CEMETERY.
I'M STEPPING ON DEAD PEOPLE.
WHERE'D THEY GO? I COULD'VE SWORN I SAW--
WHOOOOOSH
AHHH! HARPY!
Ha! THAT WAS A CLOSE ONE! CHECK YOUR POCKETS.
Shh. QUIET VOICE. LOOK...
...THE COBBLEPOT CRYPT. AND THE DOOR IS...
LA MAYYITAN MA QADIRUN YATABAQQA SARMADI

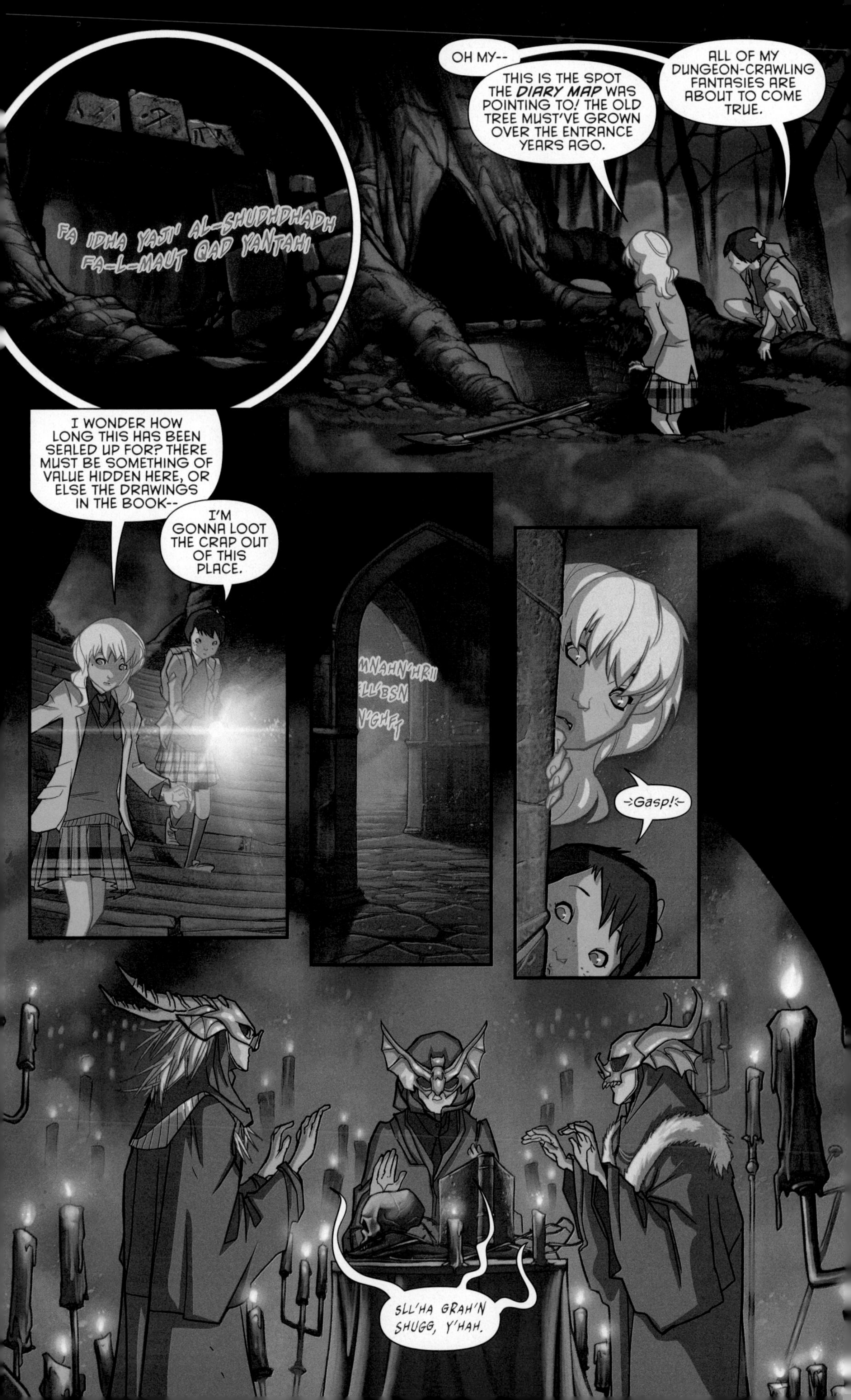
FA IDHA YAJI' AL-SHUDHDHADH
FA-L-MAUT QAD YANTAHI
OH MY--
THIS IS THE SPOT THE *DIARY MAP* WAS POINTING TO! THE OLD TREE MUST'VE GROWN OVER THE ENTRANCE YEARS AGO.
ALL OF MY DUNGEON-CRAWLING FANTASIES ARE ABOUT TO COME TRUE.
I WONDER HOW LONG THIS HAS BEEN SEALED UP FOR? THERE MUST BE SOMETHING OF VALUE HIDDEN HERE, OR ELSE THE DRAWINGS IN THE BOOK--
I'M GONNA LOOT THE CRAP OUT OF THIS PLACE.
MNAHN'HRI
ELL'BSN
N'GHFT
-Gasp!-
SLL'HA GRAH'N SHUGG, Y'HAH.

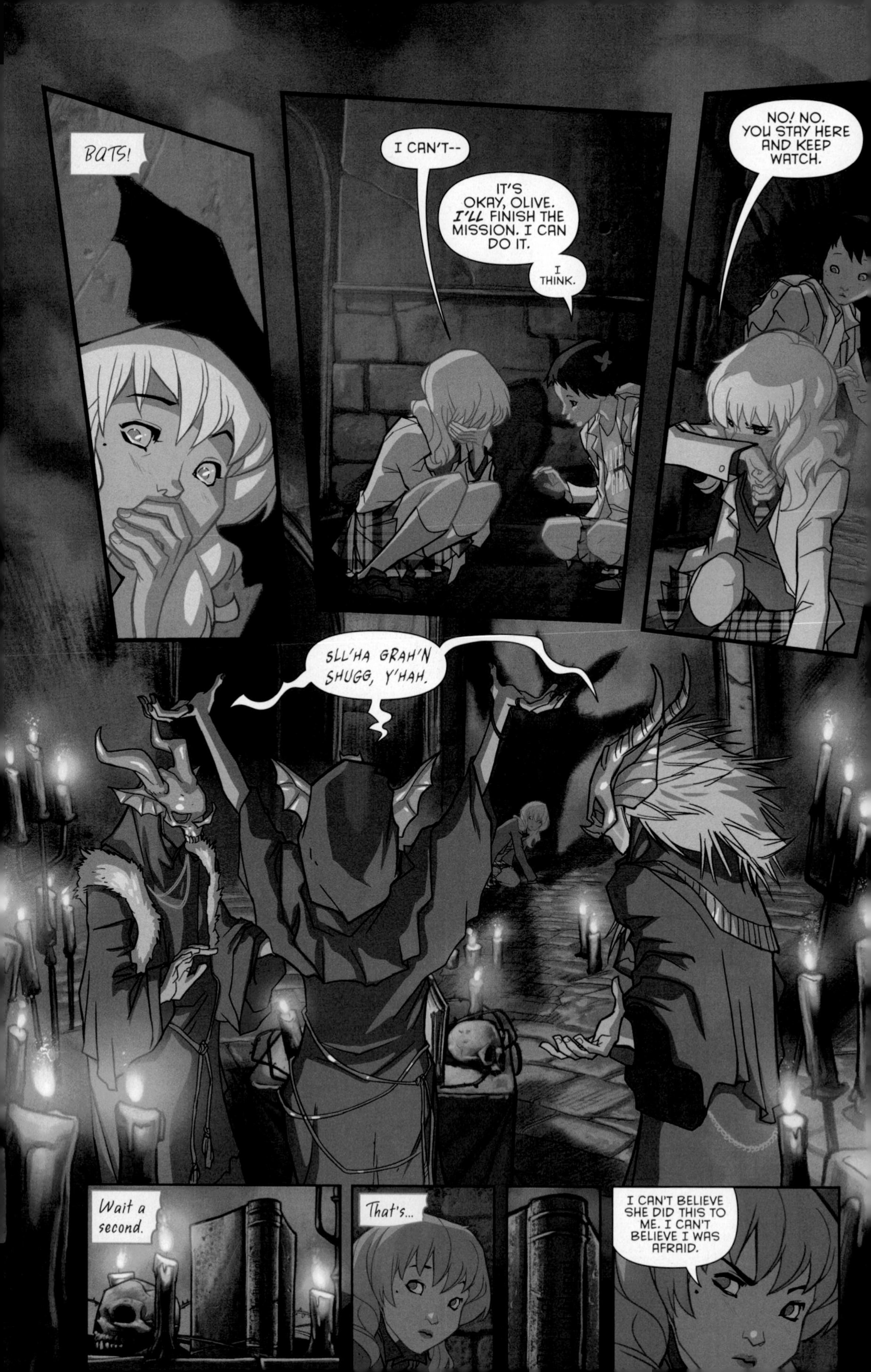
BATS!
I CAN'T--
IT'S OKAY, OLIVE. I'LL FINISH THE MISSION. I CAN DO IT.
I THINK.
NO! NO. YOU STAY HERE AND KEEP WATCH.
SLL'HA GRAH'N SHUGG, Y'HAH.
Wait a second.
That's...
I CAN'T BELIEVE SHE DID THIS TO ME. I CAN'T BELIEVE I WAS AFRAID.

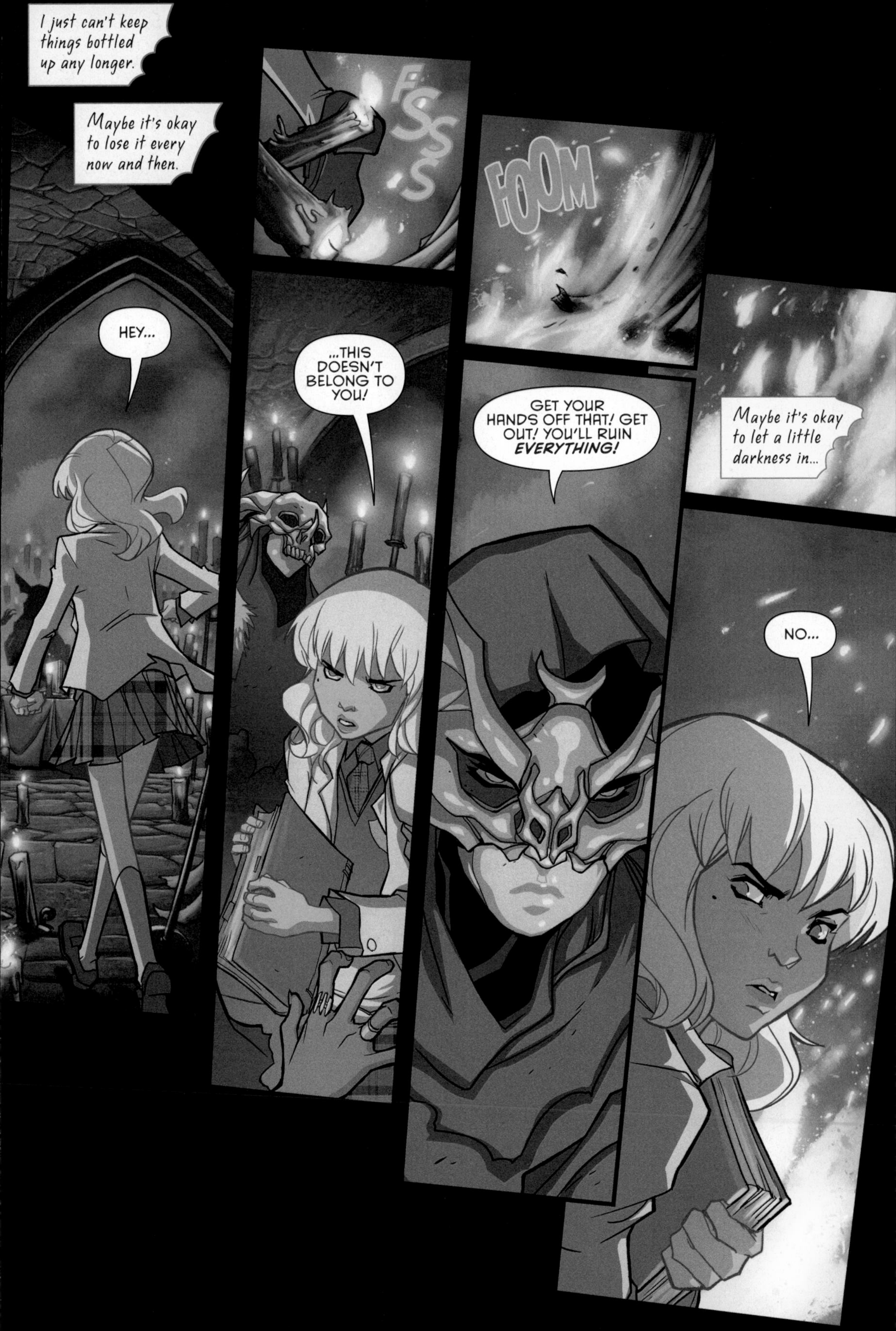
I just can't keep things bottled up any longer.
Maybe it's okay to lose it every now and then.
FSSS
FOOM
HEY...
...THIS DOESN'T BELONG TO YOU!
GET YOUR HANDS OFF THAT! GET OUT! YOU'LL RUIN EVERYTHING!
Maybe it's okay to let a little darkness in...
NO...

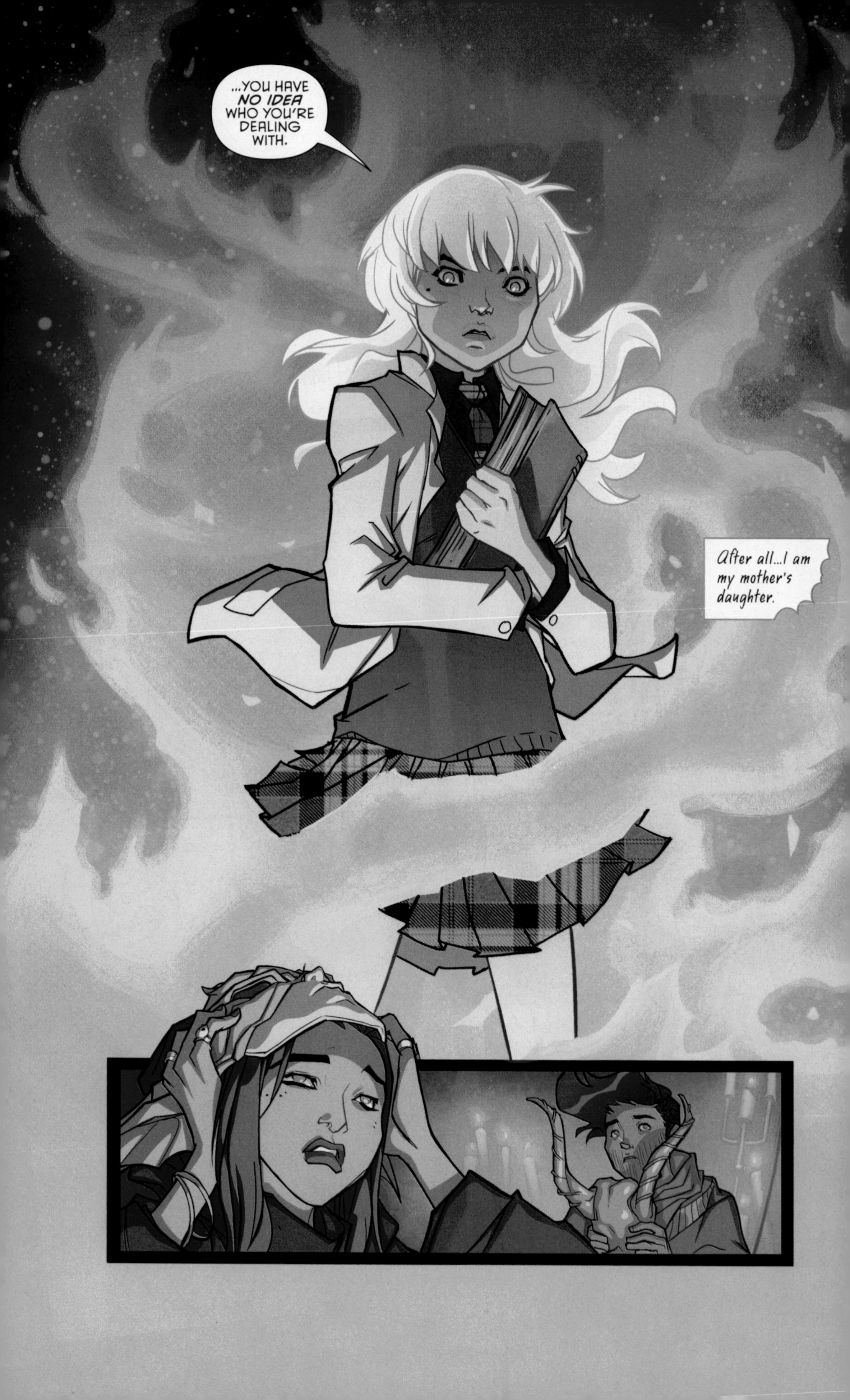
...YOU HAVE NO IDEA WHO YOU'RE DEALING WITH.
After all...I am my mother's daughter.

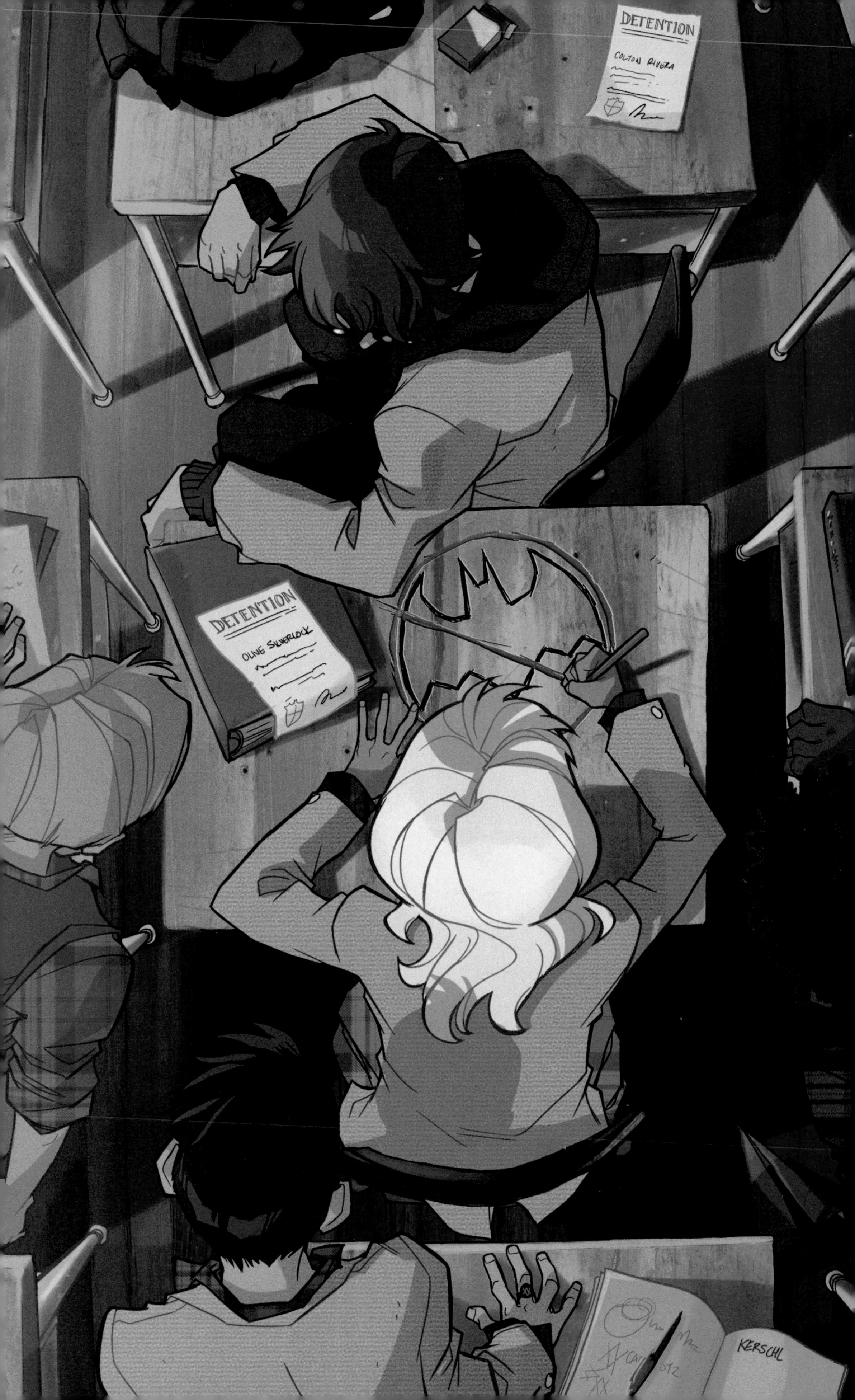
DETENTION
COLTON RIVERA
DETENTION
OLIVE SILVERLOCK
KERSCHL

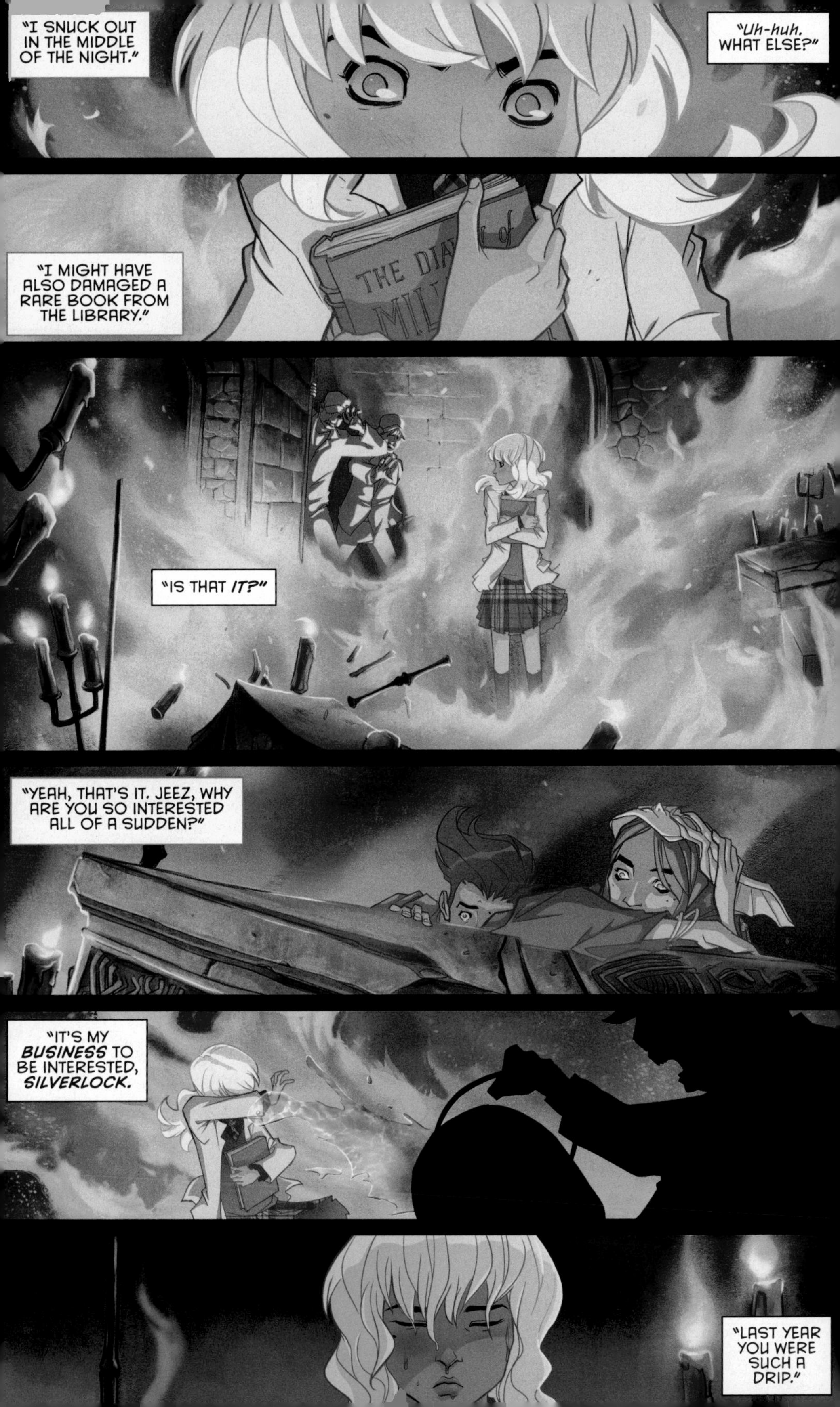
"I SNUCK OUT IN THE MIDDLE OF THE NIGHT."
"Uh-huh. WHAT ELSE?"
"I MIGHT HAVE ALSO DAMAGED A RARE BOOK FROM THE LIBRARY."
"IS THAT *IT?*"
"YEAH, THAT'S IT. JEEZ, WHY ARE YOU SO INTERESTED ALL OF A SUDDEN?"
"IT'S MY ***BUSINESS*** TO BE INTERESTED, ***SILVERLOCK.***
"LAST YEAR YOU WERE SUCH A DRIP."

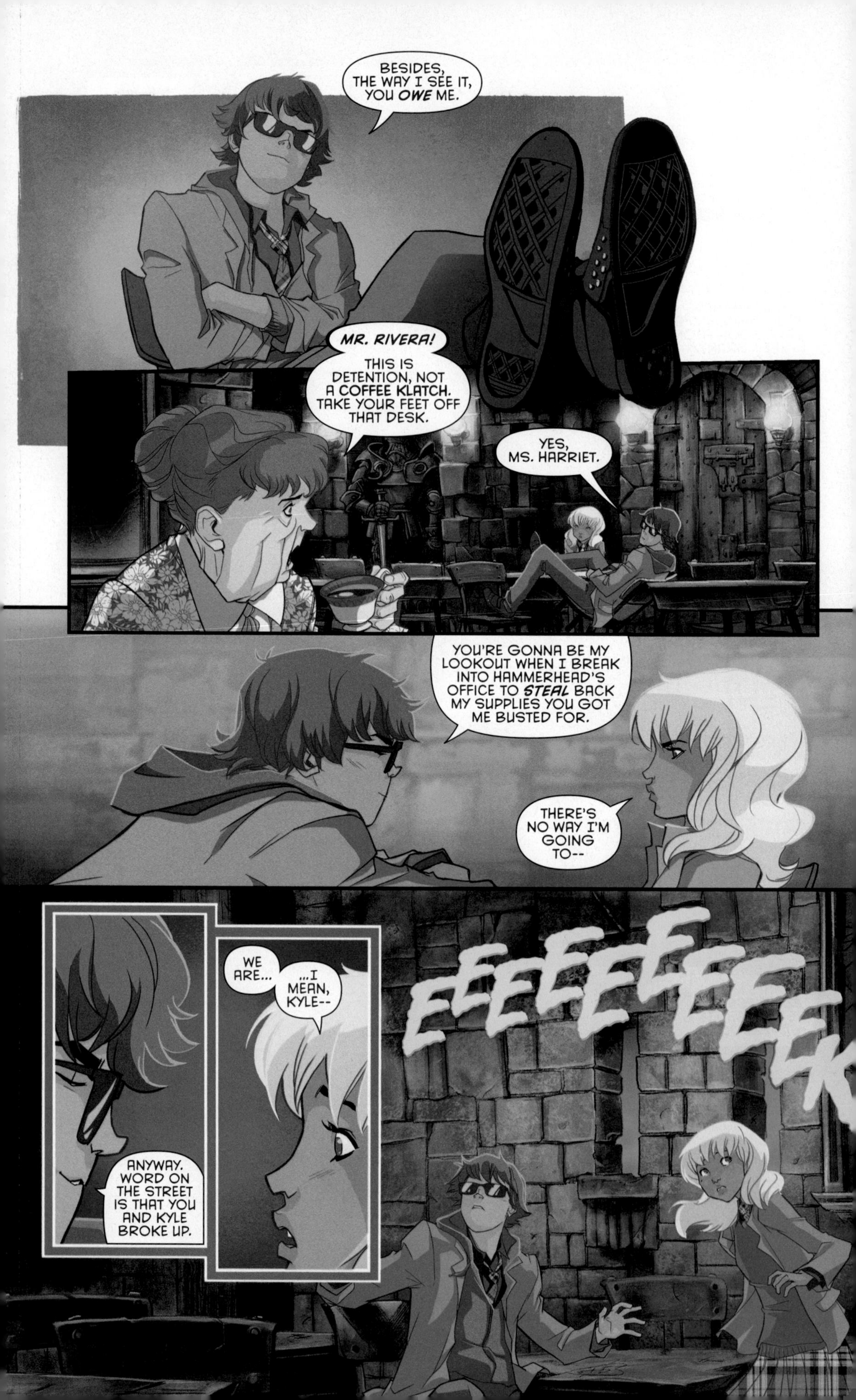
BESIDES, THE WAY I SEE IT, YOU OWE ME.
MR. RIVERA!
THIS IS DETENTION, NOT A COFFEE KLATCH. TAKE YOUR FEET OFF THAT DESK.
YES, MS. HARRIET.
YOU'RE GONNA BE MY LOOKOUT WHEN I BREAK INTO HAMMERHEAD'S OFFICE TO STEAL BACK MY SUPPLIES YOU GOT ME BUSTED FOR.
THERE'S NO WAY I'M GOING TO--
ANYWAY. WORD ON THE STREET IS THAT YOU AND KYLE BROKE UP.
WE ARE...
...I MEAN, KYLE--
EEEEEEEEEEK

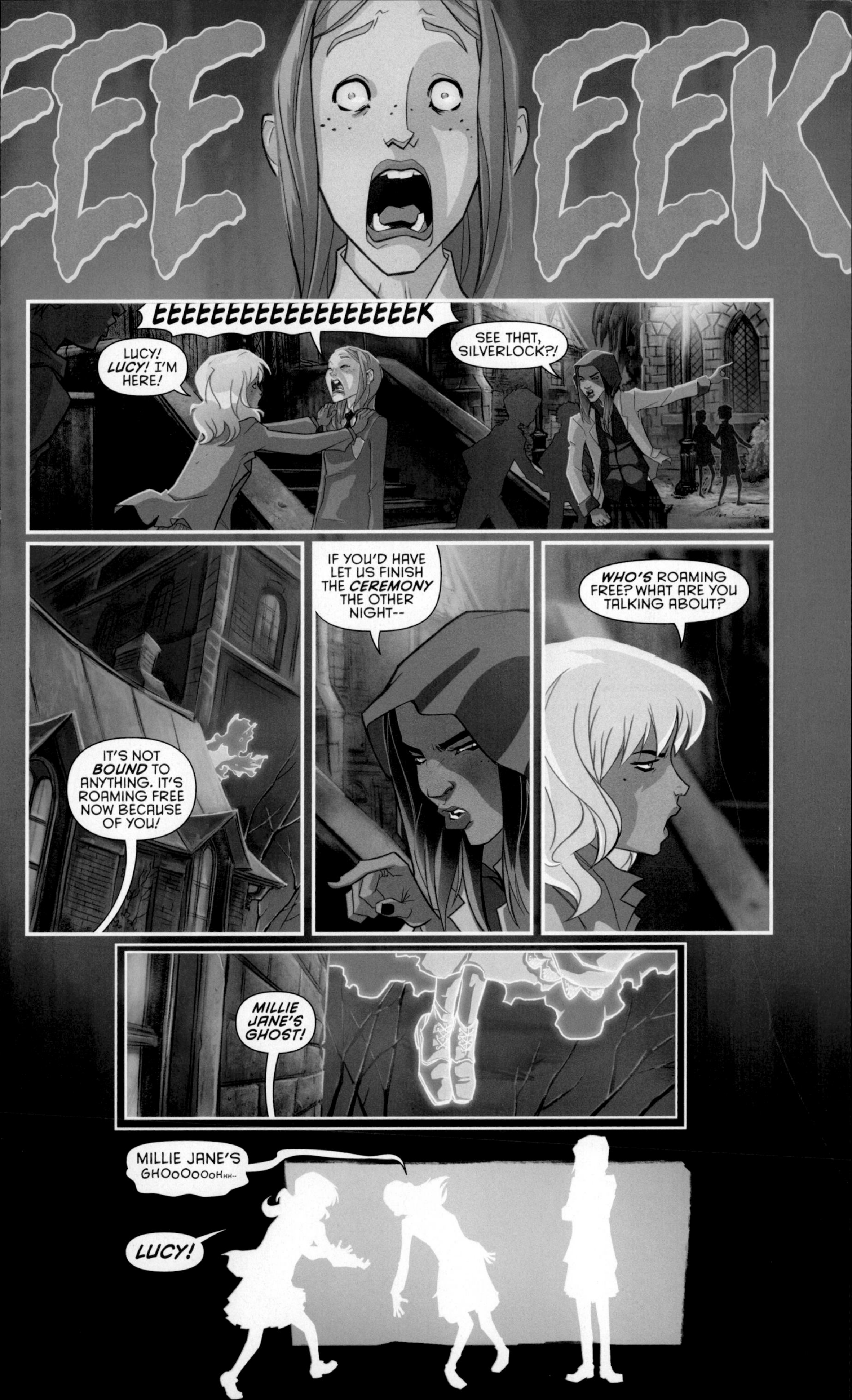
EEE EEK
EEEEEEEEEEEEEEEEEEEK
LUCY! LUCY! I'M HERE!
SEE THAT, SILVERLOCK?!
IT'S NOT BOUND TO ANYTHING. IT'S ROAMING FREE NOW BECAUSE OF YOU!
IF YOU'D HAVE LET US FINISH THE CEREMONY THE OTHER NIGHT--
WHO'S ROAMING FREE? WHAT ARE YOU TALKING ABOUT?
MILLIE JANE'S GHOST!
MILLIE JANE'S GHOOOOOOOHHH--
LUCY!

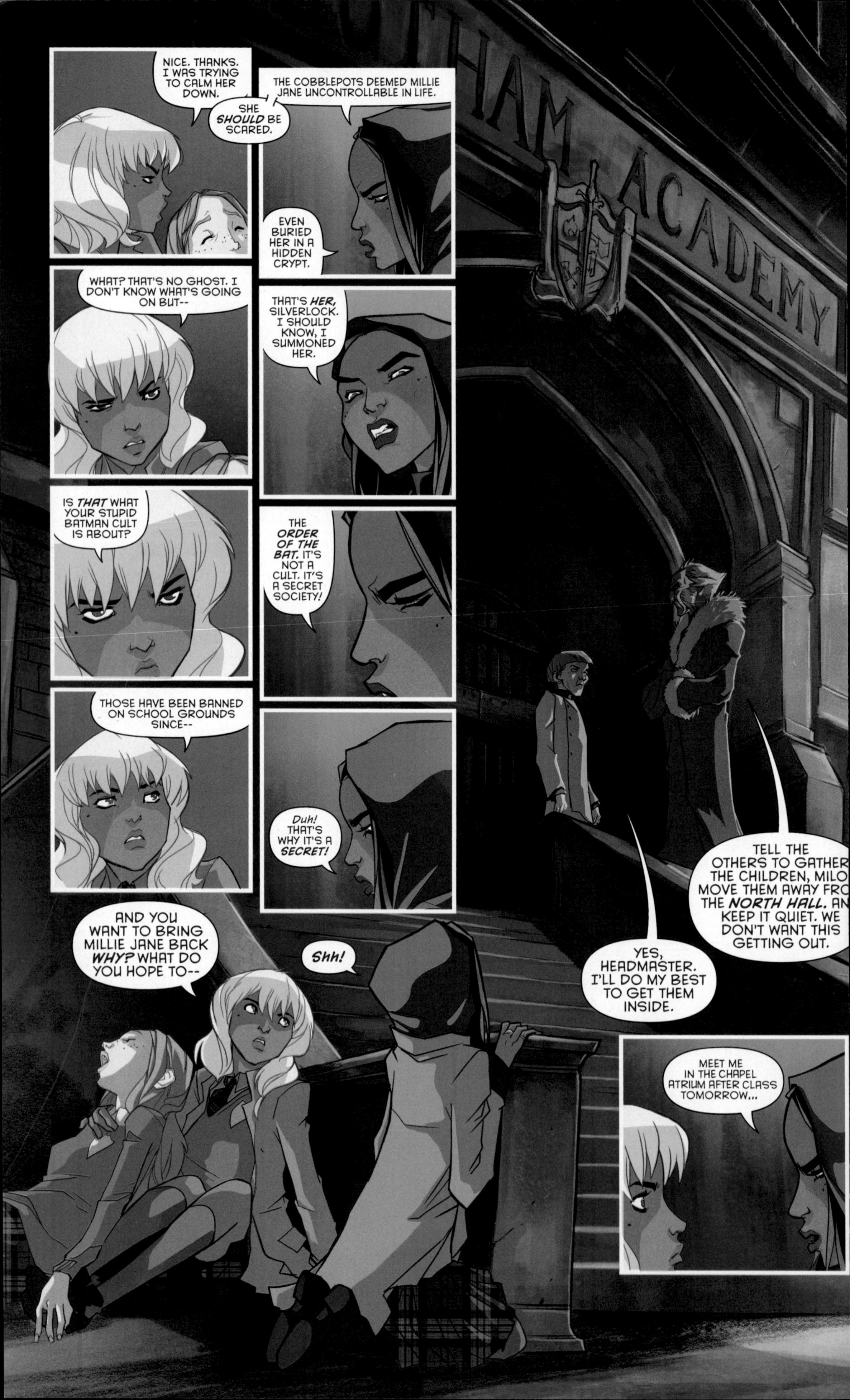
NICE. THANKS. I WAS TRYING TO CALM HER DOWN.
SHE *SHOULD* BE SCARED.
THE COBBLEPOTS DEEMED MILLIE JANE UNCONTROLLABLE IN LIFE.
EVEN BURIED HER IN A HIDDEN CRYPT.
ACADEMY
WHAT? THAT'S NO GHOST. I DON'T KNOW WHAT'S GOING ON BUT--
THAT'S *HER*, SILVERLOCK. I SHOULD KNOW, I SUMMONED HER.
IS *THAT* WHAT YOUR STUPID BATMAN CULT IS ABOUT?
THE *ORDER OF THE BAT*. IT'S NOT A CULT. IT'S A SECRET SOCIETY!
THOSE HAVE BEEN BANNED ON SCHOOL GROUNDS SINCE--
*Duh!* THAT'S WHY IT'S A *SECRET!*
AND YOU WANT TO BRING MILLIE JANE BACK *WHY?* WHAT DO YOU HOPE TO--
*Shh!*
TELL THE OTHERS TO GATHER THE CHILDREN, MILO MOVE THEM AWAY FRO THE *NORTH HALL*. AN KEEP IT QUIET. WE DON'T WANT THIS GETTING OUT.
YES, HEADMASTER. I'LL DO MY BEST TO GET THEM INSIDE.
MEET ME IN THE CHAPEL ATRIUM AFTER CLASS TOMORROW...

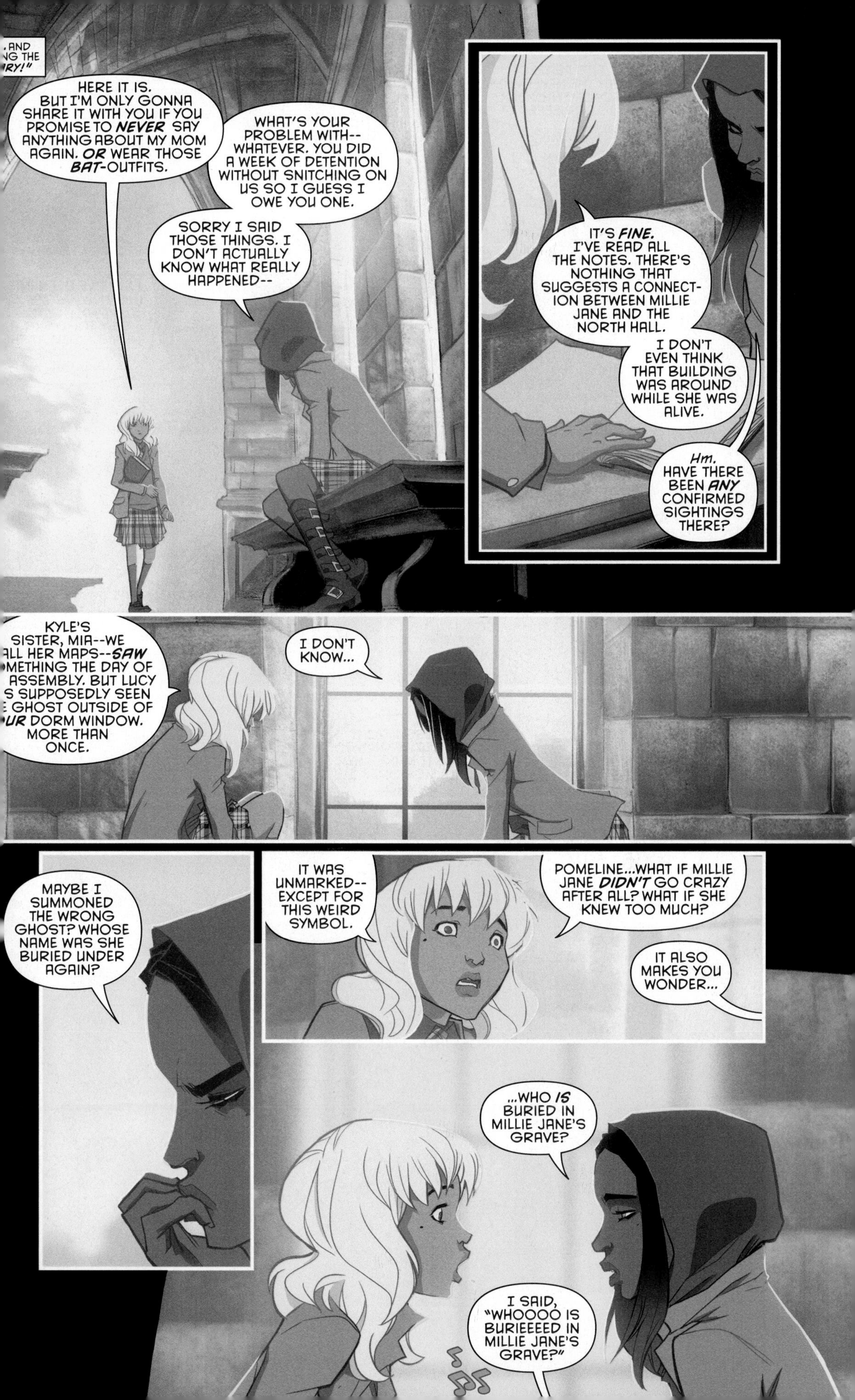
, AND
NG THE
RY!"
HERE IT IS. BUT I'M ONLY GONNA SHARE IT WITH YOU IF YOU PROMISE TO NEVER SAY ANYTHING ABOUT MY MOM AGAIN. OR WEAR THOSE BAT-OUTFITS.
WHAT'S YOUR PROBLEM WITH-- WHATEVER. YOU DID A WEEK OF DETENTION WITHOUT SNITCHING ON US SO I GUESS I OWE YOU ONE.
SORRY I SAID THOSE THINGS. I DON'T ACTUALLY KNOW WHAT REALLY HAPPENED--
IT'S FINE. I'VE READ ALL THE NOTES. THERE'S NOTHING THAT SUGGESTS A CONNECT-ION BETWEEN MILLIE JANE AND THE NORTH HALL.
I DON'T EVEN THINK THAT BUILDING WAS AROUND WHILE SHE WAS ALIVE.
Hm. HAVE THERE BEEN ANY CONFIRMED SIGHTINGS THERE?
KYLE'S SISTER, MIA--WE ALL HER MAPS--SAW METHING THE DAY OF ASSEMBLY. BUT LUCY S SUPPOSEDLY SEEN GHOST OUTSIDE OF UR DORM WINDOW. MORE THAN ONCE.
I DON'T KNOW...
MAYBE I SUMMONED THE WRONG GHOST? WHOSE NAME WAS SHE BURIED UNDER AGAIN?
IT WAS UNMARKED-- EXCEPT FOR THIS WEIRD SYMBOL.
POMELINE...WHAT IF MILLIE JANE DIDN'T GO CRAZY AFTER ALL? WHAT IF SHE KNEW TOO MUCH?
IT ALSO MAKES YOU WONDER...
...WHO IS BURIED IN MILLIE JANE'S GRAVE?
I SAID, "WHOOOO IS BURIEEEED IN MILLIE JANE'S GRAVE?"

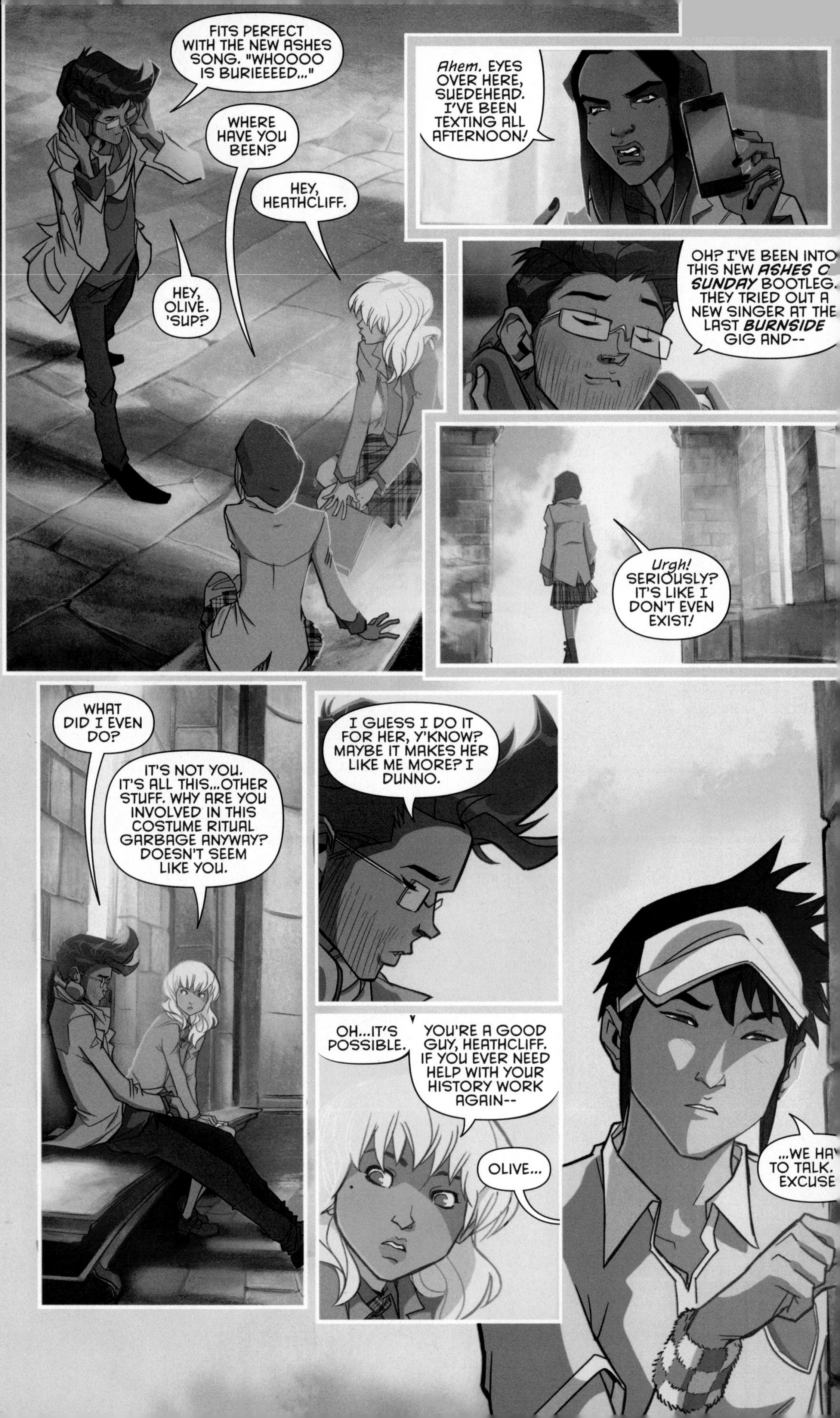

FITS PERFECT WITH THE NEW ASHES SONG. "WHOOOO IS BURIEEEED..."
WHERE HAVE YOU BEEN?
HEY, HEATHCLIFF.
HEY, OLIVE. 'SUP?
*Ahem.* EYES OVER HERE, SUEDEHEAD. I'VE BEEN TEXTING ALL AFTERNOON!
OH? I'VE BEEN INTO THIS NEW ***ASHES O SUNDAY*** BOOTLEG. THEY TRIED OUT A NEW SINGER AT THE LAST ***BURNSIDE*** GIG AND--
*Urgh!* SERIOUSLY? IT'S LIKE I DON'T EVEN EXIST!
WHAT DID I EVEN DO?
IT'S NOT YOU. IT'S ALL THIS...OTHER STUFF. WHY ARE YOU INVOLVED IN THIS COSTUME RITUAL GARBAGE ANYWAY? DOESN'T SEEM LIKE YOU.
I GUESS I DO IT FOR HER, Y'KNOW? MAYBE IT MAKES HER LIKE ME MORE? I DUNNO.
OH...IT'S POSSIBLE.
YOU'RE A GOOD GUY, HEATHCLIFF. IF YOU EVER NEED HELP WITH YOUR HISTORY WORK AGAIN--
OLIVE...
...WE HA TO TALK. EXCUSE

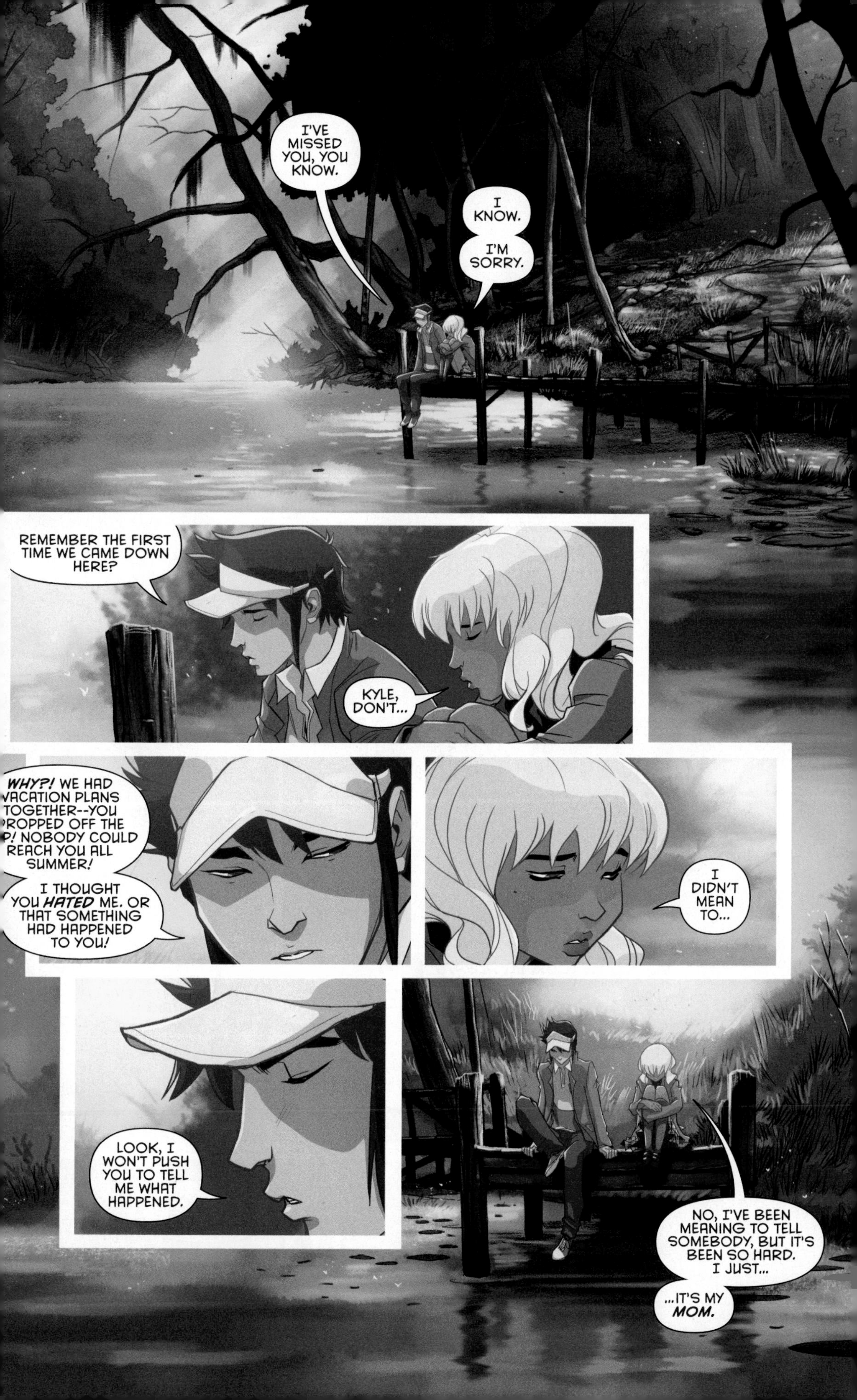
I'VE MISSED YOU, YOU KNOW.
I KNOW.
I'M SORRY.
REMEMBER THE FIRST TIME WE CAME DOWN HERE?
KYLE, DON'T...
WHY?! WE HAD VACATION PLANS TOGETHER--YOU ROPPED OFF THE P! NOBODY COULD REACH YOU ALL SUMMER!
I THOUGHT YOU HATED ME. OR THAT SOMETHING HAD HAPPENED TO YOU!
I DIDN'T MEAN TO...
LOOK, I WON'T PUSH YOU TO TELL ME WHAT HAPPENED.
NO, I'VE BEEN MEANING TO TELL SOMEBODY, BUT IT'S BEEN SO HARD. I JUST...
...IT'S MY MOM.

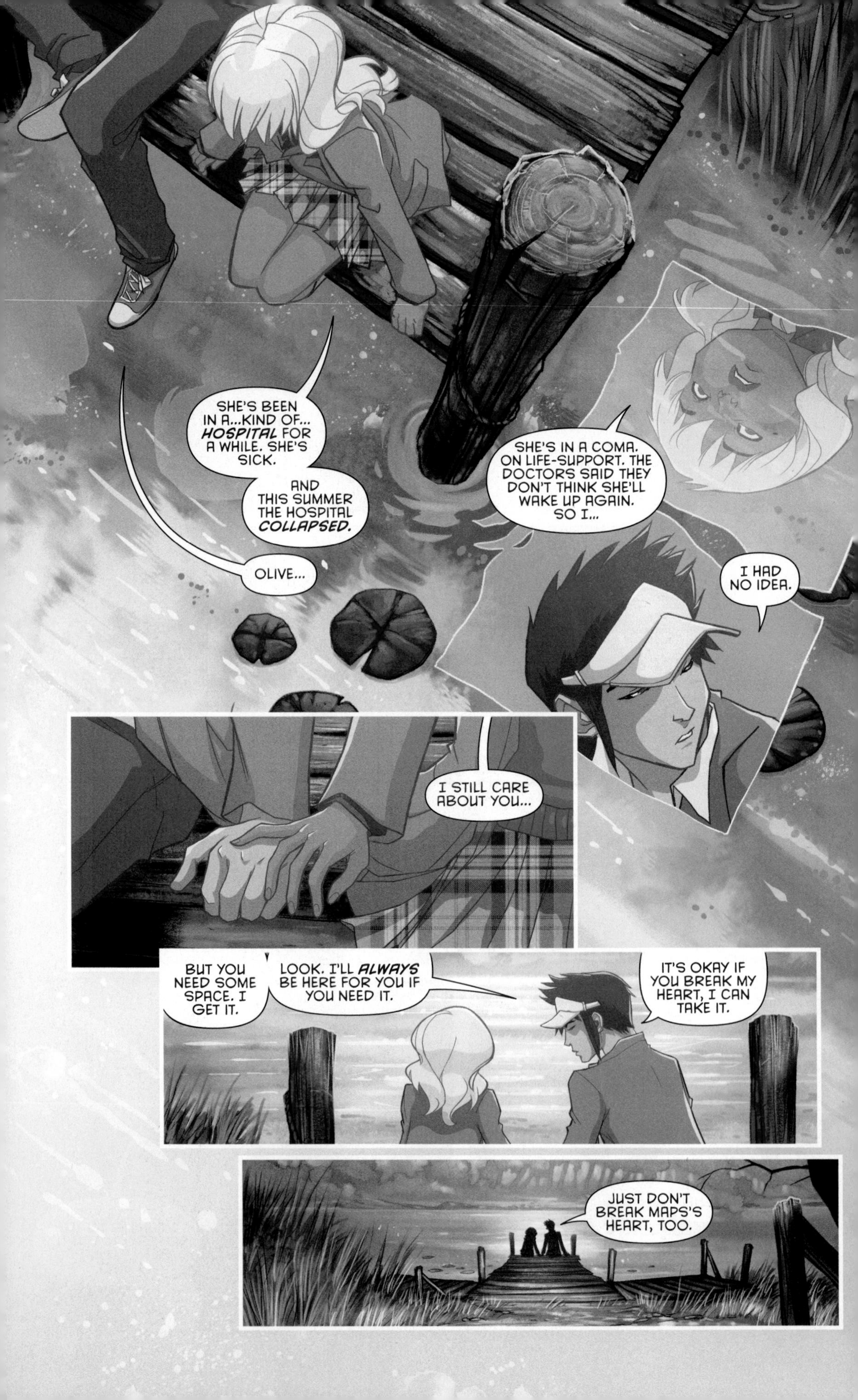
SHE'S BEEN IN A...KIND OF... HOSPITAL FOR A WHILE. SHE'S SICK.
AND THIS SUMMER THE HOSPITAL COLLAPSED.
OLIVE...
SHE'S IN A COMA. ON LIFE-SUPPORT. THE DOCTORS SAID THEY DON'T THINK SHE'LL WAKE UP AGAIN. SO I...
I HAD NO IDEA.
I STILL CARE ABOUT YOU...
BUT YOU NEED SOME SPACE. I GET IT.
LOOK. I'LL ALWAYS BE HERE FOR YOU IF YOU NEED IT.
IT'S OKAY IF YOU BREAK MY HEART, I CAN TAKE IT.
JUST DON'T BREAK MAPS'S HEART, TOO.

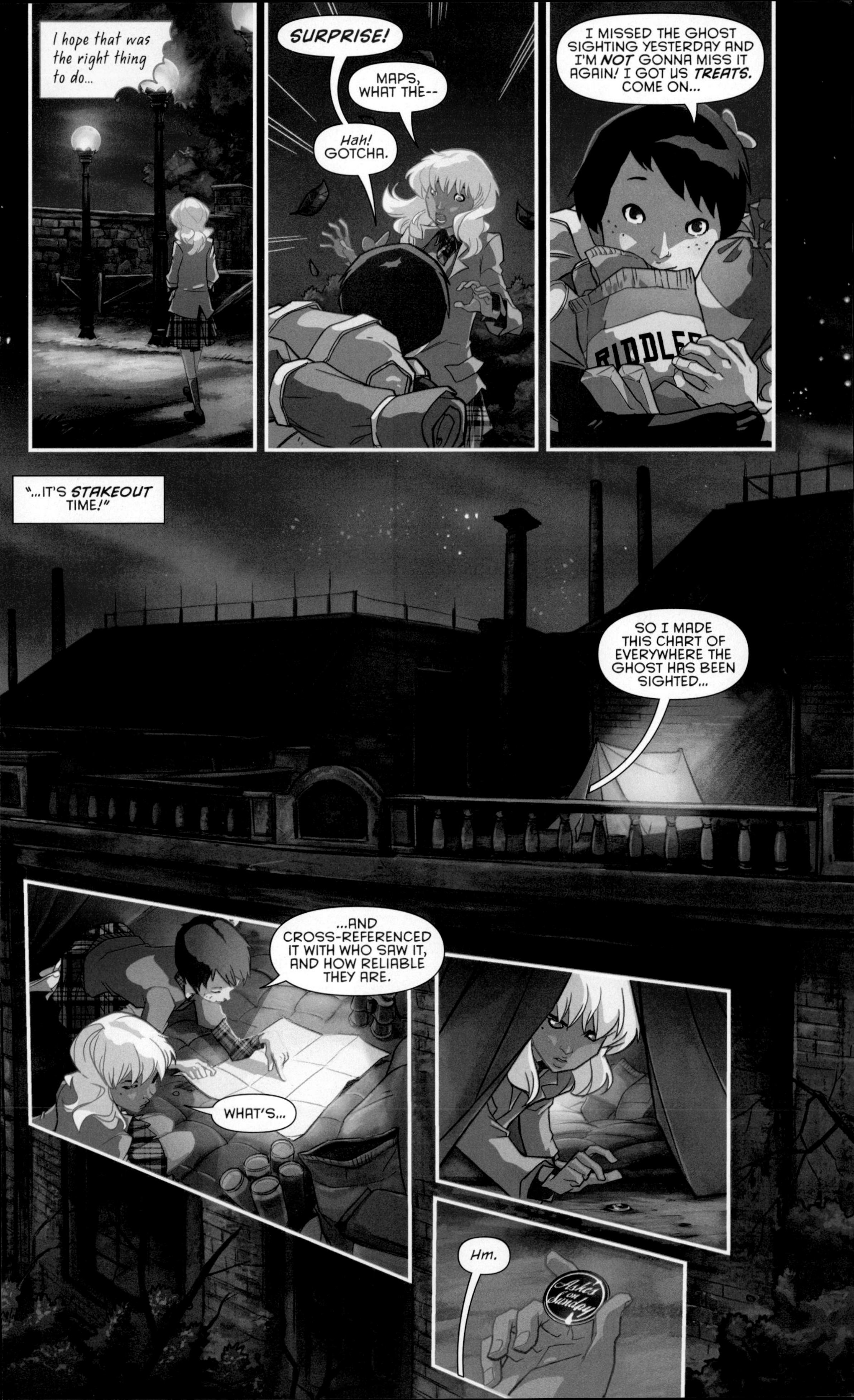
I hope that was the right thing to do...
SURPRISE!
MAPS, WHAT THE--
Hah! GOTCHA.
I MISSED THE GHOST SIGHTING YESTERDAY AND I'M NOT GONNA MISS IT AGAIN! I GOT US TREATS. COME ON...
RIDDLE
"...IT'S STAKEOUT TIME!"
SO I MADE THIS CHART OF EVERYWHERE THE GHOST HAS BEEN SIGHTED...
...AND CROSS-REFERENCED IT WITH WHO SAW IT, AND HOW RELIABLE THEY ARE.
WHAT'S...
Hm.
Ashes on Sunday

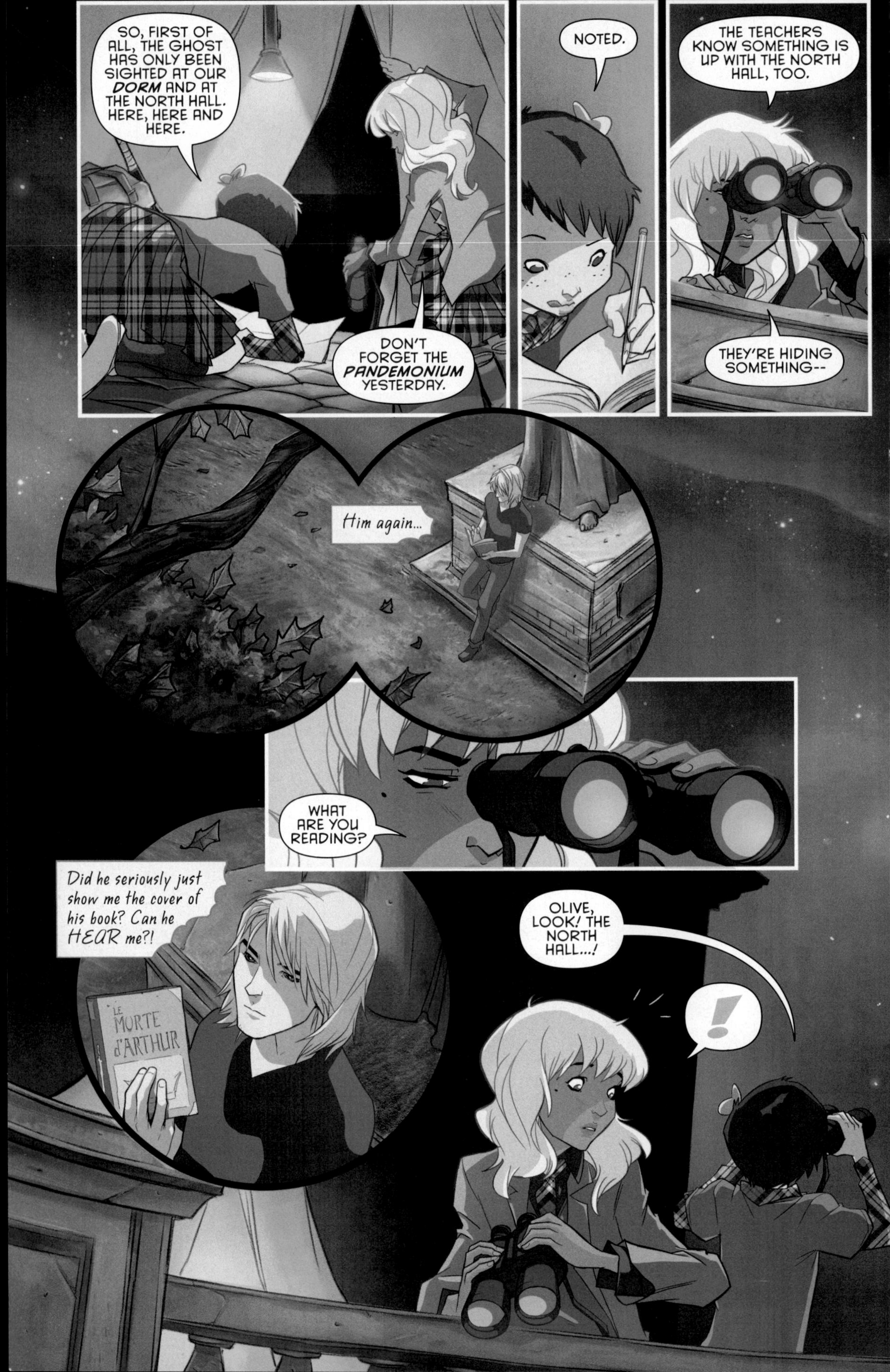

SO, FIRST OF ALL, THE GHOST HAS ONLY BEEN SIGHTED AT OUR DORM AND AT THE NORTH HALL. HERE, HERE AND HERE.
DON'T FORGET THE PANDEMONIUM YESTERDAY.
NOTED.
THE TEACHERS KNOW SOMETHING IS UP WITH THE NORTH HALL, TOO.
THEY'RE HIDING SOMETHING--
Him again...
WHAT ARE YOU READING?
Did he seriously just show me the cover of his book? Can he HEAR me?!
LE MORTE d'ARTHUR
OLIVE, LOOK! THE NORTH HALL...!
!

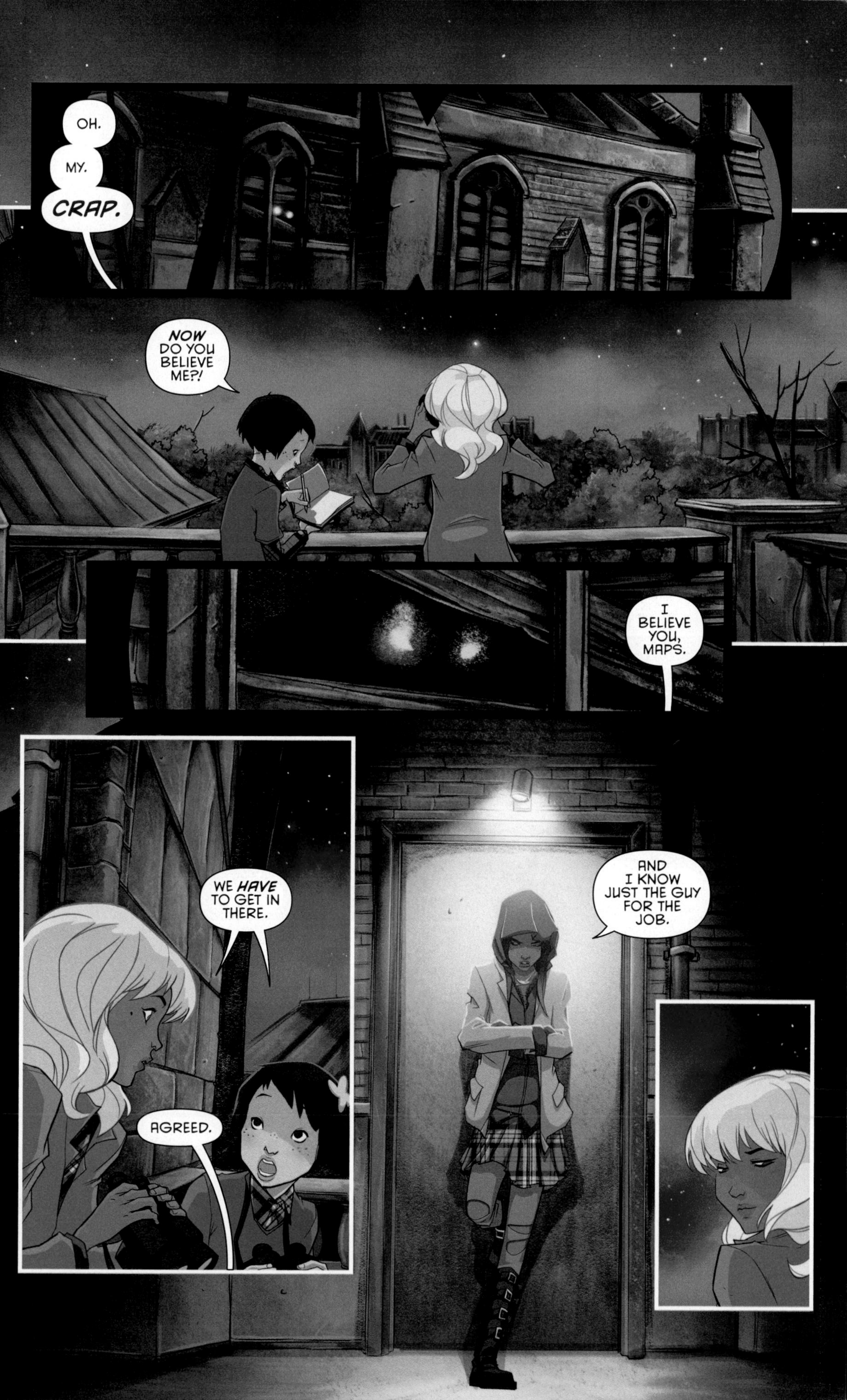
OH.
MY.
CRAP.
NOW DO YOU BELIEVE ME?!
I BELIEVE YOU, MAPS.
WE HAVE TO GET IN THERE.
AGREED.
AND I KNOW JUST THE GUY FOR THE JOB.

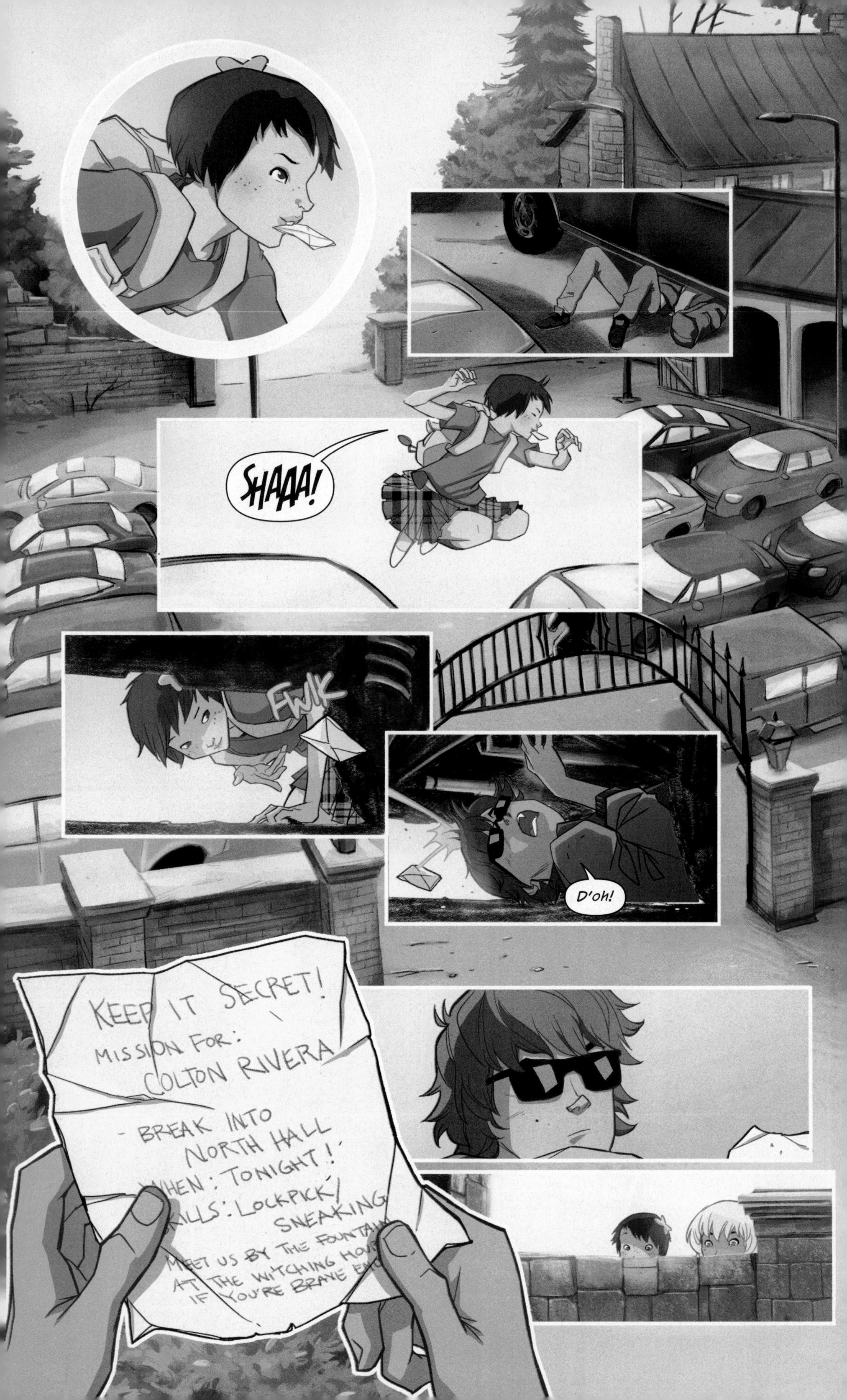
SHAAA!
FWIK
D'oh!
KEEP IT SECRET!
MISSION FOR:
COLTON RIVERA
- BREAK INTO
NORTH HALL
WHEN: TONIGHT!
SKILLS: LOCKPICK/
SNEAKING
MEET US BY THE FOUNTA
AT THE WITCHING HOU
IF YOU'RE BRAVE EN

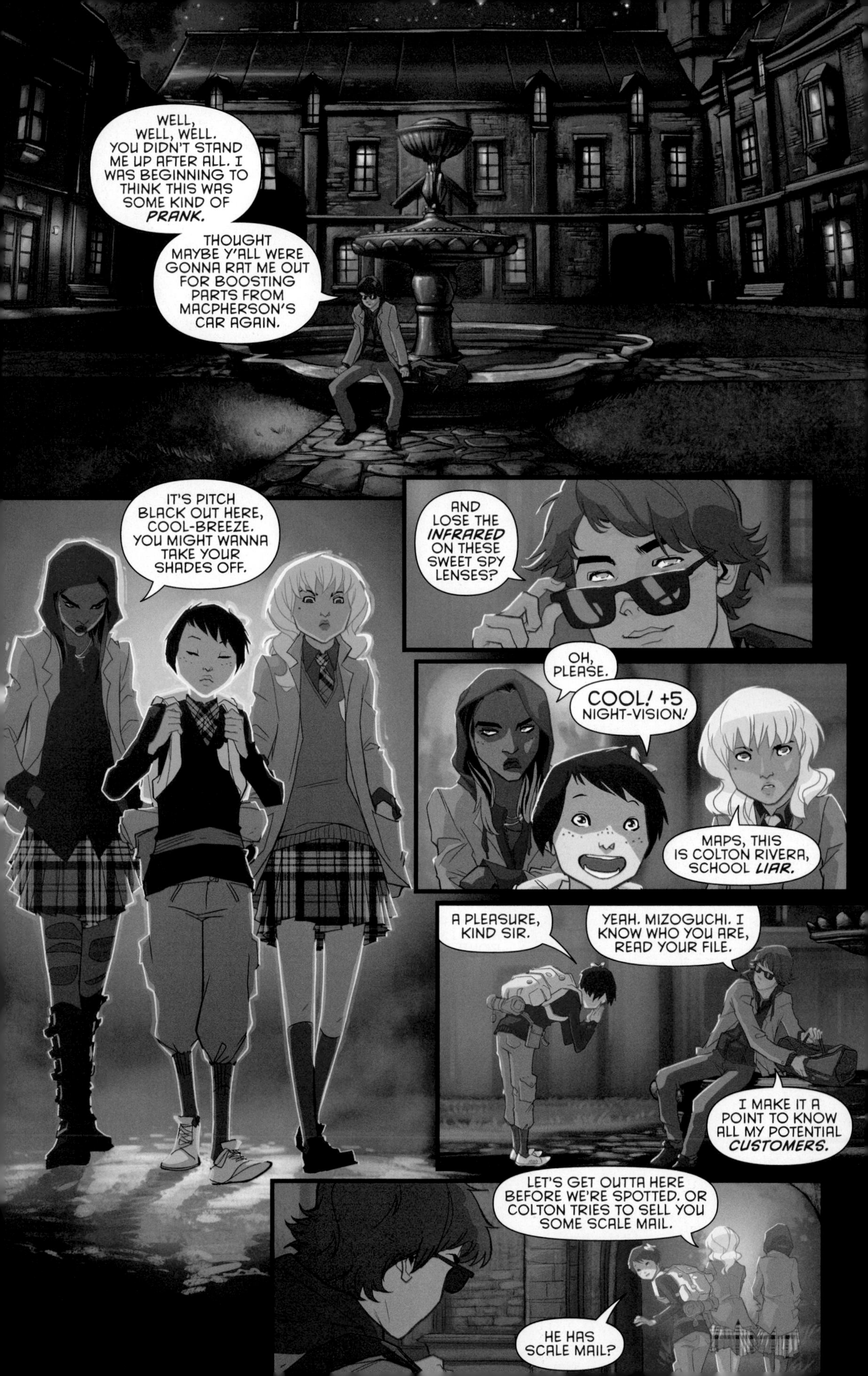
WELL, WELL, WELL. YOU DIDN'T STAND ME UP AFTER ALL. I WAS BEGINNING TO THINK THIS WAS SOME KIND OF PRANK.
THOUGHT MAYBE Y'ALL WERE GONNA RAT ME OUT FOR BOOSTING PARTS FROM MACPHERSON'S CAR AGAIN.
IT'S PITCH BLACK OUT HERE, COOL-BREEZE. YOU MIGHT WANNA TAKE YOUR SHADES OFF.
AND LOSE THE INFRARED ON THESE SWEET SPY LENSES?
OH, PLEASE.
COOL! +5 NIGHT-VISION!
MAPS, THIS IS COLTON RIVERA, SCHOOL LIAR.
A PLEASURE, KIND SIR.
YEAH. MIZOGUCHI. I KNOW WHO YOU ARE, READ YOUR FILE.
I MAKE IT A POINT TO KNOW ALL MY POTENTIAL CUSTOMERS.
LET'S GET OUTTA HERE BEFORE WE'RE SPOTTED. OR COLTON TRIES TO SELL YOU SOME SCALE MAIL.
HE HAS SCALE MAIL?

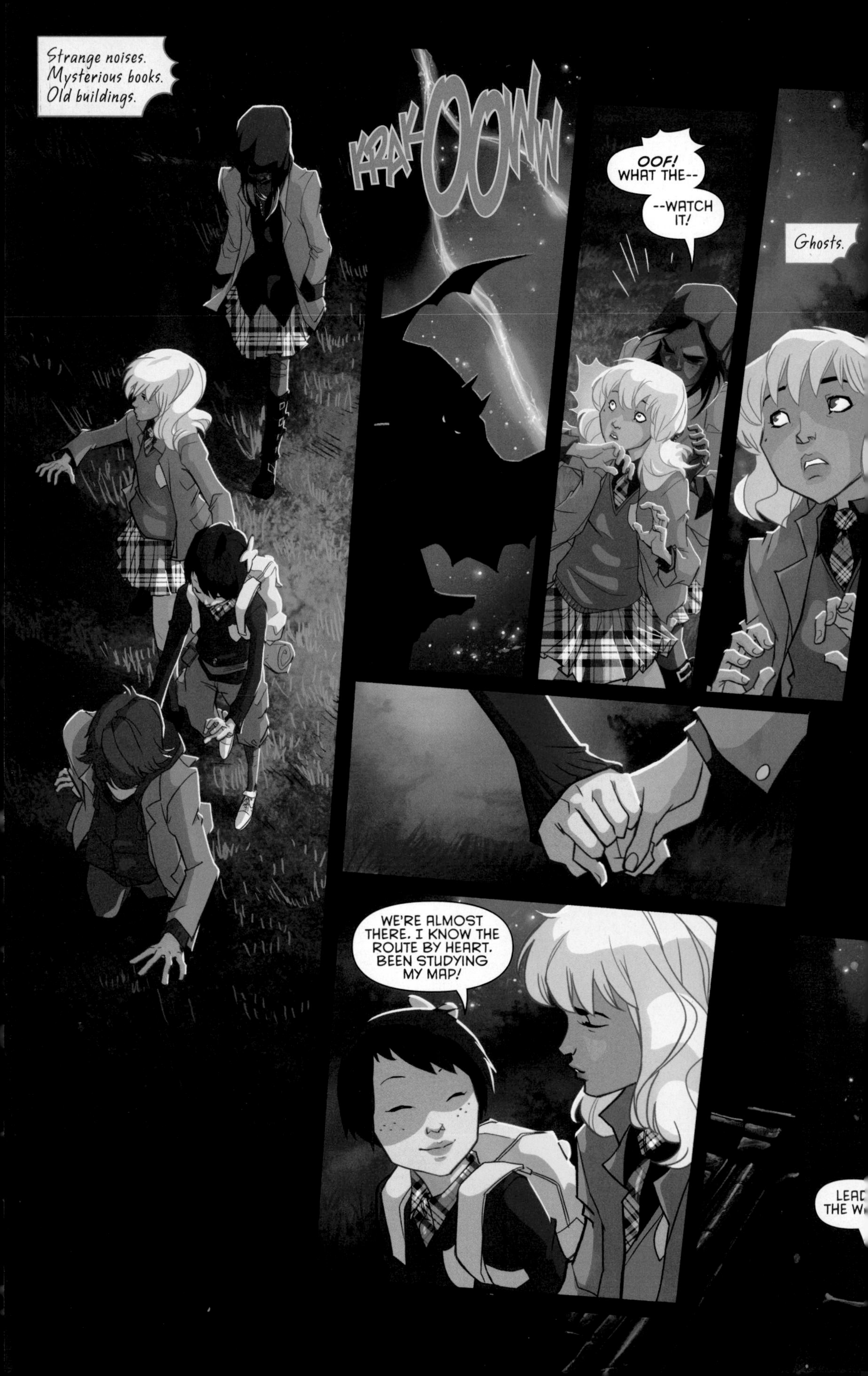
Strange noises.
Mysterious books.
Old buildings.
KRAKOOOWW
OOF! WHAT THE--
--WATCH IT!
Ghosts.
WE'RE ALMOST THERE. I KNOW THE ROUTE BY HEART. BEEN STUDYING MY MAP!

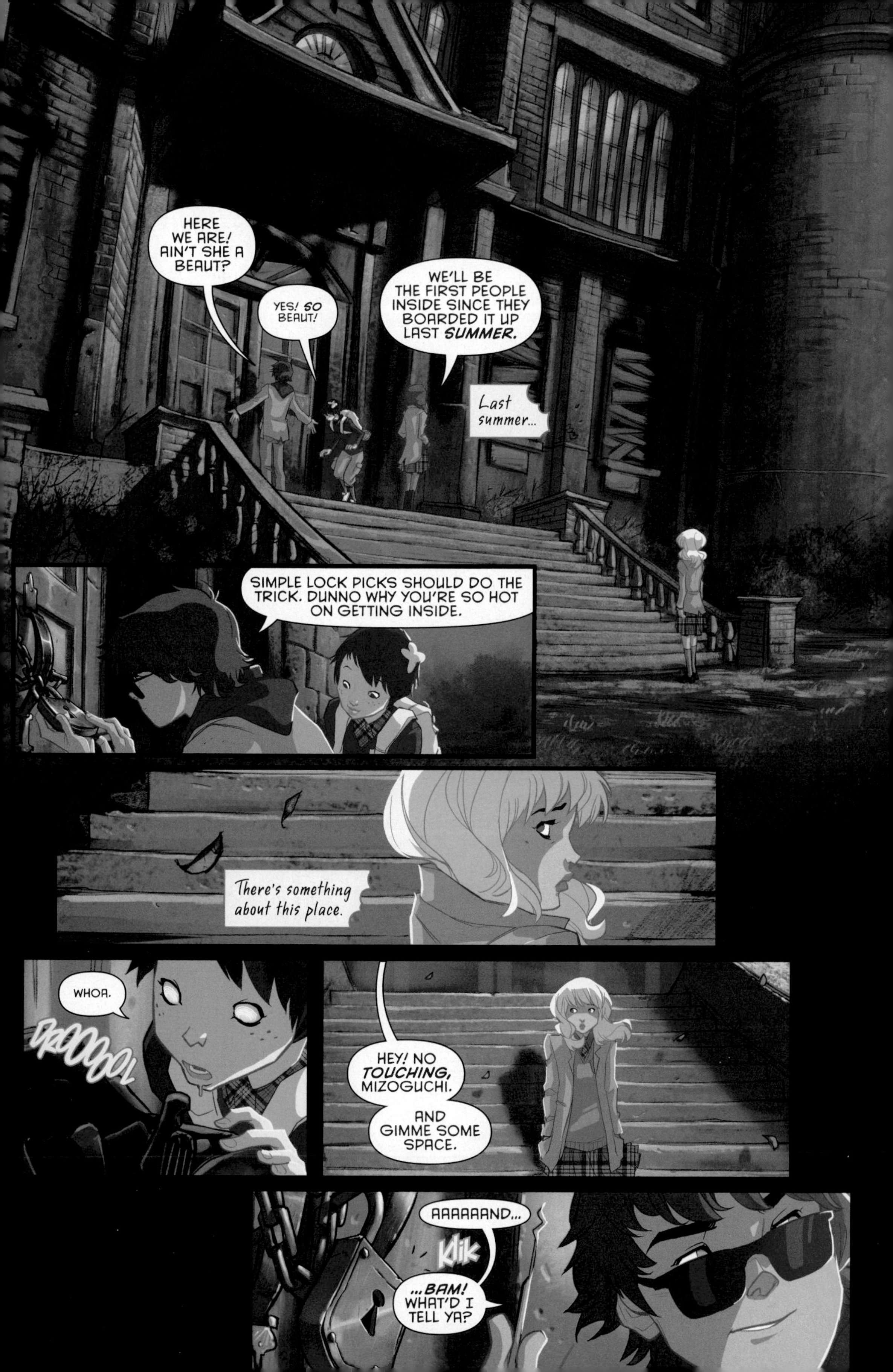
HERE WE ARE! AIN'T SHE A BEAUT?
YES! SO BEAUT!
WE'LL BE THE FIRST PEOPLE INSIDE SINCE THEY BOARDED IT UP LAST SUMMER.
Last summer...
SIMPLE LOCK PICKS SHOULD DO THE TRICK. DUNNO WHY YOU'RE SO HOT ON GETTING INSIDE.
There's something about this place.
WHOA.
DROOOOOL
HEY! NO TOUCHING, MIZOGUCHI.
AND GIMME SOME SPACE.
AAAAAAND...
KLIK
...BAM! WHAT'D I TELL YA?

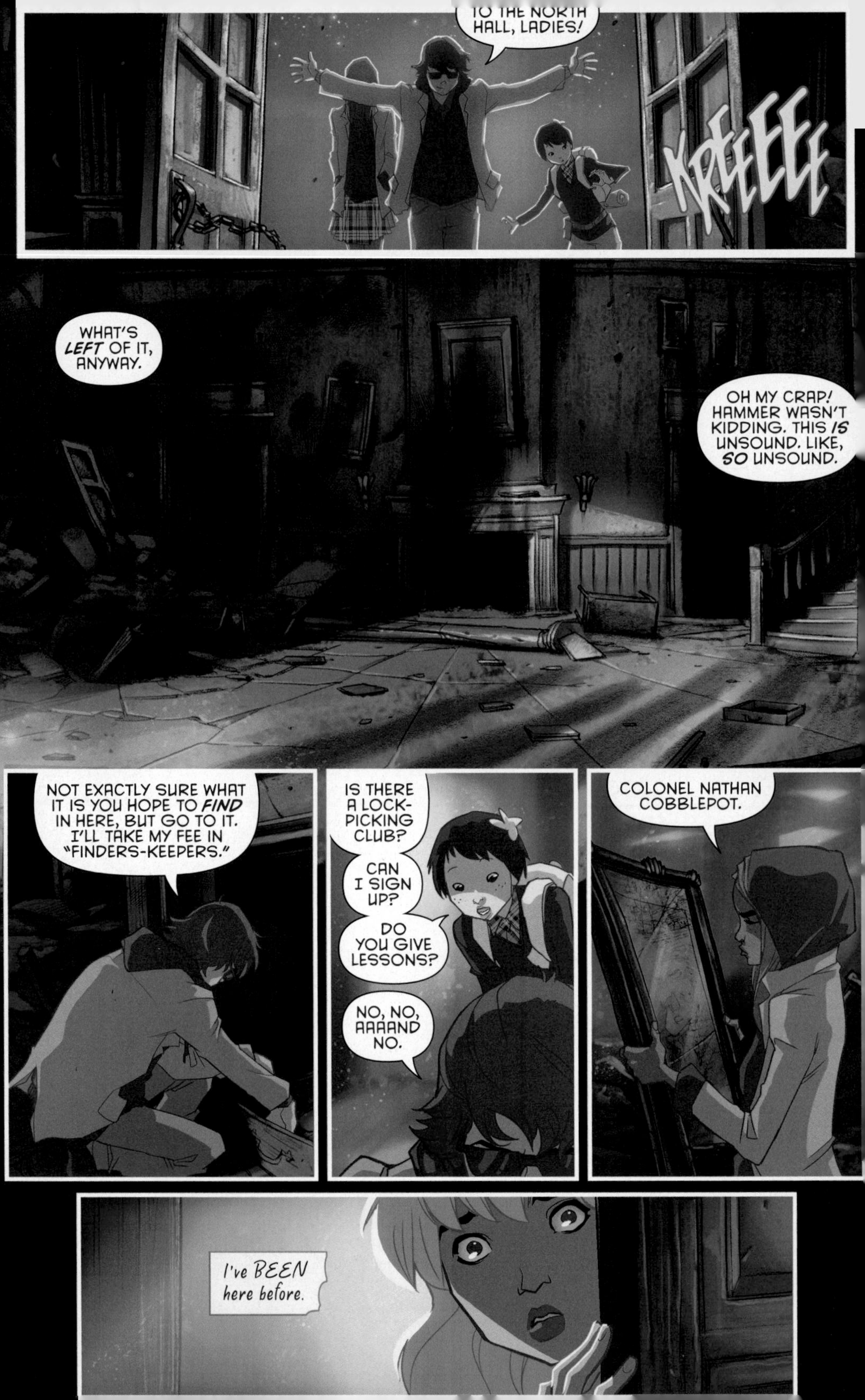
TO THE NORTH HALL, LADIES!
KREEEEE
WHAT'S LEFT OF IT, ANYWAY.
OH MY CRAP! HAMMER WASN'T KIDDING. THIS IS UNSOUND. LIKE, SO UNSOUND.
NOT EXACTLY SURE WHAT IT IS YOU HOPE TO FIND IN HERE, BUT GO TO IT. I'LL TAKE MY FEE IN "FINDERS-KEEPERS."
IS THERE A LOCK-PICKING CLUB?
CAN I SIGN UP?
DO YOU GIVE LESSONS?
NO, NO, AAAAND NO.
COLONEL NATHAN COBBLEPOT.
I've BEEN here before.

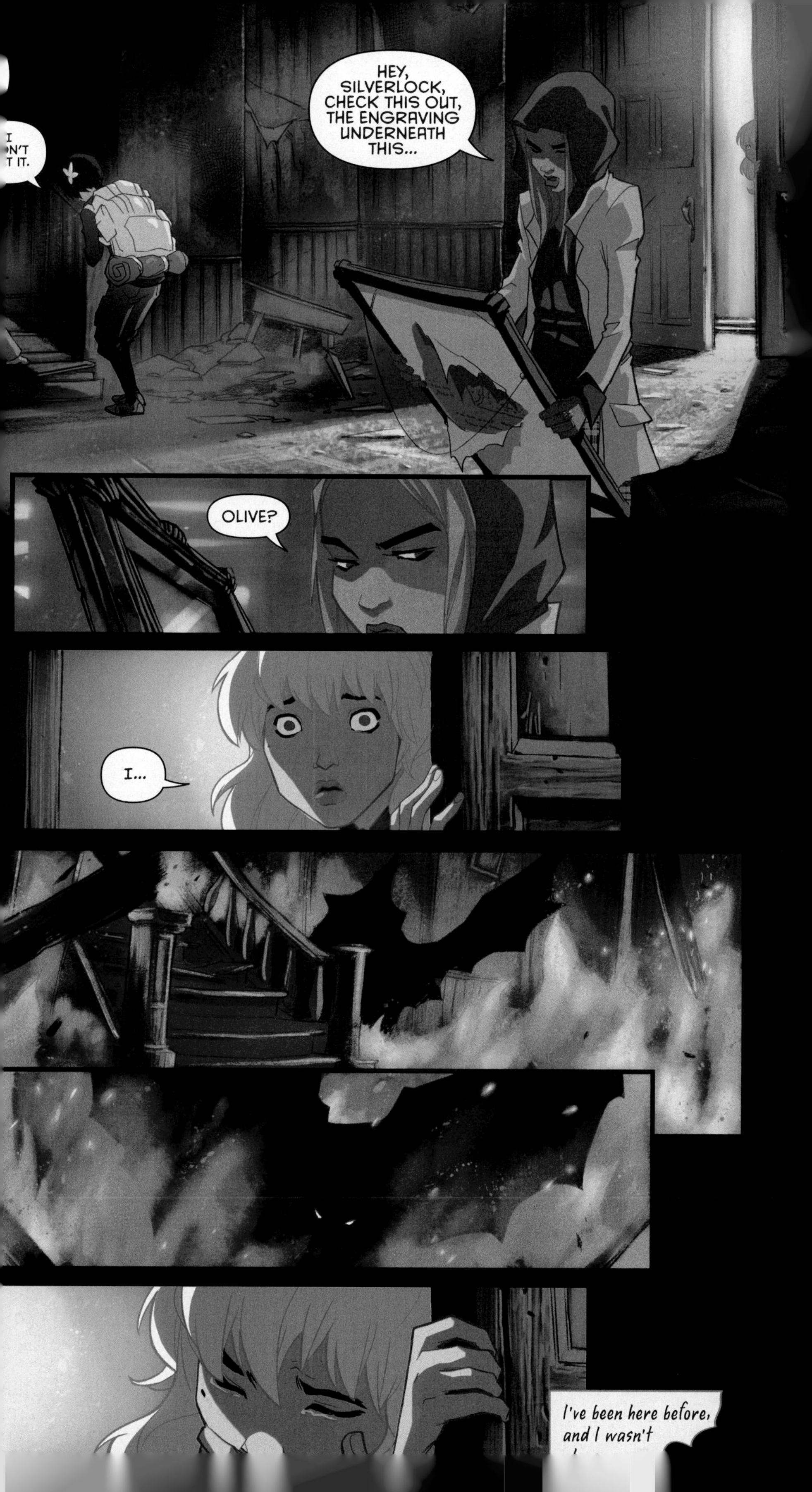
I
...N'T
...T IT.
HEY, SILVERLOCK, CHECK THIS OUT, THE ENGRAVING UNDERNEATH THIS...
OLIVE?
I...
I've been here before, and I wasn't

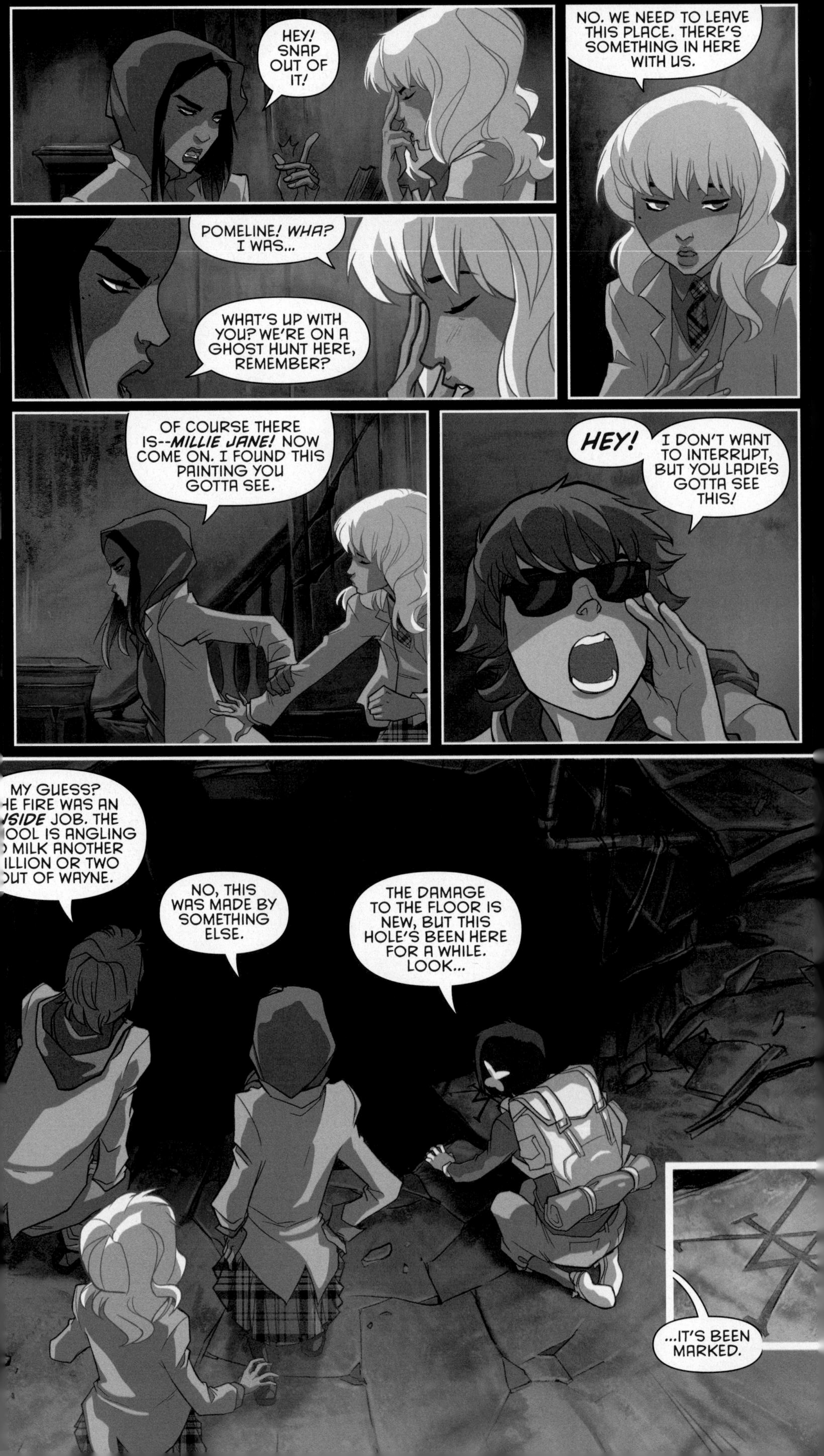

HEY! SNAP OUT OF IT!
NO. WE NEED TO LEAVE THIS PLACE. THERE'S SOMETHING IN HERE WITH US.
POMELINE! WHA? I WAS...
WHAT'S UP WITH YOU? WE'RE ON A GHOST HUNT HERE, REMEMBER?
OF COURSE THERE IS--MILLIE JANE! NOW COME ON. I FOUND THIS PAINTING YOU GOTTA SEE.
HEY!
I DON'T WANT TO INTERRUPT, BUT YOU LADIES GOTTA SEE THIS!
MY GUESS? HE FIRE WAS AN SIDE JOB. THE OOL IS ANGLING O MILK ANOTHER ILLION OR TWO UT OF WAYNE.
NO, THIS WAS MADE BY SOMETHING ELSE.
THE DAMAGE TO THE FLOOR IS NEW, BUT THIS HOLE'S BEEN HERE FOR A WHILE. LOOK...
...IT'S BEEN MARKED.

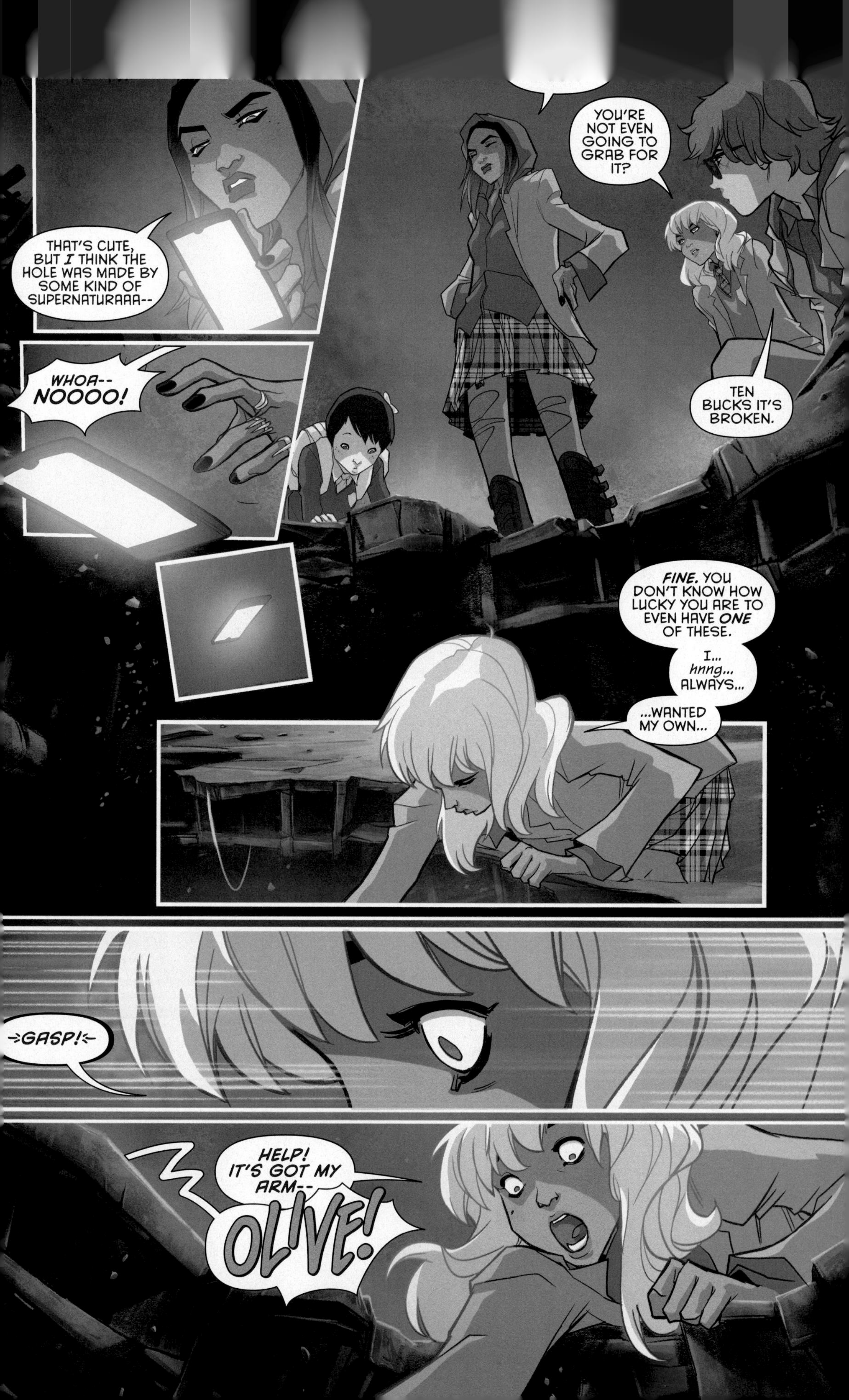
YOU'RE NOT EVEN GOING TO GRAB FOR IT?
THAT'S CUTE, BUT I THINK THE HOLE WAS MADE BY SOME KIND OF SUPERNATURAAA--
WHOA-- NOOOO!
TEN BUCKS IT'S BROKEN.
FINE. YOU DON'T KNOW HOW LUCKY YOU ARE TO EVEN HAVE ONE OF THESE.
I... hnng... ALWAYS...
...WANTED MY OWN...
GASP!
HELP! IT'S GOT MY ARM--
OLIVE!

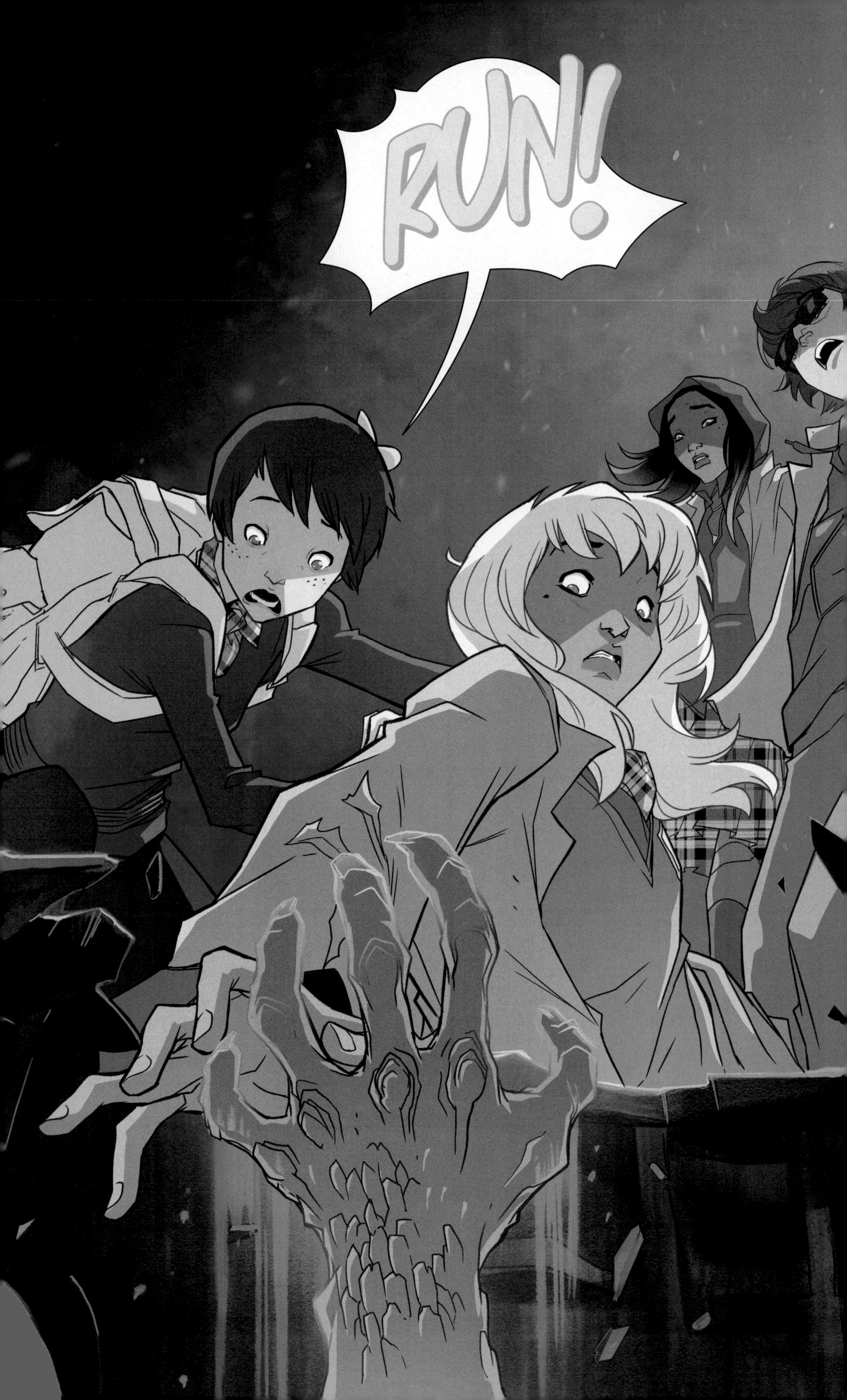
RUN!

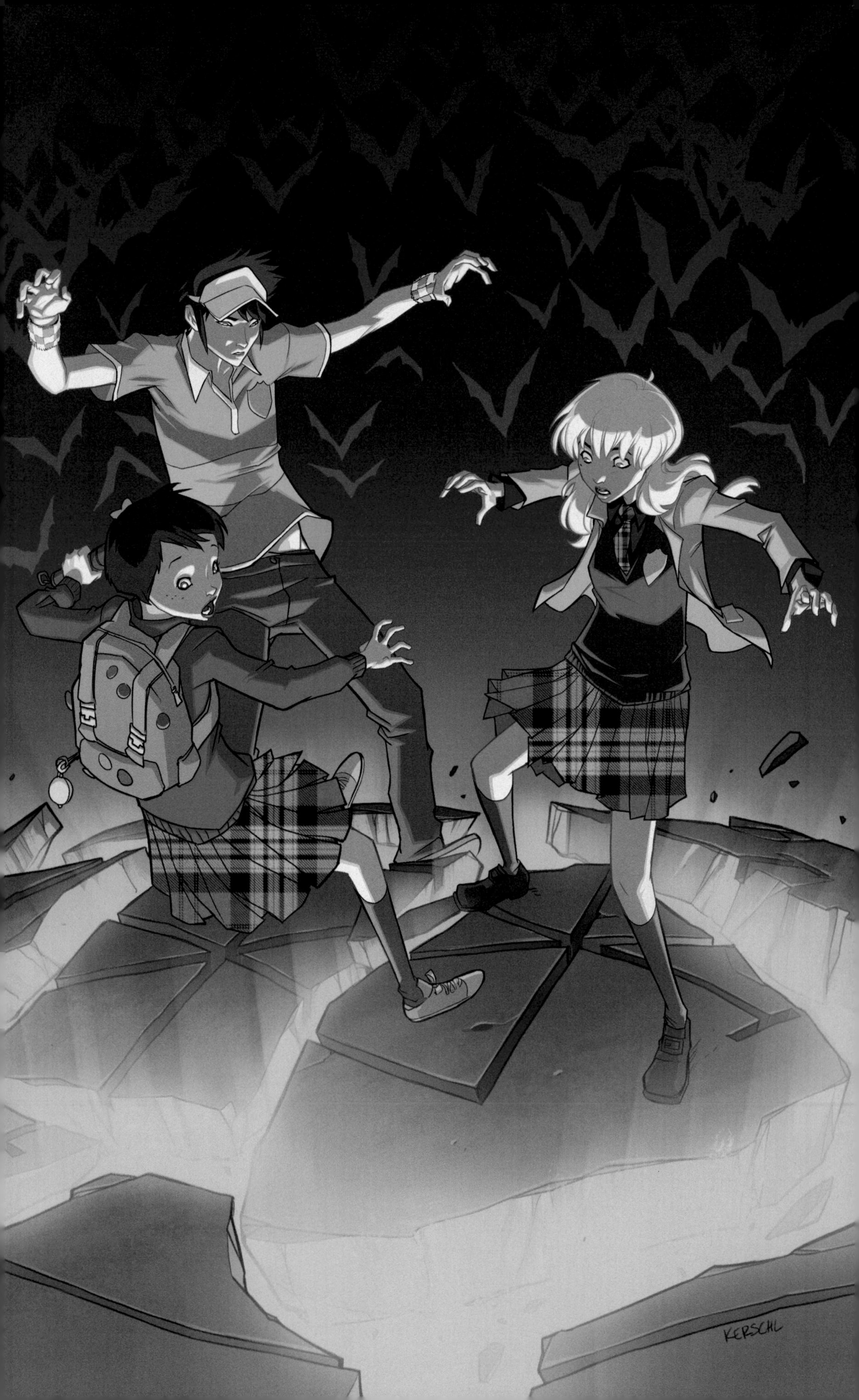
KERSCHL

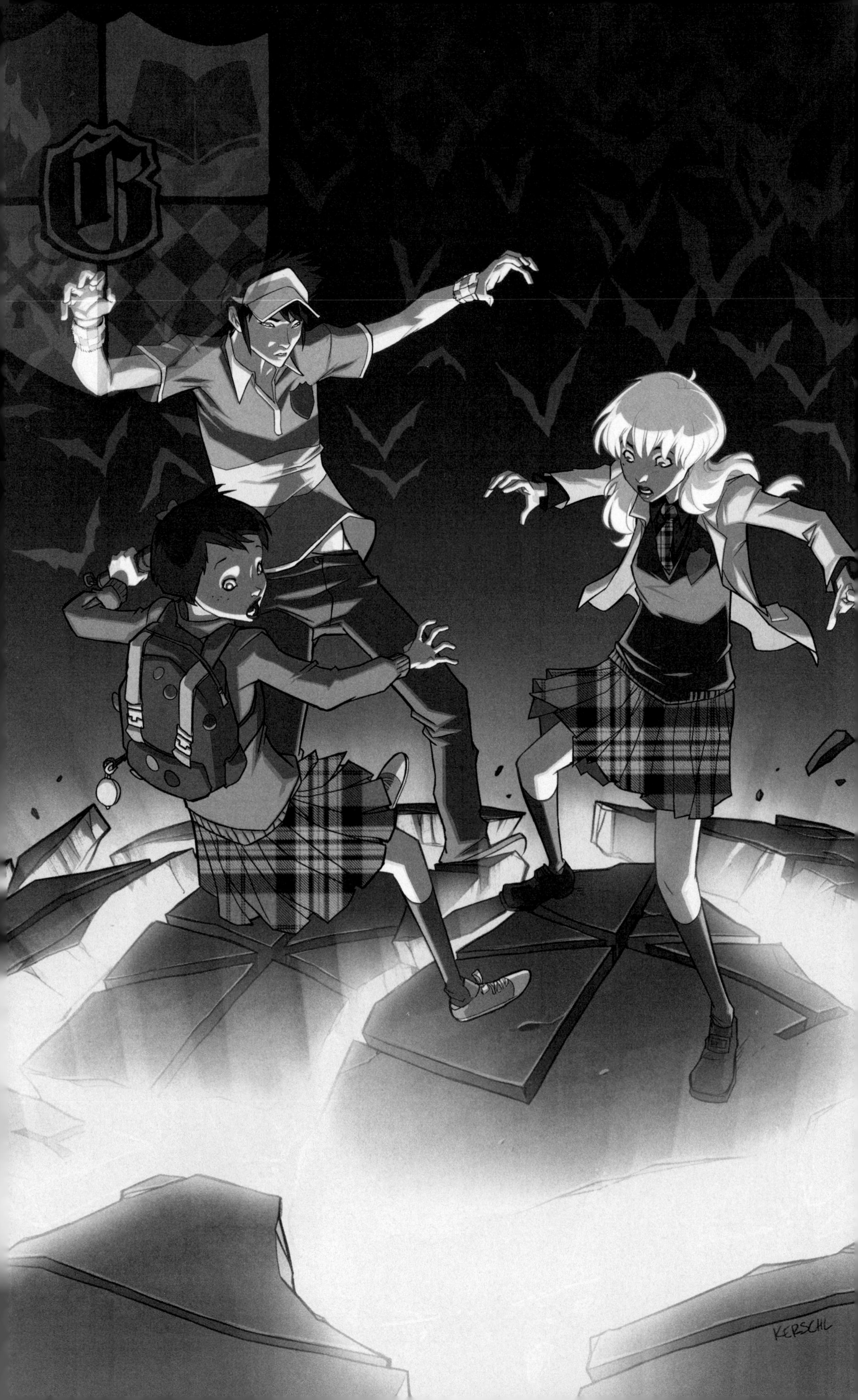
KERSCHL

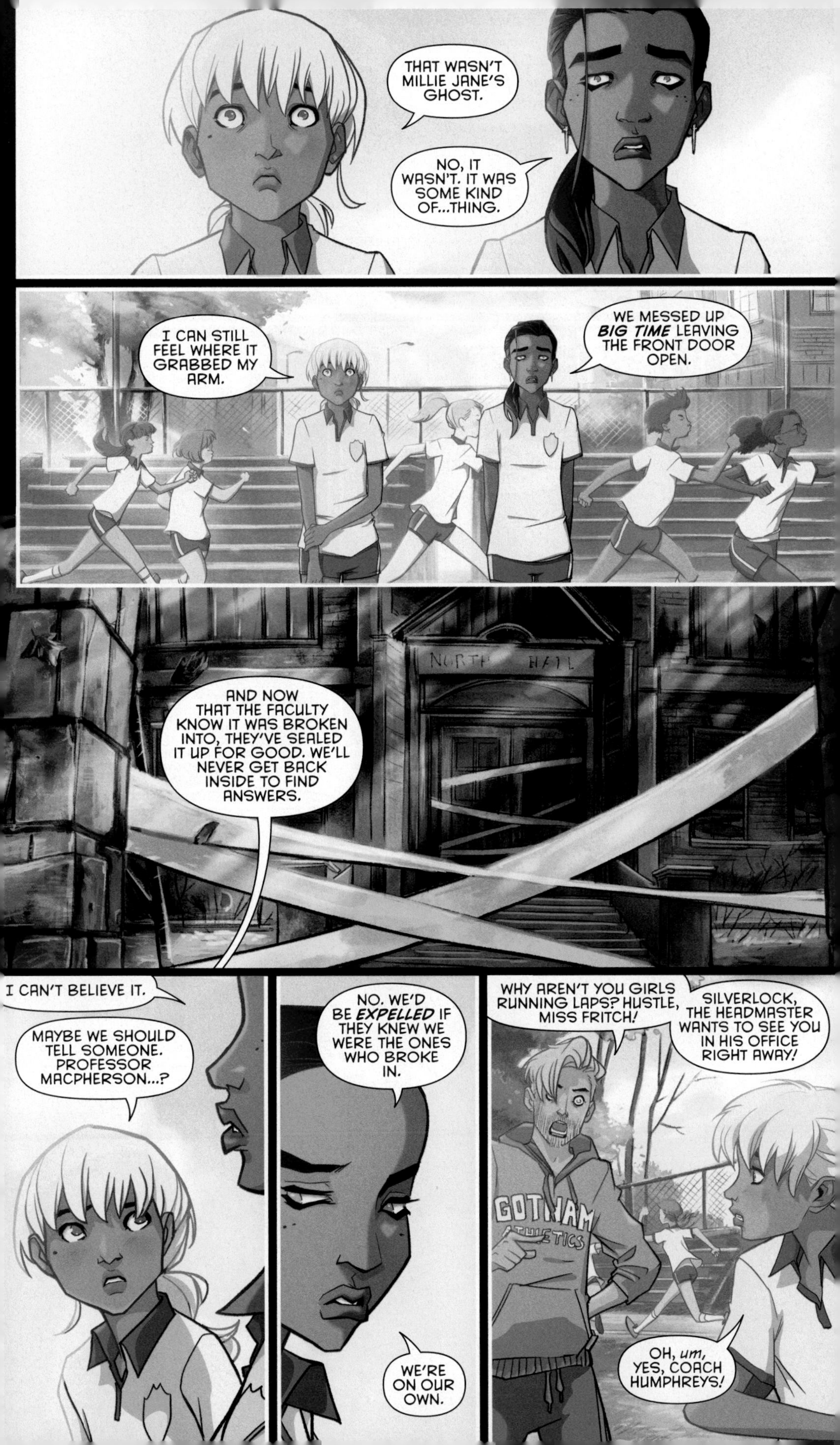
THAT WASN'T MILLIE JANE'S GHOST.
NO, IT WASN'T. IT WAS SOME KIND OF...THING.
I CAN STILL FEEL WHERE IT GRABBED MY ARM.
WE MESSED UP *BIG TIME* LEAVING THE FRONT DOOR OPEN.
NORTH HALL
AND NOW THAT THE FACULTY KNOW IT WAS BROKEN INTO, THEY'VE SEALED IT UP FOR GOOD. WE'LL NEVER GET BACK INSIDE TO FIND ANSWERS.
I CAN'T BELIEVE IT.
MAYBE WE SHOULD TELL SOMEONE. PROFESSOR MACPHERSON...?
NO. WE'D BE *EXPELLED* IF THEY KNEW WE WERE THE ONES WHO BROKE IN.
WE'RE ON OUR OWN.
WHY AREN'T YOU GIRLS RUNNING LAPS? HUSTLE, MISS FRITCH!
SILVERLOCK, THE HEADMASTER WANTS TO SEE YOU IN HIS OFFICE RIGHT AWAY!
GOTHAM ATHLETICS
OH, *um*, YES, COACH HUMPHREYS!

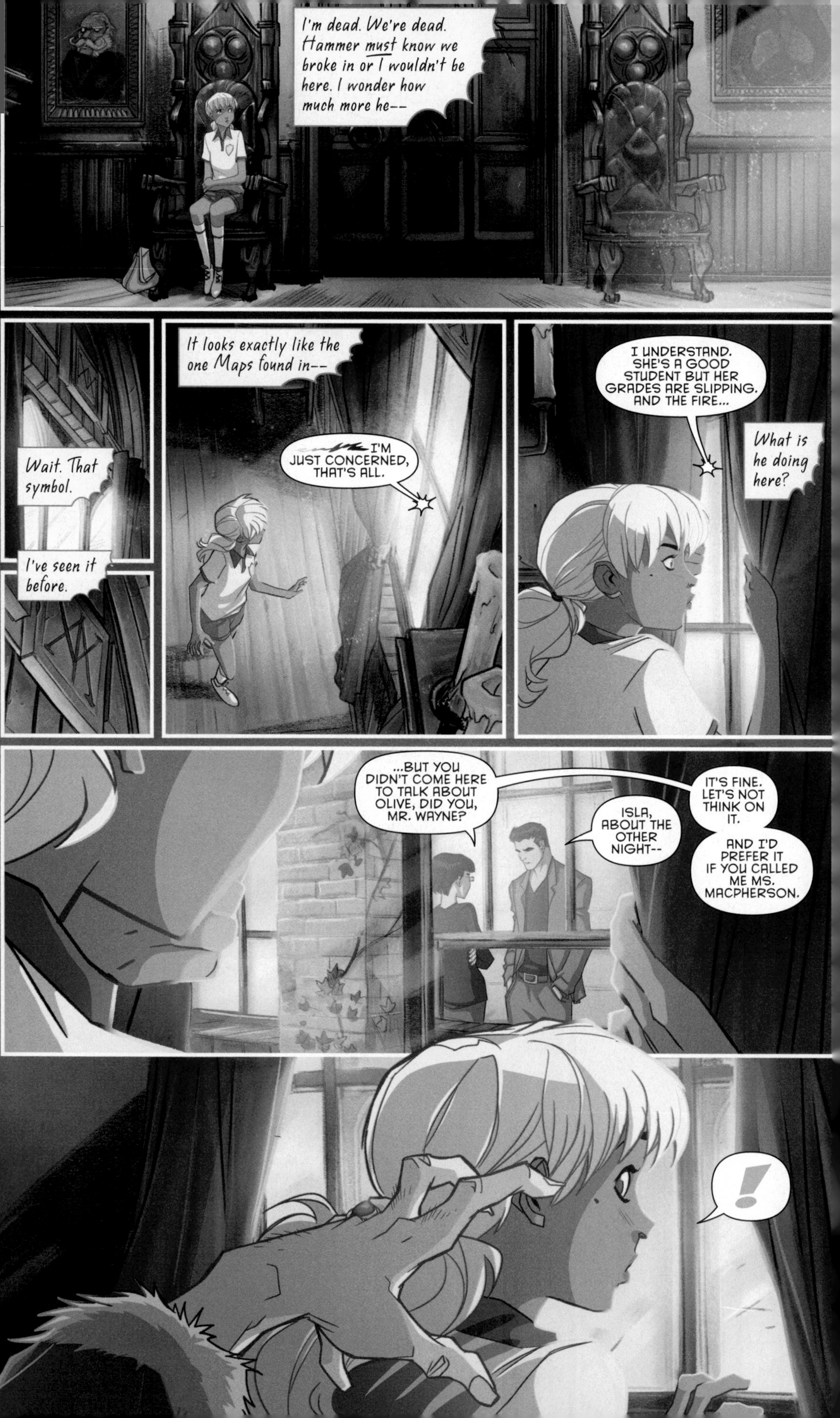
I'm dead. We're dead. Hammer must know we broke in or I wouldn't be here. I wonder how much more he--
Wait. That symbol.
I've seen it before.
It looks exactly like the one Maps found in--
I'M JUST CONCERNED, THAT'S ALL.
I UNDERSTAND. SHE'S A GOOD STUDENT BUT HER GRADES ARE SLIPPING. AND THE FIRE...
What is he doing here?
...BUT YOU DIDN'T COME HERE TO TALK ABOUT OLIVE, DID YOU, MR. WAYNE?
ISLA, ABOUT THE OTHER NIGHT--
IT'S FINE. LET'S NOT THINK ON IT.
AND I'D PREFER IT IF YOU CALLED ME MS. MACPHERSON.
!

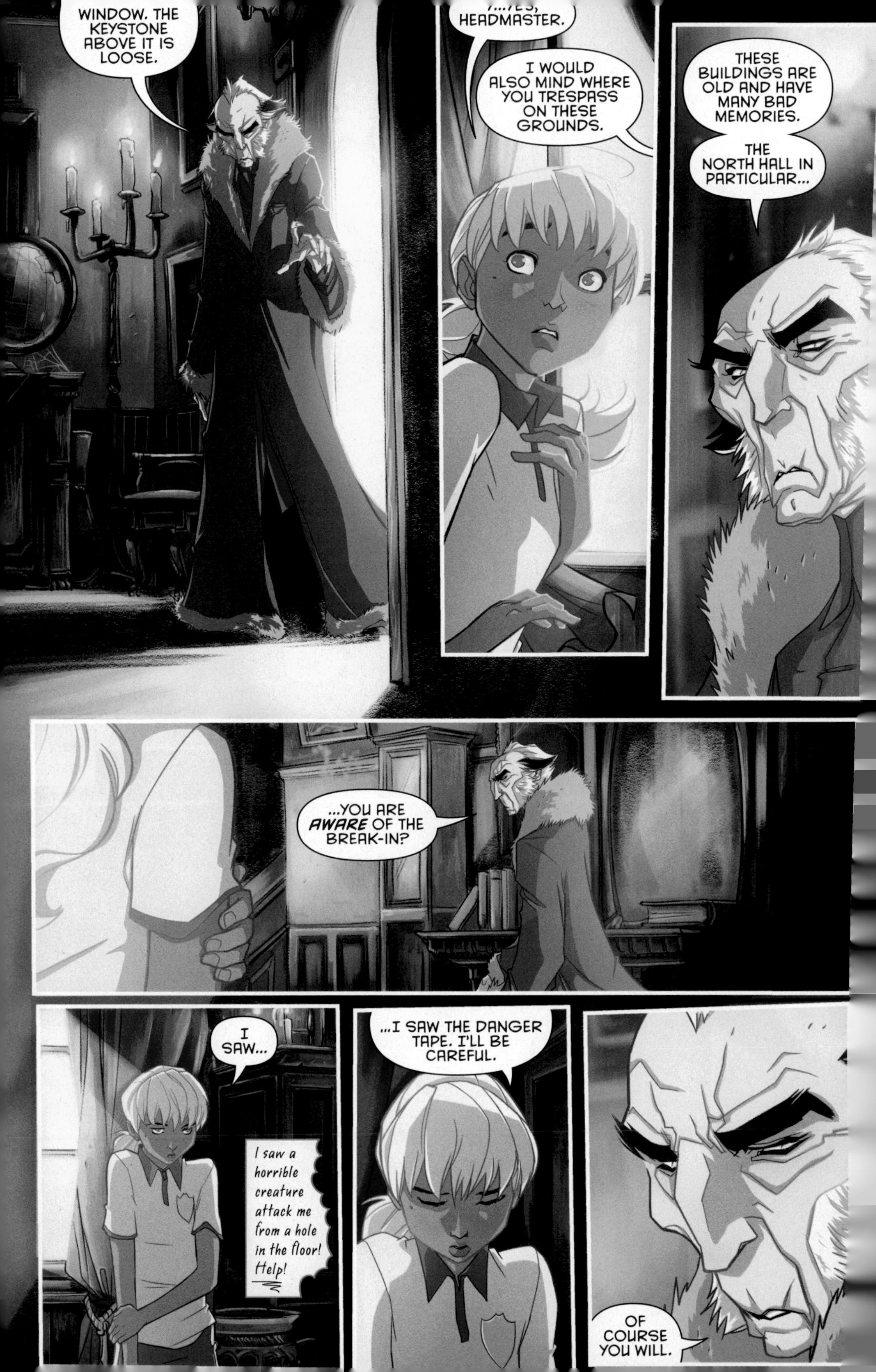

WINDOW. THE KEYSTONE ABOVE IT IS LOOSE.
HEADMASTER.
I WOULD ALSO MIND WHERE YOU TRESPASS ON THESE GROUNDS.
THESE BUILDINGS ARE OLD AND HAVE MANY BAD MEMORIES.
THE NORTH HALL IN PARTICULAR...
...YOU ARE AWARE OF THE BREAK-IN?
I SAW...
I saw a horrible creature attack me from a hole in the floor! Help!
...I SAW THE DANGER TAPE. I'LL BE CAREFUL.
OF COURSE YOU WILL.

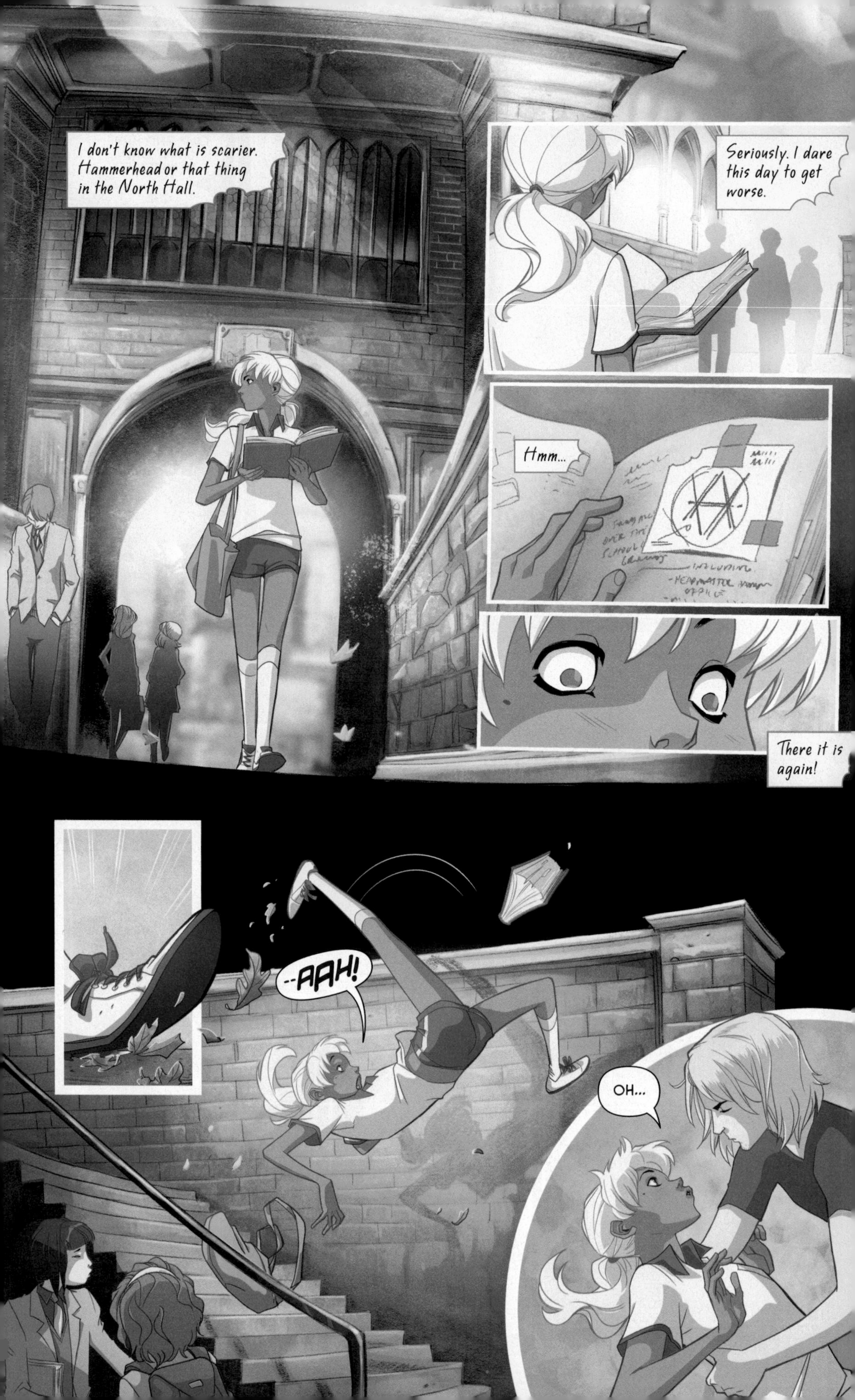

I don't know what is scarier. Hammerhead or that thing in the North Hall.
Seriously. I dare this day to get worse.
Hmm...
There it is again!
--AAH!
OH...

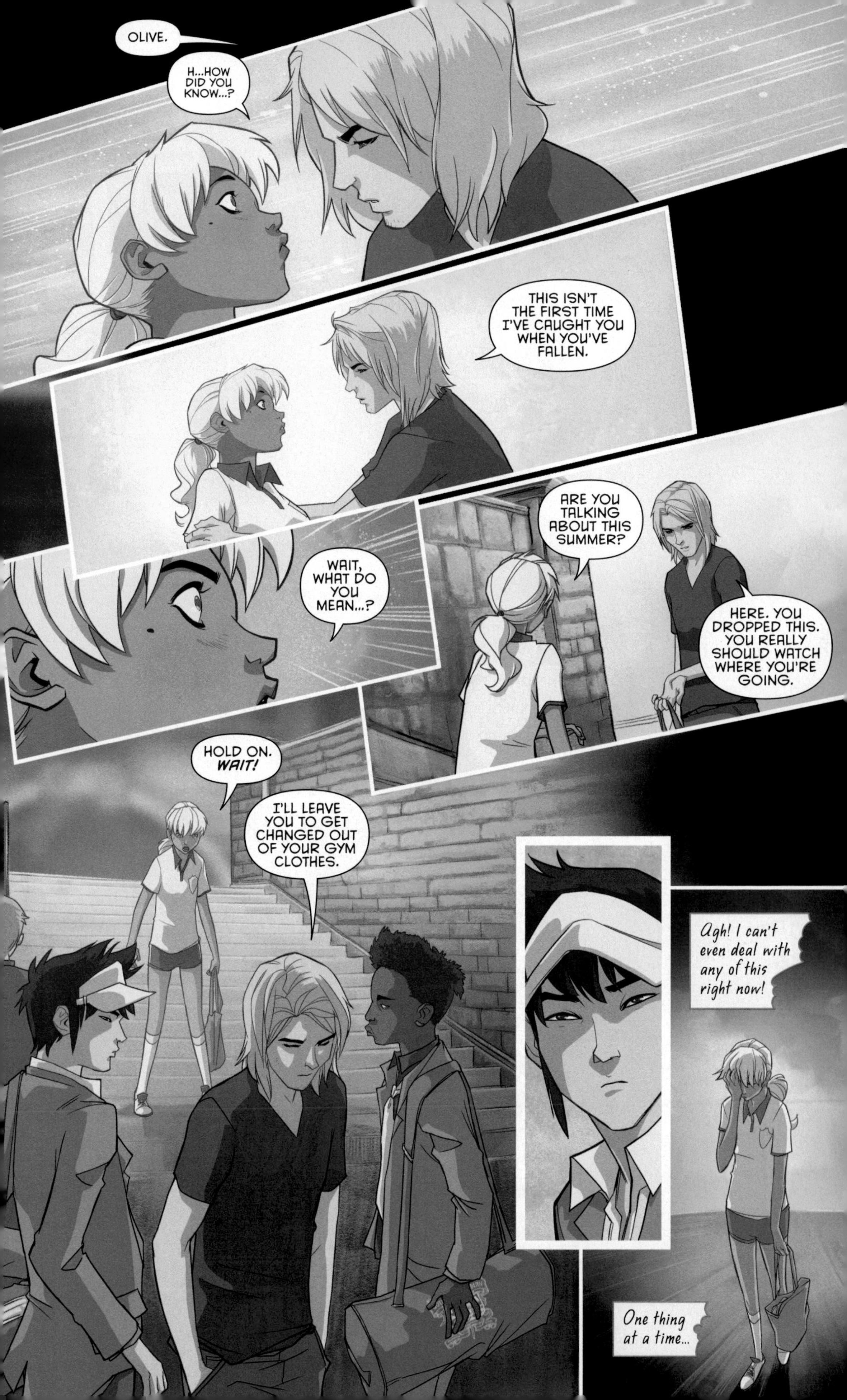
OLIVE.
H...HOW DID YOU KNOW...?
THIS ISN'T THE FIRST TIME I'VE CAUGHT YOU WHEN YOU'VE FALLEN.
WAIT, WHAT DO YOU MEAN...?
ARE YOU TALKING ABOUT THIS SUMMER?
HERE. YOU DROPPED THIS. YOU REALLY SHOULD WATCH WHERE YOU'RE GOING.
HOLD ON. WAIT!
I'LL LEAVE YOU TO GET CHANGED OUT OF YOUR GYM CLOTHES.
Agh! I can't even deal with any of this right now!
One thing at a time...

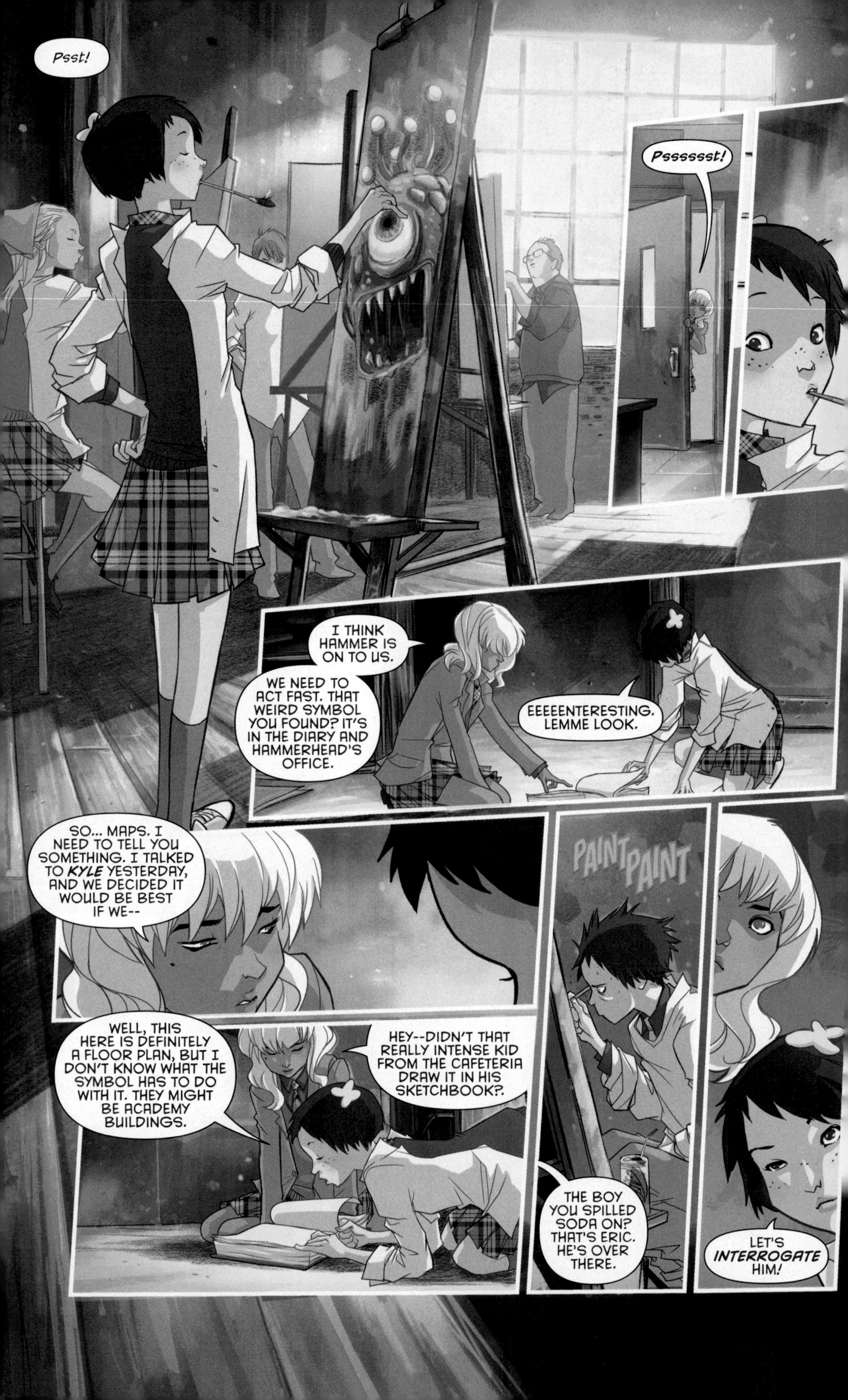
Psst!
Pssssst!
I THINK HAMMER IS ON TO US.
WE NEED TO ACT FAST. THAT WEIRD SYMBOL YOU FOUND? IT'S IN THE DIARY AND HAMMERHEAD'S OFFICE.
EEEEENTERESTING. LEMME LOOK.
SO... MAPS. I NEED TO TELL YOU SOMETHING. I TALKED TO KYLE YESTERDAY, AND WE DECIDED IT WOULD BE BEST IF WE--
PAINT PAINT
WELL, THIS HERE IS DEFINITELY A FLOOR PLAN, BUT I DON'T KNOW WHAT THE SYMBOL HAS TO DO WITH IT. THEY MIGHT BE ACADEMY BUILDINGS.
HEY--DIDN'T THAT REALLY INTENSE KID FROM THE CAFETERIA DRAW IT IN HIS SKETCHBOOK?.
THE BOY YOU SPILLED SODA ON? THAT'S ERIC. HE'S OVER THERE.
LET'S INTERROGATE HIM!

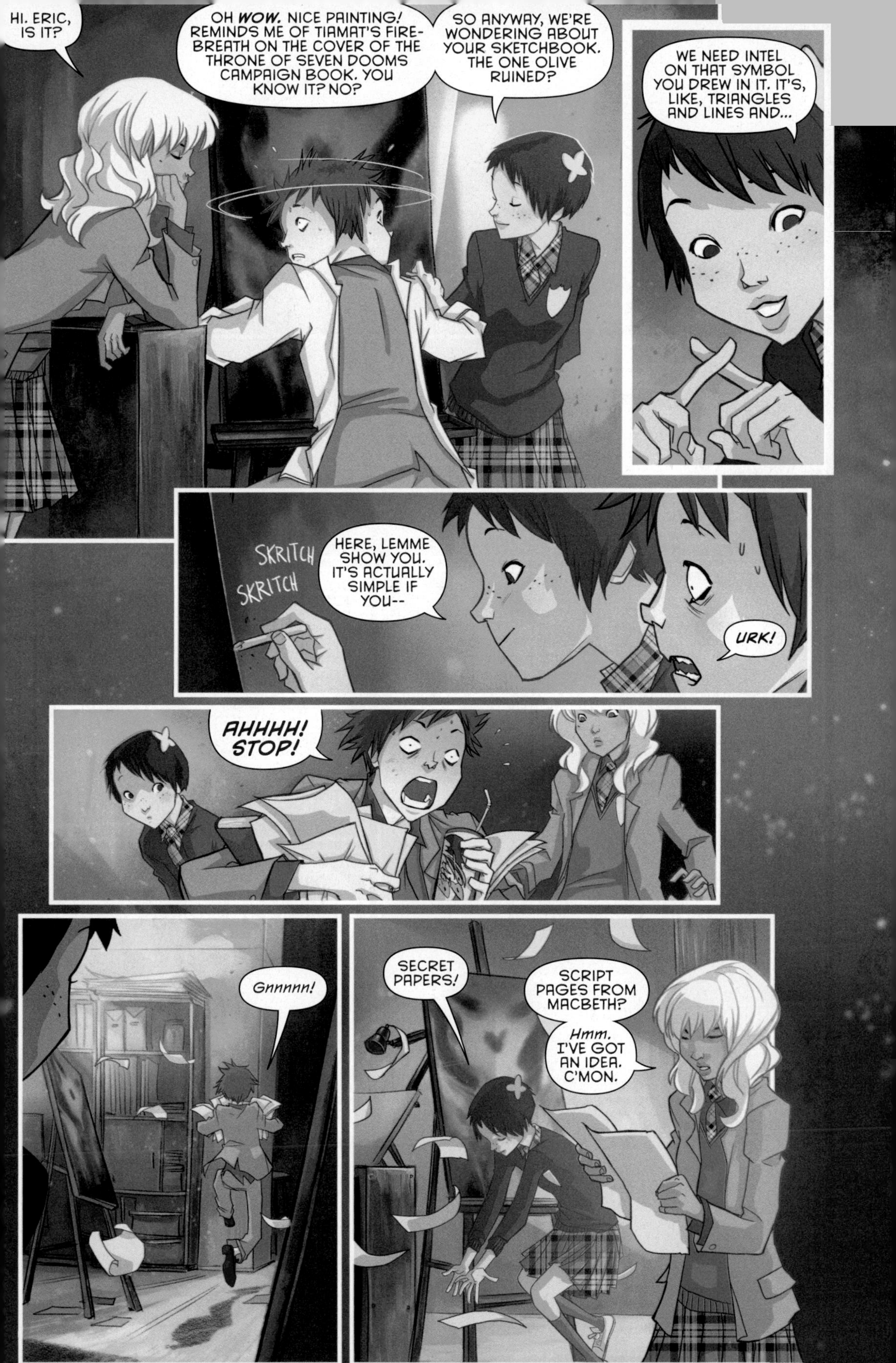
HI. ERIC, IS IT?
OH *WOW.* NICE PAINTING! REMINDS ME OF TIAMAT'S FIRE-BREATH ON THE COVER OF THE THRONE OF SEVEN DOOMS CAMPAIGN BOOK. YOU KNOW IT? NO?
SO ANYWAY, WE'RE WONDERING ABOUT YOUR SKETCHBOOK. THE ONE OLIVE RUINED?
WE NEED INTEL ON THAT SYMBOL YOU DREW IN IT. IT'S, LIKE, TRIANGLES AND LINES AND...
SKRITCH
SKRITCH
HERE, LEMME SHOW YOU. IT'S ACTUALLY SIMPLE IF YOU--
URK!
AHHHH! STOP!
Gnnnnn!
SECRET PAPERS!
SCRIPT PAGES FROM MACBETH?
*Hmm.* I'VE GOT AN IDEA. C'MON.

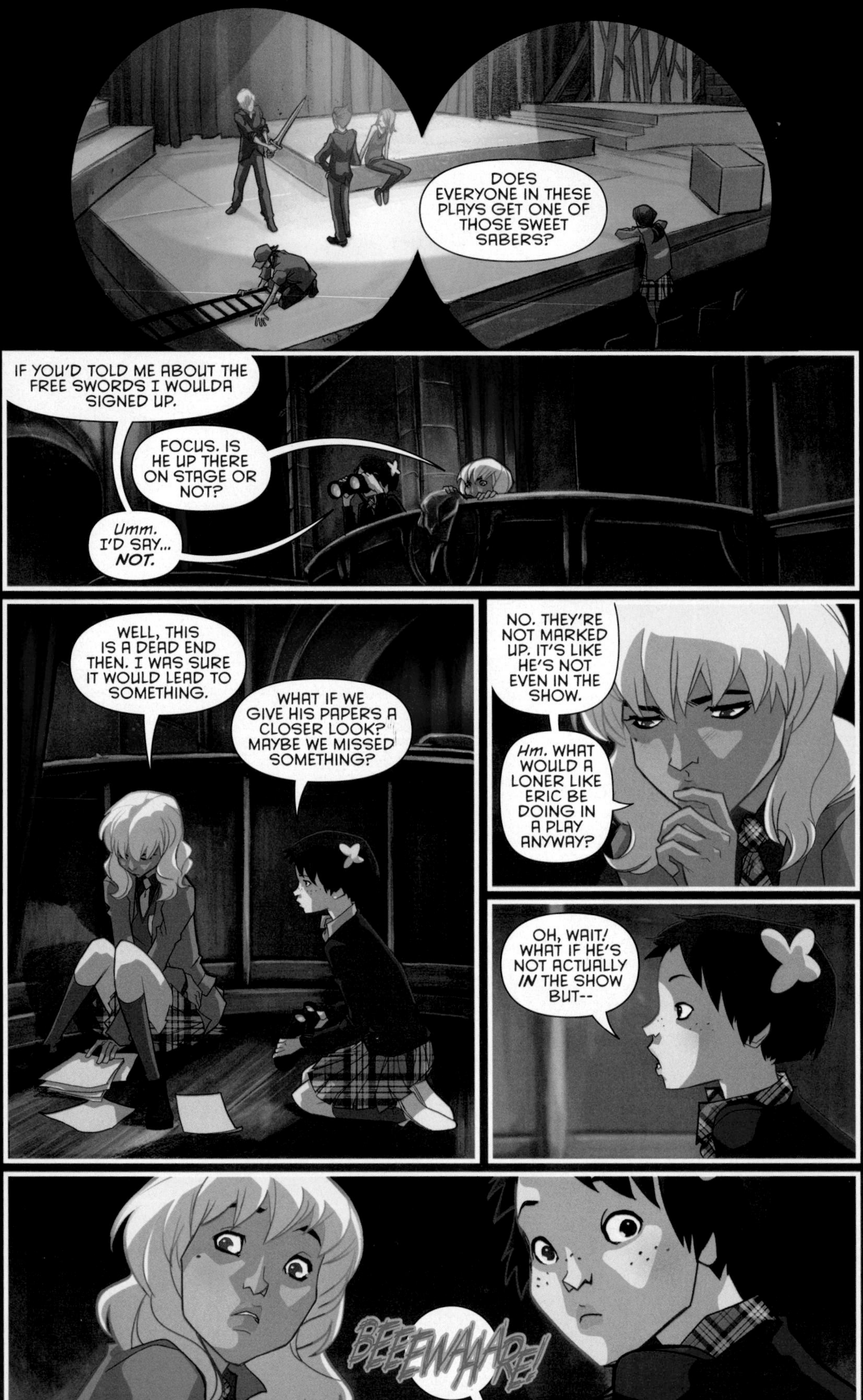
DOES EVERYONE IN THESE PLAYS GET ONE OF THOSE SWEET SABERS?
IF YOU'D TOLD ME ABOUT THE FREE SWORDS I WOULDA SIGNED UP.
FOCUS. IS HE UP THERE ON STAGE OR NOT?
*Umm.* I'D SAY... ***NOT.***
WELL, THIS IS A DEAD END THEN. I WAS SURE IT WOULD LEAD TO SOMETHING.
WHAT IF WE GIVE HIS PAPERS A CLOSER LOOK? MAYBE WE MISSED SOMETHING?
NO. THEY'RE NOT MARKED UP. IT'S LIKE HE'S NOT EVEN IN THE SHOW.
*Hm.* WHAT WOULD A LONER LIKE ERIC BE DOING IN A PLAY ANYWAY?
OH, WAIT! WHAT IF HE'S NOT ACTUALLY ***IN*** THE SHOW BUT--
BEEEWAAARE!

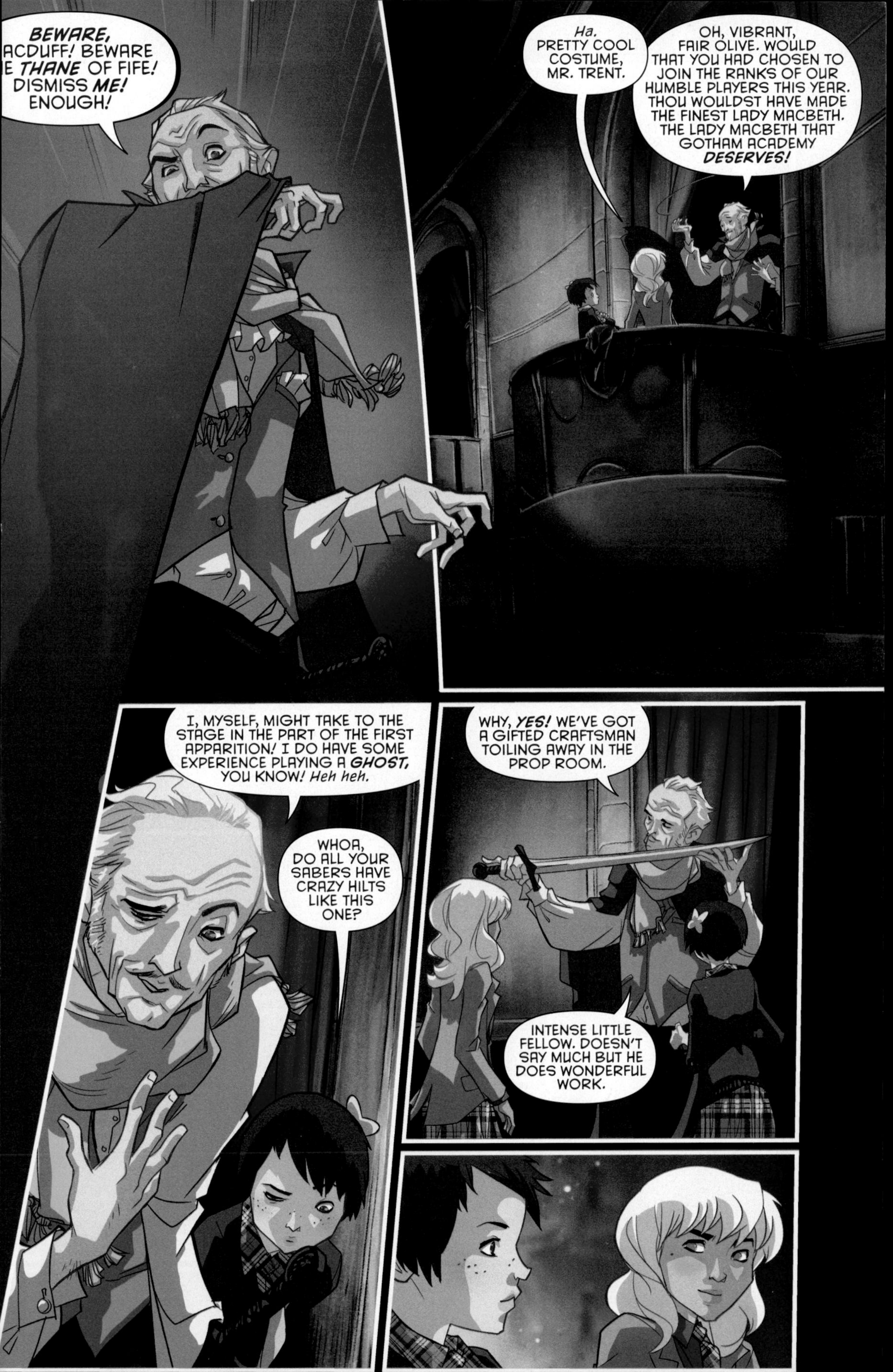
BEWARE, ACDUFF! BEWARE E THANE OF FIFE! DISMISS ME! ENOUGH!
Ha. PRETTY COOL COSTUME, MR. TRENT.
OH, VIBRANT, FAIR OLIVE. WOULD THAT YOU HAD CHOSEN TO JOIN THE RANKS OF OUR HUMBLE PLAYERS THIS YEAR. THOU WOULDST HAVE MADE THE FINEST LADY MACBETH. THE LADY MACBETH THAT GOTHAM ACADEMY DESERVES!
I, MYSELF, MIGHT TAKE TO THE STAGE IN THE PART OF THE FIRST APPARITION! I DO HAVE SOME EXPERIENCE PLAYING A GHOST, YOU KNOW! Heh heh.
WHOA, DO ALL YOUR SABERS HAVE CRAZY HILTS LIKE THIS ONE?
WHY, YES! WE'VE GOT A GIFTED CRAFTSMAN TOILING AWAY IN THE PROP ROOM.
INTENSE LITTLE FELLOW. DOESN'T SAY MUCH BUT HE DOES WONDERFUL WORK.

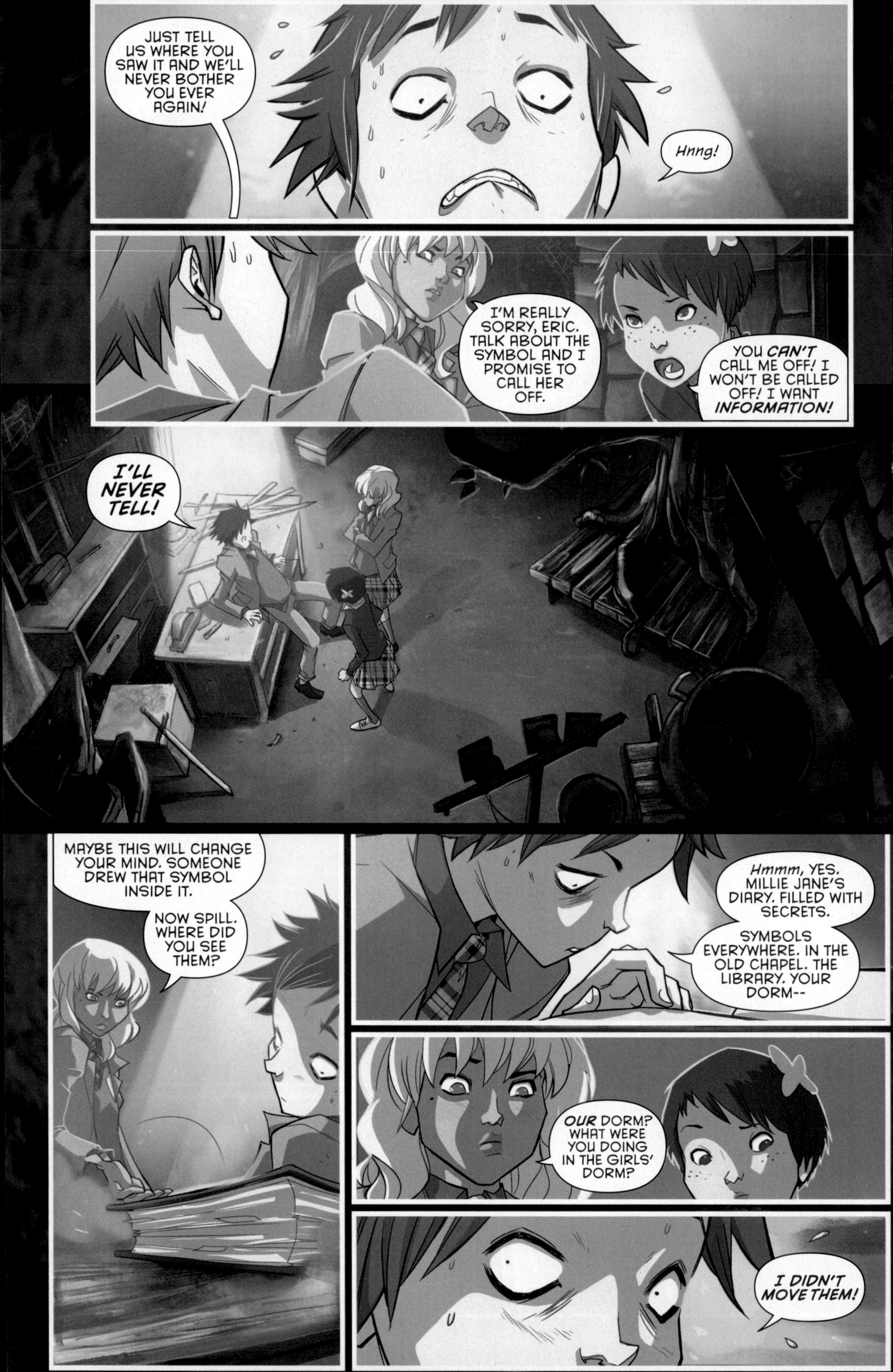
JUST TELL US WHERE YOU SAW IT AND WE'LL NEVER BOTHER YOU EVER AGAIN!
Hnng!
I'M REALLY SORRY, ERIC. TALK ABOUT THE SYMBOL AND I PROMISE TO CALL HER OFF.
YOU CAN'T CALL ME OFF! I WON'T BE CALLED OFF! I WANT INFORMATION!
I'LL NEVER TELL!
MAYBE THIS WILL CHANGE YOUR MIND. SOMEONE DREW THAT SYMBOL INSIDE IT.
NOW SPILL. WHERE DID YOU SEE THEM?
Hmmm, YES. MILLIE JANE'S DIARY. FILLED WITH SECRETS.
SYMBOLS EVERYWHERE. IN THE OLD CHAPEL. THE LIBRARY. YOUR DORM--
OUR DORM? WHAT WERE YOU DOING IN THE GIRLS' DORM?
I DIDN'T MOVE THEM!

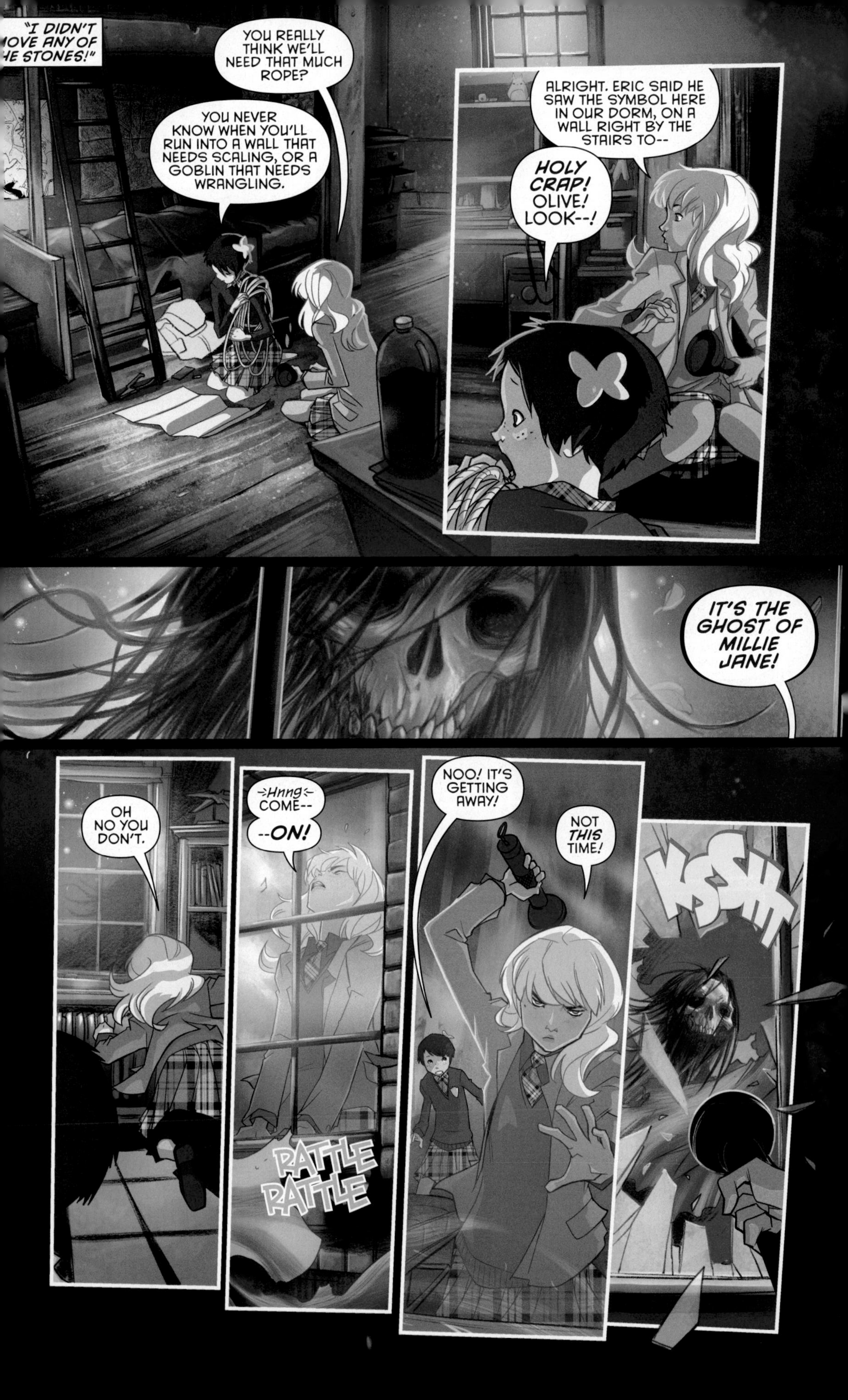
"I DIDN'T
MOVE ANY OF
THE STONES!"
YOU REALLY THINK WE'LL NEED THAT MUCH ROPE?
YOU NEVER KNOW WHEN YOU'LL RUN INTO A WALL THAT NEEDS SCALING, OR A GOBLIN THAT NEEDS WRANGLING.
ALRIGHT. ERIC SAID HE SAW THE SYMBOL HERE IN OUR DORM, ON A WALL RIGHT BY THE STAIRS TO--
HOLY CRAP! OLIVE! LOOK--!
IT'S THE GHOST OF MILLIE JANE!
OH NO YOU DON'T.
Hnng COME--
--ON!
RATTLE RATTLE
NOO! IT'S GETTING AWAY!
NOT THIS TIME!
KSSH

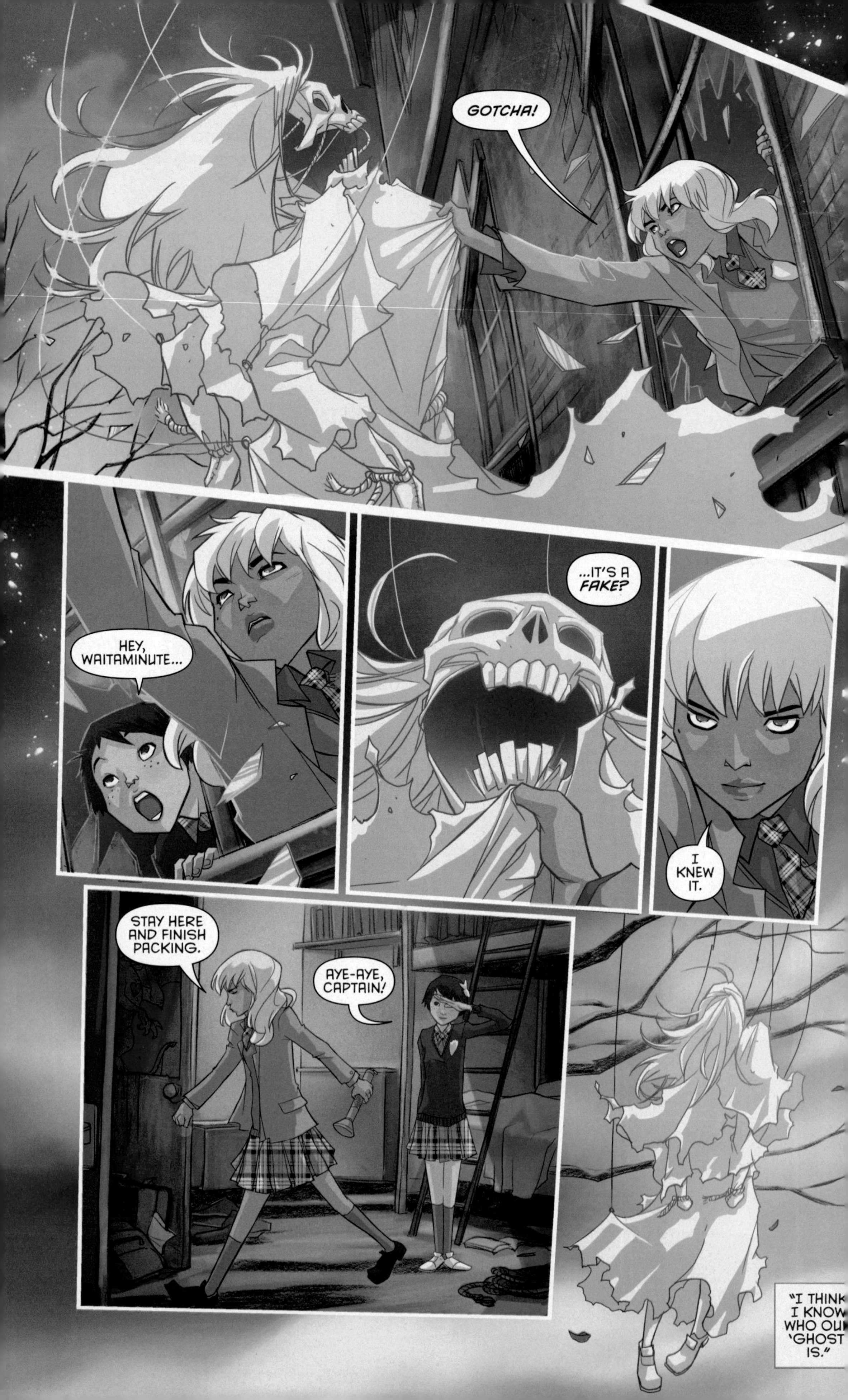
GOTCHA!
HEY, WAITAMINUTE...
...IT'S A FAKE?
I KNEW IT.
STAY HERE AND FINISH PACKING.
AYE-AYE, CAPTAIN!
"I THINK I KNOW WHO OU 'GHOST IS."

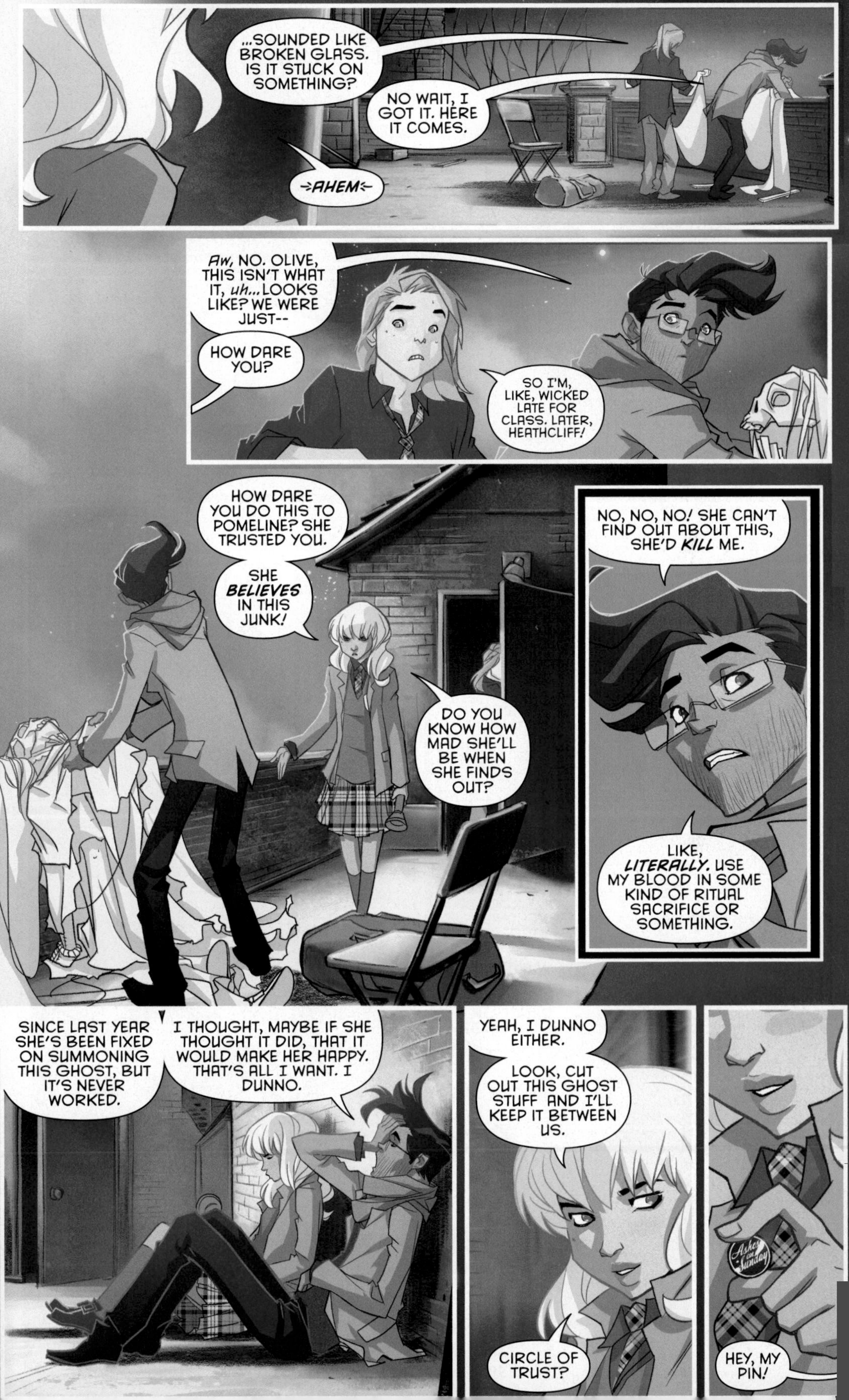
...SOUNDED LIKE BROKEN GLASS. IS IT STUCK ON SOMETHING?
NO WAIT, I GOT IT. HERE IT COMES.
AHEM
*Aw,* NO. OLIVE, THIS ISN'T WHAT IT, *uh*... LOOKS LIKE? WE WERE JUST--
HOW DARE YOU?
SO I'M, LIKE, WICKED LATE FOR CLASS. LATER, HEATHCLIFF!
HOW DARE YOU DO THIS TO POMELINE? SHE TRUSTED YOU.
SHE ***BELIEVES*** IN THIS JUNK!
DO YOU KNOW HOW MAD SHE'LL BE WHEN SHE FINDS OUT?
NO, NO, NO! SHE CAN'T FIND OUT ABOUT THIS, SHE'D ***KILL*** ME.
LIKE, ***LITERALLY.*** USE MY BLOOD IN SOME KIND OF RITUAL SACRIFICE OR SOMETHING.
SINCE LAST YEAR SHE'S BEEN FIXED ON SUMMONING THIS GHOST, BUT IT'S NEVER WORKED.
I THOUGHT, MAYBE IF SHE THOUGHT IT DID, THAT IT WOULD MAKE HER HAPPY. THAT'S ALL I WANT. I DUNNO.
YEAH, I DUNNO EITHER.
LOOK, CUT OUT THIS GHOST STUFF AND I'LL KEEP IT BETWEEN US.
CIRCLE OF TRUST?
Ashes on Sunday
HEY, MY PIN!

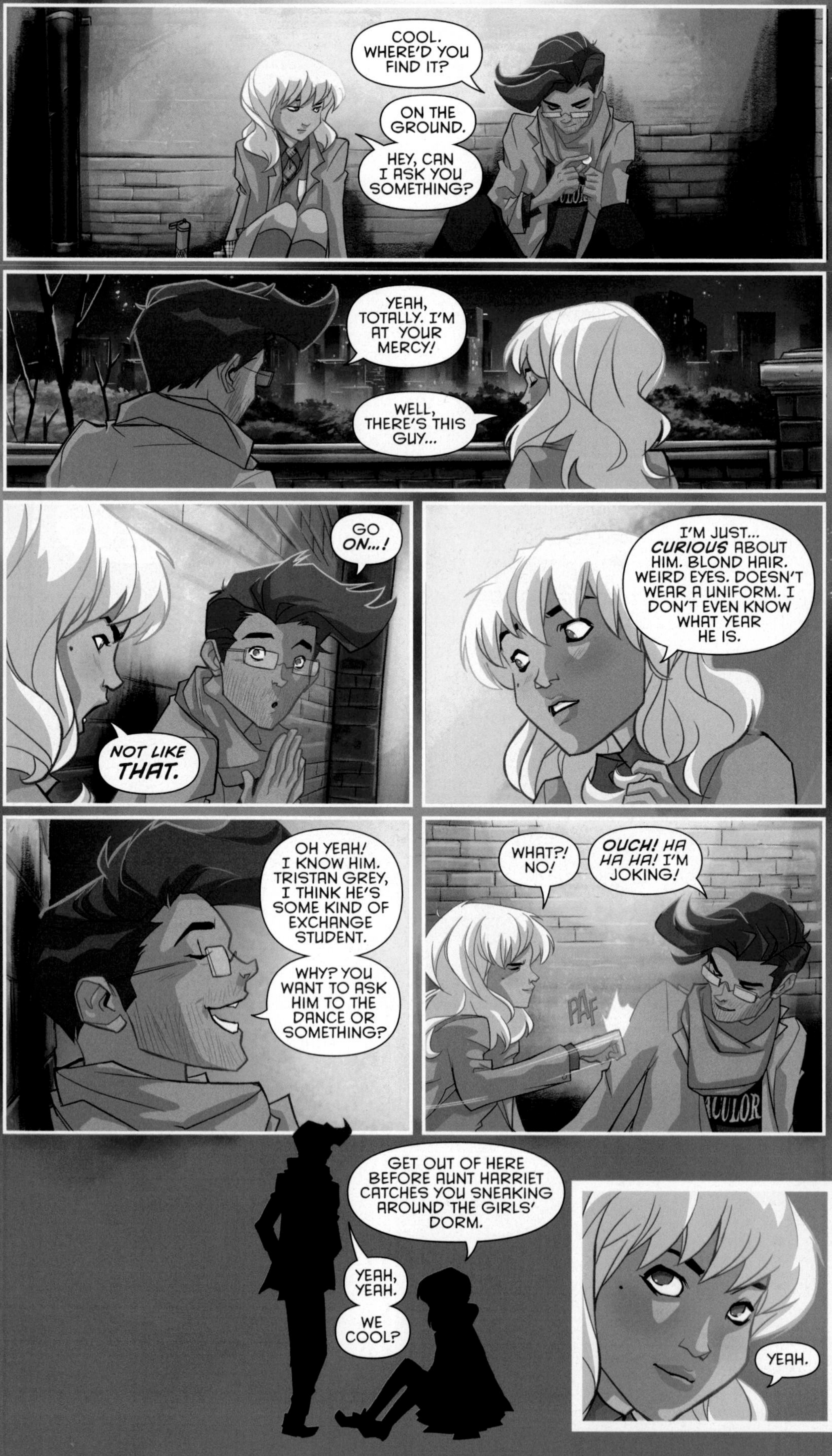
COOL. WHERE'D YOU FIND IT?
ON THE GROUND.
HEY, CAN I ASK YOU SOMETHING?
YEAH, TOTALLY. I'M AT YOUR MERCY!
WELL, THERE'S THIS GUY...
GO ON...!
NOT LIKE THAT.
I'M JUST... CURIOUS ABOUT HIM. BLOND HAIR. WEIRD EYES. DOESN'T WEAR A UNIFORM. I DON'T EVEN KNOW WHAT YEAR HE IS.
OH YEAH! I KNOW HIM. TRISTAN GREY, I THINK HE'S SOME KIND OF EXCHANGE STUDENT.
WHY? YOU WANT TO ASK HIM TO THE DANCE OR SOMETHING?
WHAT?! NO!
PAF
OUCH! HA HA HA! I'M JOKING!
GET OUT OF HERE BEFORE AUNT HARRIET CATCHES YOU SNEAKING AROUND THE GIRLS' DORM.
YEAH, YEAH.
WE COOL?
YEAH.

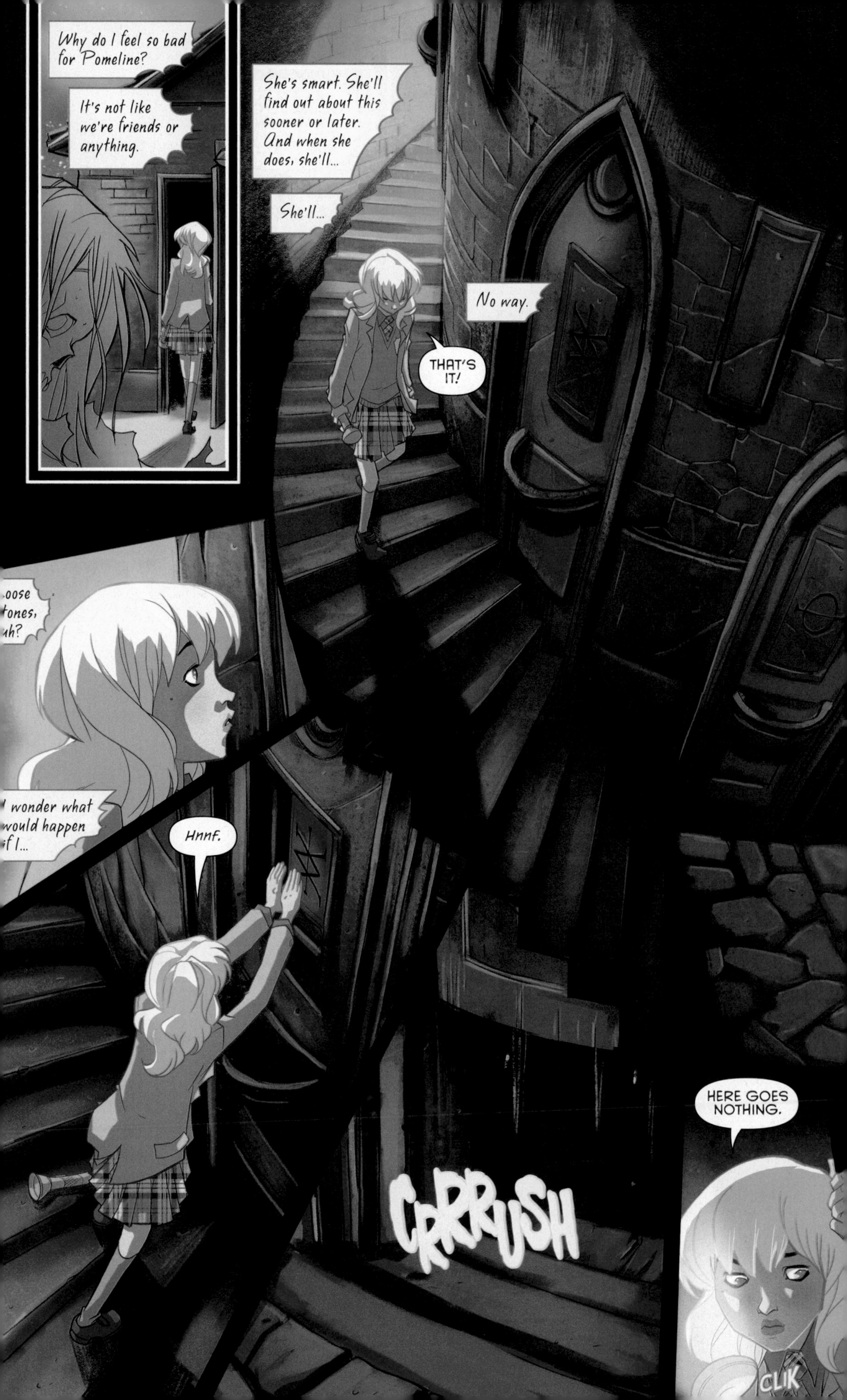

Why do I feel so bad for Pomeline?
It's not like we're friends or anything.
She's smart. She'll find out about this sooner or later. And when she does, she'll...
She'll...
No way.
THAT'S IT!
oose tones, uh?
I wonder what would happen if I...
Hnnf.
CRRRUSH
HERE GOES NOTHING.
CLIK

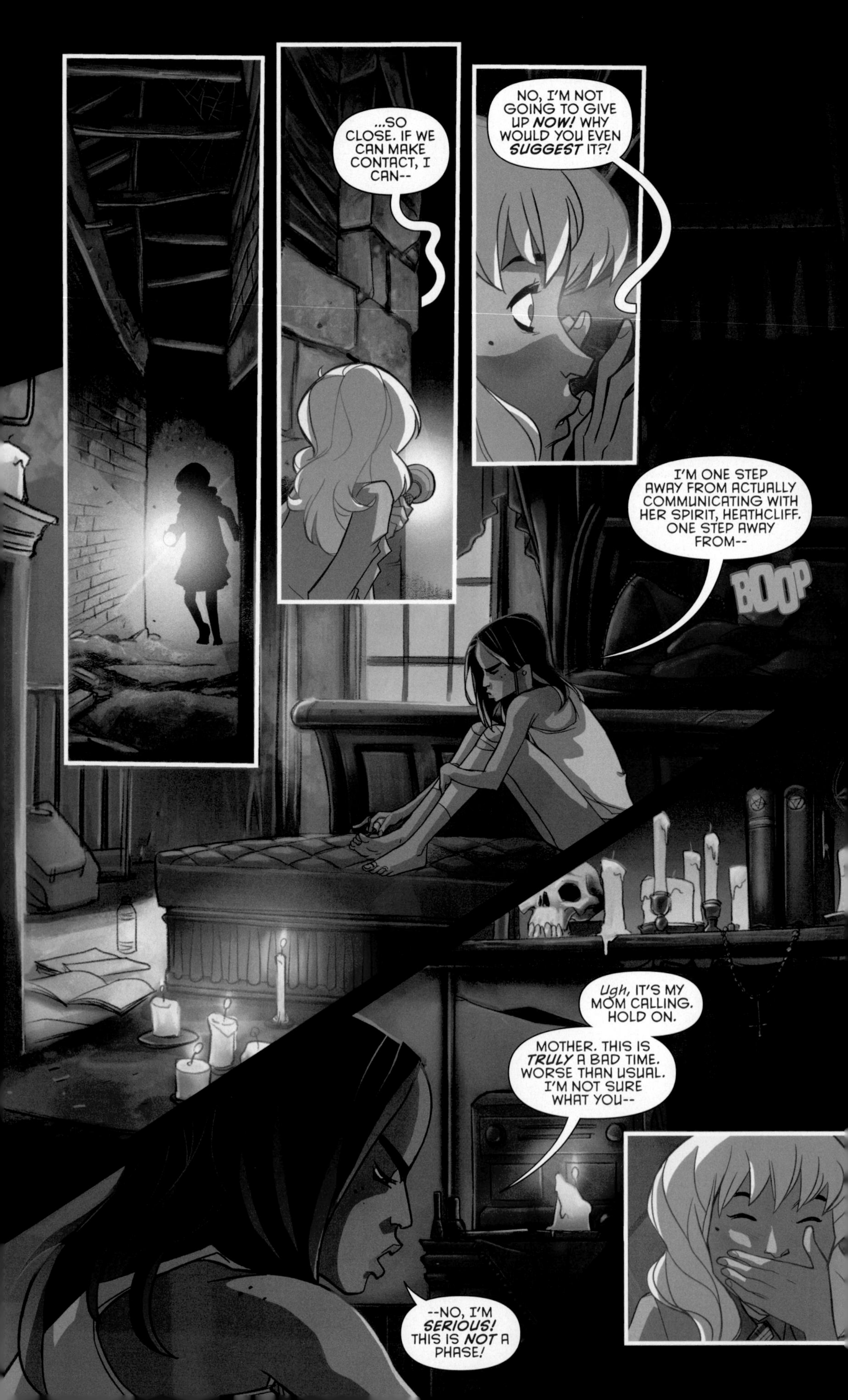
...SO CLOSE. IF WE CAN MAKE CONTACT, I CAN--
NO, I'M NOT GOING TO GIVE UP NOW! WHY WOULD YOU EVEN SUGGEST IT?!
I'M ONE STEP AWAY FROM ACTUALLY COMMUNICATING WITH HER SPIRIT, HEATHCLIFF. ONE STEP AWAY FROM--
BOOP
Ugh, IT'S MY MOM CALLING. HOLD ON.
MOTHER. THIS IS TRULY A BAD TIME. WORSE THAN USUAL. I'M NOT SURE WHAT YOU--
--NO, I'M SERIOUS! THIS IS NOT A PHASE!

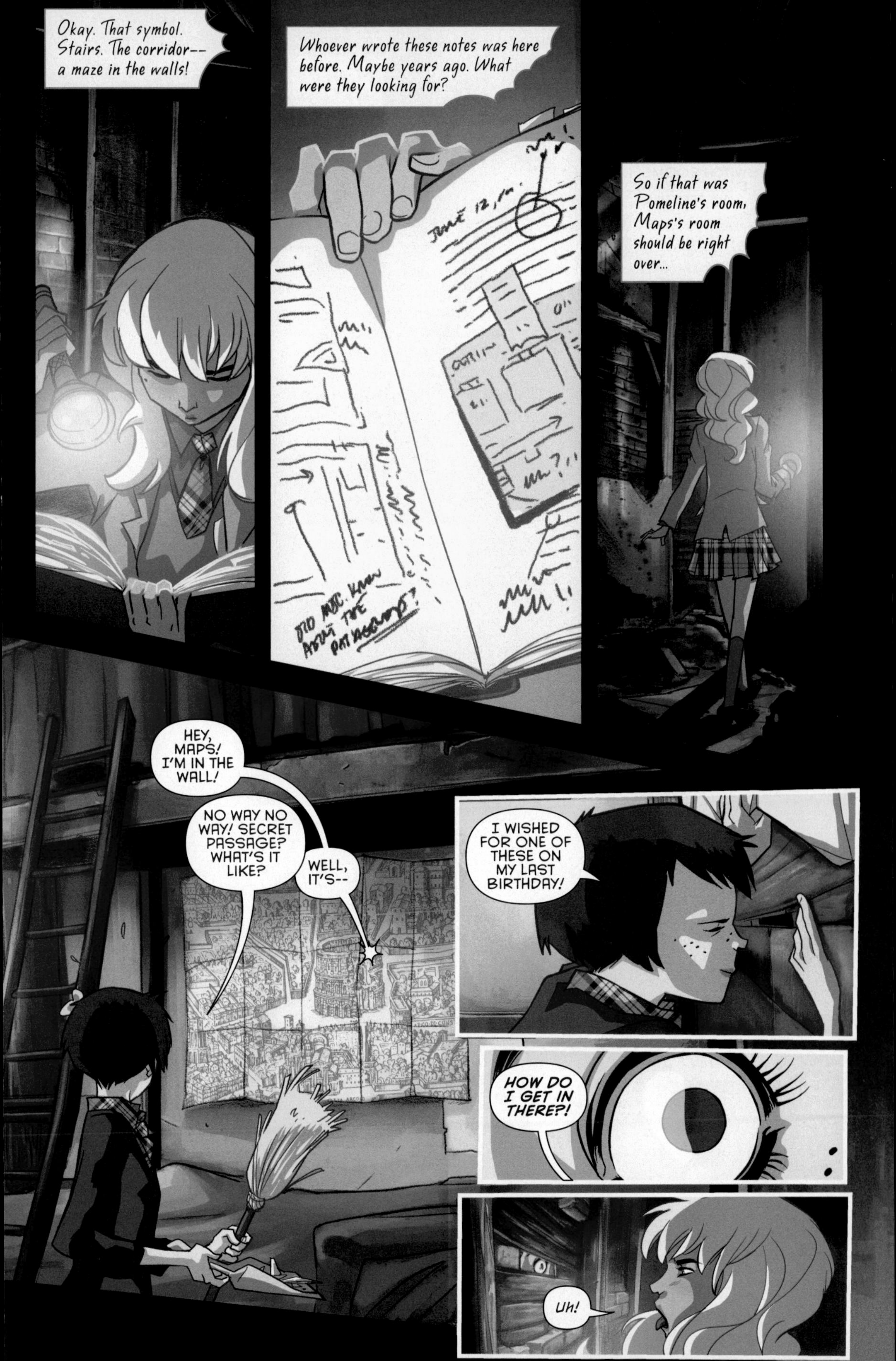
Okay. That symbol. Stairs. The corridor-- a maze in the walls!
Whoever wrote these notes was here before. Maybe years ago. What were they looking for?
So if that was Pomeline's room, Maps's room should be right over...
HEY, MAPS! I'M IN THE WALL!
NO WAY NO WAY! SECRET PASSAGE? WHAT'S IT LIKE?
WELL, IT'S--
I WISHED FOR ONE OF THESE ON MY LAST BIRTHDAY!
HOW DO I GET IN THERE?!
Uh!

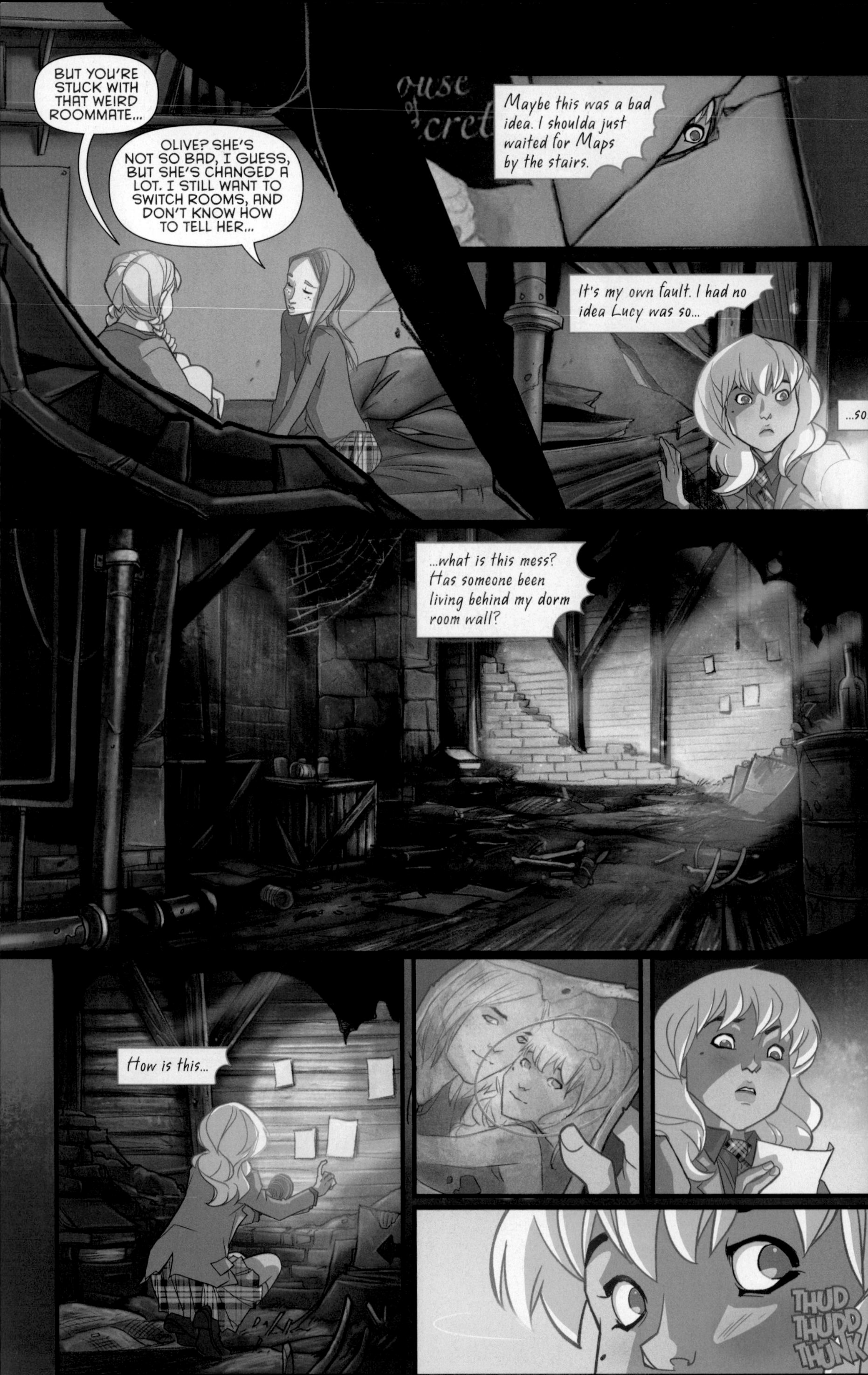

BUT YOU'RE STUCK WITH THAT WEIRD ROOMMATE...
OLIVE? SHE'S NOT SO BAD, I GUESS, BUT SHE'S CHANGED A LOT. I STILL WANT TO SWITCH ROOMS, AND DON'T KNOW HOW TO TELL HER...
Maybe this was a bad idea. I shoulda just waited for Maps by the stairs.
It's my own fault. I had no idea Lucy was so...
...so
...what is this mess? Has someone been living behind my dorm room wall?
How is this...
THUD
THUDD
THUNK

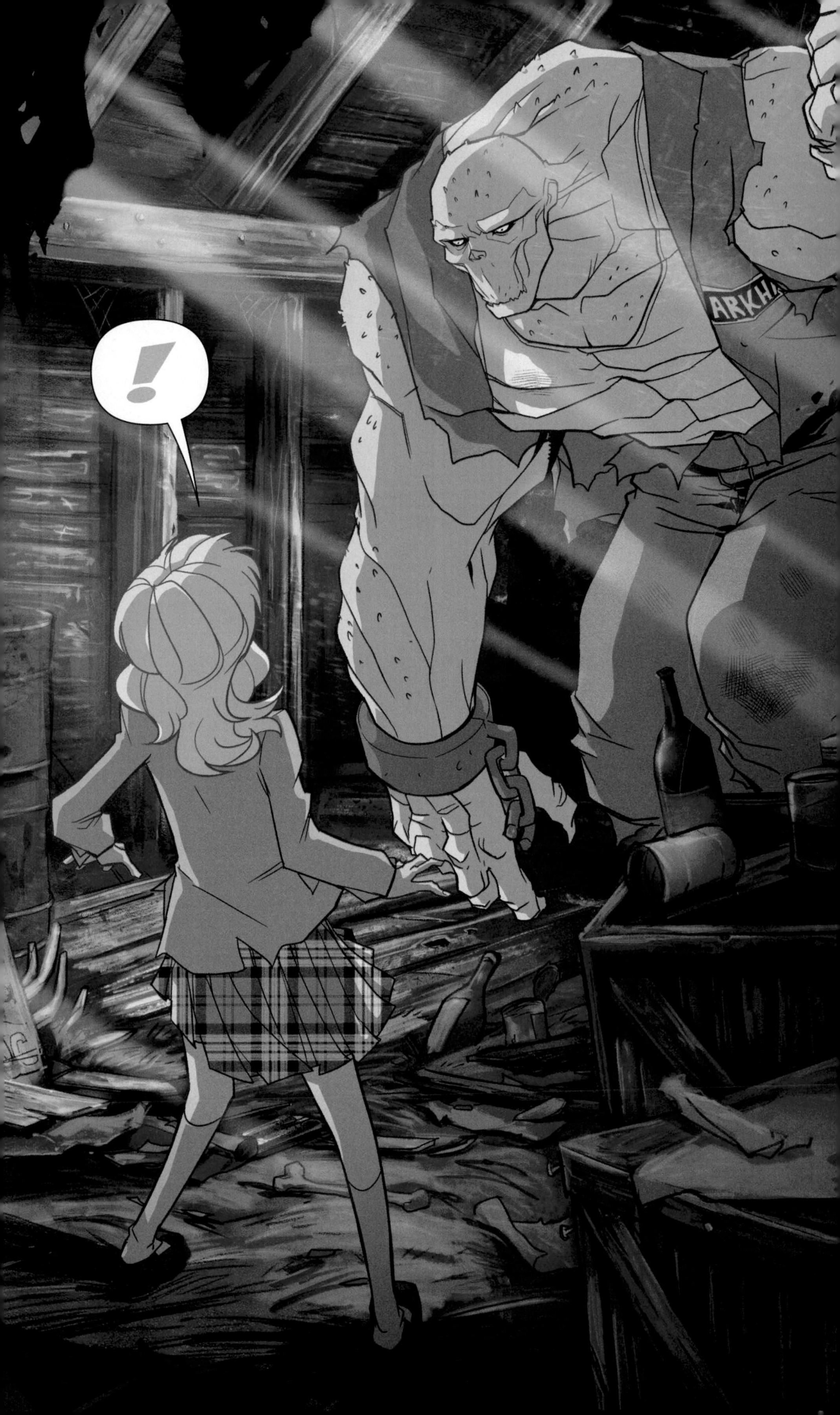
!
ARKH

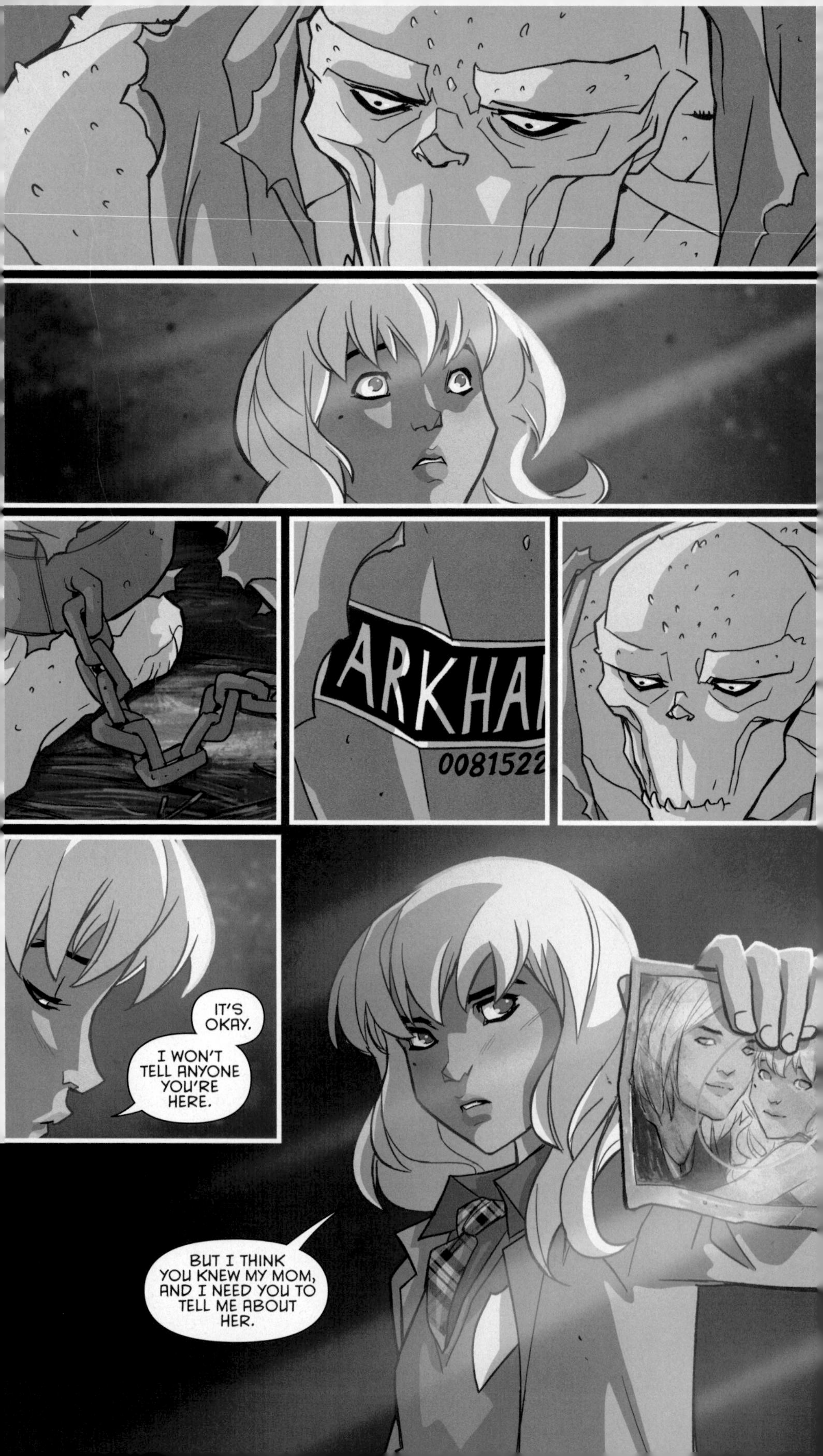
ARKHA
0081522
IT'S OKAY.
I WON'T TELL ANYONE YOU'RE HERE.
BUT I THINK YOU KNEW MY MOM, AND I NEED YOU TO TELL ME ABOUT HER.

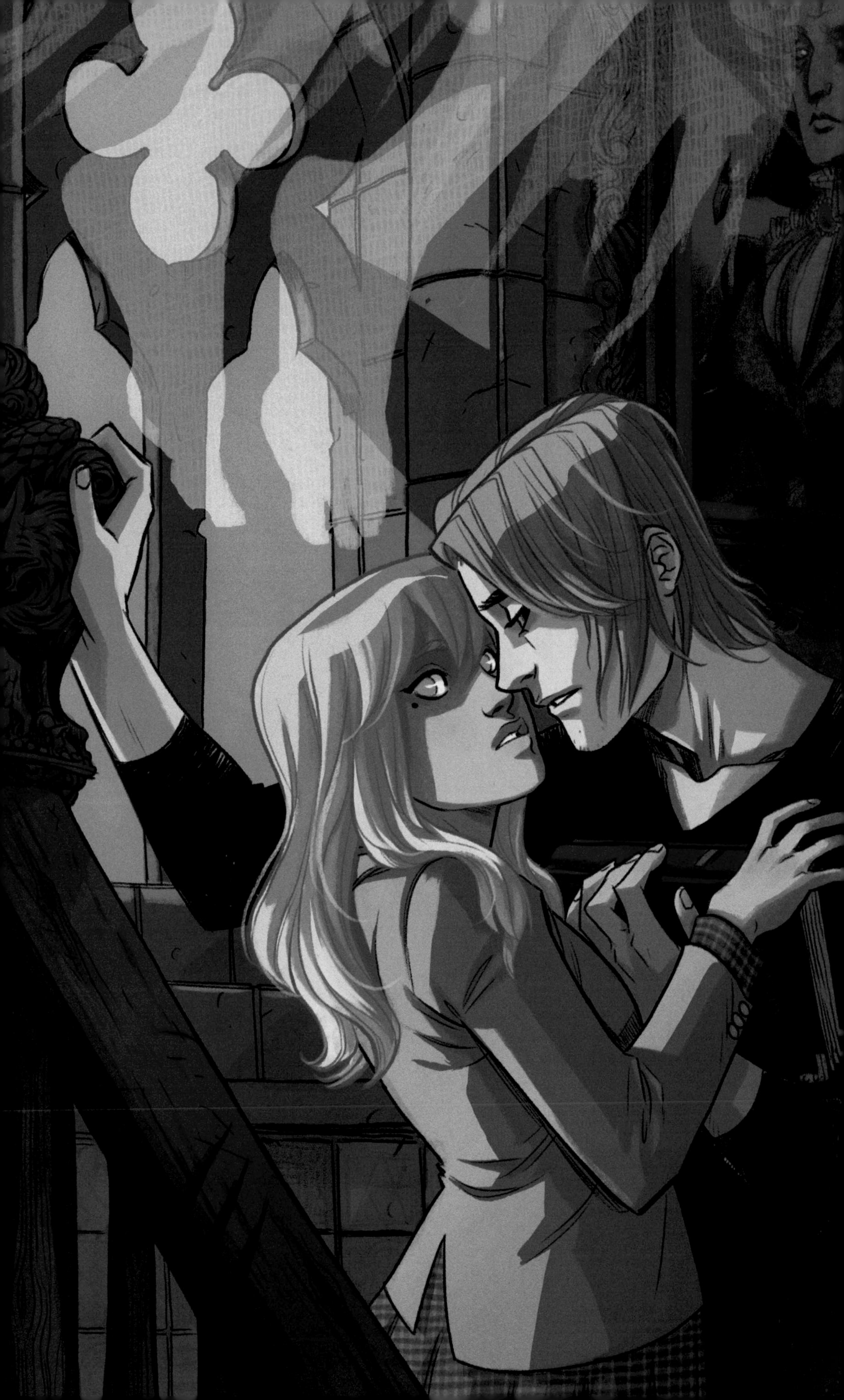

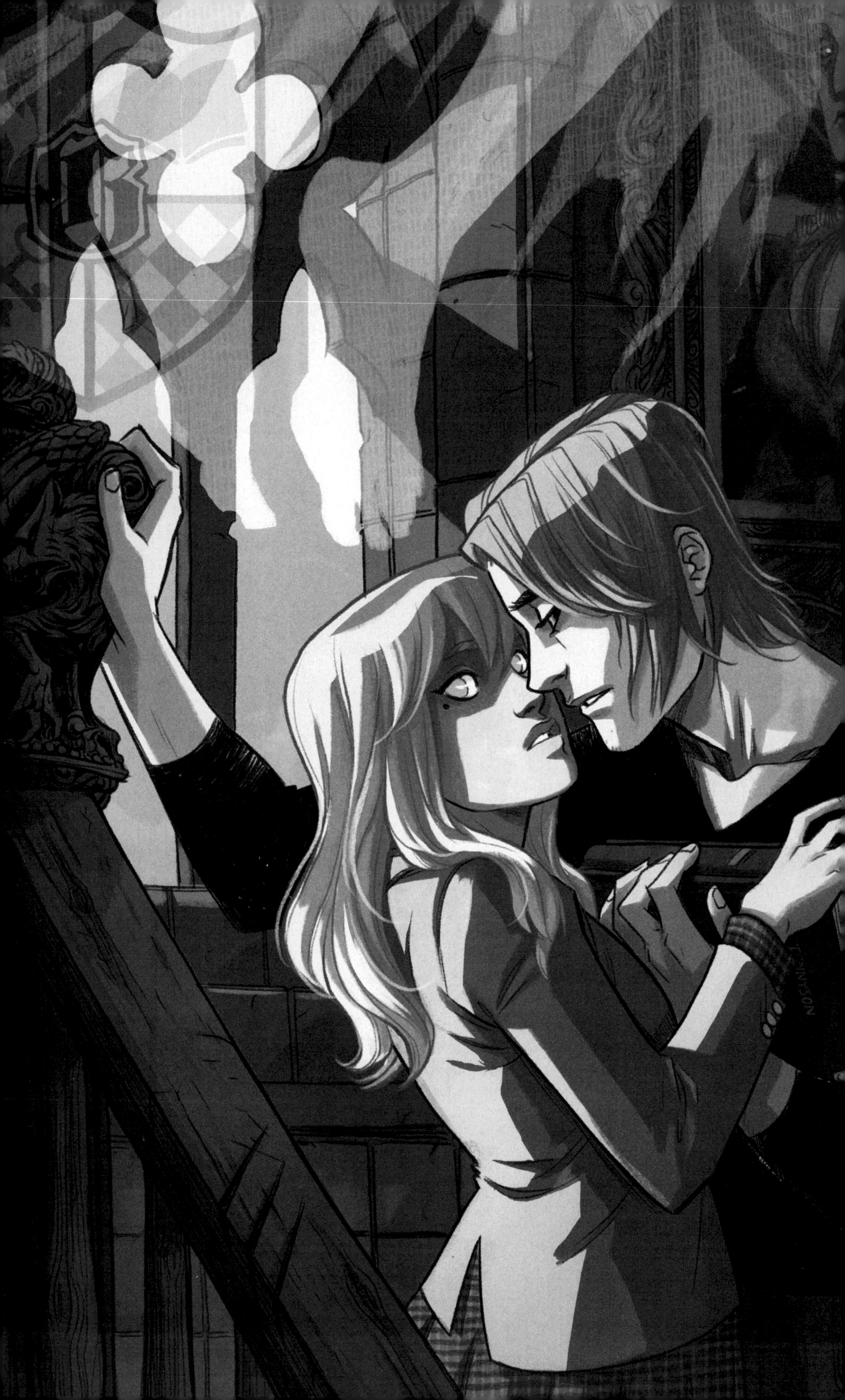

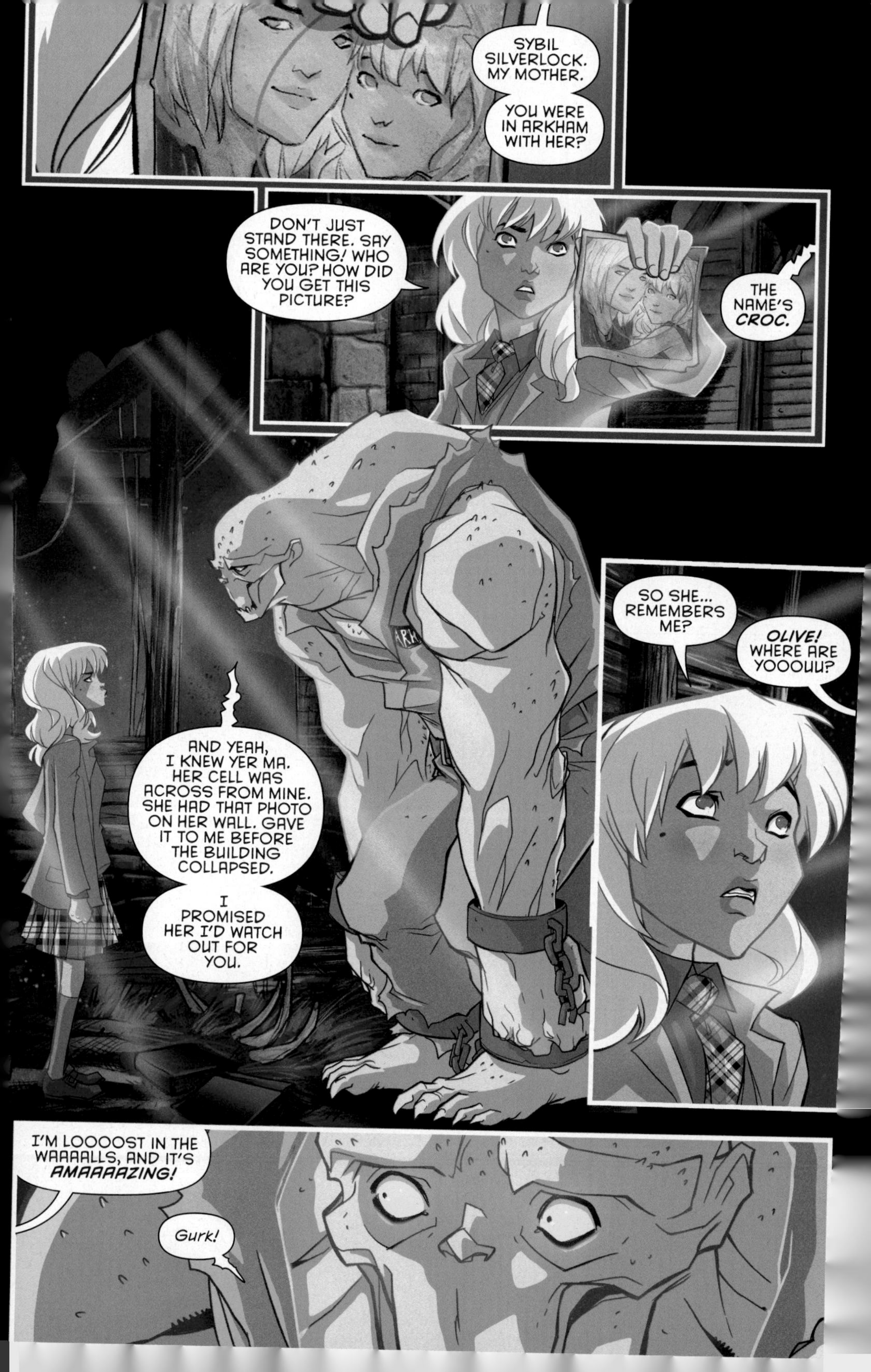

SYBIL SILVERLOCK. MY MOTHER.
YOU WERE IN ARKHAM WITH HER?
DON'T JUST STAND THERE. SAY SOMETHING! WHO ARE YOU? HOW DID YOU GET THIS PICTURE?
THE NAME'S *CROC.*
AND YEAH, I KNEW YER MA. HER CELL WAS ACROSS FROM MINE. SHE HAD THAT PHOTO ON HER WALL. GAVE IT TO ME BEFORE THE BUILDING COLLAPSED.
I PROMISED HER I'D WATCH OUT FOR YOU.
SO SHE... REMEMBERS ME?
*OLIVE!* WHERE ARE YOOOUU?
I'M LOOOOST IN THE WAAAALLS, AND IT'S *AMAAAAZING!*
*Gurk!*

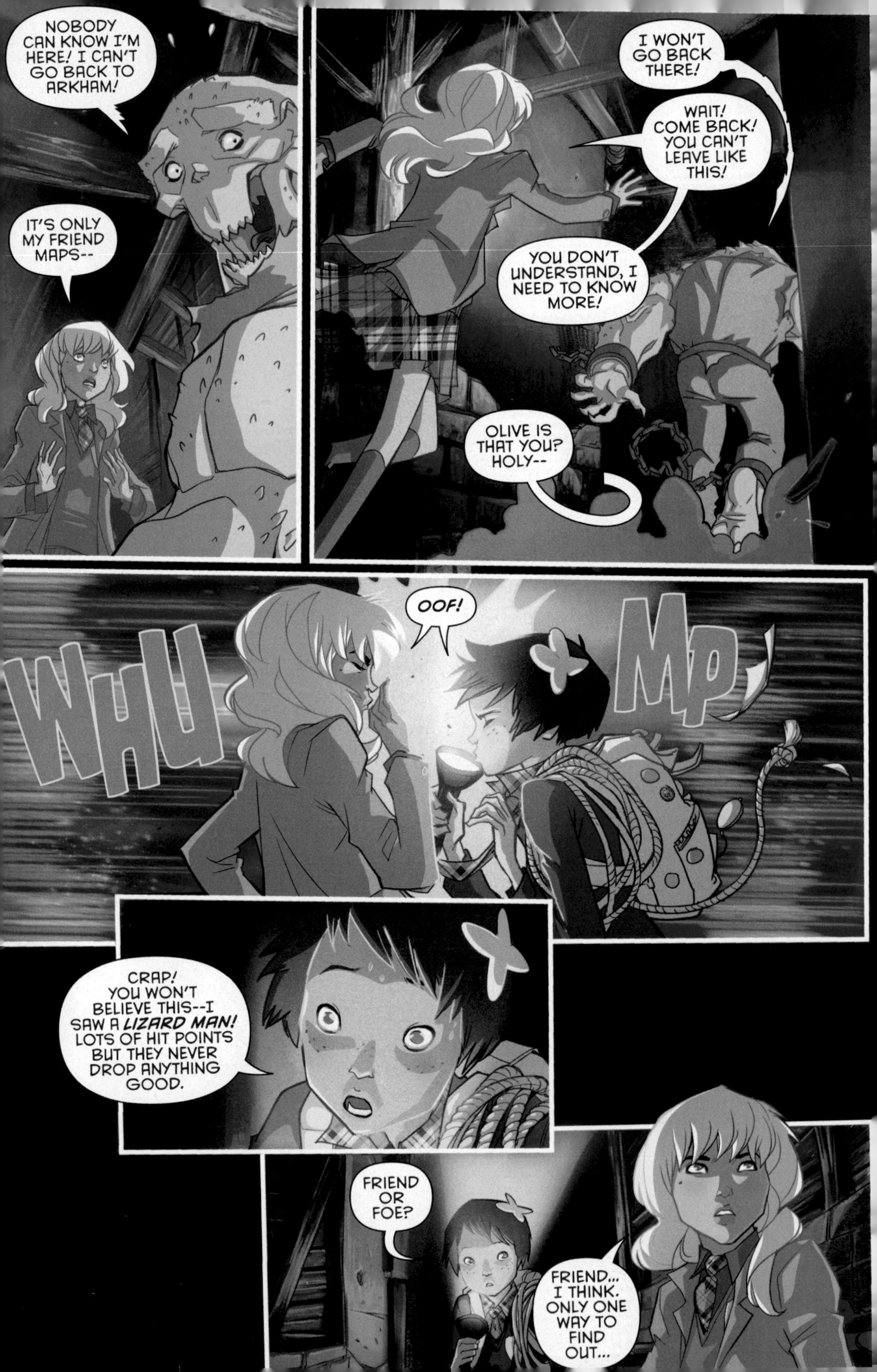
NOBODY CAN KNOW I'M HERE! I CAN'T GO BACK TO ARKHAM!
IT'S ONLY MY FRIEND MAPS--
I WON'T GO BACK THERE!
WAIT! COME BACK! YOU CAN'T LEAVE LIKE THIS!
YOU DON'T UNDERSTAND, I NEED TO KNOW MORE!
OLIVE IS THAT YOU? HOLY--
WHU
OOF!
MP
CRAP! YOU WON'T BELIEVE THIS--I SAW A *LIZARD MAN!* LOTS OF HIT POINTS BUT THEY NEVER DROP ANYTHING GOOD.
FRIEND OR FOE?
FRIEND... I THINK. ONLY ONE WAY TO FIND OUT...

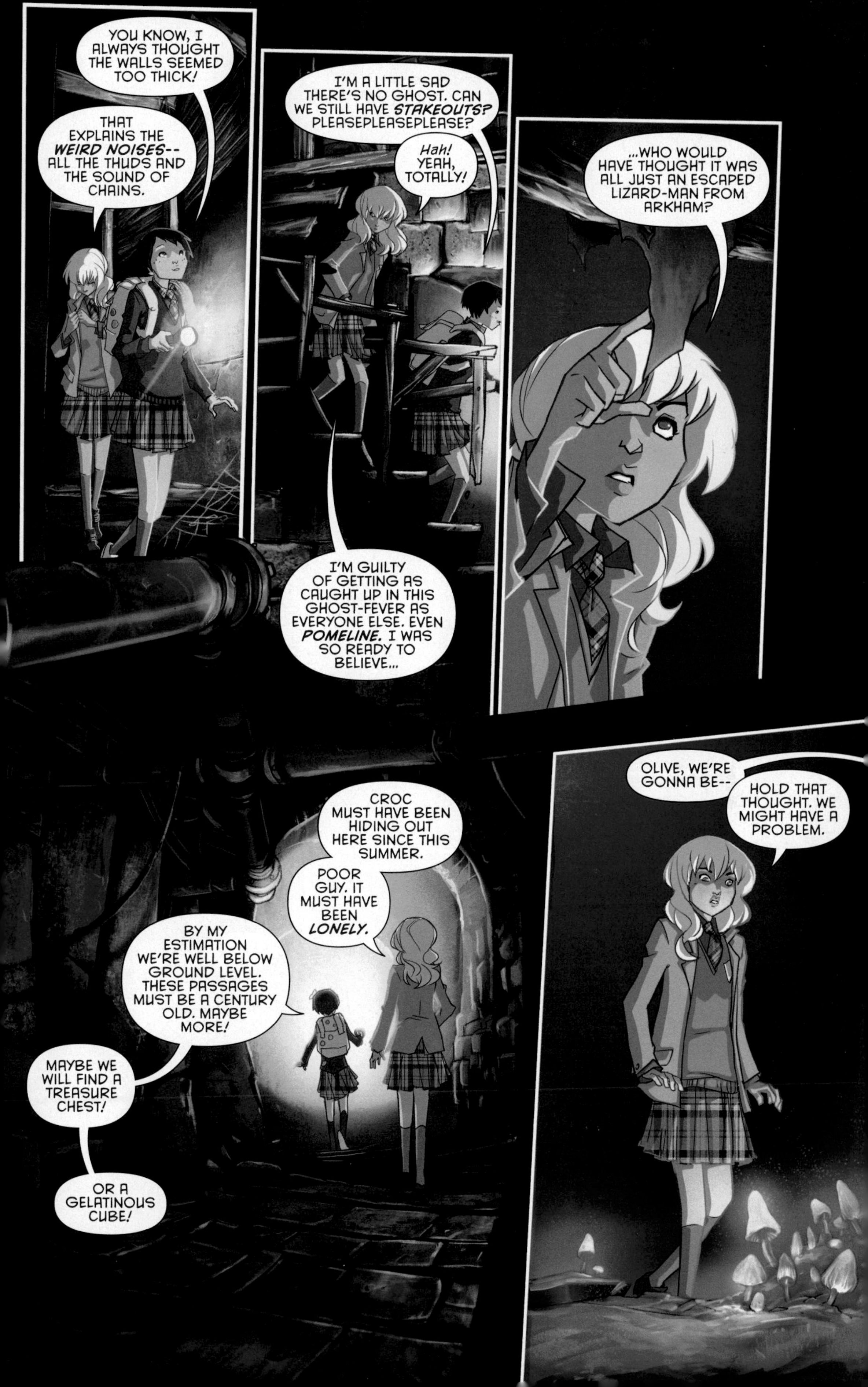
YOU KNOW, I ALWAYS THOUGHT THE WALLS SEEMED TOO THICK!
THAT EXPLAINS THE WEIRD NOISES-- ALL THE THUDS AND THE SOUND OF CHAINS.
I'M A LITTLE SAD THERE'S NO GHOST. CAN WE STILL HAVE STAKEOUTS? PLEASEPLEASEPLEASE?
Hah! YEAH, TOTALLY!
I'M GUILTY OF GETTING AS CAUGHT UP IN THIS GHOST-FEVER AS EVERYONE ELSE. EVEN POMELINE. I WAS SO READY TO BELIEVE...
...WHO WOULD HAVE THOUGHT IT WAS ALL JUST AN ESCAPED LIZARD-MAN FROM ARKHAM?
CROC MUST HAVE BEEN HIDING OUT HERE SINCE THIS SUMMER.
POOR GUY. IT MUST HAVE BEEN LONELY.
BY MY ESTIMATION WE'RE WELL BELOW GROUND LEVEL. THESE PASSAGES MUST BE A CENTURY OLD. MAYBE MORE!
MAYBE WE WILL FIND A TREASURE CHEST!
OR A GELATINOUS CUBE!
OLIVE, WE'RE GONNA BE--
HOLD THAT THOUGHT. WE MIGHT HAVE A PROBLEM.

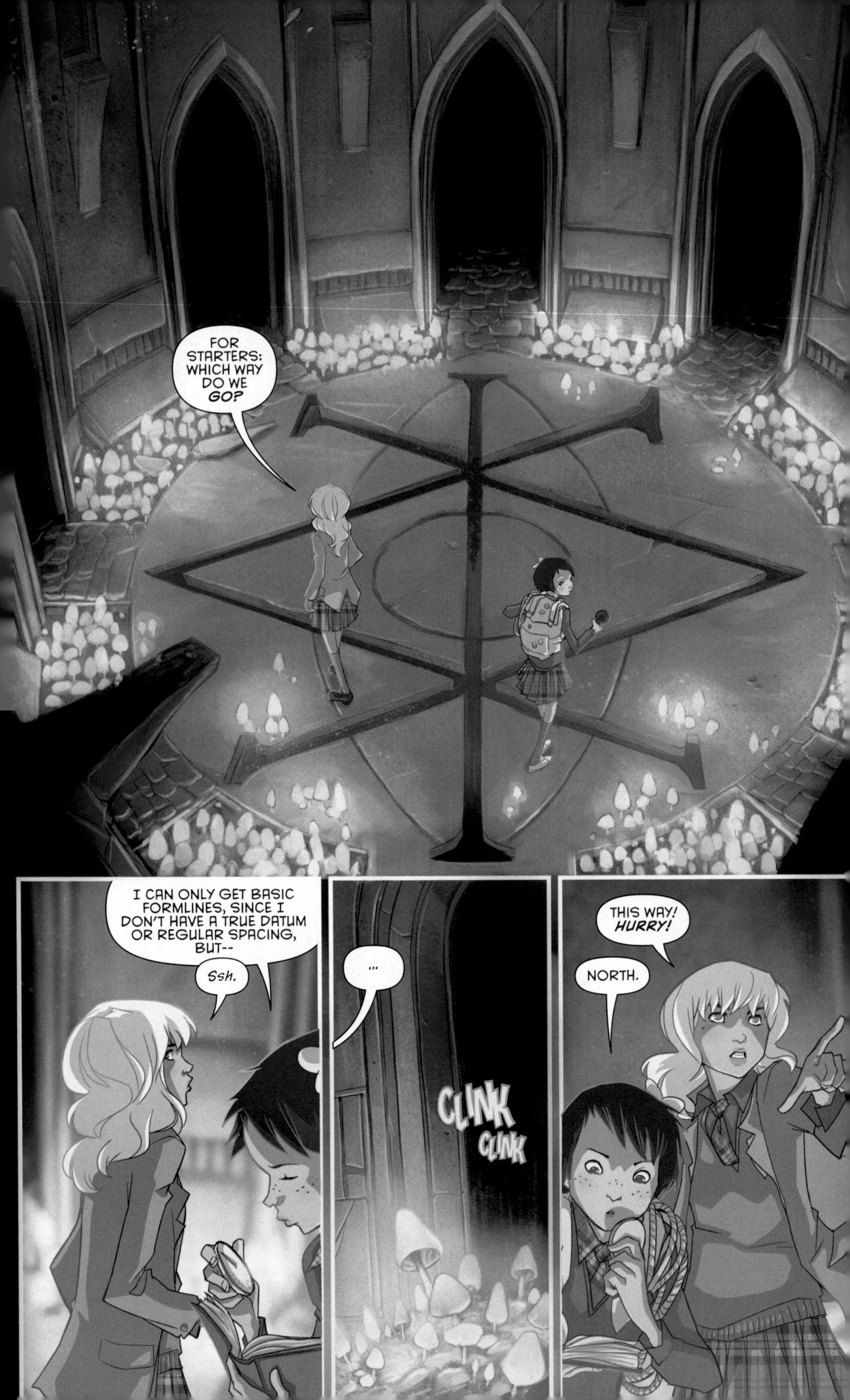

FOR STARTERS: WHICH WAY DO WE GO?
I CAN ONLY GET BASIC FORMLINES, SINCE I DON'T HAVE A TRUE DATUM OR REGULAR SPACING, BUT--
Ssh.
...
CLINK
CLINK
THIS WAY! HURRY!
NORTH.

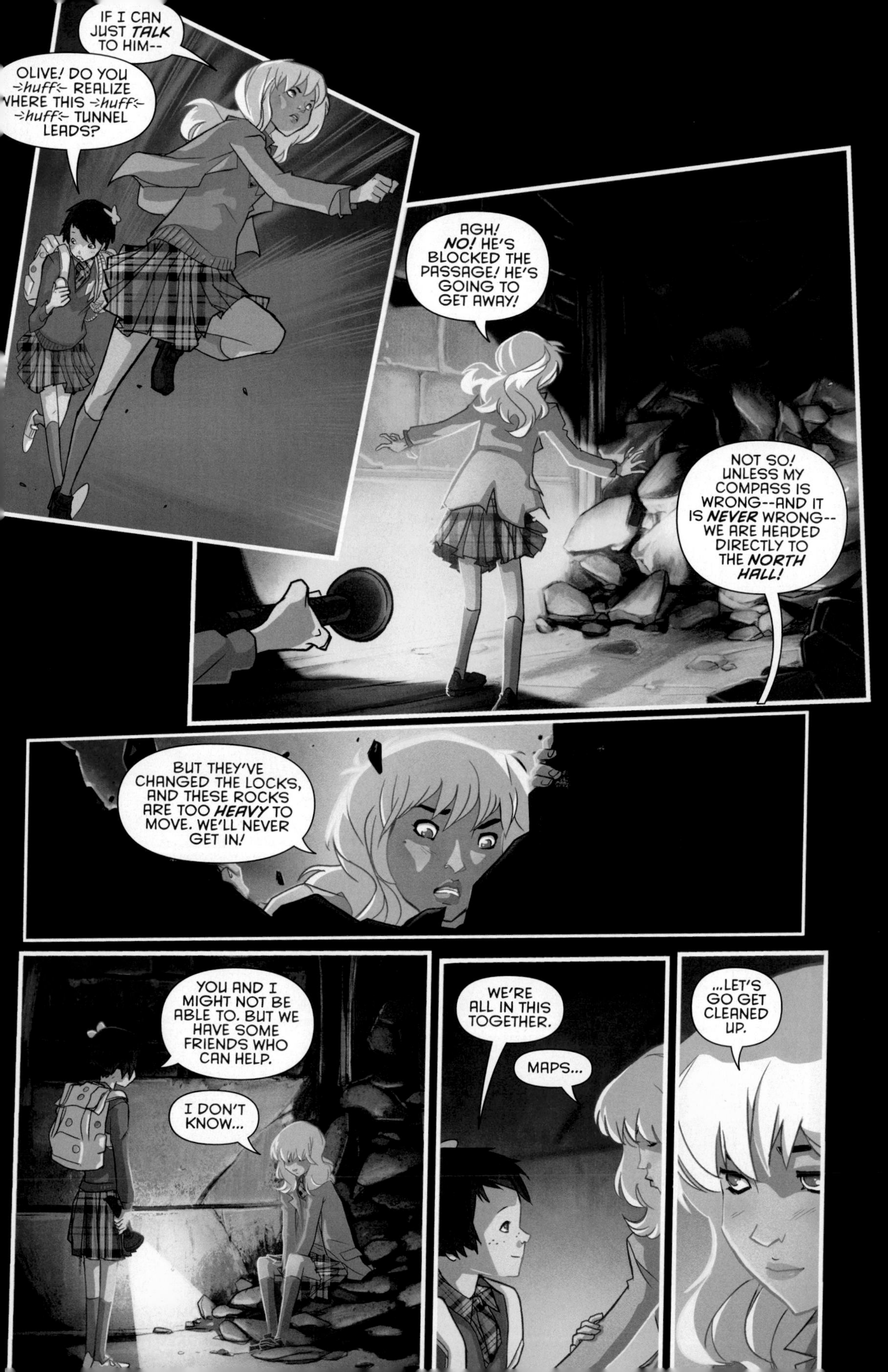
IF I CAN JUST *TALK* TO HIM--
OLIVE! DO YOU ->*huff*<- REALIZE WHERE THIS ->*huff*<- ->*huff*<- TUNNEL LEADS?
AGH! *NO!* HE'S BLOCKED THE PASSAGE! HE'S GOING TO GET AWAY!
NOT SO! UNLESS MY COMPASS IS WRONG--AND IT IS *NEVER* WRONG--WE ARE HEADED DIRECTLY TO THE *NORTH HALL!*
BUT THEY'VE CHANGED THE LOCKS, AND THESE ROCKS ARE TOO *HEAVY* TO MOVE. WE'LL NEVER GET IN!
YOU AND I MIGHT NOT BE ABLE TO. BUT WE HAVE SOME FRIENDS WHO CAN HELP.
I DON'T KNOW...
WE'RE ALL IN THIS TOGETHER.
MAPS...
...LET'S GO GET CLEANED UP.

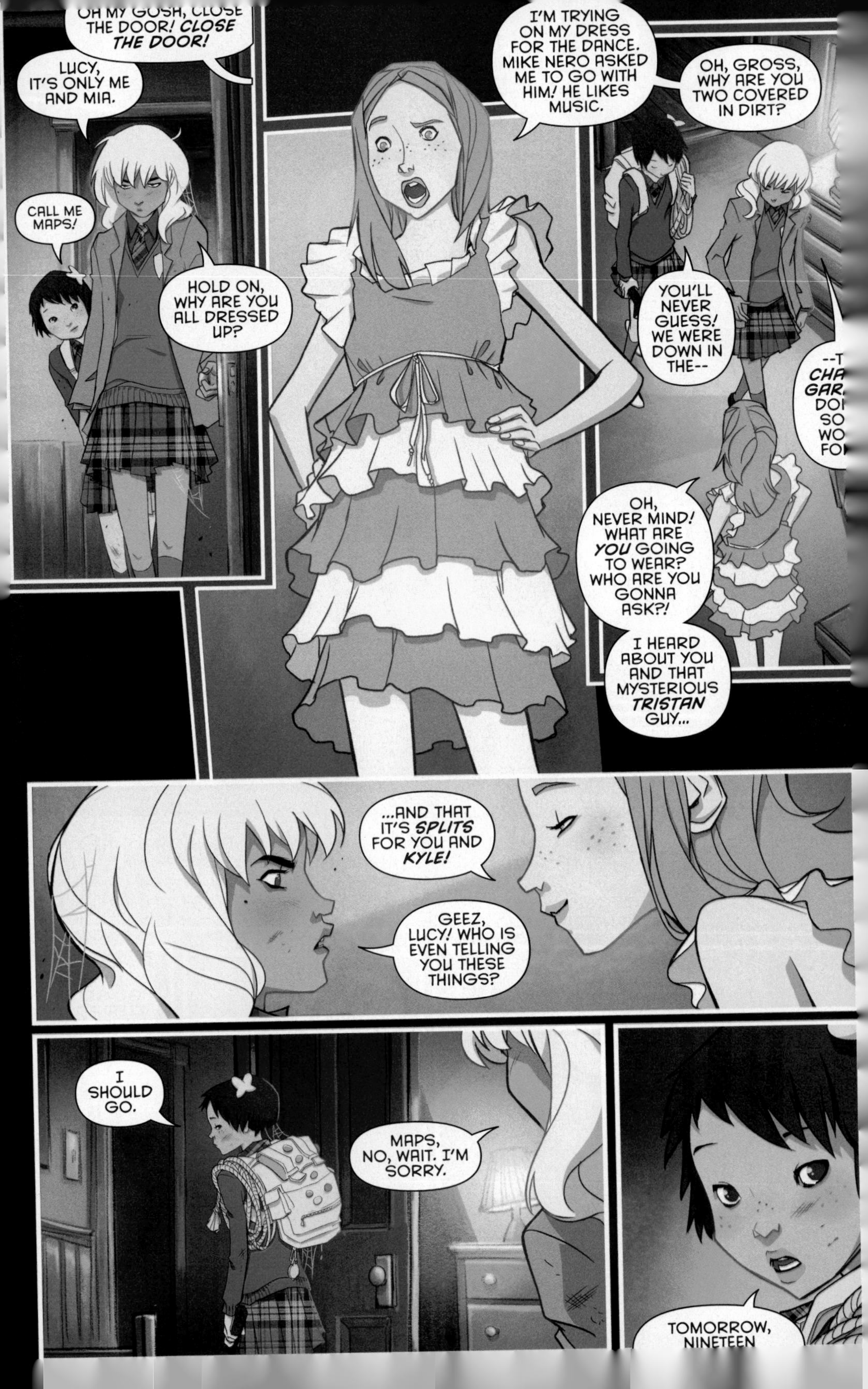
OH MY GOSH, CLOSE THE DOOR! CLOSE THE DOOR!
LUCY, IT'S ONLY ME AND MIA.
CALL ME MAPS!
HOLD ON, WHY ARE YOU ALL DRESSED UP?
I'M TRYING ON MY DRESS FOR THE DANCE. MIKE NERO ASKED ME TO GO WITH HIM! HE LIKES MUSIC.
OH, GROSS, WHY ARE YOU TWO COVERED IN DIRT?
YOU'LL NEVER GUESS! WE WERE DOWN IN THE--
OH, NEVER MIND! WHAT ARE YOU GOING TO WEAR? WHO ARE YOU GONNA ASK?!
I HEARD ABOUT YOU AND THAT MYSTERIOUS TRISTAN GUY...
...AND THAT IT'S SPLITS FOR YOU AND KYLE!
GEEZ, LUCY! WHO IS EVEN TELLING YOU THESE THINGS?
I SHOULD GO.
MAPS, NO, WAIT. I'M SORRY.
TOMORROW, NINETEEN

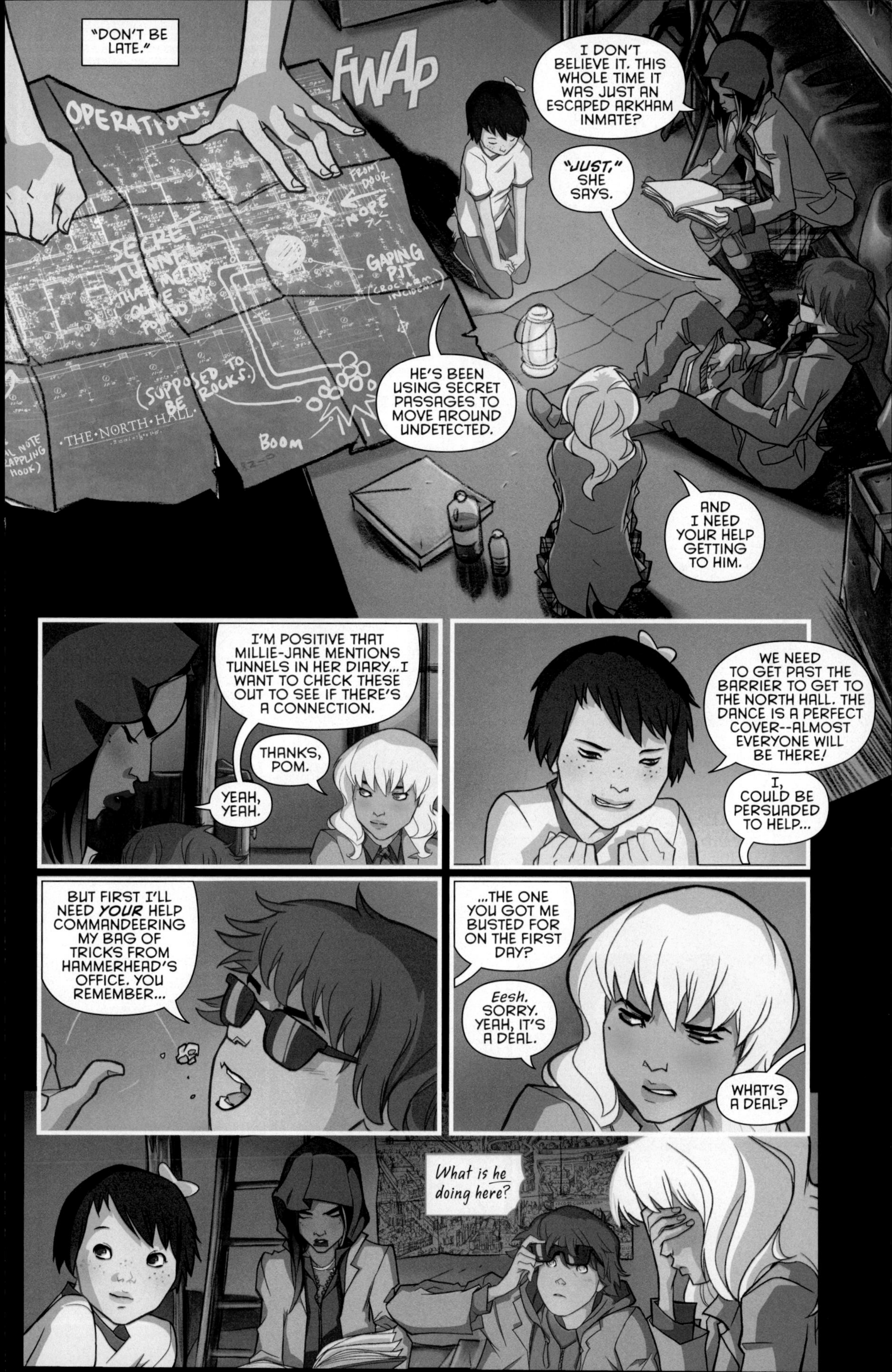
"DON'T BE LATE."
FWAP
OPERATION:
FRONT DOOR
NOPE
GAPING PIT (CROC-ARM INCIDENT)
(SUPPOSED TO BE ROCKS.)
BOOM
THE·NORTH·HALL
I DON'T BELIEVE IT. THIS WHOLE TIME IT WAS JUST AN ESCAPED ARKHAM INMATE?
"JUST," SHE SAYS.
HE'S BEEN USING SECRET PASSAGES TO MOVE AROUND UNDETECTED.
AND I NEED YOUR HELP GETTING TO HIM.
I'M POSITIVE THAT MILLIE-JANE MENTIONS TUNNELS IN HER DIARY...I WANT TO CHECK THESE OUT TO SEE IF THERE'S A CONNECTION.
THANKS, POM.
YEAH, YEAH.
WE NEED TO GET PAST THE BARRIER TO GET TO THE NORTH HALL. THE DANCE IS A PERFECT COVER--ALMOST EVERYONE WILL BE THERE!
I, COULD BE PERSUADED TO HELP...
BUT FIRST I'LL NEED *YOUR* HELP COMMANDEERING MY BAG OF TRICKS FROM HAMMERHEAD'S OFFICE. YOU REMEMBER...
...THE ONE YOU GOT ME BUSTED FOR ON THE FIRST DAY?
*Eesh.* SORRY. YEAH, IT'S A DEAL.
WHAT'S A DEAL?
*What is he doing here?*

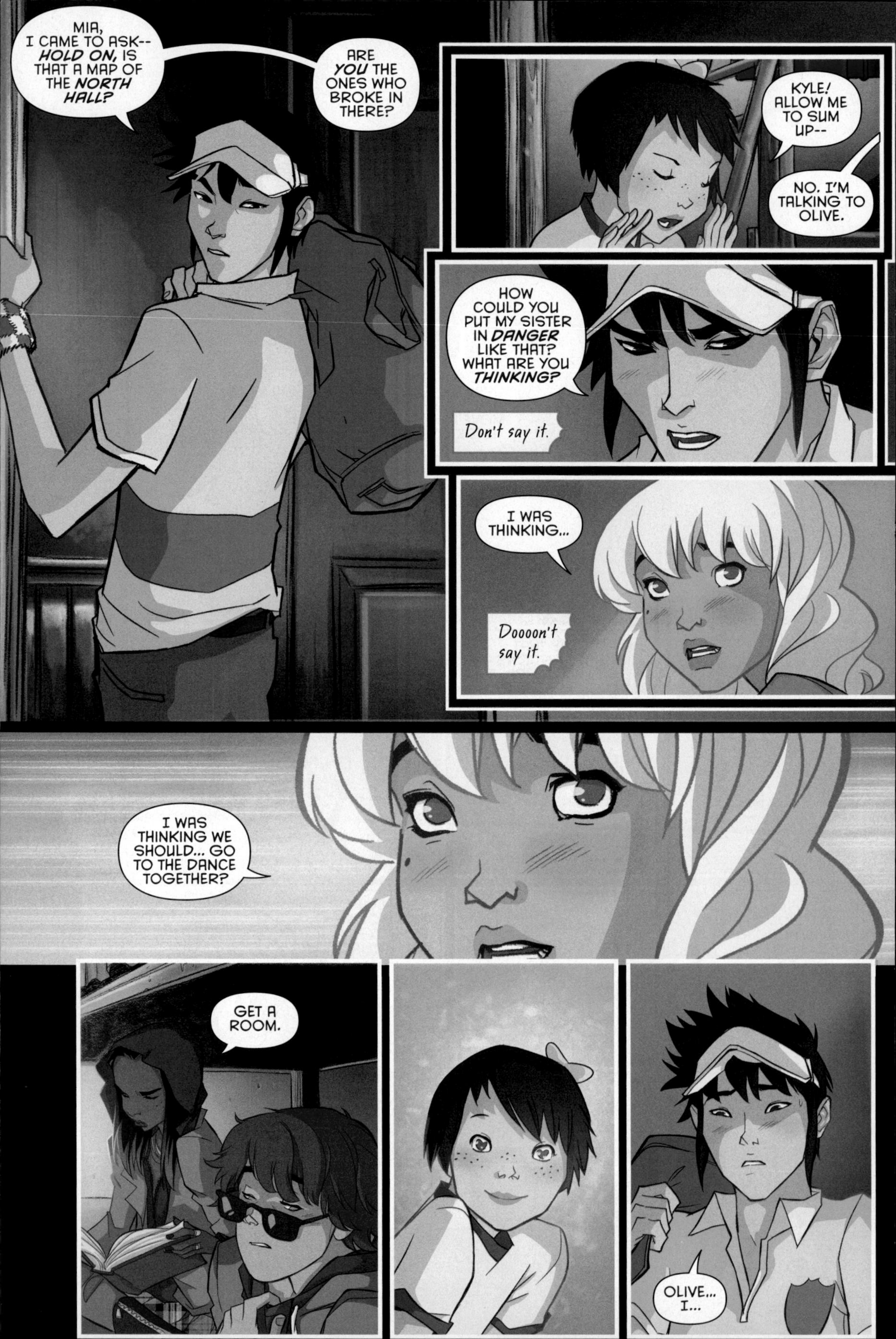
MIA, I CAME TO ASK-- HOLD ON, IS THAT A MAP OF THE NORTH HALL?
ARE YOU THE ONES WHO BROKE IN THERE?
KYLE! ALLOW ME TO SUM UP--
NO. I'M TALKING TO OLIVE.
HOW COULD YOU PUT MY SISTER IN DANGER LIKE THAT? WHAT ARE YOU THINKING?
Don't say it.
I WAS THINKING...
Doooon't say it.
I WAS THINKING WE SHOULD... GO TO THE DANCE TOGETHER?
GET A ROOM.
OLIVE... I...

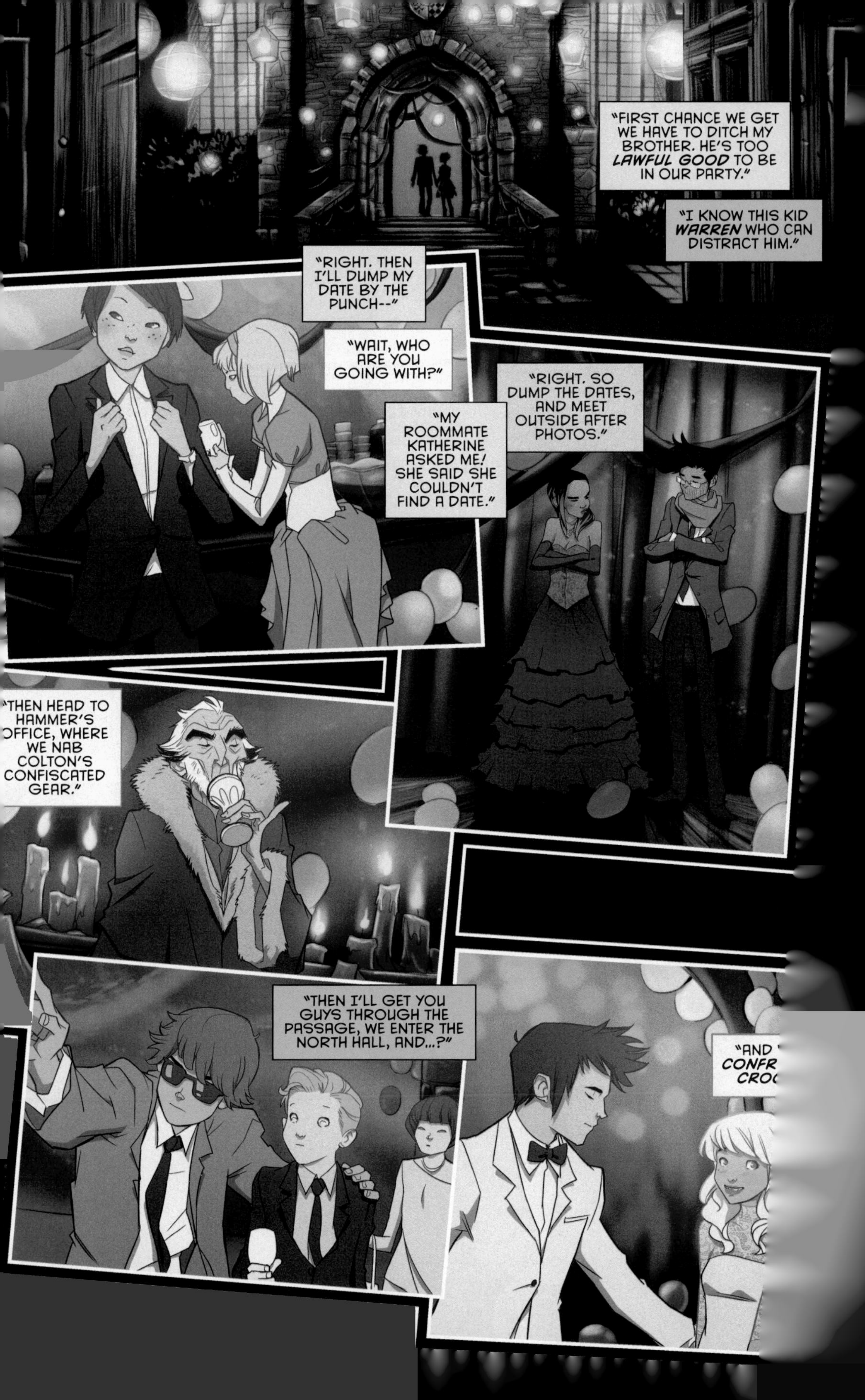

"FIRST CHANCE WE GET WE HAVE TO DITCH MY BROTHER. HE'S TOO *LAWFUL GOOD* TO BE IN OUR PARTY."
"I KNOW THIS KID *WARREN* WHO CAN DISTRACT HIM."
"RIGHT. THEN I'LL DUMP MY DATE BY THE PUNCH--"
"WAIT, WHO ARE YOU GOING WITH?"
"MY ROOMMATE KATHERINE ASKED ME! SHE SAID SHE COULDN'T FIND A DATE."
"RIGHT. SO DUMP THE DATES, AND MEET OUTSIDE AFTER PHOTOS."
"THEN HEAD TO HAMMER'S OFFICE, WHERE WE NAB COLTON'S CONFISCATED GEAR."
"THEN I'LL GET YOU GUYS THROUGH THE PASSAGE, WE ENTER THE NORTH HALL, AND...?"

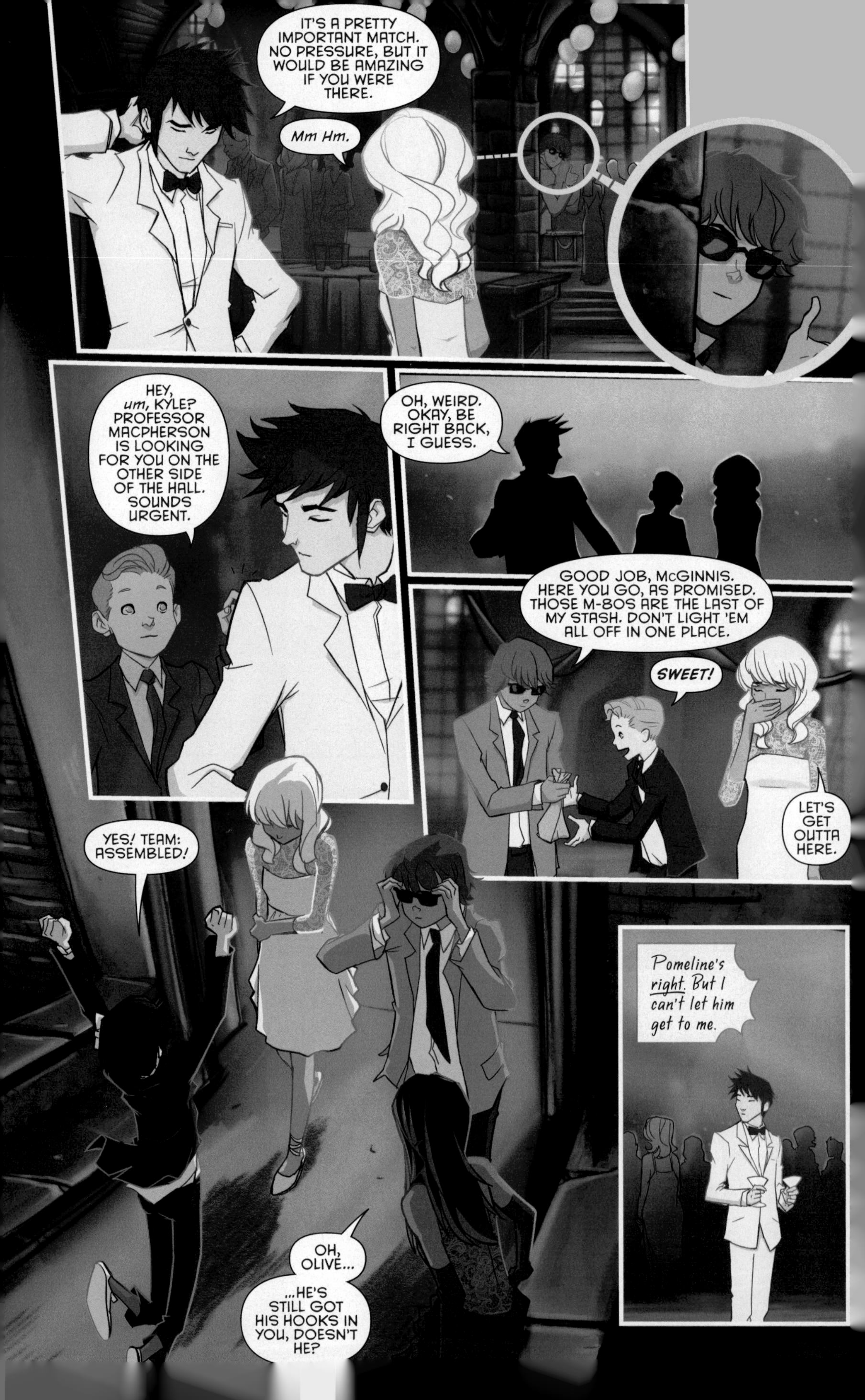
IT'S A PRETTY IMPORTANT MATCH. NO PRESSURE, BUT IT WOULD BE AMAZING IF YOU WERE THERE.
Mm Hm.
HEY, um, KYLE? PROFESSOR MACPHERSON IS LOOKING FOR YOU ON THE OTHER SIDE OF THE HALL. SOUNDS URGENT.
OH, WEIRD. OKAY, BE RIGHT BACK, I GUESS.
GOOD JOB, McGINNIS. HERE YOU GO, AS PROMISED. THOSE M-80S ARE THE LAST OF MY STASH. DON'T LIGHT 'EM ALL OFF IN ONE PLACE.
SWEET!
LET'S GET OUTTA HERE.
YES! TEAM: ASSEMBLED!
OH, OLIVE...
...HE'S STILL GOT HIS HOOKS IN YOU, DOESN'T HE?
Pomeline's right. But I can't let him get to me.

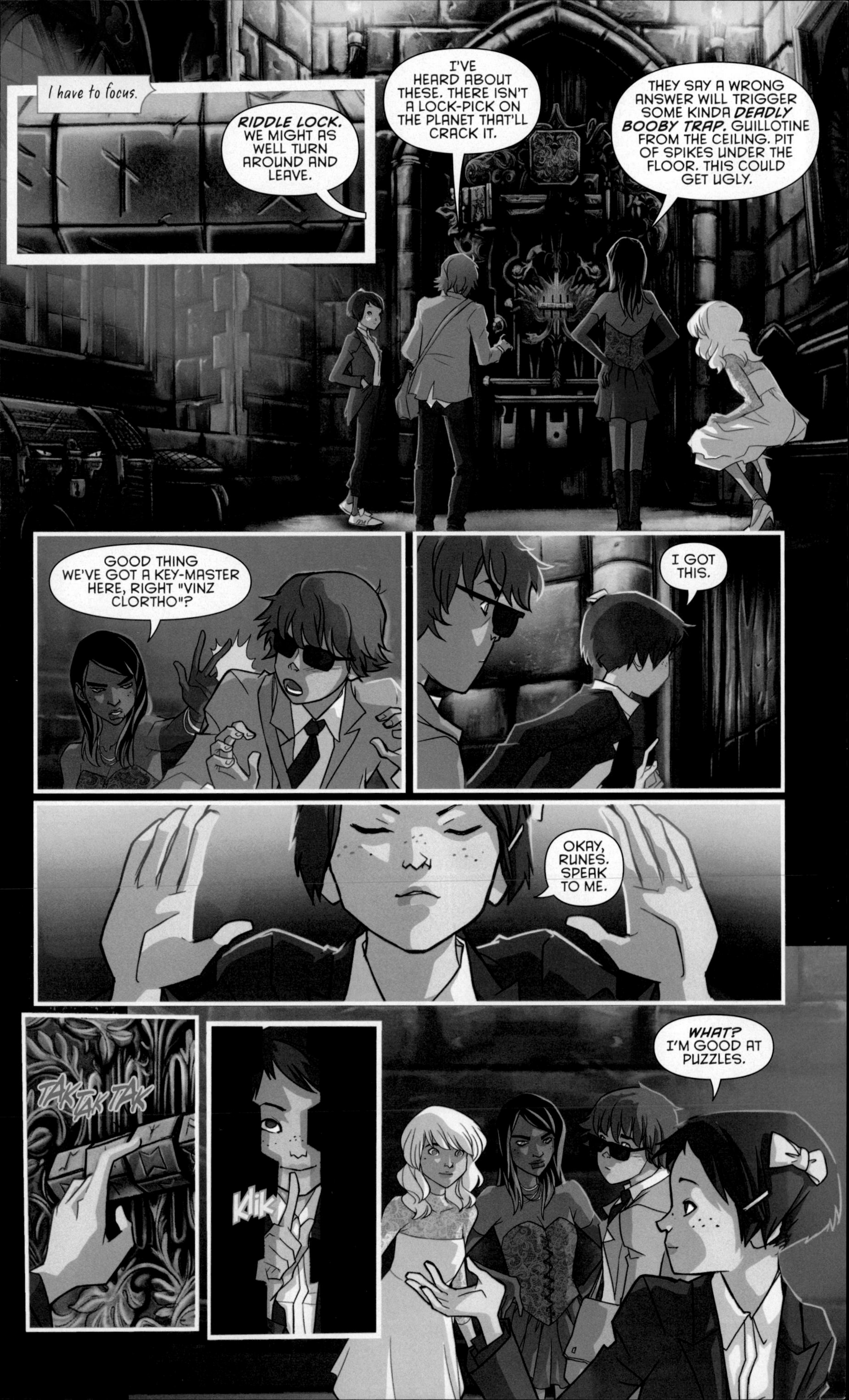
I have to focus.
RIDDLE LOCK. WE MIGHT AS WELL TURN AROUND AND LEAVE.
I'VE HEARD ABOUT THESE. THERE ISN'T A LOCK-PICK ON THE PLANET THAT'LL CRACK IT.
THEY SAY A WRONG ANSWER WILL TRIGGER SOME KINDA DEADLY BOOBY TRAP. GUILLOTINE FROM THE CEILING. PIT OF SPIKES UNDER THE FLOOR. THIS COULD GET UGLY.
GOOD THING WE'VE GOT A KEY-MASTER HERE, RIGHT "VINZ CLORTHO"?
I GOT THIS.
OKAY, RUNES. SPEAK TO ME.
TAK TAK TAK
KLIK
WHAT? I'M GOOD AT PUZZLES.

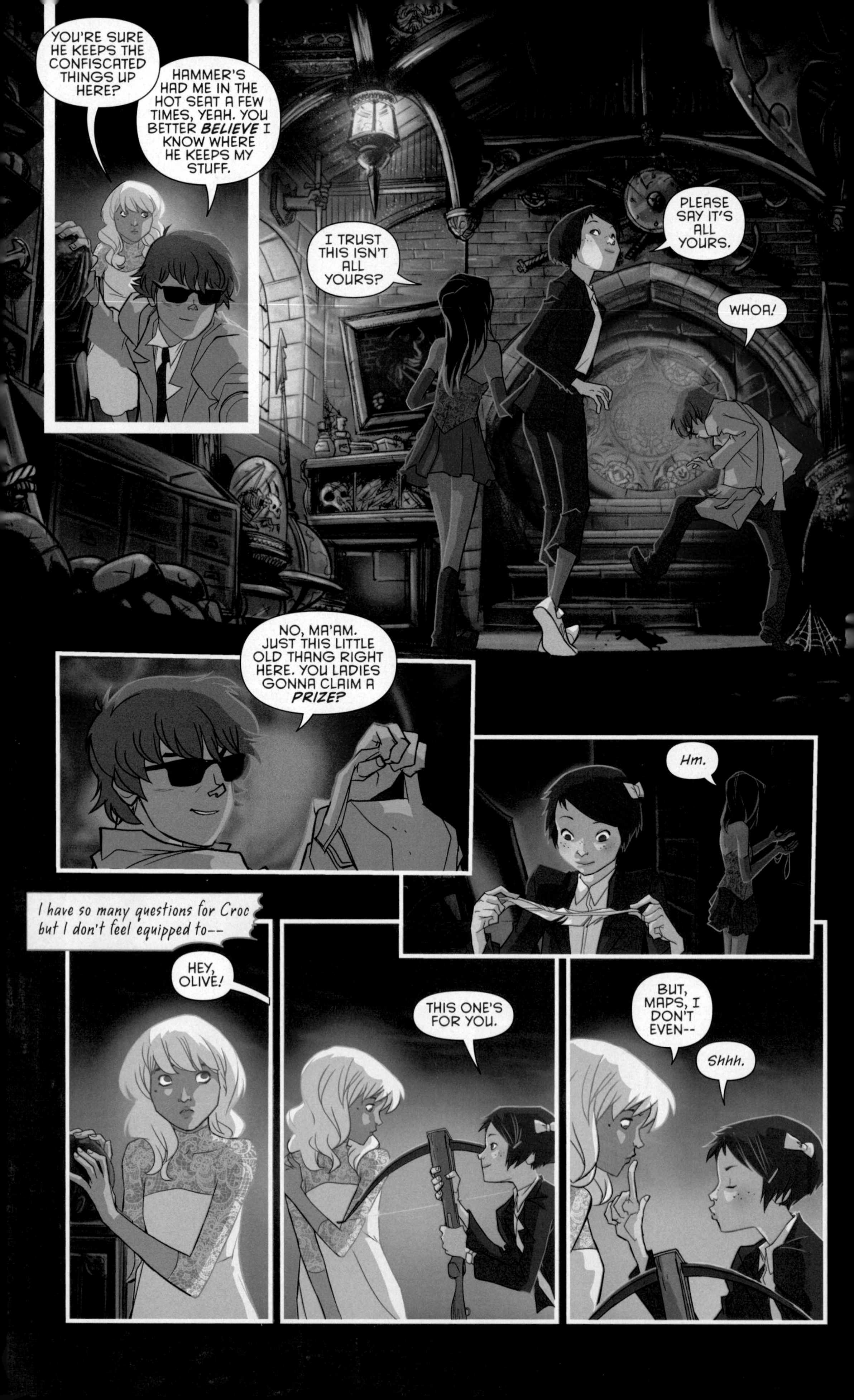
YOU'RE SURE HE KEEPS THE CONFISCATED THINGS UP HERE?
HAMMER'S HAD ME IN THE HOT SEAT A FEW TIMES, YEAH. YOU BETTER BELIEVE I KNOW WHERE HE KEEPS MY STUFF.
I TRUST THIS ISN'T ALL YOURS?
PLEASE SAY IT'S ALL YOURS.
WHOA!
NO, MA'AM. JUST THIS LITTLE OLD THANG RIGHT HERE. YOU LADIES GONNA CLAIM A PRIZE?
Hm.
I have so many questions for Croc but I don't feel equipped to--
HEY, OLIVE!
THIS ONE'S FOR YOU.
BUT, MAPS, I DON'T EVEN--
Shhh.

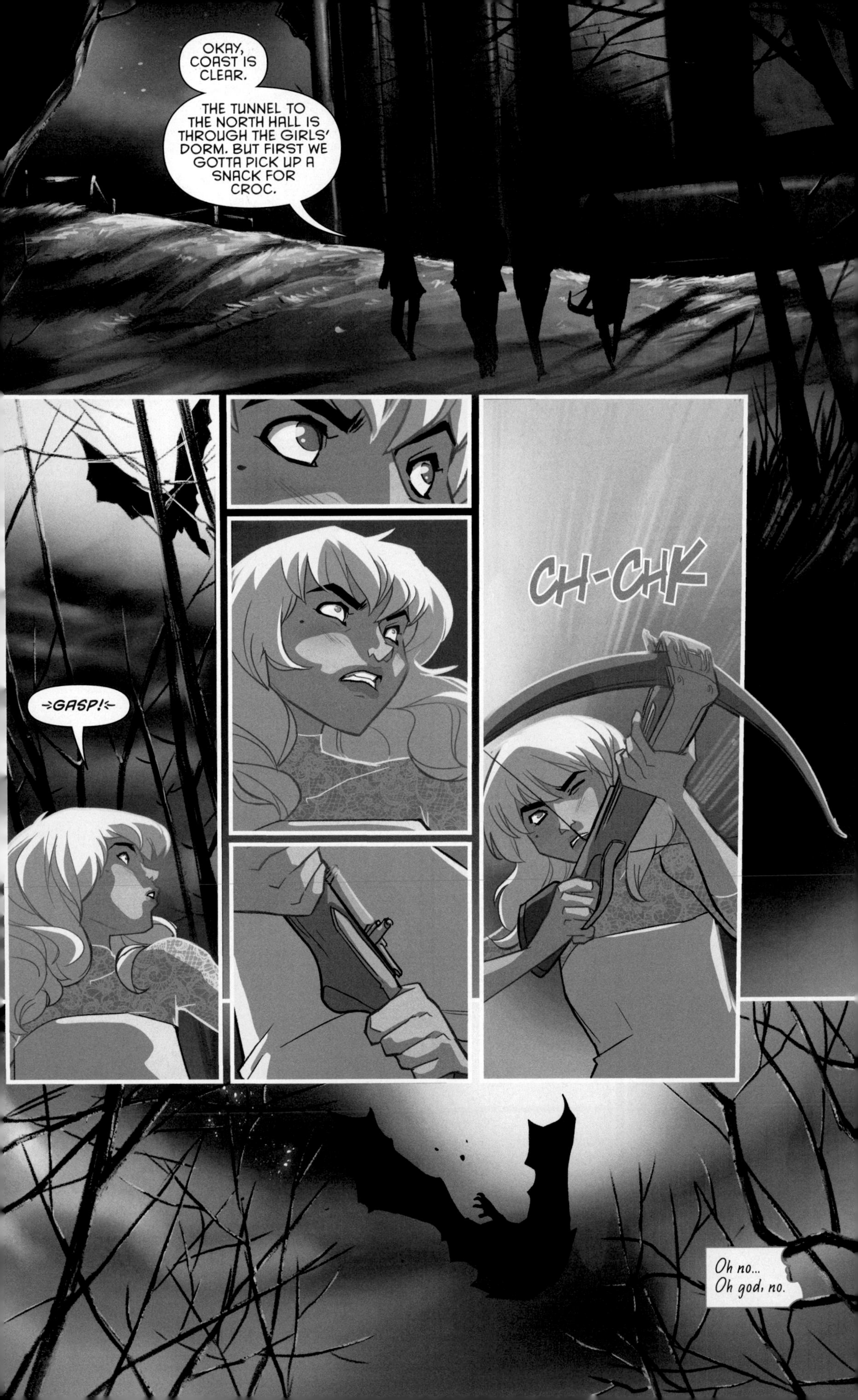
OKAY, COAST IS CLEAR.
THE TUNNEL TO THE NORTH HALL IS THROUGH THE GIRLS' DORM. BUT FIRST WE GOTTA PICK UP A SNACK FOR CROC.
-GASP!-
CH-CHK
Oh no... Oh god, no.

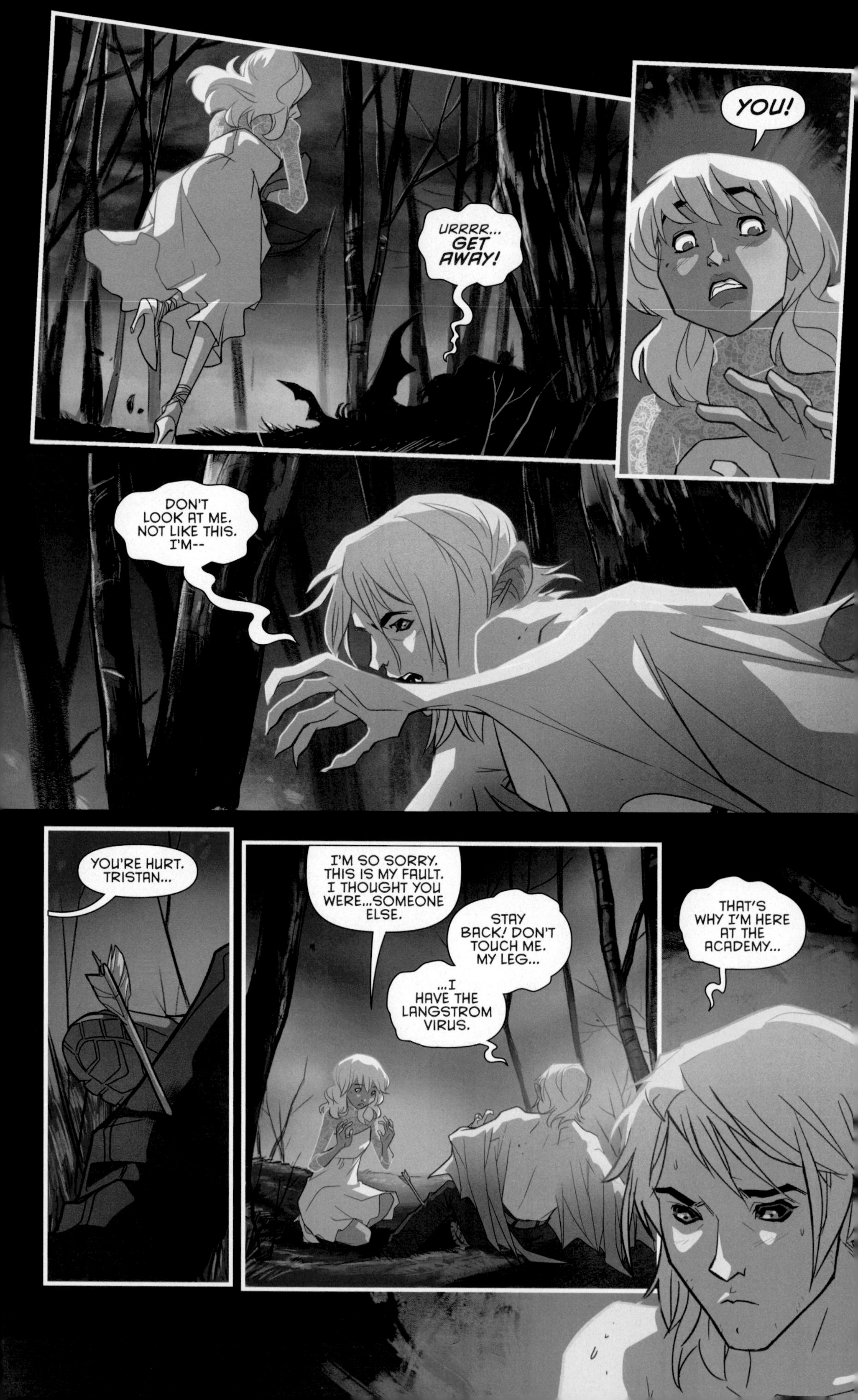
URRRR... GET AWAY!
YOU!
DON'T LOOK AT ME. NOT LIKE THIS. I'M--
YOU'RE HURT. TRISTAN...
I'M SO SORRY. THIS IS MY FAULT. I THOUGHT YOU WERE...SOMEONE ELSE.
STAY BACK! DON'T TOUCH ME. MY LEG...
...I HAVE THE LANGSTROM VIRUS.
THAT'S WHY I'M HERE AT THE ACADEMY...

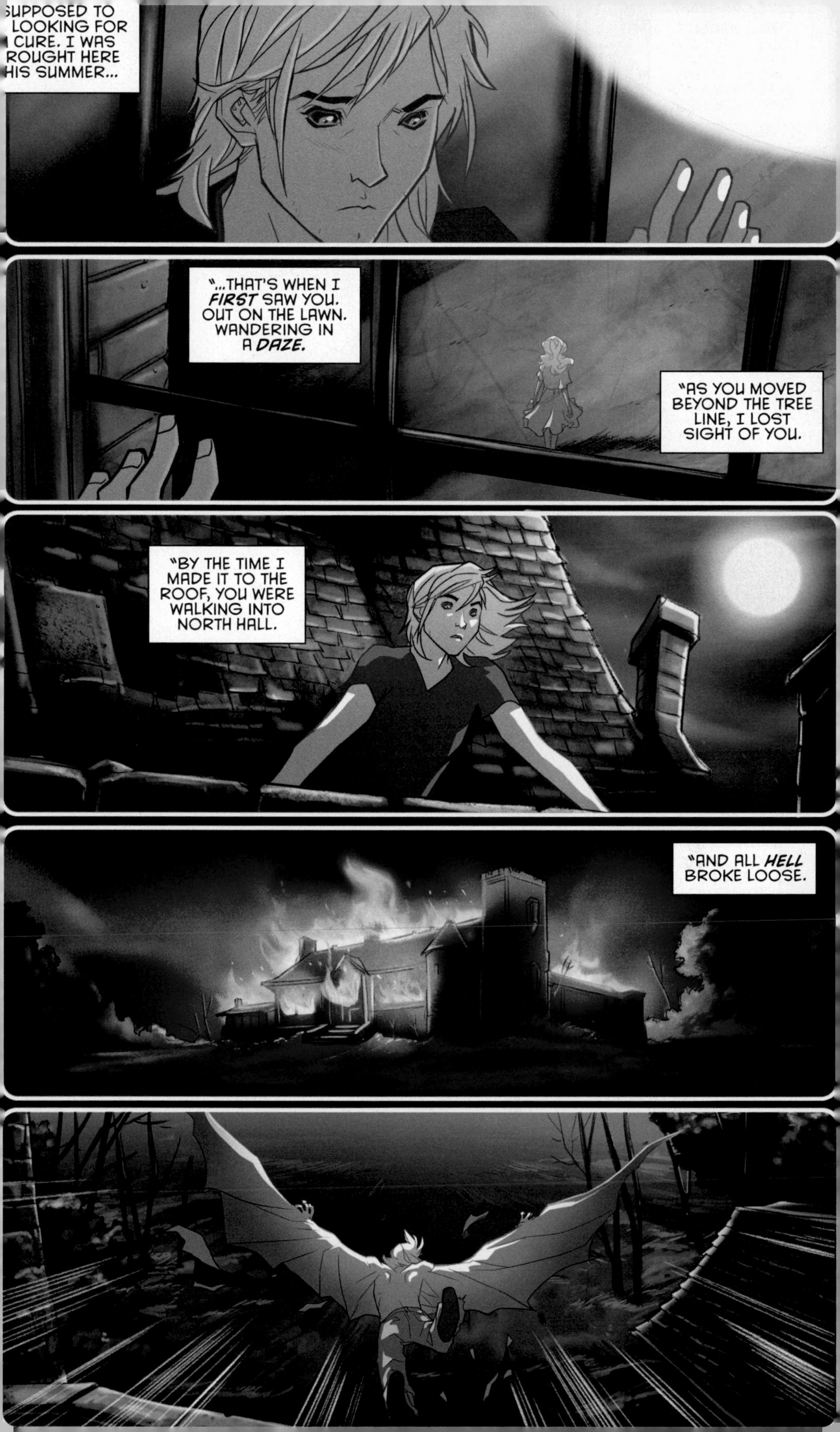
SUPPOSED TO LOOKING FOR CURE. I WAS ROUGHT HERE HIS SUMMER...
"...THAT'S WHEN I FIRST SAW YOU. OUT ON THE LAWN. WANDERING IN A DAZE.
"AS YOU MOVED BEYOND THE TREE LINE, I LOST SIGHT OF YOU.
"BY THE TIME I MADE IT TO THE ROOF, YOU WERE WALKING INTO NORTH HALL.
"AND ALL HELL BROKE LOOSE.

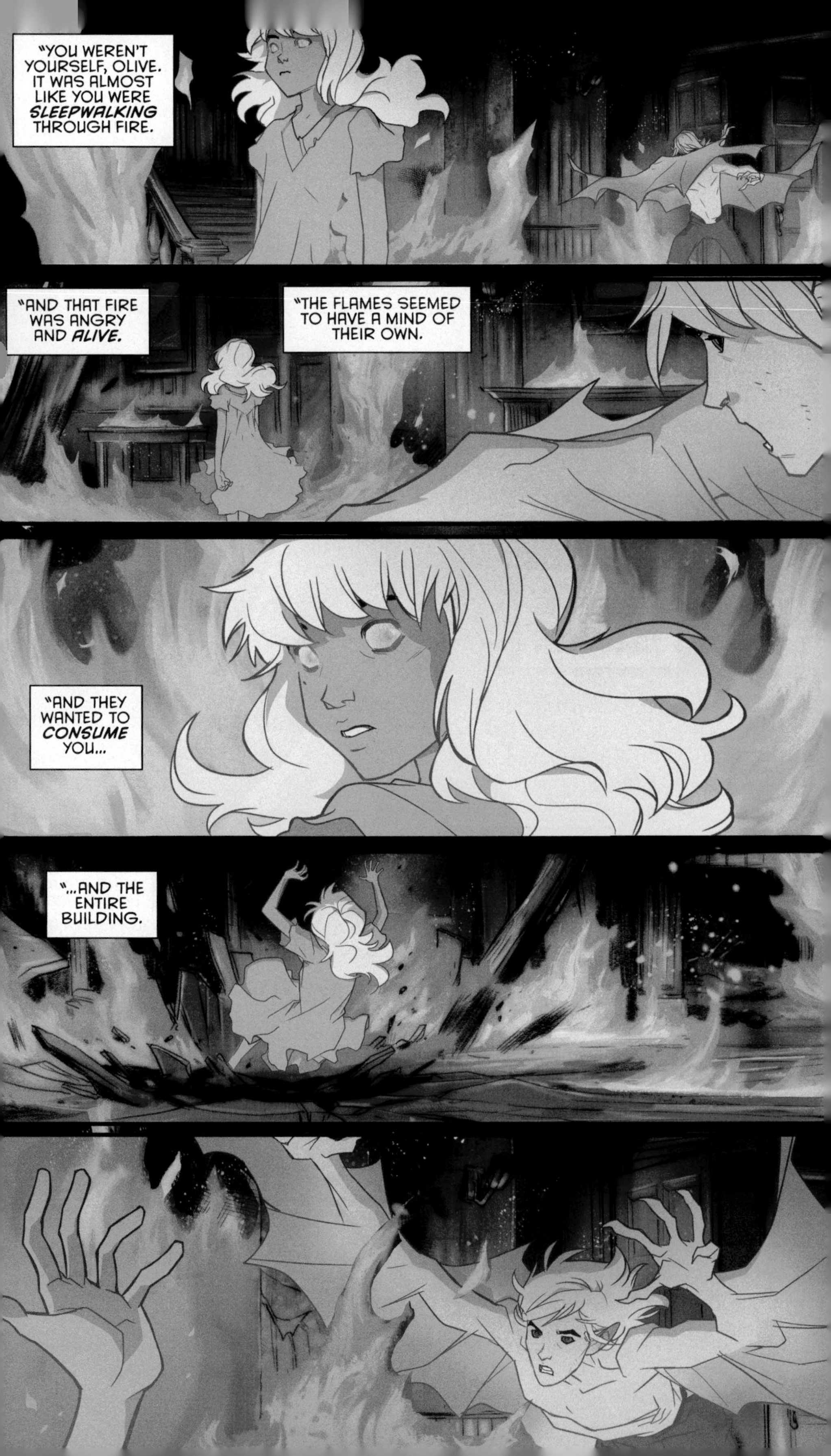
"YOU WEREN'T YOURSELF, OLIVE. IT WAS ALMOST LIKE YOU WERE *SLEEPWALKING* THROUGH FIRE.
"AND THAT FIRE WAS ANGRY AND *ALIVE.*
"THE FLAMES SEEMED TO HAVE A MIND OF THEIR OWN.
"AND THEY WANTED TO *CONSUME* YOU...
"...AND THE ENTIRE BUILDING.

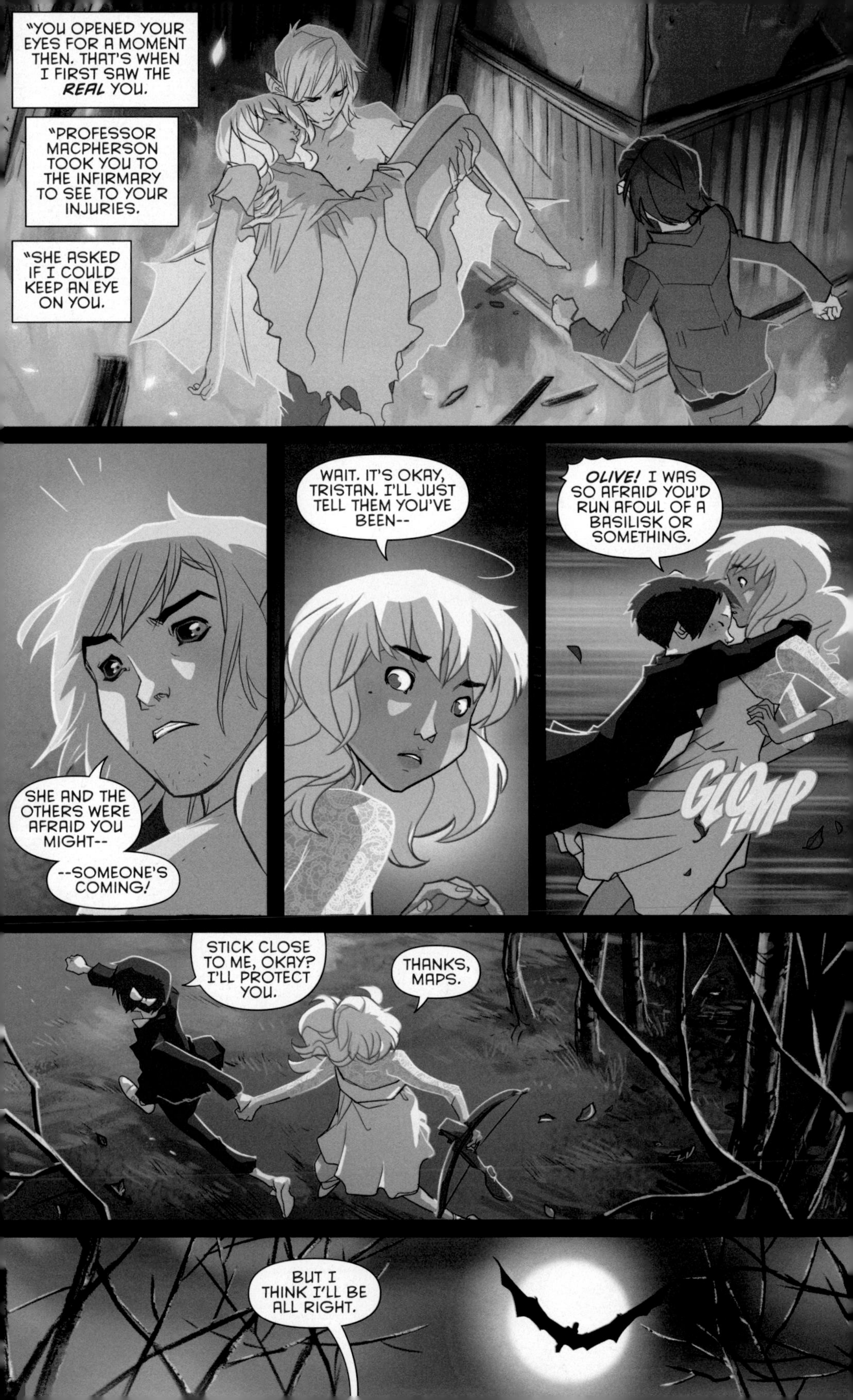
"YOU OPENED YOUR EYES FOR A MOMENT THEN. THAT'S WHEN I FIRST SAW THE *REAL* YOU.
"PROFESSOR MACPHERSON TOOK YOU TO THE INFIRMARY TO SEE TO YOUR INJURIES.
"SHE ASKED IF I COULD KEEP AN EYE ON YOU.
SHE AND THE OTHERS WERE AFRAID YOU MIGHT--
--SOMEONE'S COMING!
WAIT. IT'S OKAY, TRISTAN. I'LL JUST TELL THEM YOU'VE BEEN--
*OLIVE!* I WAS SO AFRAID YOU'D RUN AFOUL OF A BASILISK OR SOMETHING.
GLOMP
STICK CLOSE TO ME, OKAY? I'LL PROTECT YOU.
THANKS, MAPS.
BUT I THINK I'LL BE ALL RIGHT.

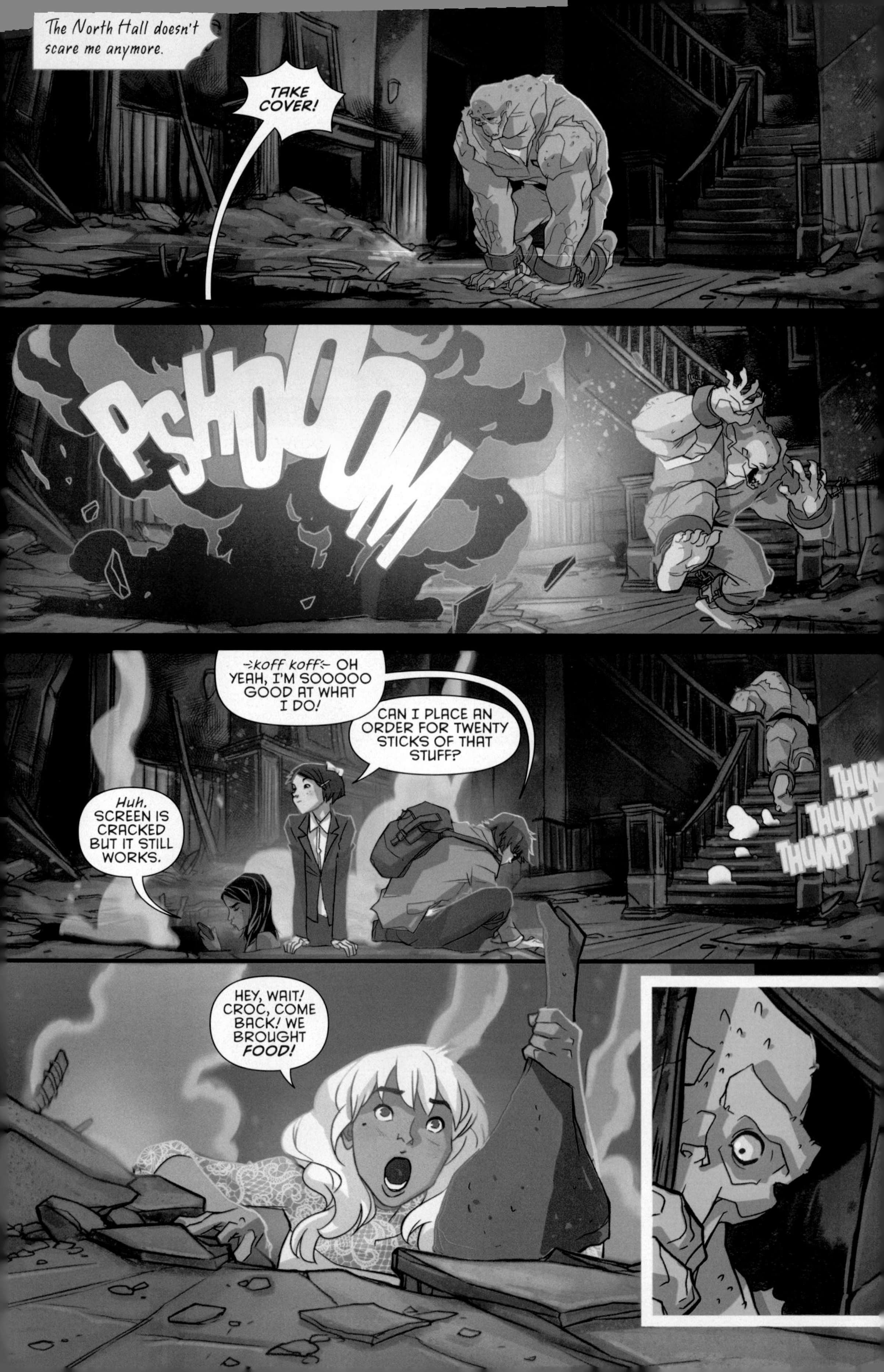
The North Hall doesn't scare me anymore.
TAKE COVER!
PSHOOOM
-koff koff- OH YEAH, I'M SOOOOO GOOD AT WHAT I DO!
CAN I PLACE AN ORDER FOR TWENTY STICKS OF THAT STUFF?
Huh. SCREEN IS CRACKED BUT IT STILL WORKS.
THUMP THUMP
HEY, WAIT! CROC, COME BACK! WE BROUGHT FOOD!

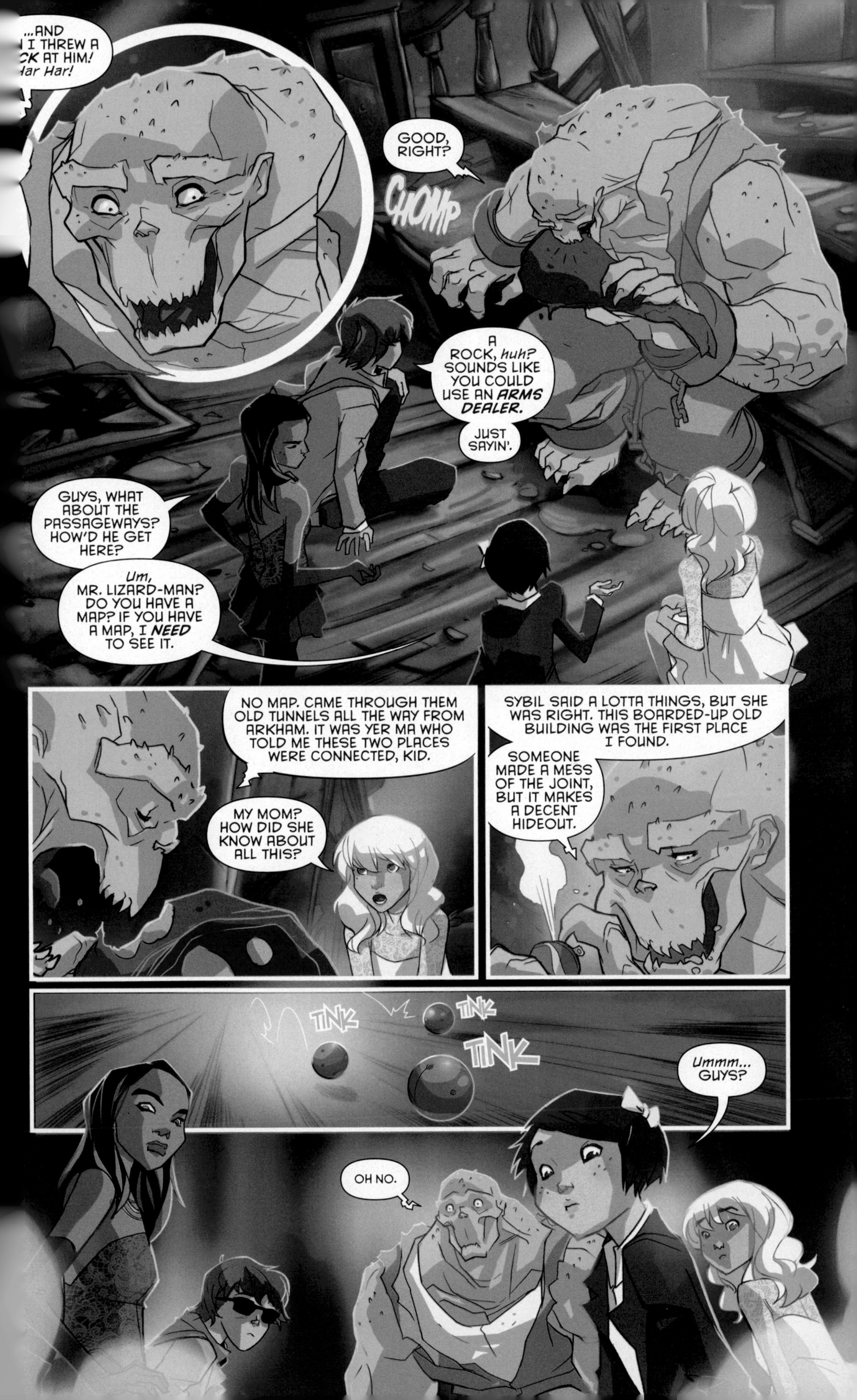
...AND
I THREW A
CK AT HIM!
Har Har!
GOOD, RIGHT?
CHOMP
A ROCK, huh? SOUNDS LIKE YOU COULD USE AN ARMS DEALER.
JUST SAYIN'.
GUYS, WHAT ABOUT THE PASSAGEWAYS? HOW'D HE GET HERE?
Um, MR. LIZARD-MAN? DO YOU HAVE A MAP? IF YOU HAVE A MAP, I NEED TO SEE IT.
NO MAP. CAME THROUGH THEM OLD TUNNELS ALL THE WAY FROM ARKHAM. IT WAS YER MA WHO TOLD ME THESE TWO PLACES WERE CONNECTED, KID.
MY MOM? HOW DID SHE KNOW ABOUT ALL THIS?
SYBIL SAID A LOTTA THINGS, BUT SHE WAS RIGHT. THIS BOARDED-UP OLD BUILDING WAS THE FIRST PLACE I FOUND.
SOMEONE MADE A MESS OF THE JOINT, BUT IT MAKES A DECENT HIDEOUT.
TINK
TINK
TINK
Ummm... GUYS?
OH NO.

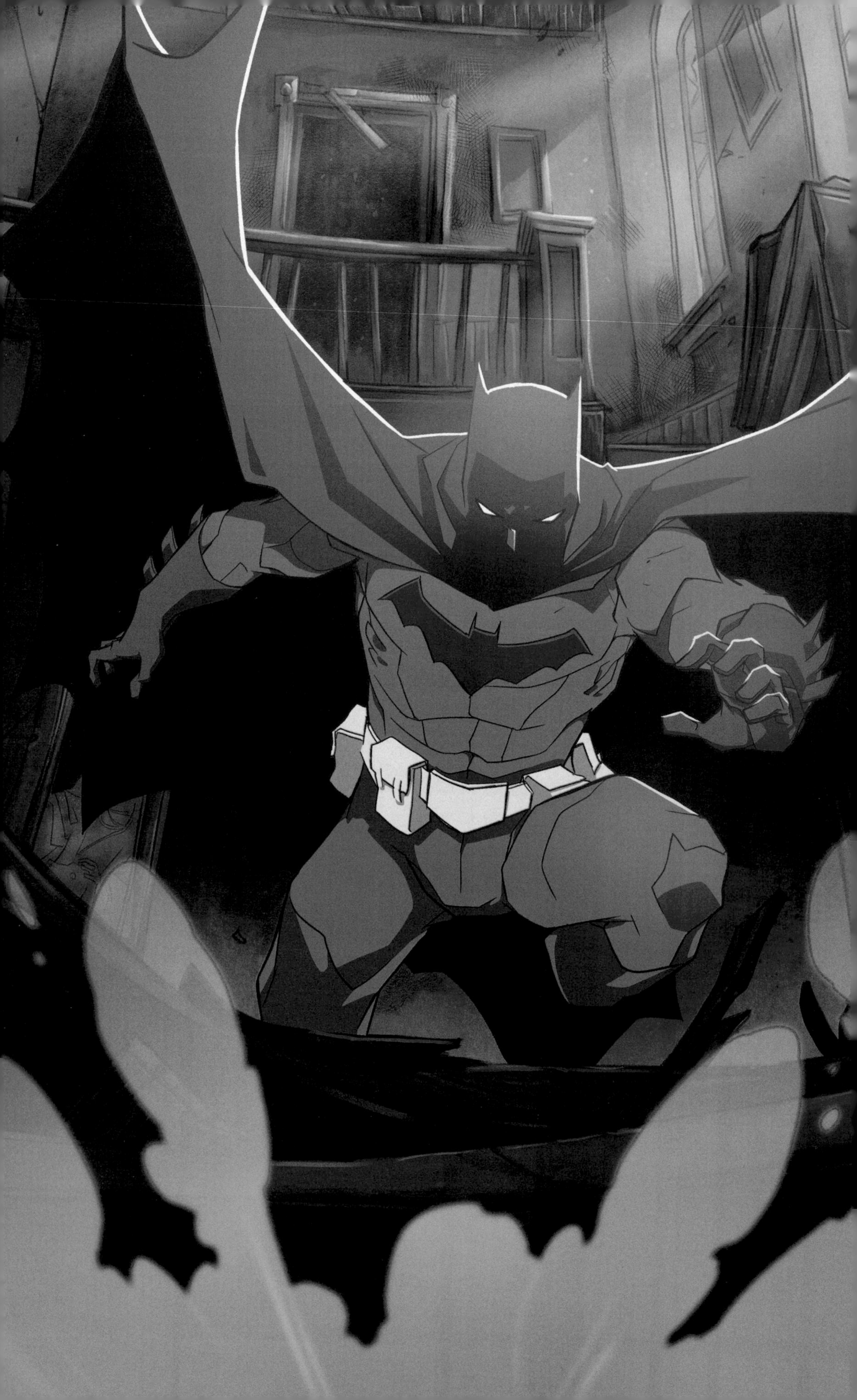

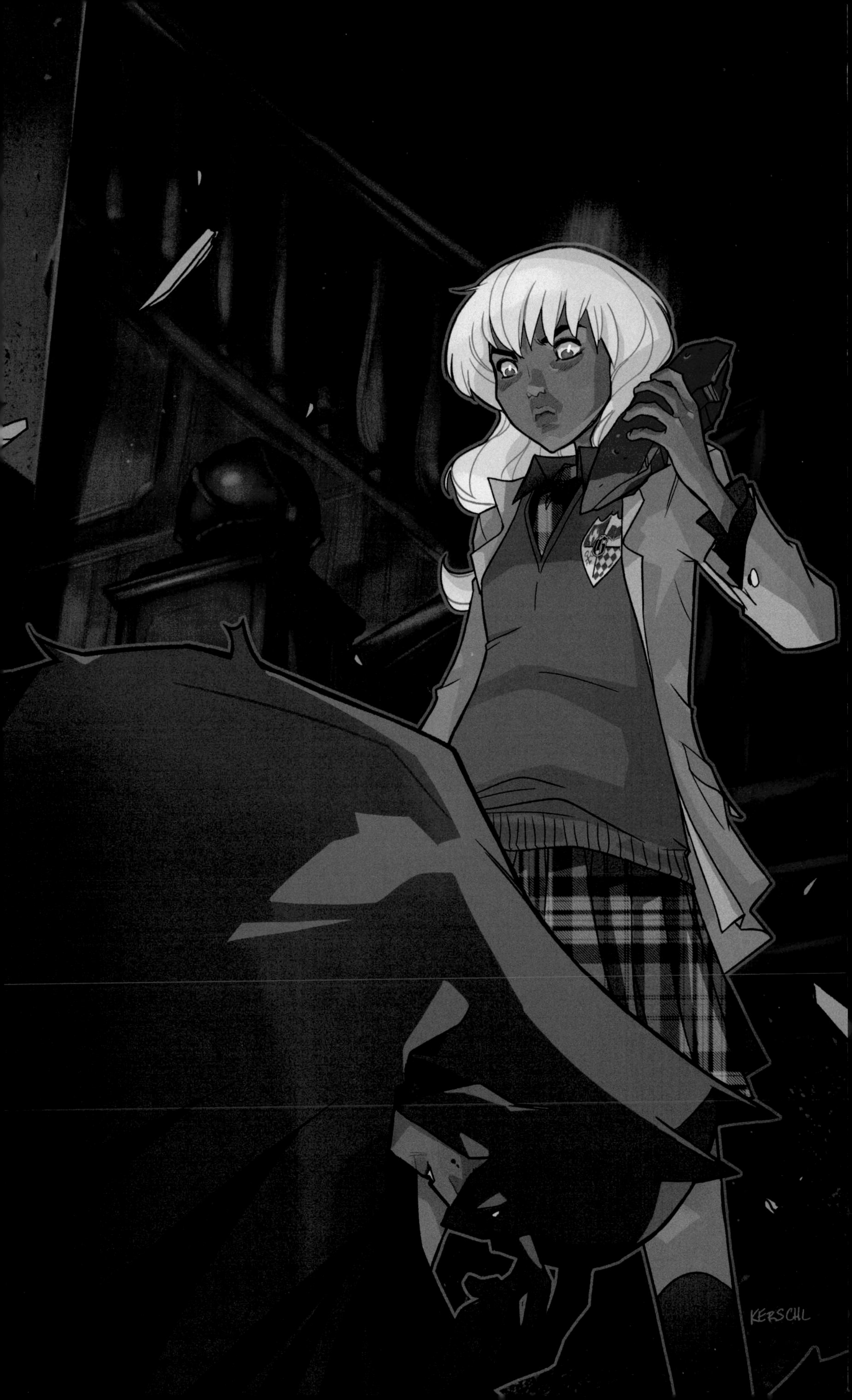
KERSCHL

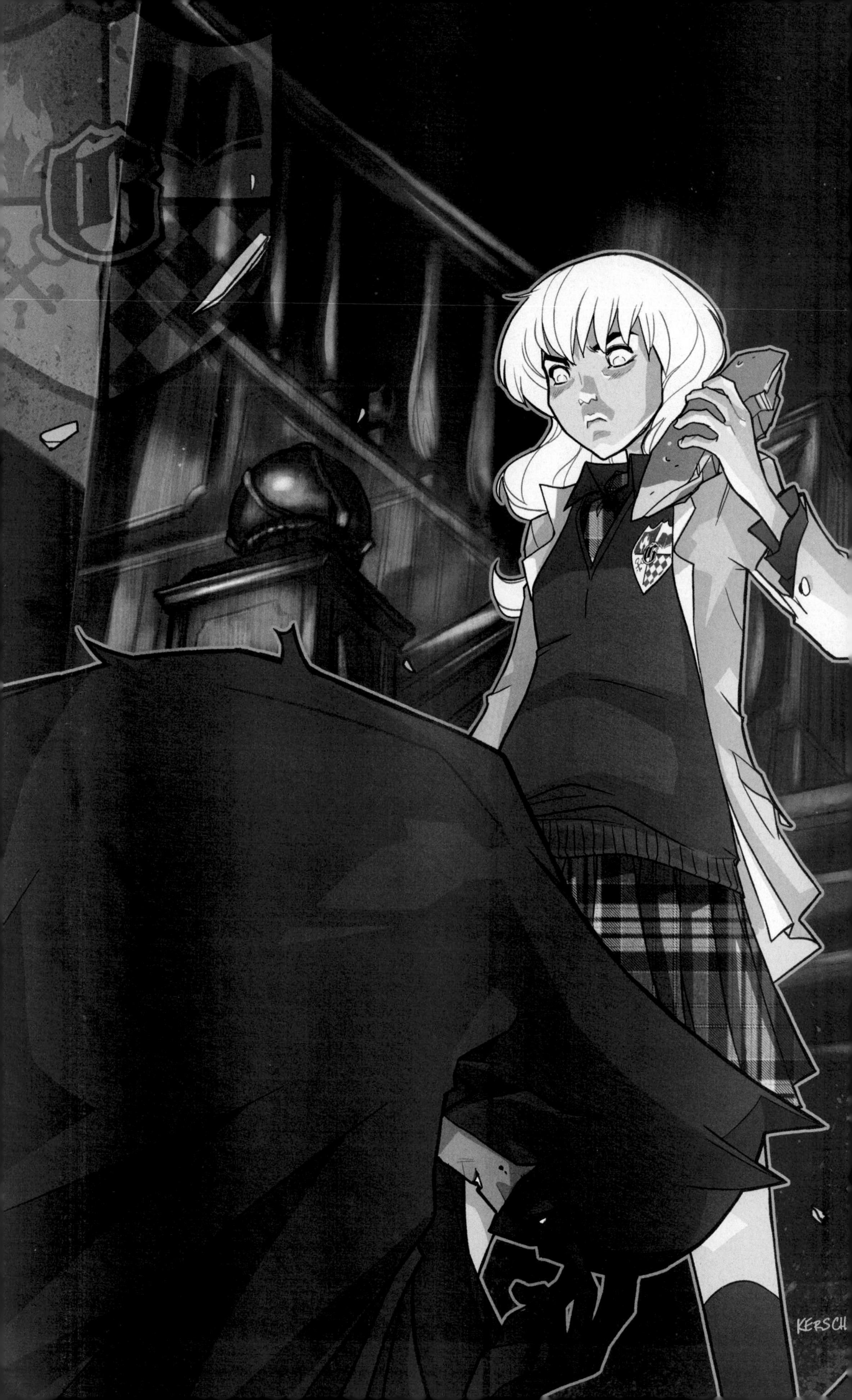
KERSCH

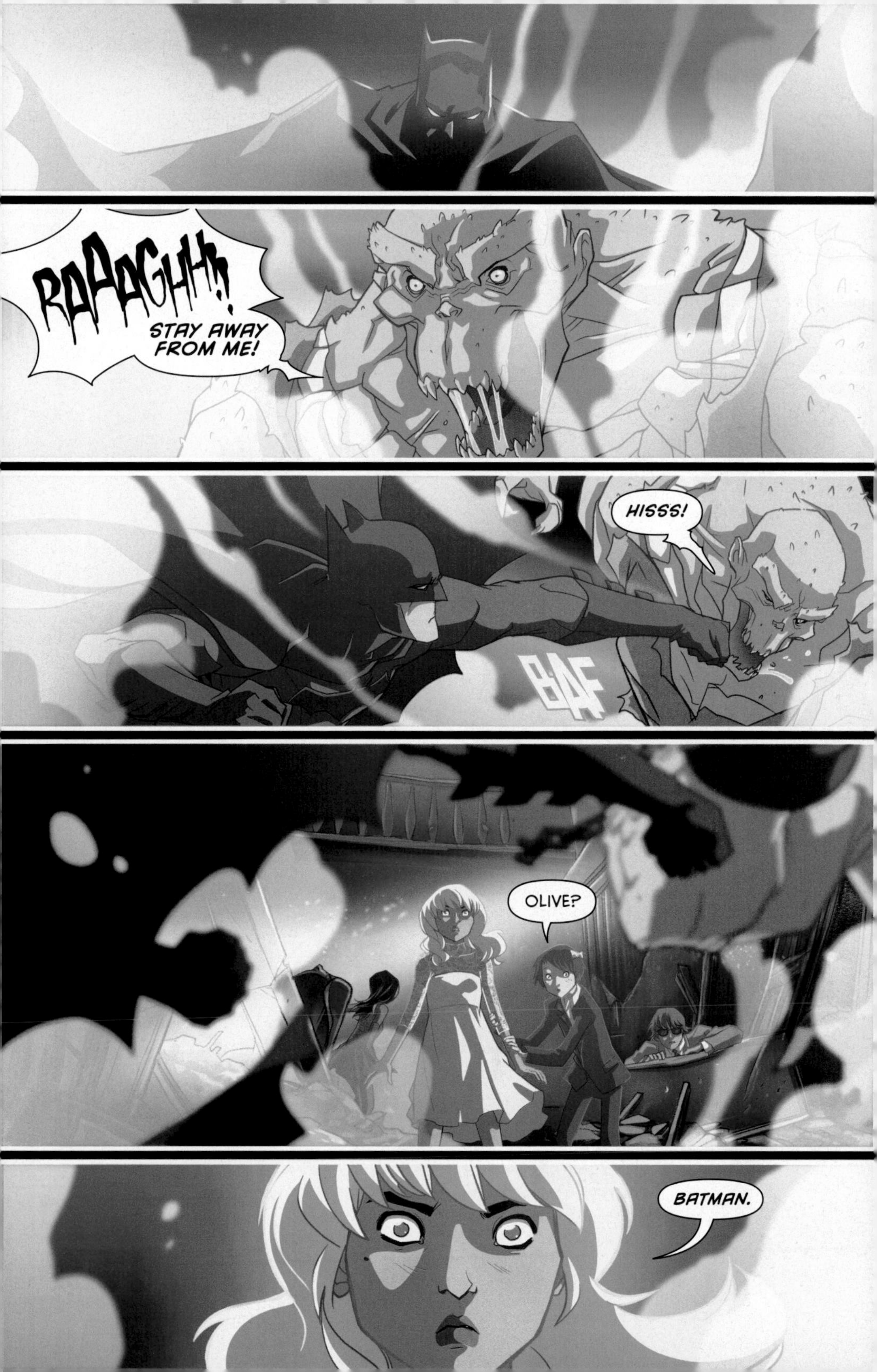
RAAAGHHH!
STAY AWAY FROM ME!
HISSS!
BAF
OLIVE?
BATMAN.

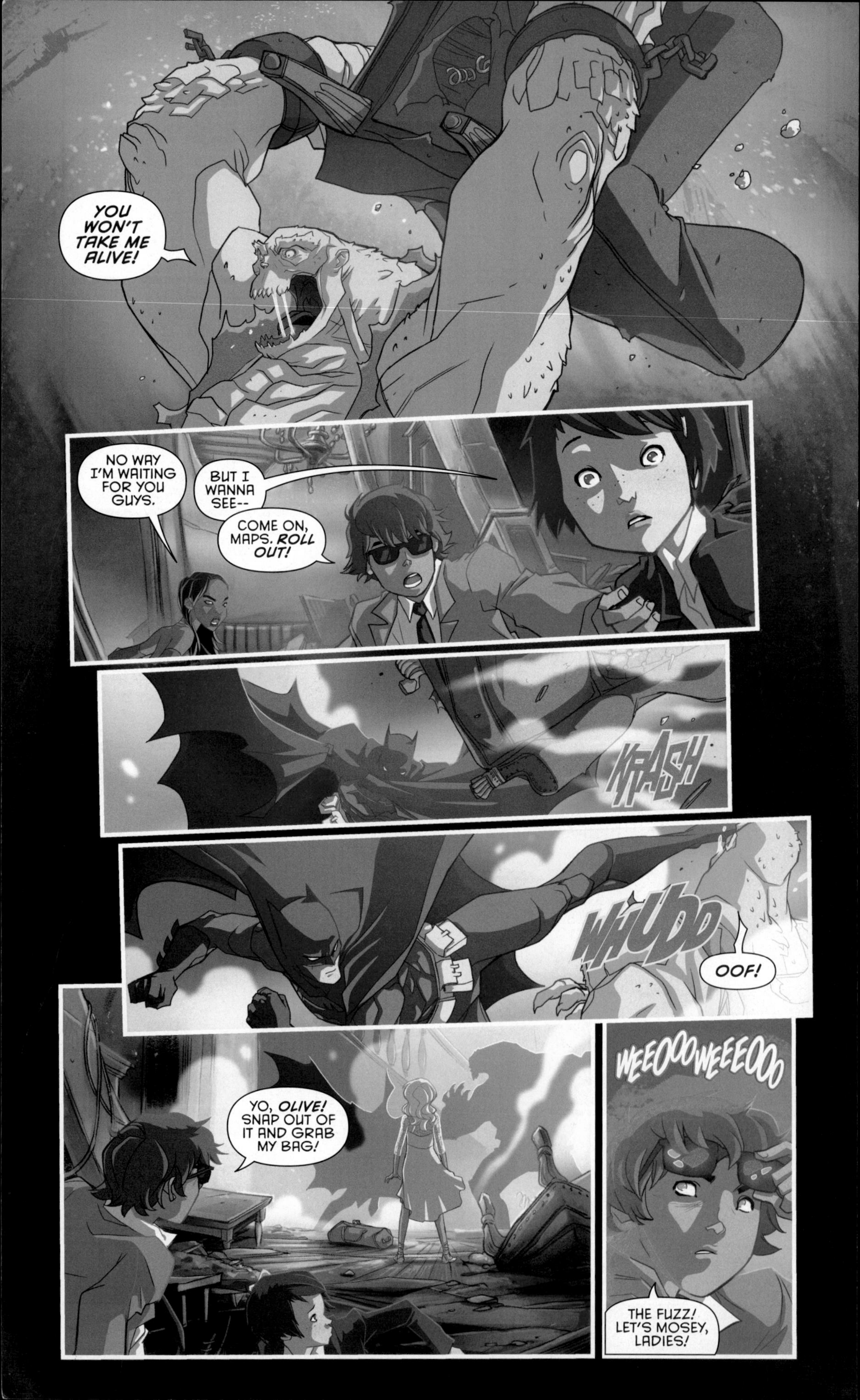
YOU WON'T TAKE ME ALIVE!
NO WAY I'M WAITING FOR YOU GUYS.
BUT I WANNA SEE--
COME ON, MAPS. ROLL OUT!
KRASH
WHUDD
OOF!
YO, OLIVE! SNAP OUT OF IT AND GRAB MY BAG!
WEEOOOWEEEOOO
THE FUZZ! LET'S MOSEY, LADIES!

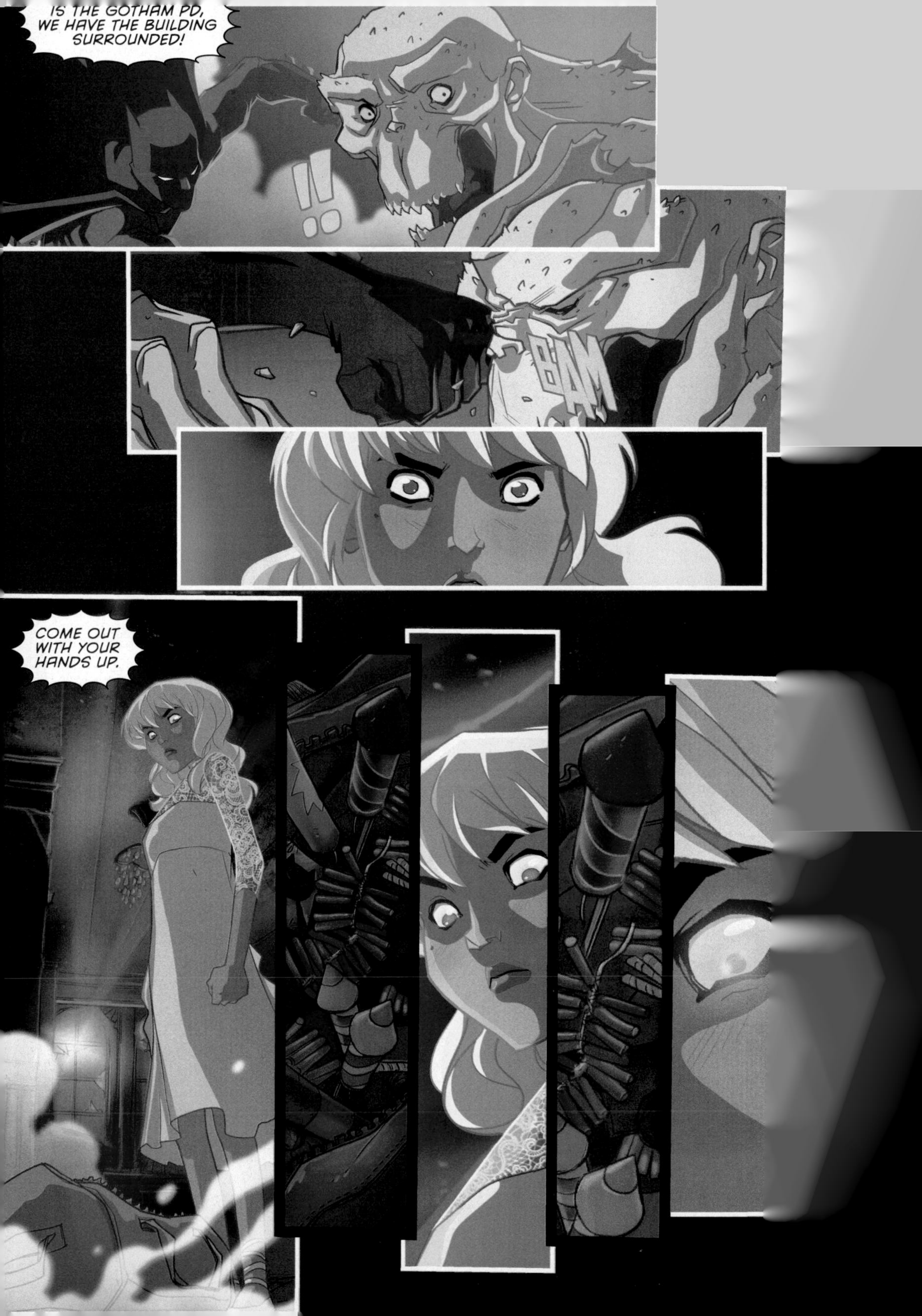
IS THE GOTHAM PD, WE HAVE THE BUILDING SURROUNDED!
!!
BAM
COME OUT WITH YOUR HANDS UP.

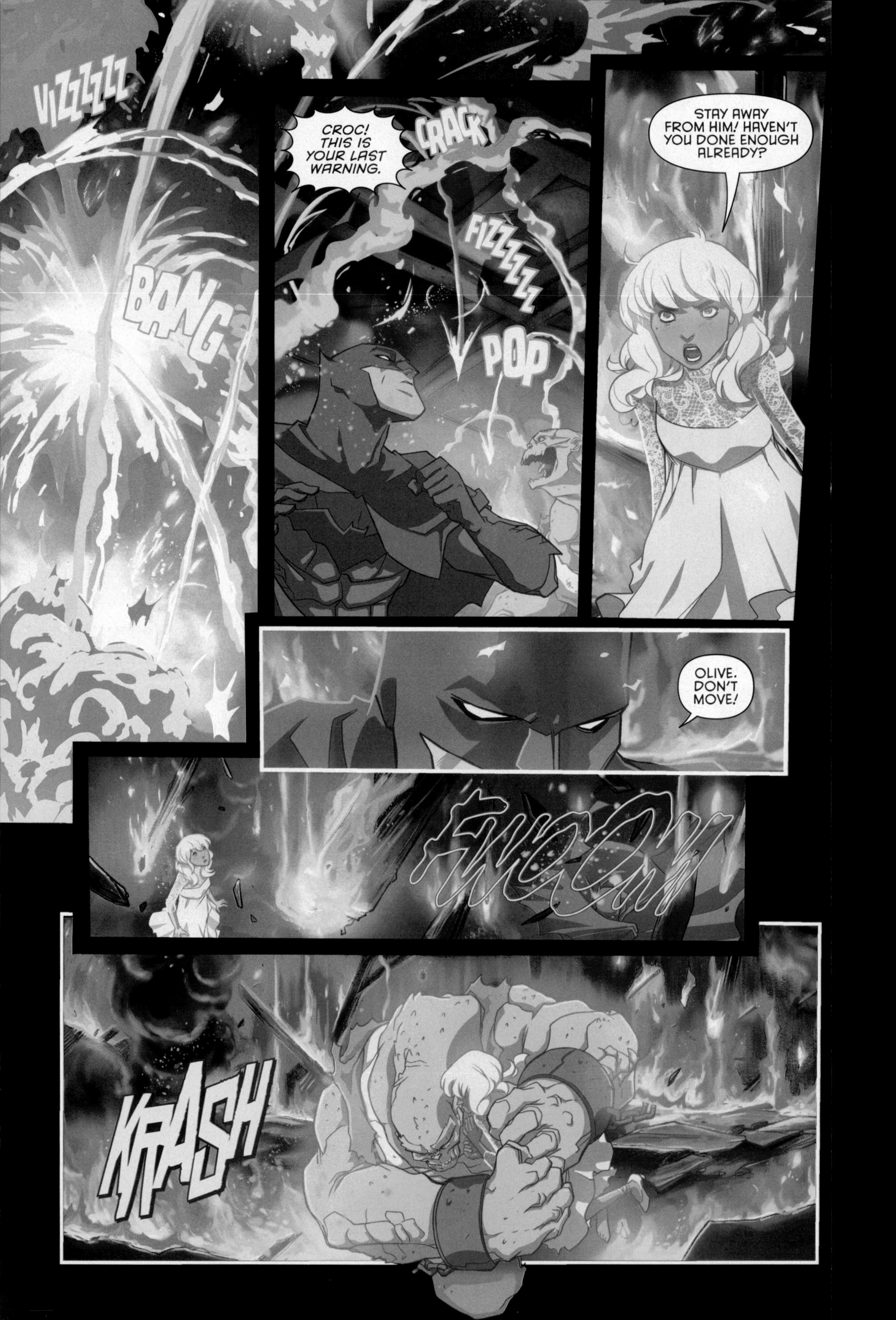
VIZZZZZZ
BANG
CROC! THIS IS YOUR LAST WARNING.
CRACK
FIZZZZZZ
POP
STAY AWAY FROM HIM! HAVEN'T YOU DONE ENOUGH ALREADY?
OLIVE. DON'T MOVE!
KRASH

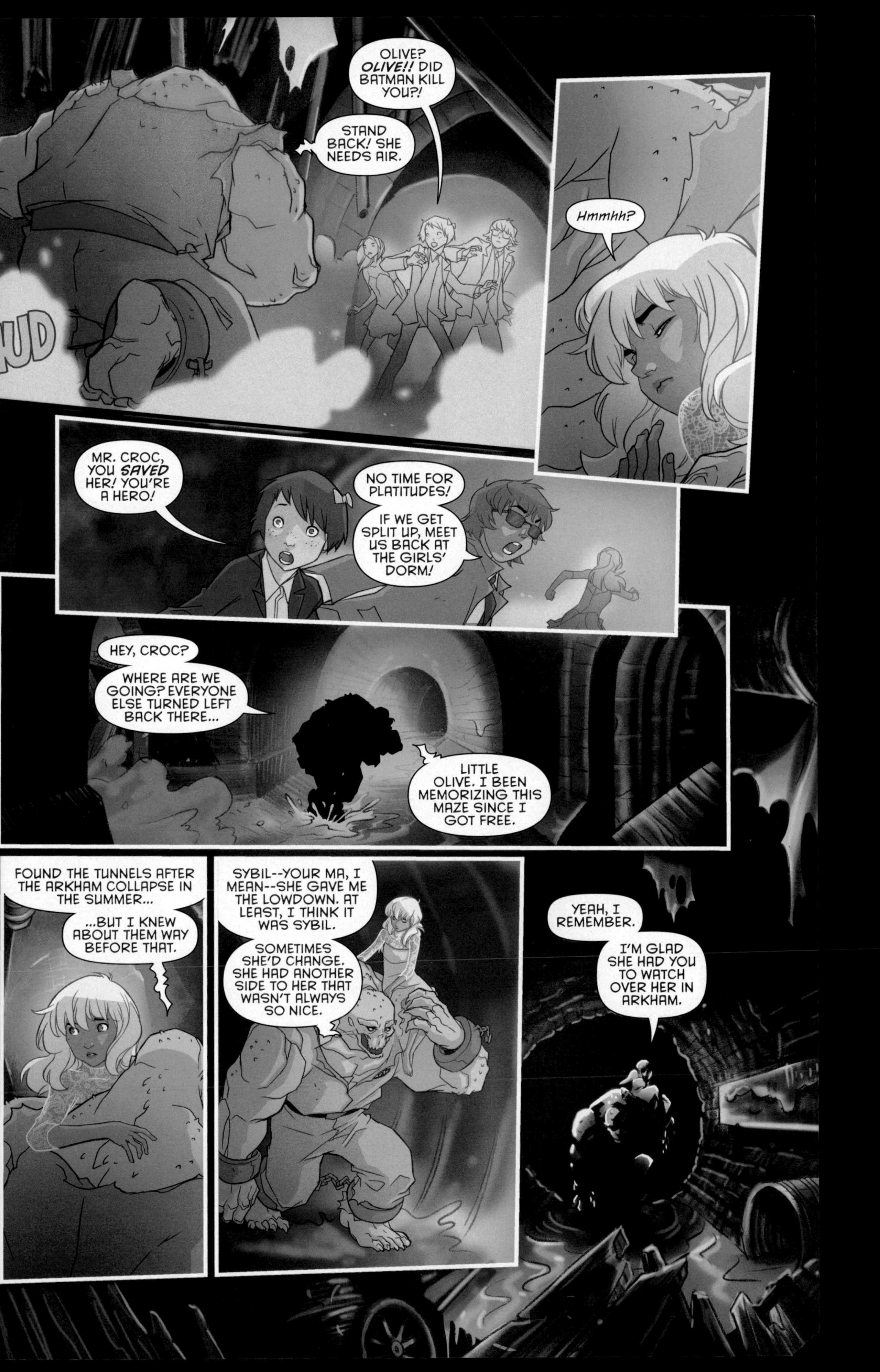
OLIVE? OLIVE!! DID BATMAN KILL YOU?!
STAND BACK! SHE NEEDS AIR.
HUD
Hmmhh?
MR. CROC, YOU SAVED HER! YOU'RE A HERO!
NO TIME FOR PLATITUDES!
IF WE GET SPLIT UP, MEET US BACK AT THE GIRLS' DORM!
HEY, CROC?
WHERE ARE WE GOING? EVERYONE ELSE TURNED LEFT BACK THERE...
LITTLE OLIVE. I BEEN MEMORIZING THIS MAZE SINCE I GOT FREE.
FOUND THE TUNNELS AFTER THE ARKHAM COLLAPSE IN THE SUMMER...
...BUT I KNEW ABOUT THEM WAY BEFORE THAT.
SYBIL--YOUR MA, I MEAN--SHE GAVE ME THE LOWDOWN. AT LEAST, I THINK IT WAS SYBIL.
SOMETIMES SHE'D CHANGE. SHE HAD ANOTHER SIDE TO HER THAT WASN'T ALWAYS SO NICE.
YEAH, I REMEMBER.
I'M GLAD SHE HAD YOU TO WATCH OVER HER IN ARKHAM.

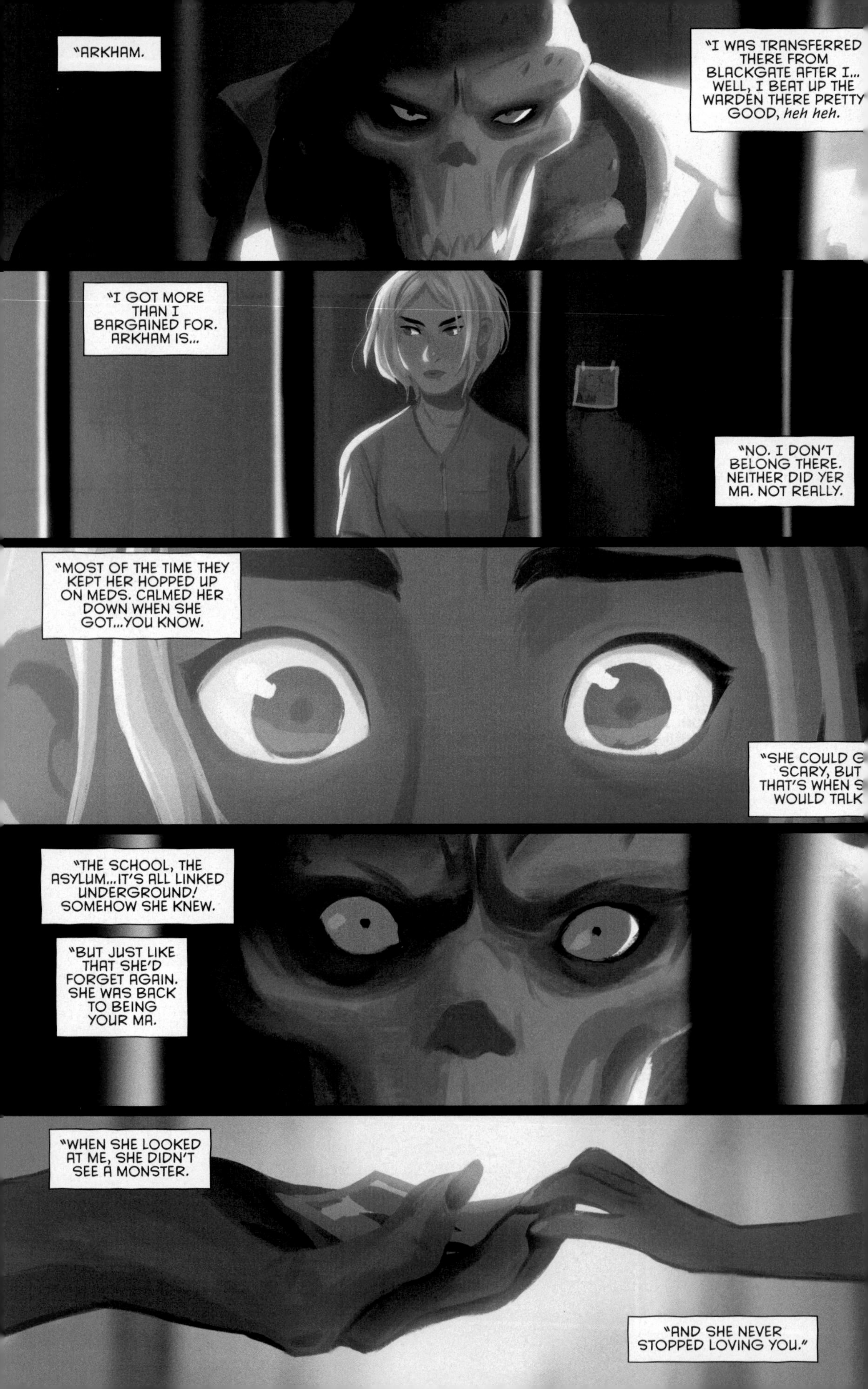
"ARKHAM.
"I WAS TRANSFERRED THERE FROM BLACKGATE AFTER I... WELL, I BEAT UP THE WARDEN THERE PRETTY GOOD, *heh heh.*
"I GOT MORE THAN I BARGAINED FOR. ARKHAM IS...
"NO. I DON'T BELONG THERE. NEITHER DID YER MA. NOT REALLY.
"MOST OF THE TIME THEY KEPT HER HOPPED UP ON MEDS. CALMED HER DOWN WHEN SHE GOT...YOU KNOW.
"SHE COULD G SCARY, BUT THAT'S WHEN S WOULD TALK
"THE SCHOOL, THE ASYLUM...IT'S ALL LINKED UNDERGROUND! SOMEHOW SHE KNEW.
"BUT JUST LIKE THAT SHE'D FORGET AGAIN. SHE WAS BACK TO BEING YOUR MA.
"WHEN SHE LOOKED AT ME, SHE DIDN'T SEE A MONSTER.
"AND SHE NEVER STOPPED LOVING YOU."

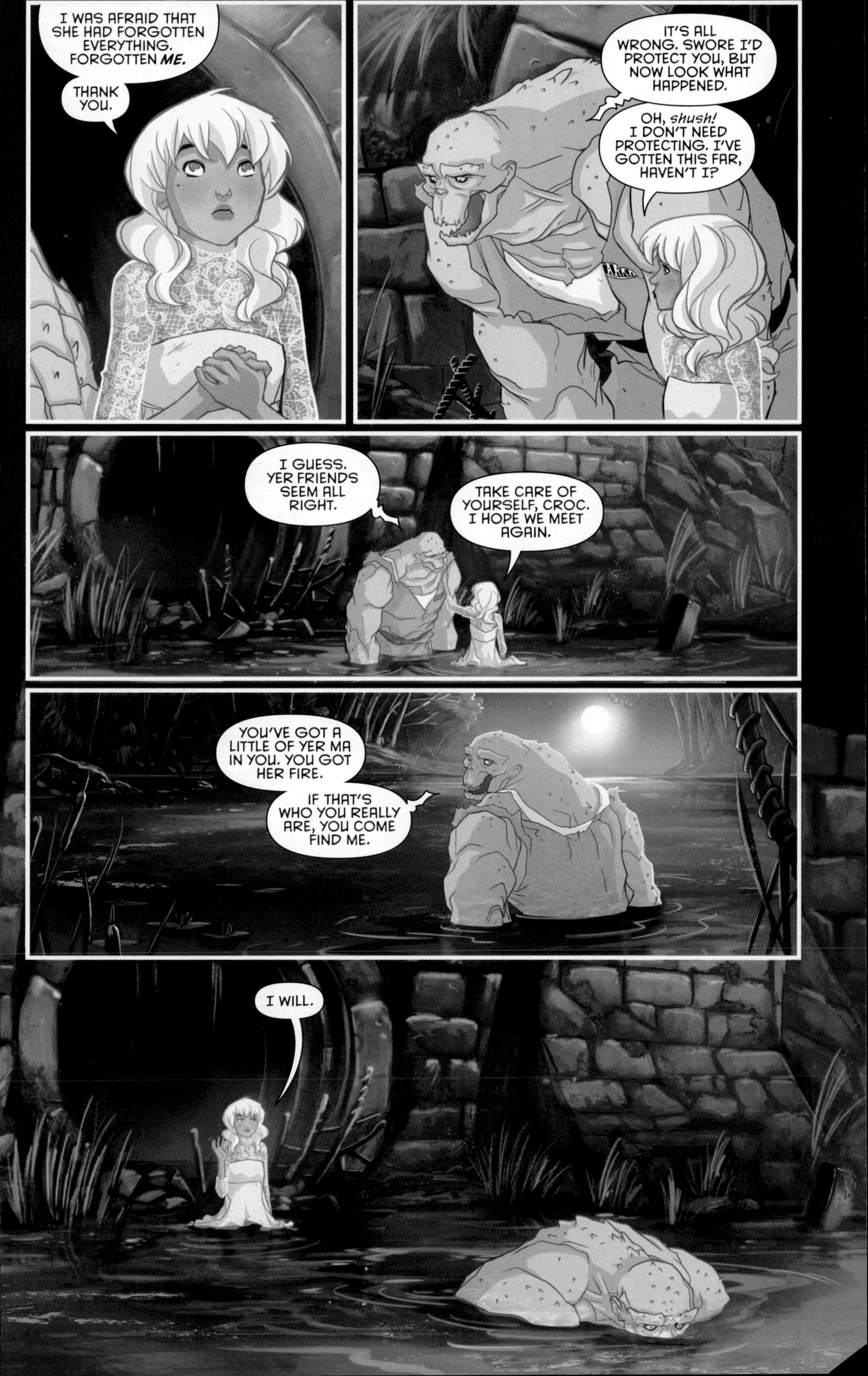
I WAS AFRAID THAT SHE HAD FORGOTTEN EVERYTHING. FORGOTTEN *ME.*
THANK YOU.
IT'S ALL WRONG. SWORE I'D PROTECT YOU, BUT NOW LOOK WHAT HAPPENED.
OH, *shush!* I DON'T NEED PROTECTING. I'VE GOTTEN THIS FAR, HAVEN'T I?
I GUESS. YER FRIENDS SEEM ALL RIGHT.
TAKE CARE OF YOURSELF, CROC. I HOPE WE MEET AGAIN.
YOU'VE GOT A LITTLE OF YER MA IN YOU. YOU GOT HER FIRE.
IF THAT'S WHO YOU REALLY ARE, YOU COME FIND ME.
I WILL.

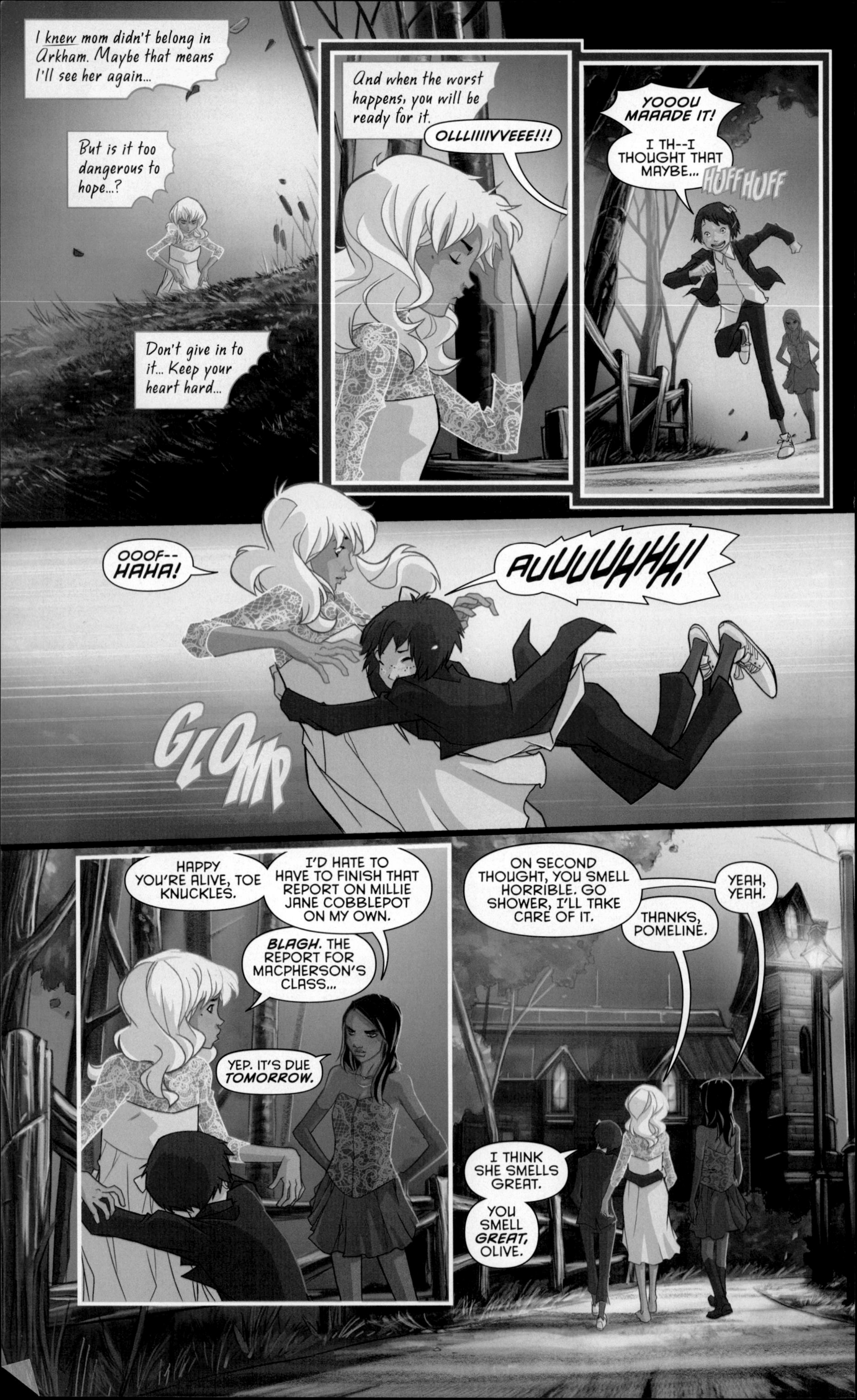

I knew mom didn't belong in Arkham. Maybe that means I'll see her again...
But is it too dangerous to hope...?
Don't give in to it... Keep your heart hard...
And when the worst happens, you will be ready for it.
OLLLIIIIVVEEE!!!
YOOOU MAAADE IT!
I TH--I THOUGHT THAT MAYBE...
HUFF HUFF
OOOF-- HAHA!
AUUUUHHH!
GLOMP
HAPPY YOU'RE ALIVE, TOE KNUCKLES.
I'D HATE TO HAVE TO FINISH THAT REPORT ON MILLIE JANE COBBLEPOT ON MY OWN.
BLAGH. THE REPORT FOR MACPHERSON'S CLASS...
YEP. IT'S DUE TOMORROW.
ON SECOND THOUGHT, YOU SMELL HORRIBLE. GO SHOWER, I'LL TAKE CARE OF IT.
YEAH, YEAH.
THANKS, POMELINE.
I THINK SHE SMELLS GREAT.
YOU SMELL GREAT, OLIVE.

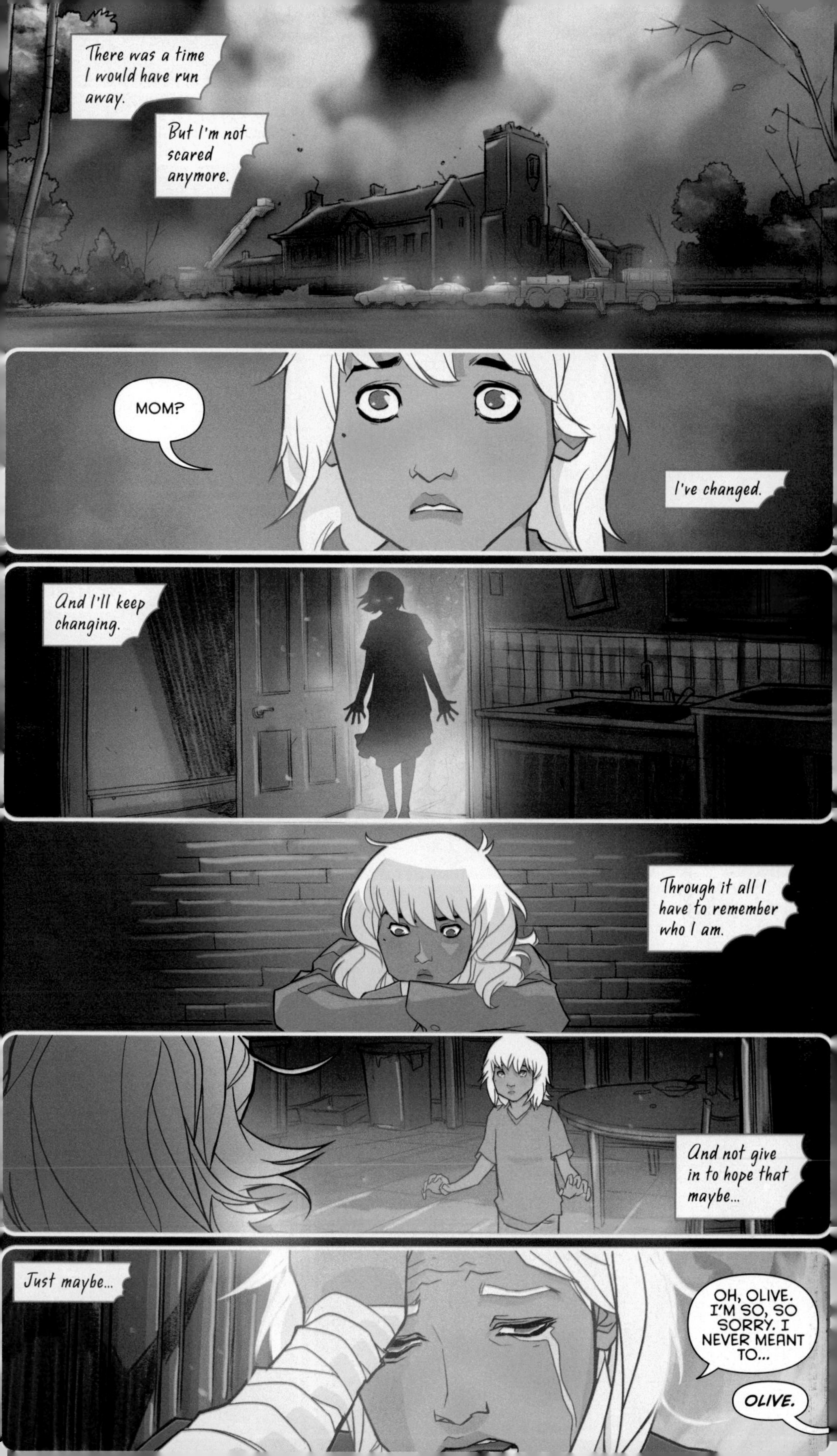
There was a time I would have run away.
But I'm not scared anymore.
MOM?
I've changed.
And I'll keep changing.
Through it all I have to remember who I am.
And not give in to hope that maybe...
Just maybe...
OH, OLIVE. I'M SO, SO SORRY. I NEVER MEANT TO...
OLIVE.

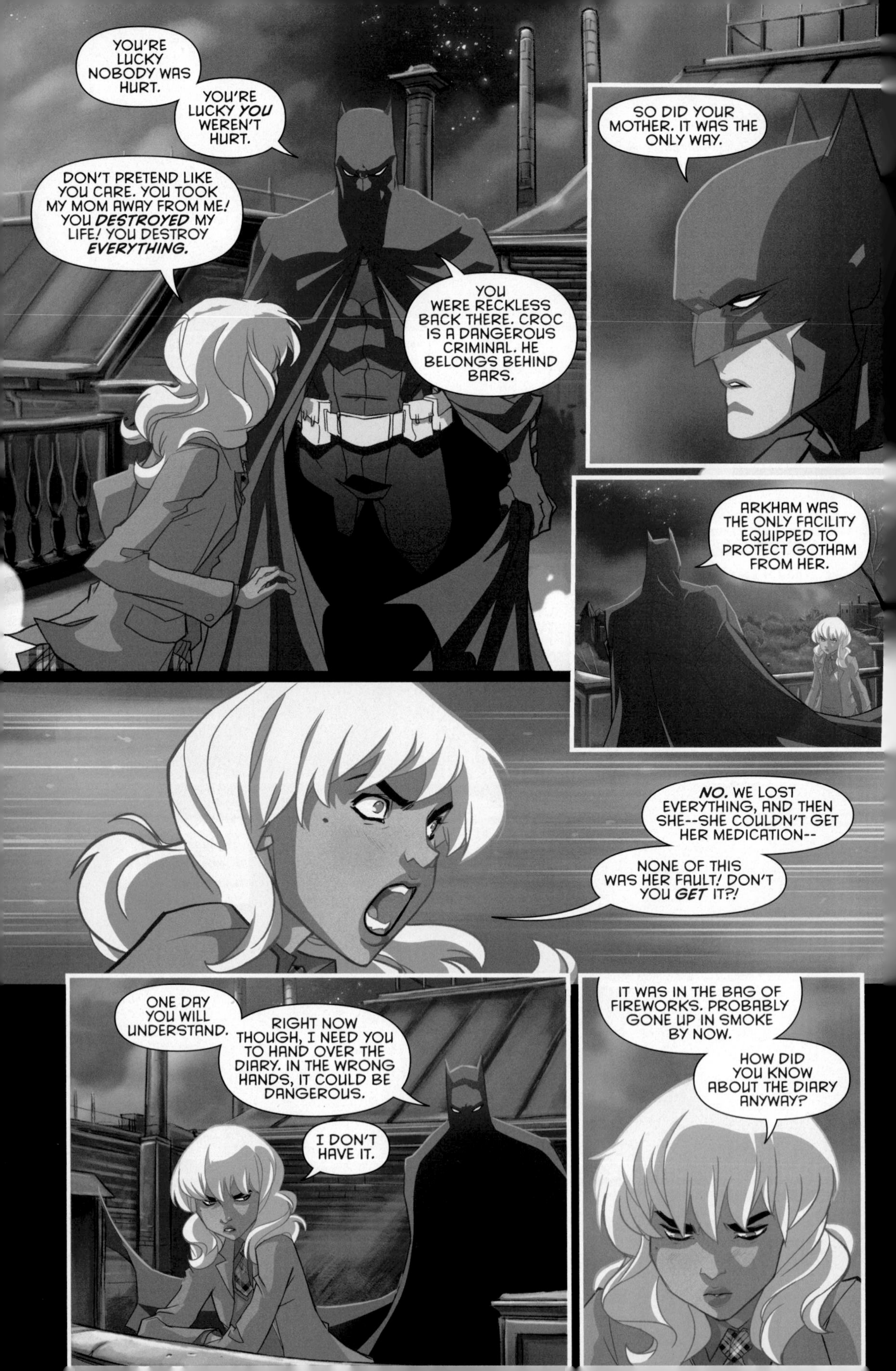

YOU'RE LUCKY NOBODY WAS HURT.
YOU'RE LUCKY *YOU* WEREN'T HURT.
DON'T PRETEND LIKE YOU CARE. YOU TOOK MY MOM AWAY FROM ME! YOU *DESTROYED* MY LIFE! YOU DESTROY *EVERYTHING.*
YOU WERE RECKLESS BACK THERE. CROC IS A DANGEROUS CRIMINAL. HE BELONGS BEHIND BARS.
SO DID YOUR MOTHER. IT WAS THE ONLY WAY.
ARKHAM WAS THE ONLY FACILITY EQUIPPED TO PROTECT GOTHAM FROM HER.
*NO.* WE LOST EVERYTHING, AND THEN SHE--SHE COULDN'T GET HER MEDICATION--
NONE OF THIS WAS HER FAULT! DON'T YOU *GET* IT?!
ONE DAY YOU WILL UNDERSTAND.
RIGHT NOW THOUGH, I NEED YOU TO HAND OVER THE DIARY. IN THE WRONG HANDS, IT COULD BE DANGEROUS.
I DON'T HAVE IT.
IT WAS IN THE BAG OF FIREWORKS. PROBABLY GONE UP IN SMOKE BY NOW.
HOW DID YOU KNOW ABOUT THE DIARY ANYWAY?

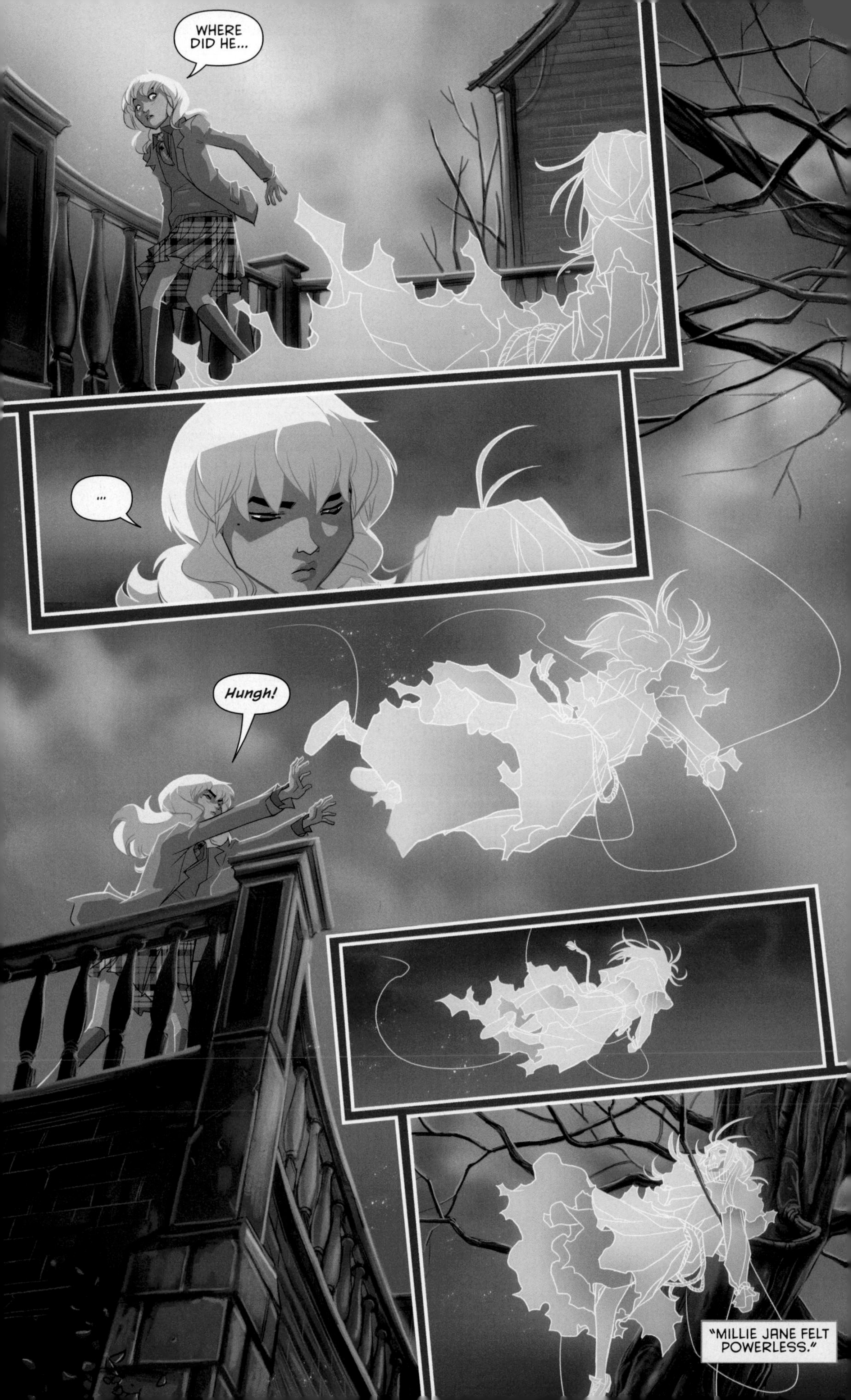
WHERE DID HE...
...
Hungh!
"MILLIE JANE FELT POWERLESS."

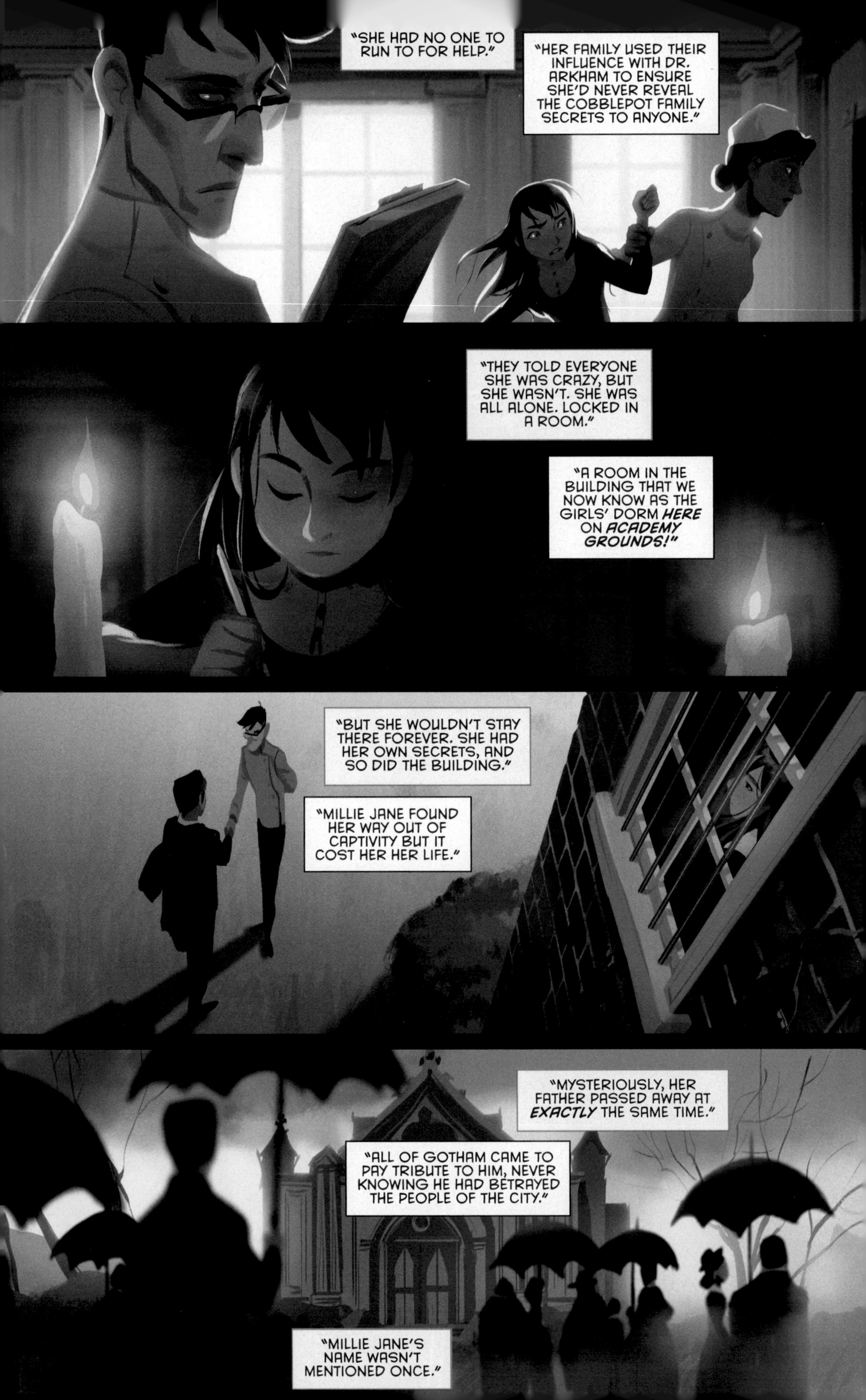
"SHE HAD NO ONE TO RUN TO FOR HELP."
"HER FAMILY USED THEIR INFLUENCE WITH DR. ARKHAM TO ENSURE SHE'D NEVER REVEAL THE COBBLEPOT FAMILY SECRETS TO ANYONE."
"THEY TOLD EVERYONE SHE WAS CRAZY, BUT SHE WASN'T. SHE WAS ALL ALONE. LOCKED IN A ROOM."
"A ROOM IN THE BUILDING THAT WE NOW KNOW AS THE GIRLS' DORM *HERE* ON *ACADEMY GROUNDS!*"
"BUT SHE WOULDN'T STAY THERE FOREVER. SHE HAD HER OWN SECRETS, AND SO DID THE BUILDING."
"MILLIE JANE FOUND HER WAY OUT OF CAPTIVITY BUT IT COST HER HER LIFE."
"MYSTERIOUSLY, HER FATHER PASSED AWAY AT *EXACTLY* THE SAME TIME."
"ALL OF GOTHAM CAME TO PAY TRIBUTE TO HIM, NEVER KNOWING HE HAD BETRAYED THE PEOPLE OF THE CITY."
"MILLIE JANE'S NAME WASN'T MENTIONED ONCE."

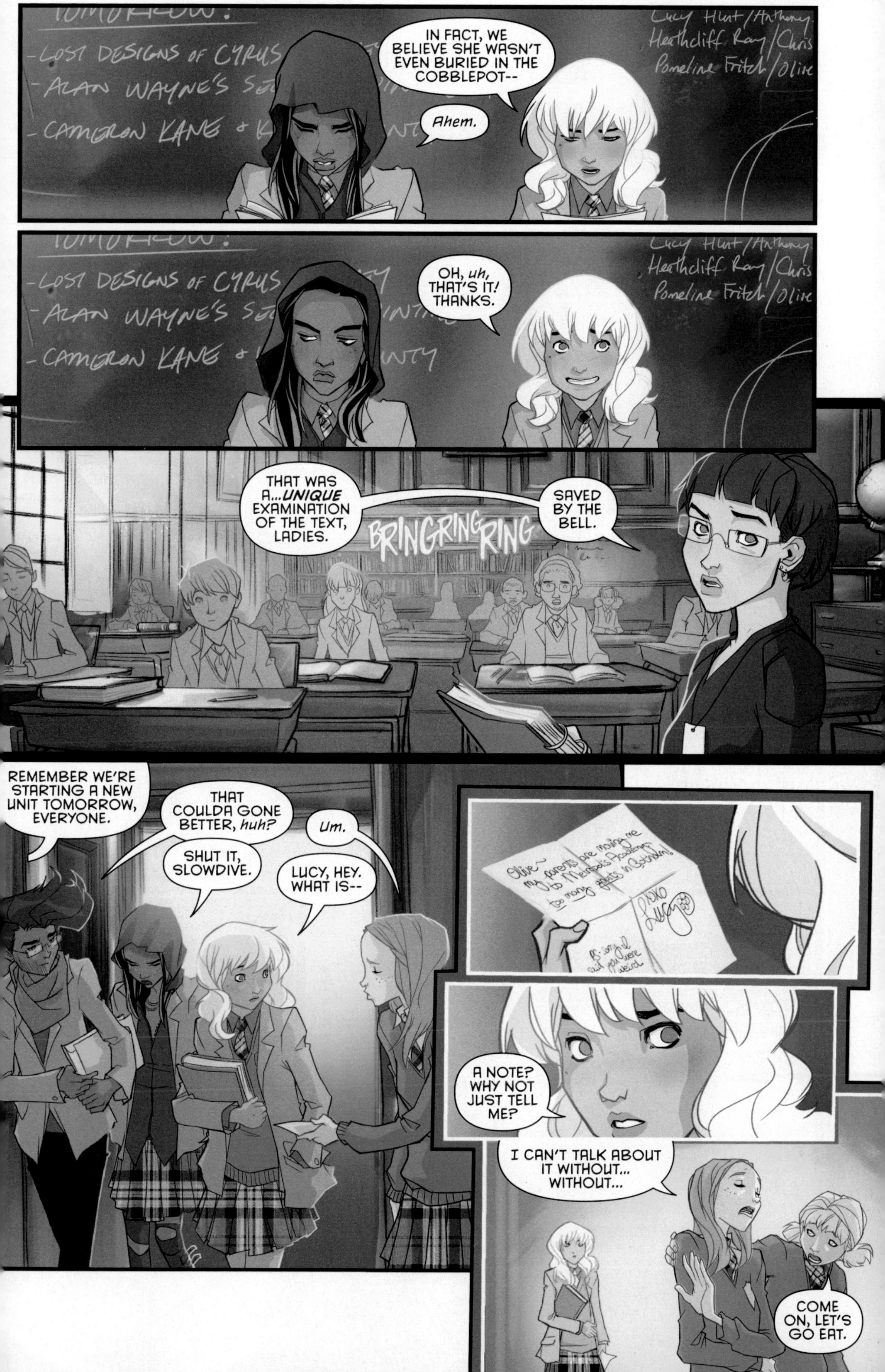
IN FACT, WE BELIEVE SHE WASN'T EVEN BURIED IN THE COBBLEPOT--
Ahem.
OH, uh, THAT'S IT! THANKS.
THAT WAS A...UNIQUE EXAMINATION OF THE TEXT, LADIES.
BRINGRINGRING
SAVED BY THE BELL.
REMEMBER WE'RE STARTING A NEW UNIT TOMORROW, EVERYONE.
THAT COULDA GONE BETTER, huh?
SHUT IT, SLOWDIVE.
Um.
LUCY, HEY. WHAT IS--
A NOTE? WHY NOT JUST TELL ME?
I CAN'T TALK ABOUT IT WITHOUT... WITHOUT...
COME ON, LET'S GO EAT.

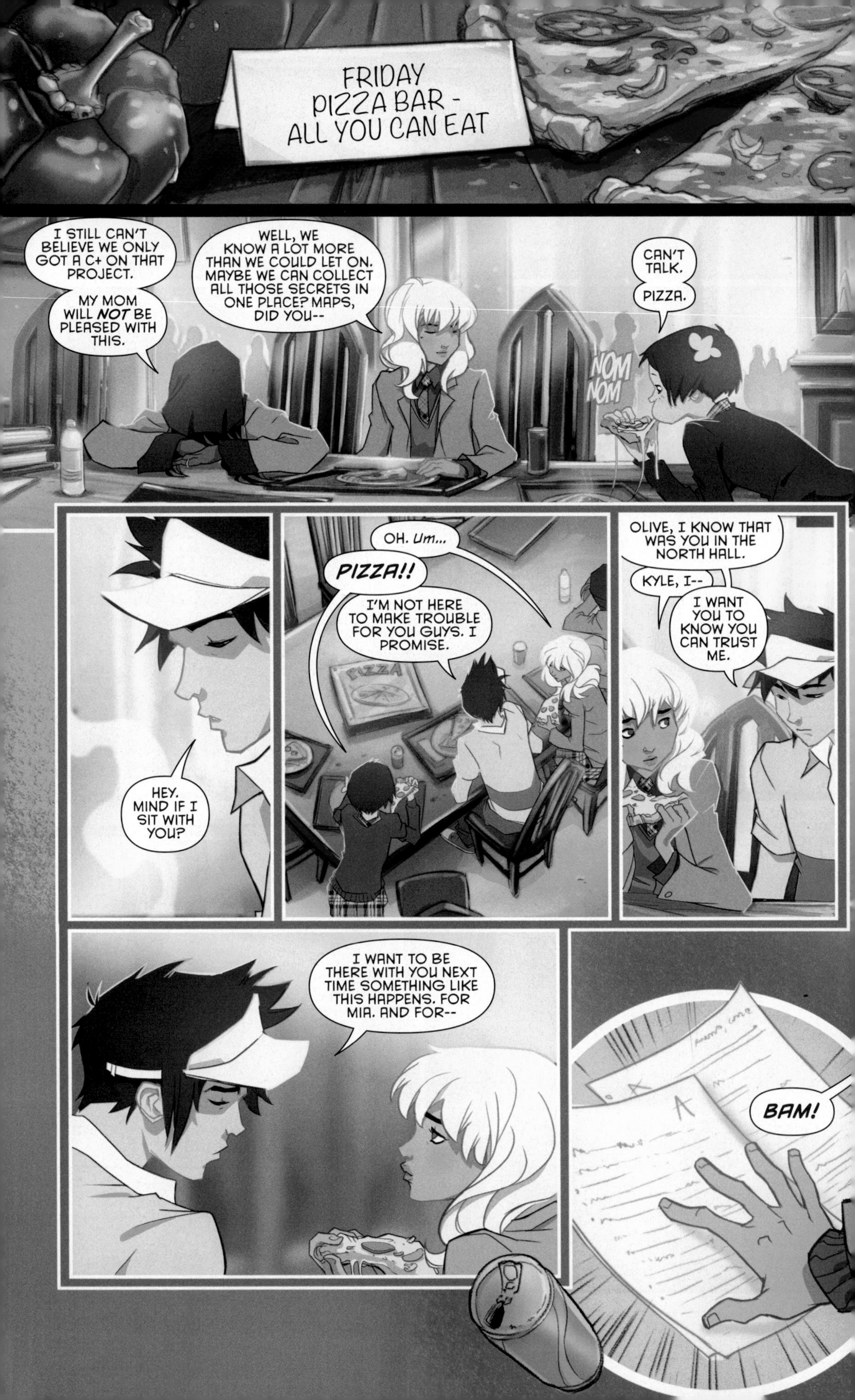
FRIDAY
PIZZA BAR -
ALL YOU CAN EAT
I STILL CAN'T BELIEVE WE ONLY GOT A C+ ON THAT PROJECT.
MY MOM WILL *NOT* BE PLEASED WITH THIS.
WELL, WE KNOW A LOT MORE THAN WE COULD LET ON. MAYBE WE CAN COLLECT ALL THOSE SECRETS IN ONE PLACE? MAPS, DID YOU--
CAN'T TALK.
PIZZA.
NOM NOM
HEY. MIND IF I SIT WITH YOU?
OH. *Um...*
PIZZA!!
I'M NOT HERE TO MAKE TROUBLE FOR YOU GUYS. I PROMISE.
PIZZA
OLIVE, I KNOW THAT WAS YOU IN THE NORTH HALL.
KYLE, I--
I WANT YOU TO KNOW YOU CAN TRUST ME.
I WANT TO BE THERE WITH YOU NEXT TIME SOMETHING LIKE THIS HAPPENS. FOR MIA. AND FOR--
BAM!

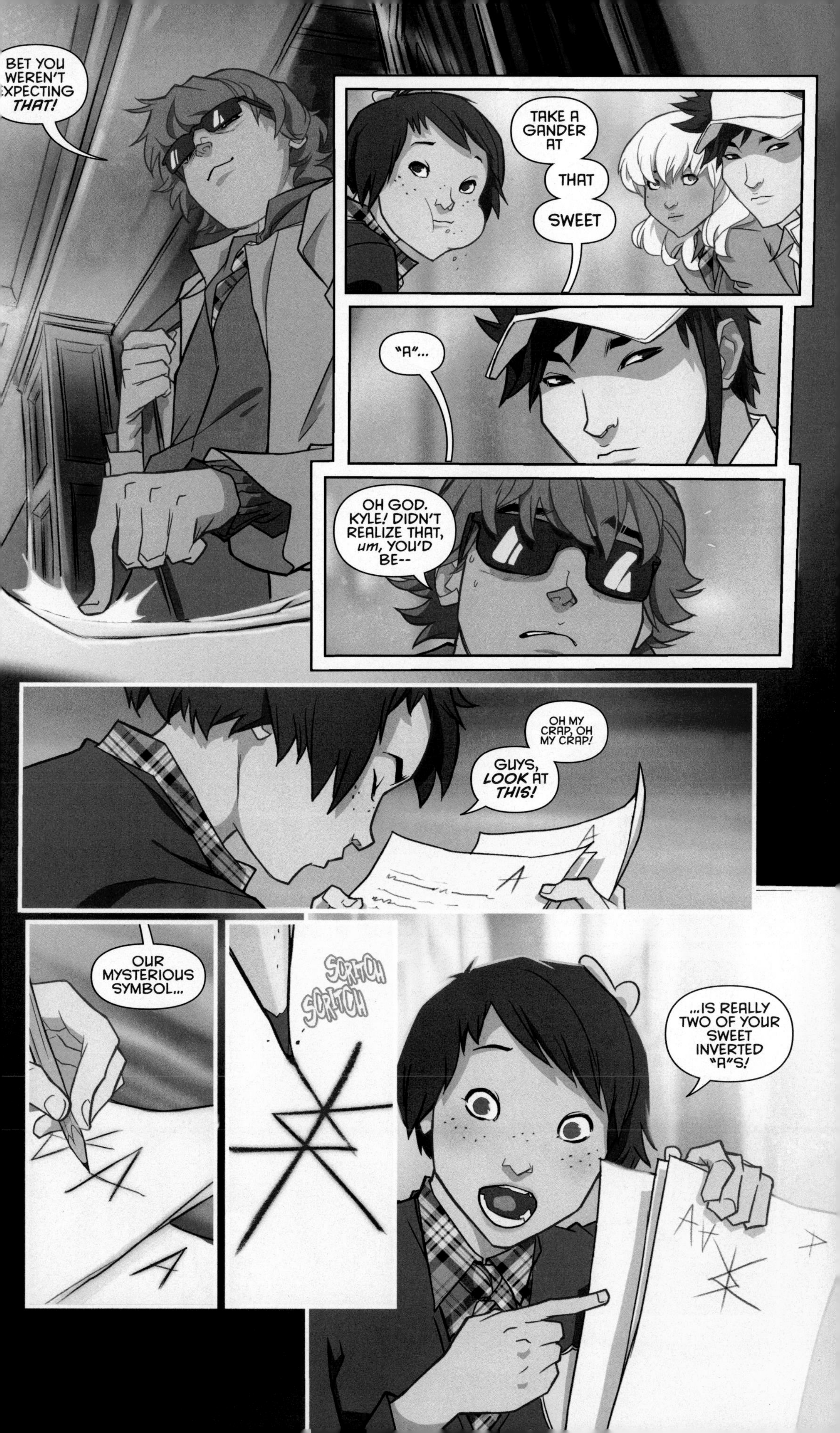
BET YOU WEREN'T EXPECTING *THAT!*
TAKE A GANDER AT
THAT
SWEET
"A"...
OH GOD. KYLE! DIDN'T REALIZE THAT, *um*, YOU'D BE--
OH MY CRAP, OH MY CRAP!
GUYS, *LOOK* AT *THIS!*
OUR MYSTERIOUS SYMBOL...
SCRITCH SCRITCH
...IS REALLY TWO OF YOUR SWEET INVERTED "A"S!

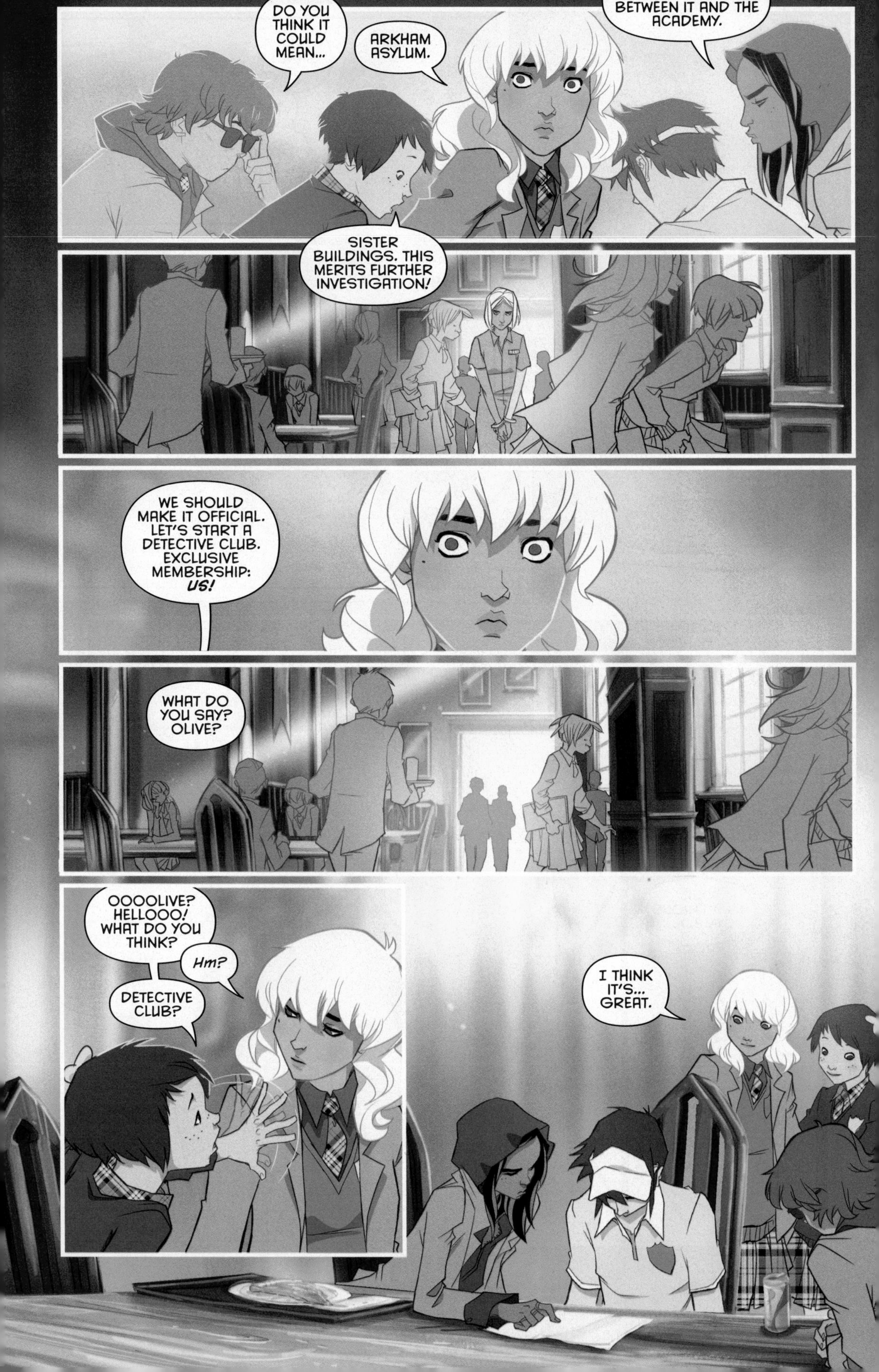
DO YOU THINK IT COULD MEAN...
ARKHAM ASYLUM.
EXPLAINS THE CONNECTION BETWEEN IT AND THE ACADEMY.
SISTER BUILDINGS. THIS MERITS FURTHER INVESTIGATION!
WE SHOULD MAKE IT OFFICIAL. LET'S START A DETECTIVE CLUB. EXCLUSIVE MEMBERSHIP: US!
WHAT DO YOU SAY? OLIVE?
OOOOLIVE? HELLOOO! WHAT DO YOU THINK?
Hm?
DETECTIVE CLUB?
I THINK IT'S... GREAT.

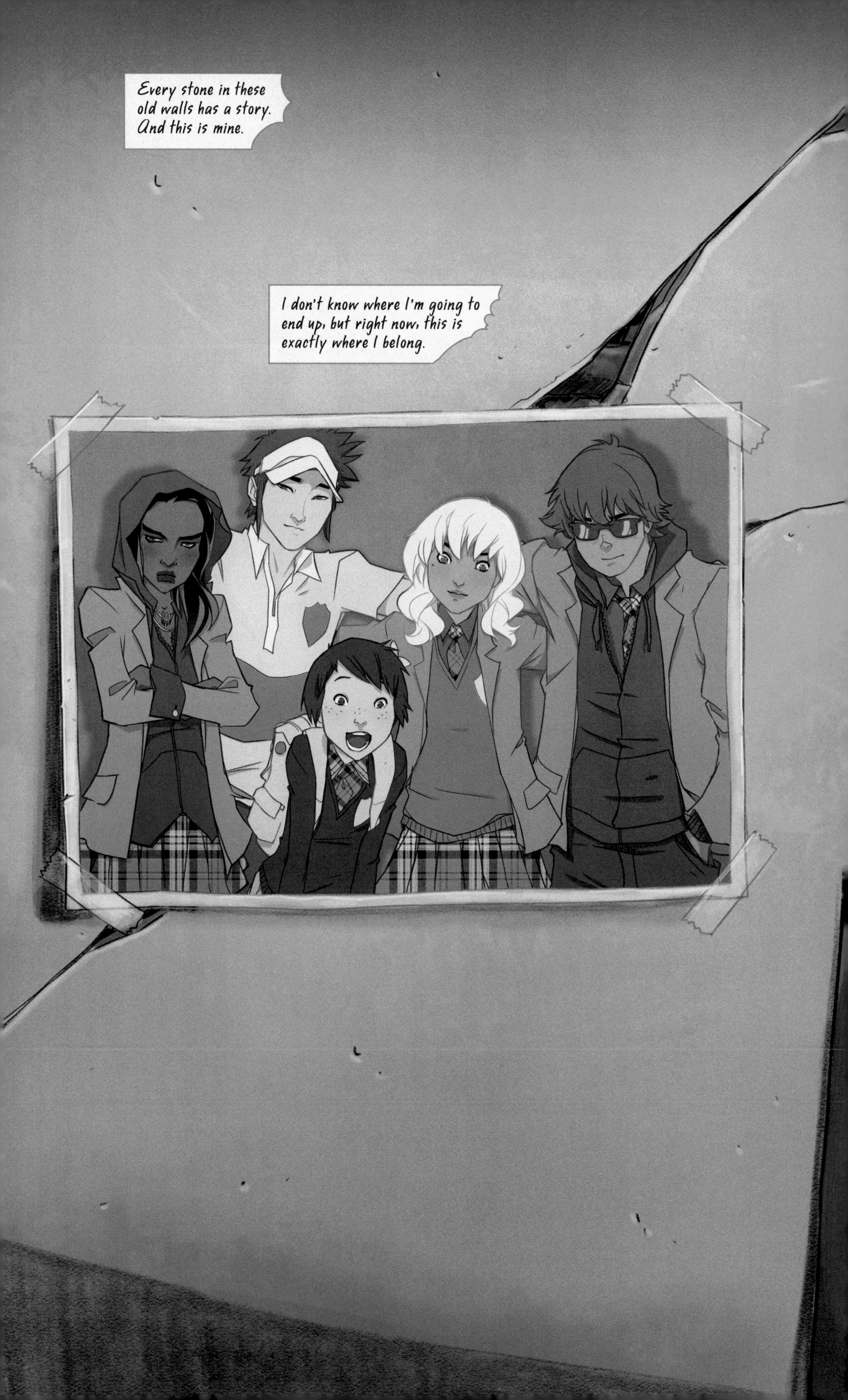
Every stone in these old walls has a story. And this is mine.
I don't know where I'm going to end up, but right now, this is exactly where I belong.

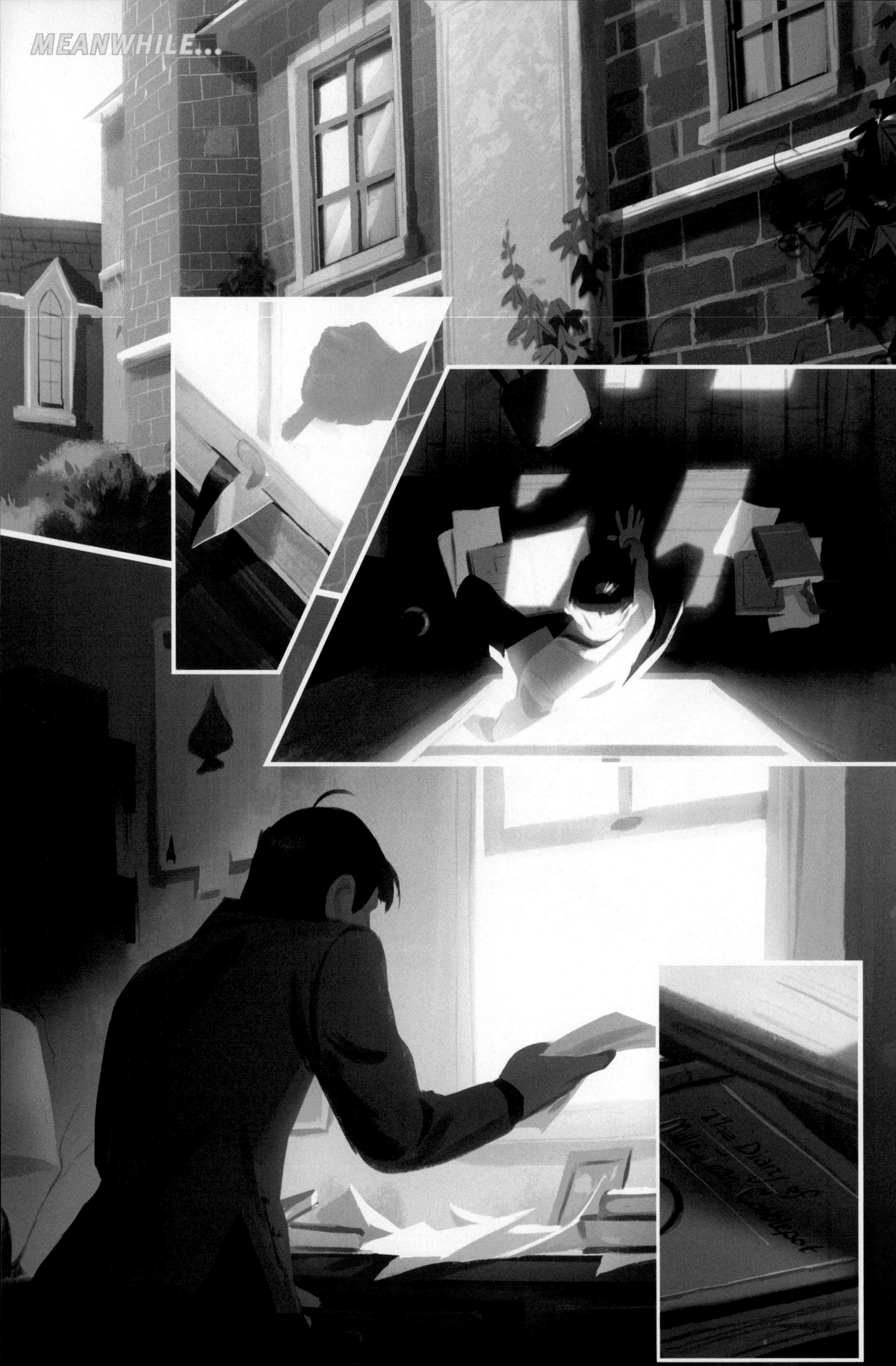
MEANWHILE...
The Diary of

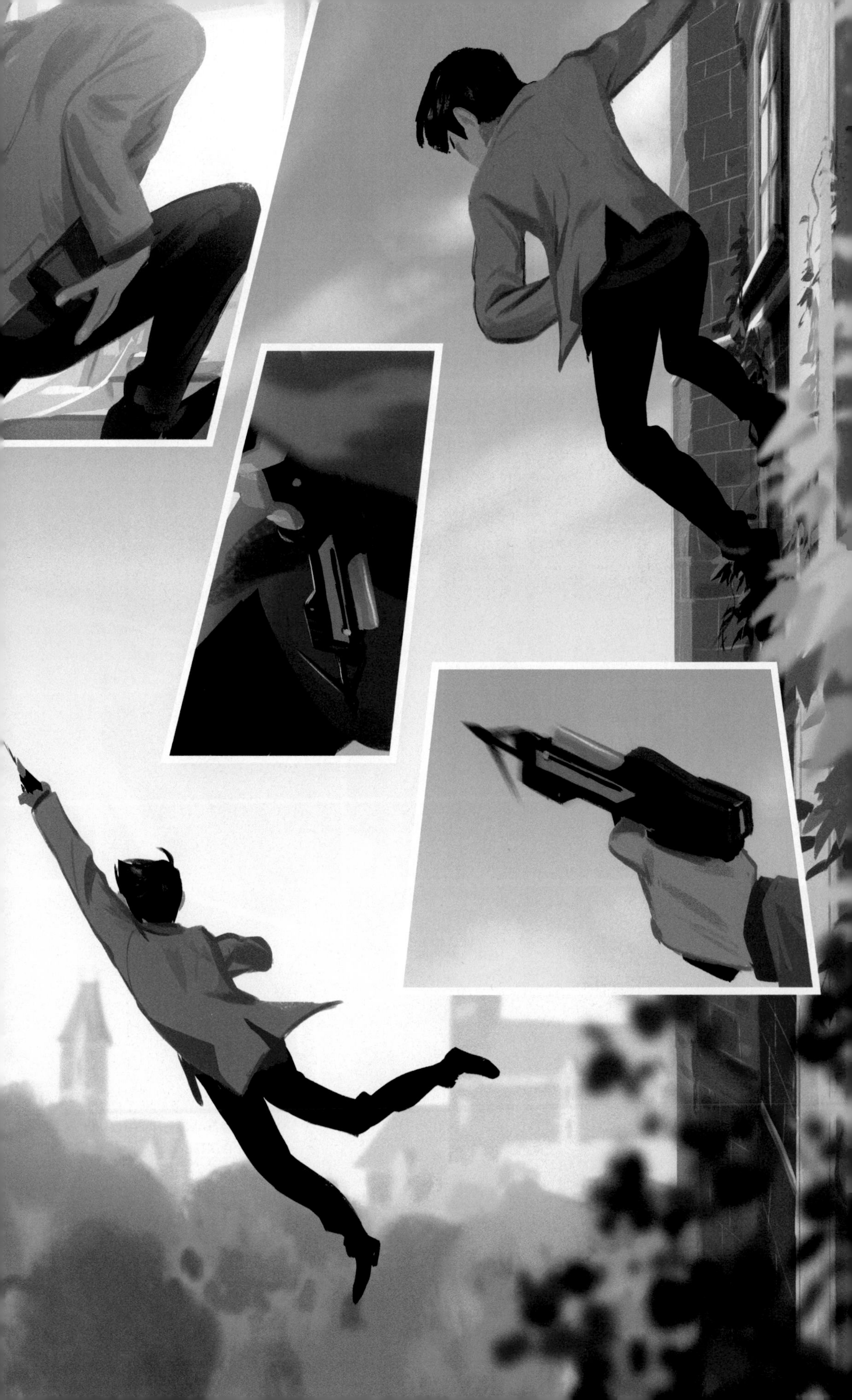

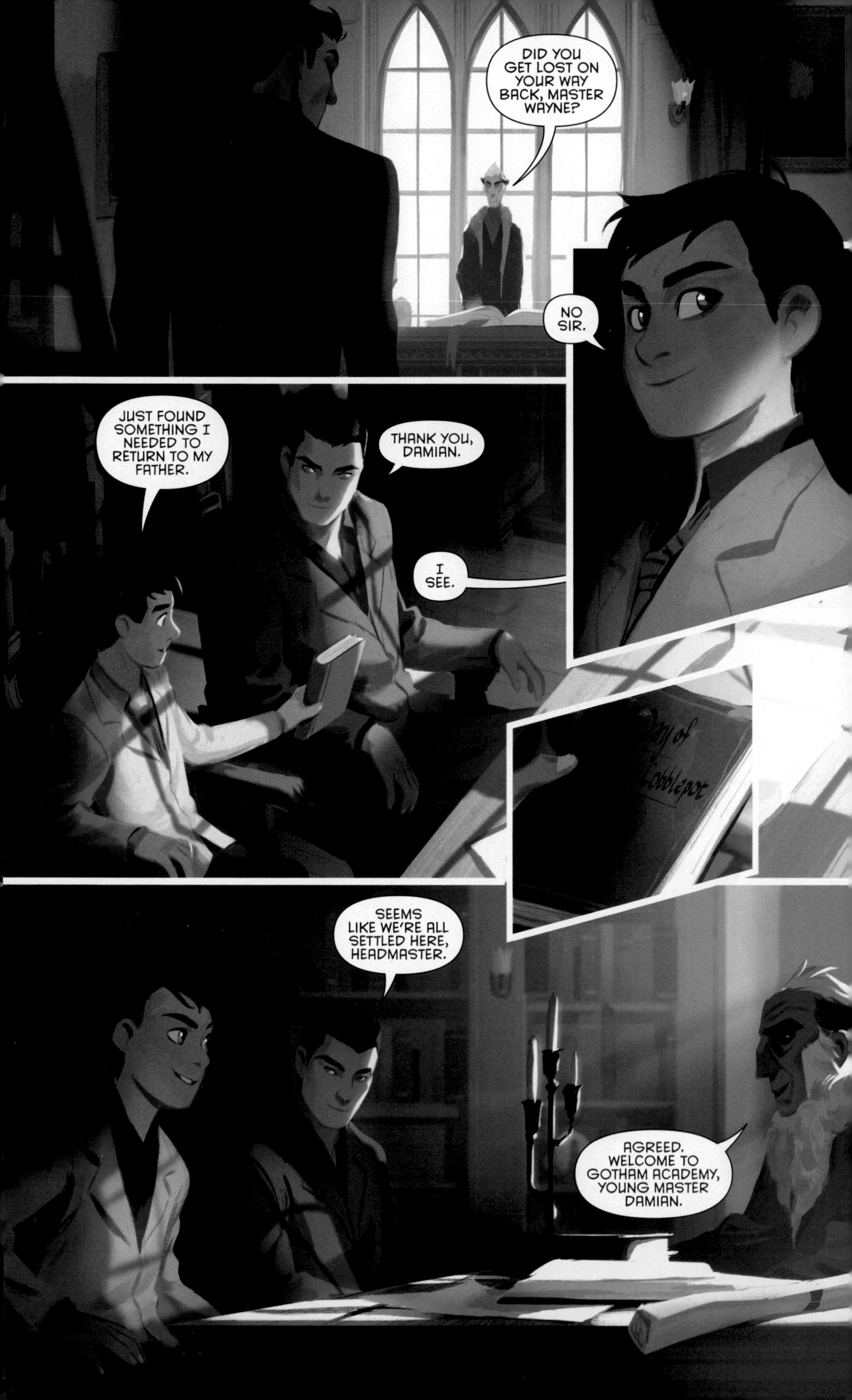
DID YOU GET LOST ON YOUR WAY BACK, MASTER WAYNE?
NO SIR.
JUST FOUND SOMETHING I NEEDED TO RETURN TO MY FATHER.
THANK YOU, DAMIAN.
I SEE.
SEEMS LIKE WE'RE ALL SETTLED HERE, HEADMASTER.
AGREED. WELCOME TO GOTHAM ACADEMY, YOUNG MASTER DAMIAN.

# VARIANT COVER GALLERY

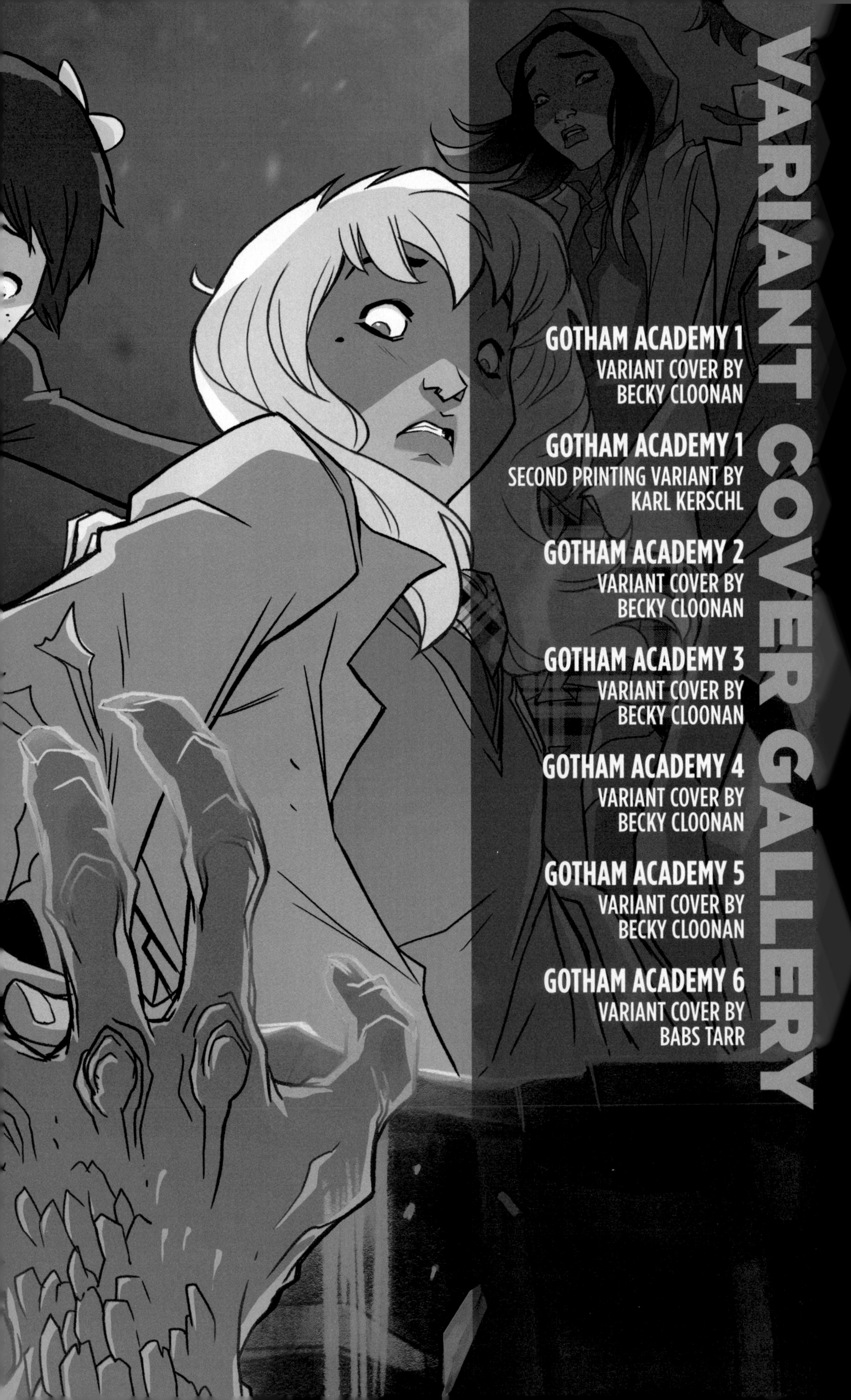

**GOTHAM ACADEMY 1**
VARIANT COVER BY
BECKY CLOONAN

**GOTHAM ACADEMY 1**
SECOND PRINTING VARIANT BY
KARL KERSCHL

**GOTHAM ACADEMY 2**
VARIANT COVER BY
BECKY CLOONAN

**GOTHAM ACADEMY 3**
VARIANT COVER BY
BECKY CLOONAN

**GOTHAM ACADEMY 4**
VARIANT COVER BY
BECKY CLOONAN

**GOTHAM ACADEMY 5**
VARIANT COVER BY
BECKY CLOONAN

**GOTHAM ACADEMY 6**
VARIANT COVER BY
BABS TARR

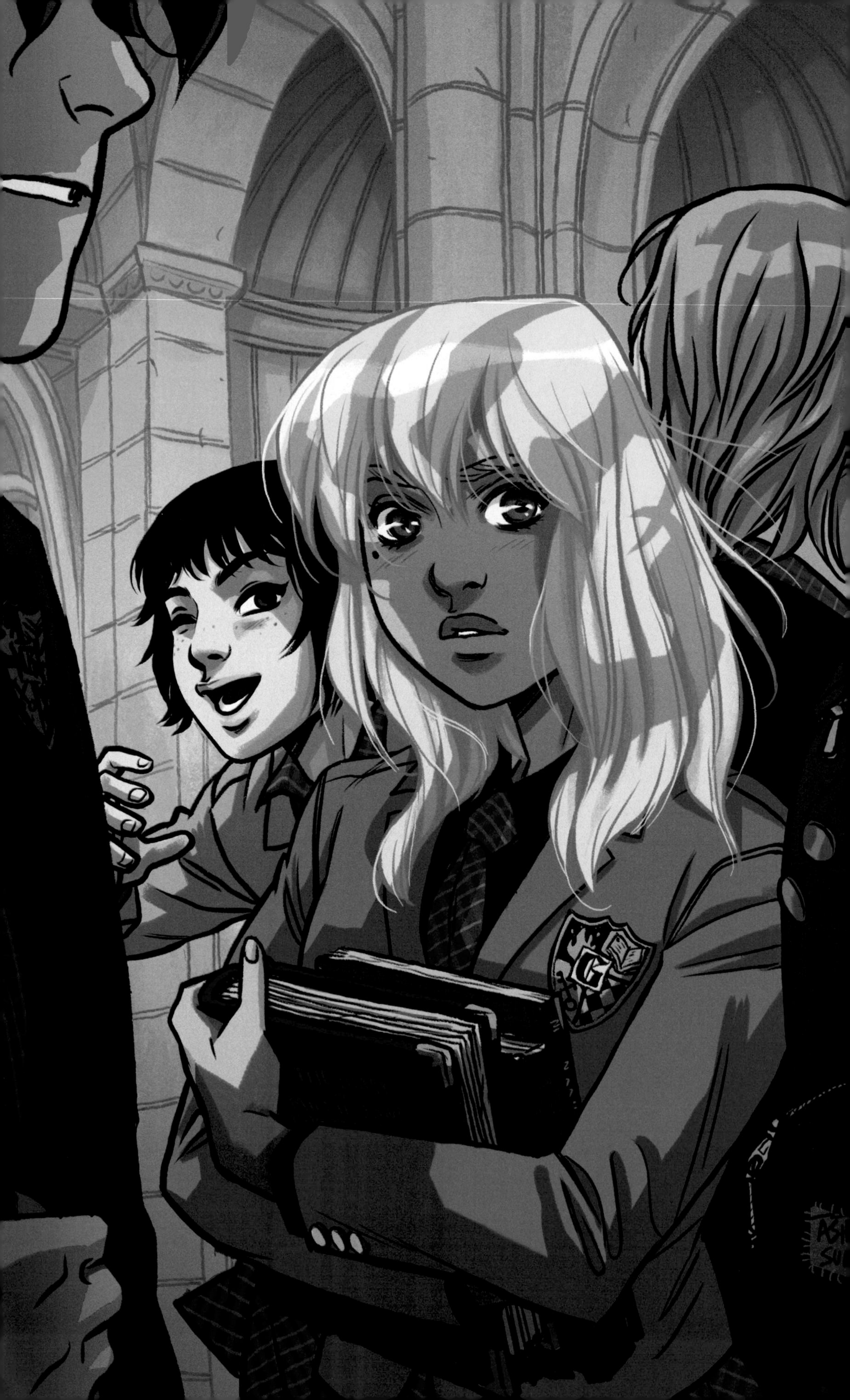

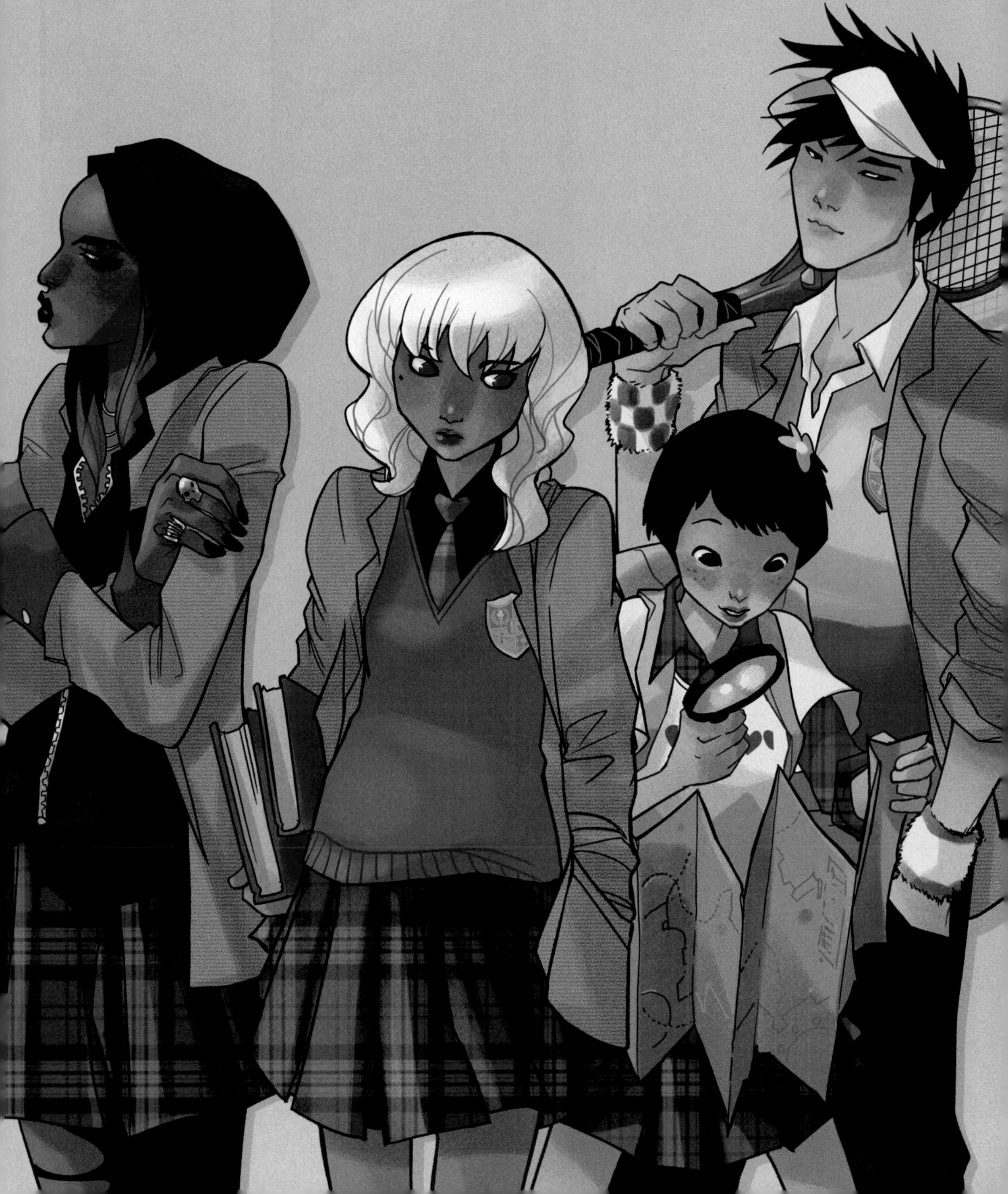

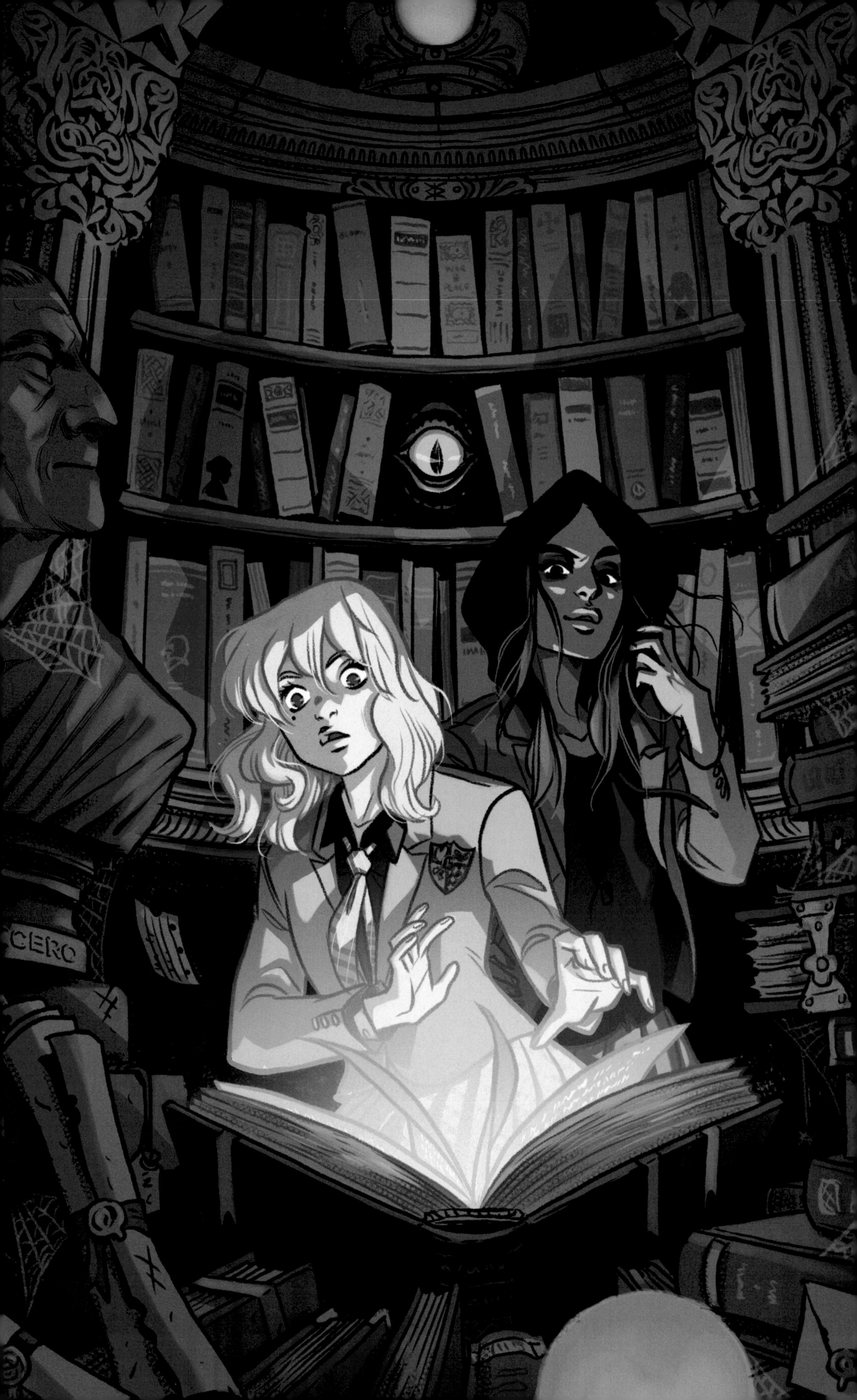
CERO

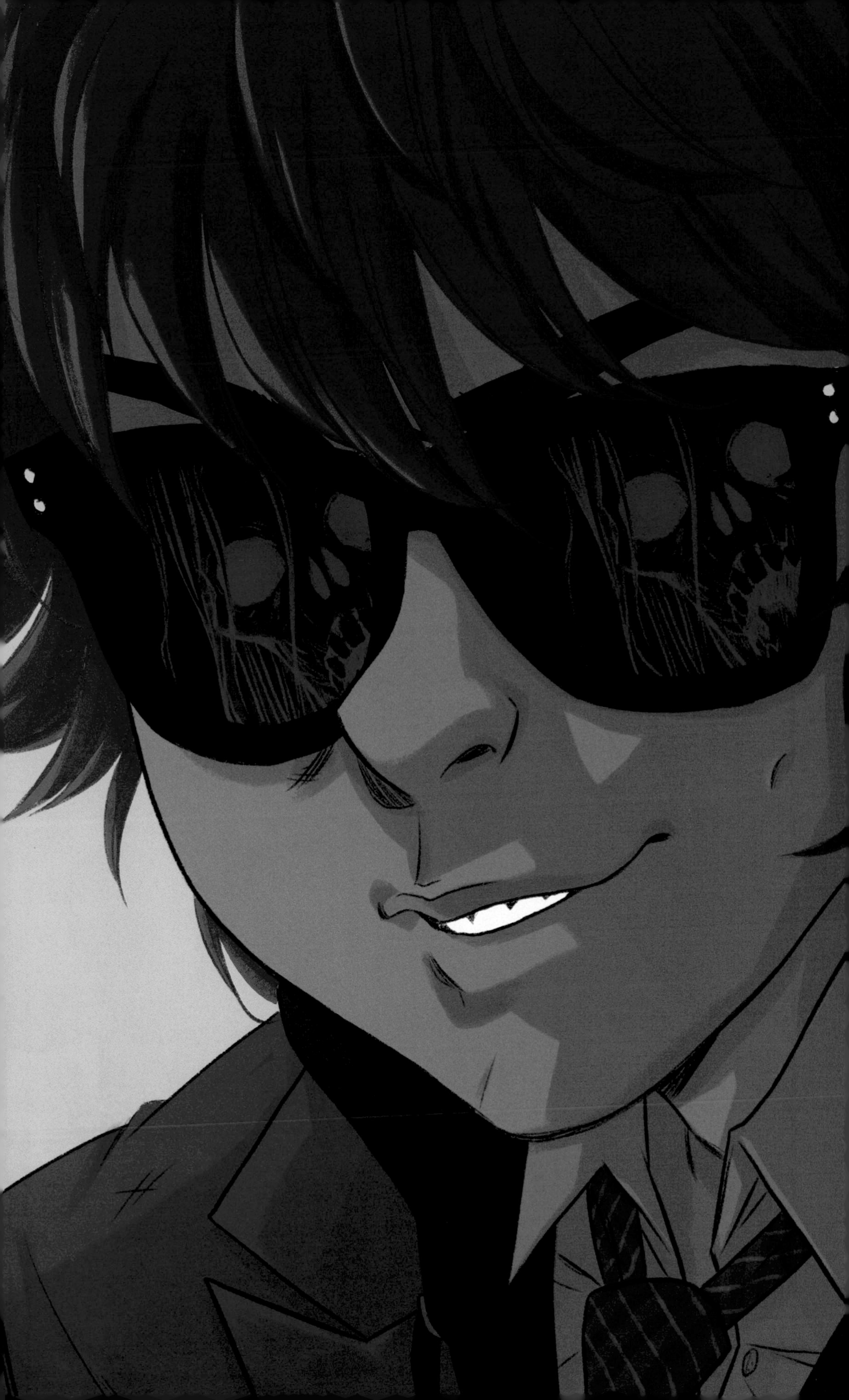

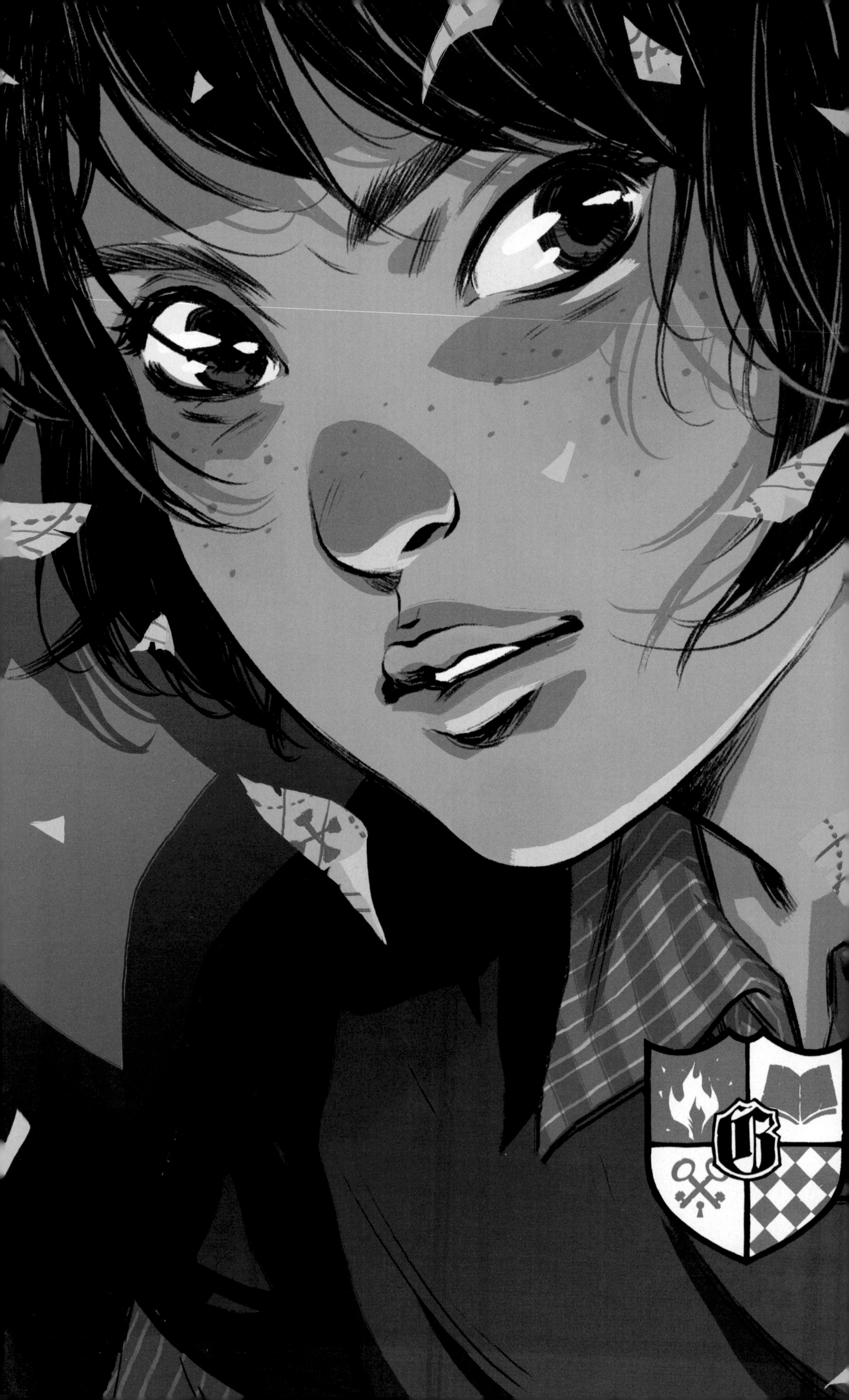

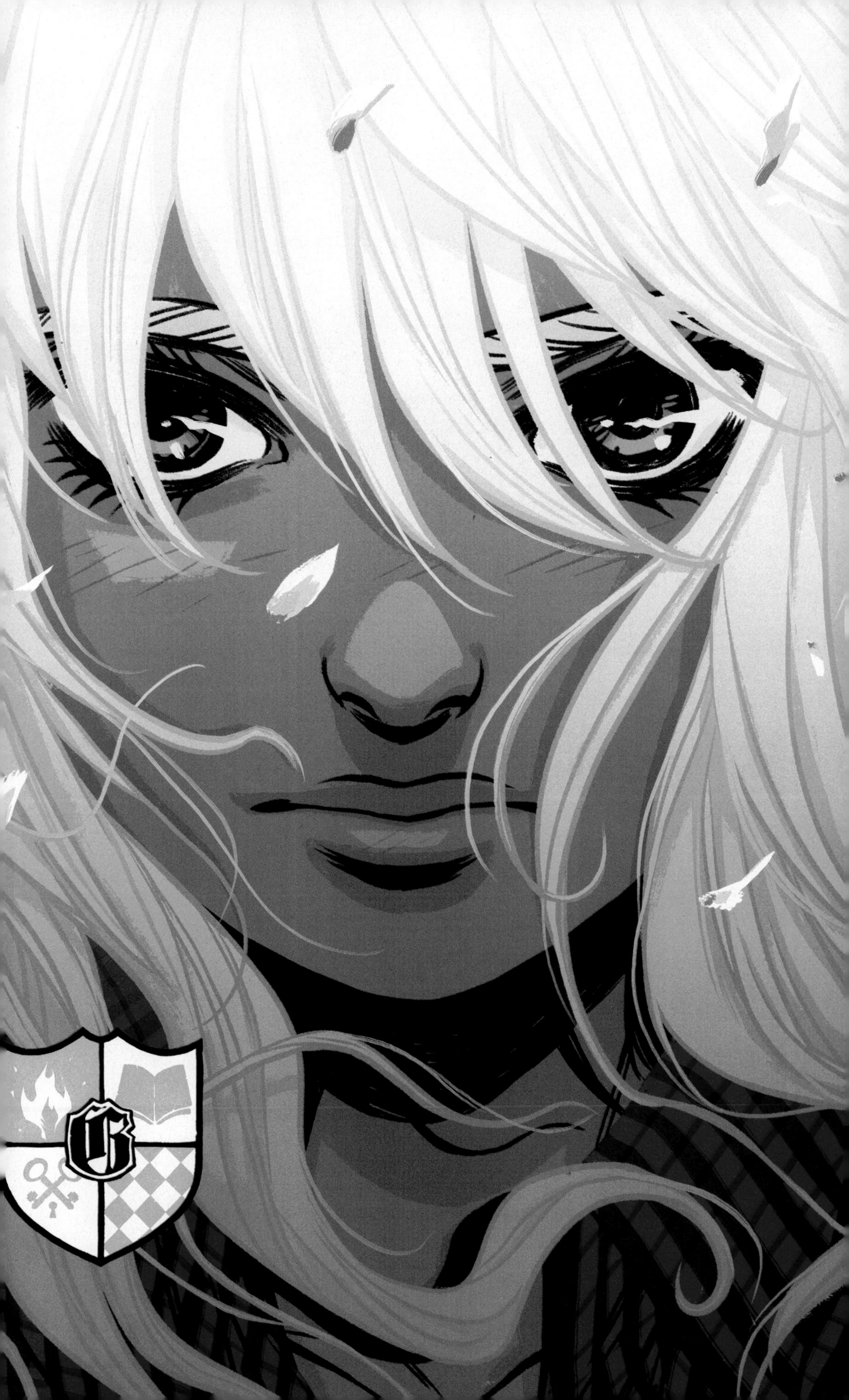

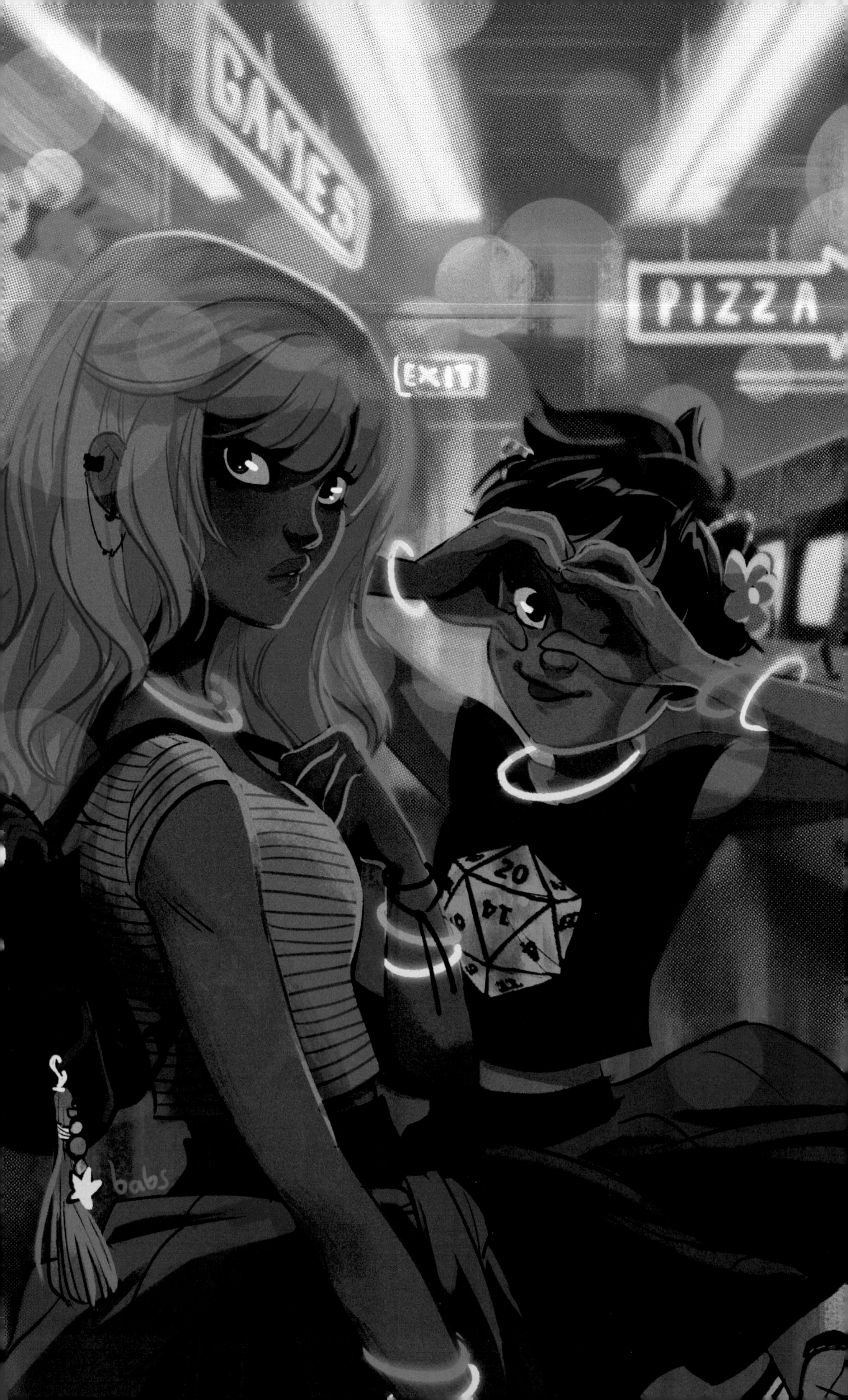
PIZZA
EXIT
20
babs

# BUILDING GOTHAM ACADEMY

WITH ART BY KARL KERSCHL & BECKY CLOONAN
and COMMENTARY BY BRENDEN FLETCHER & KARL KERSCHL

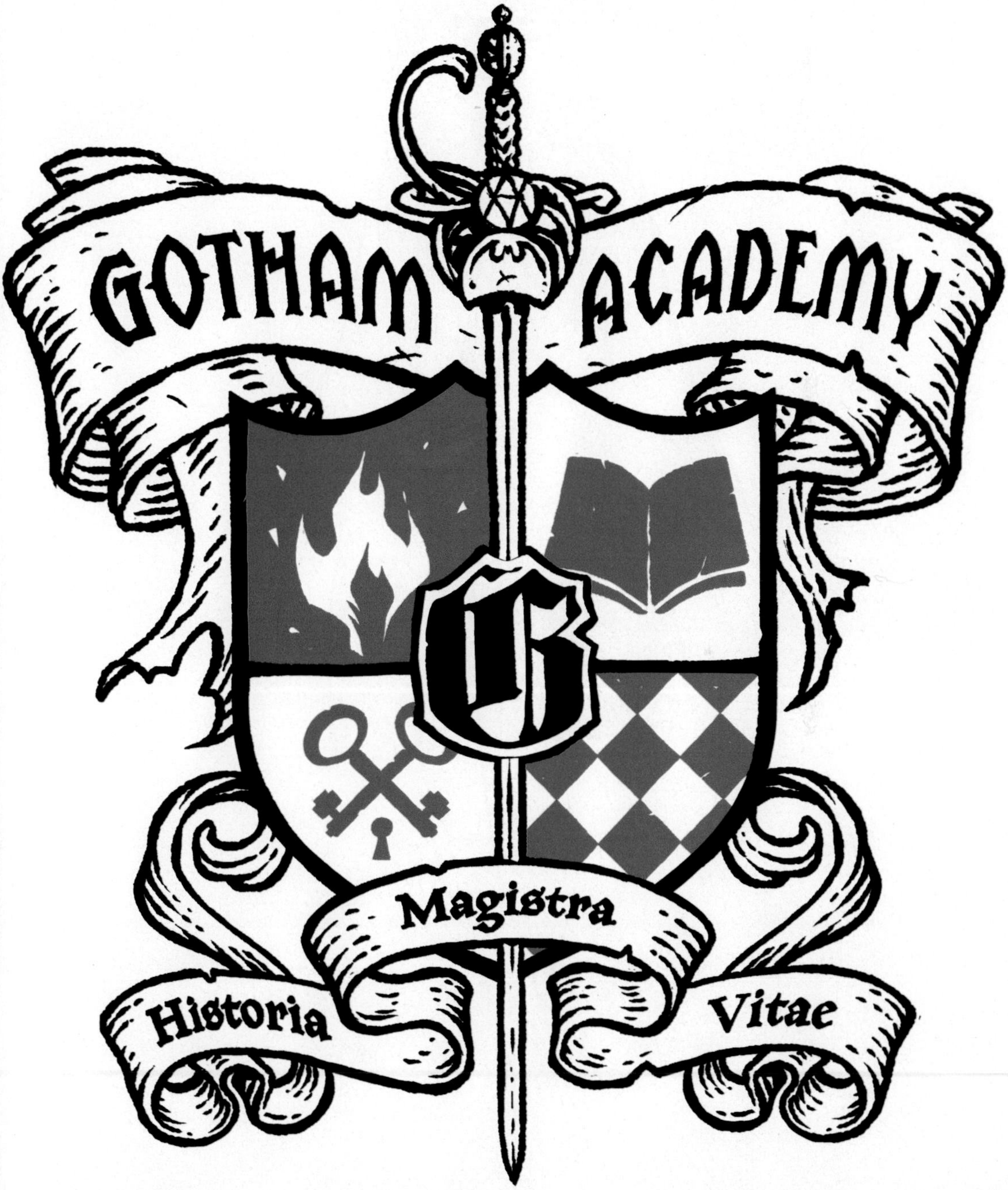
GOTHAM ACADEMY
Magistra
Historia
Vitae

We always knew the school crest would be a critical design for the series. This full version with banners and sword appears occasionally within the story but was originally intended to feature as our series logo! Look closely and you'll find secrets hidden within it. Secrets that might reveal clues to the future of Gotham Academy.

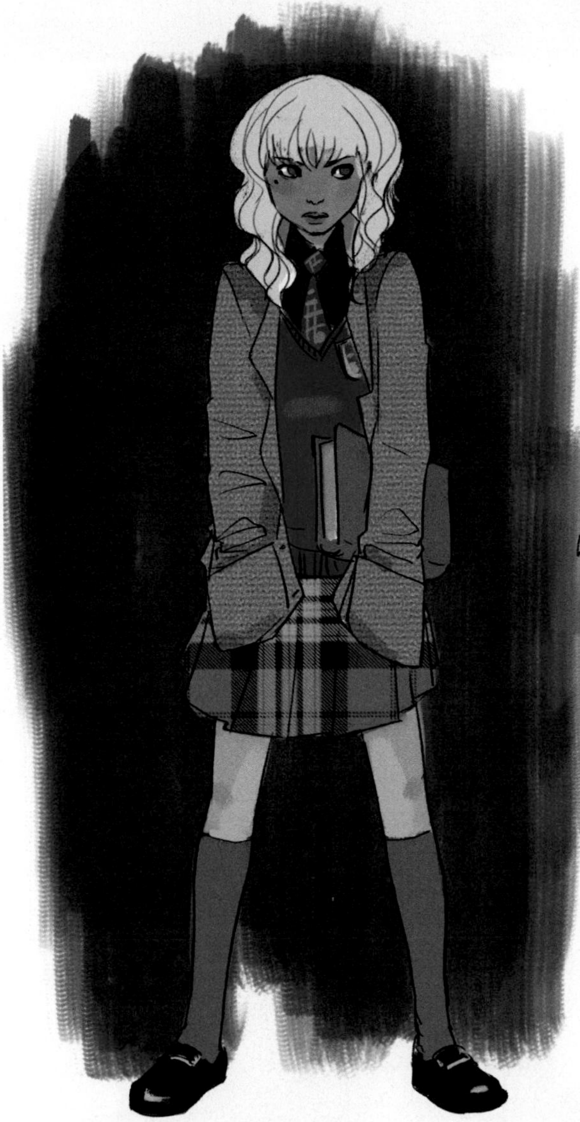

OLIVE

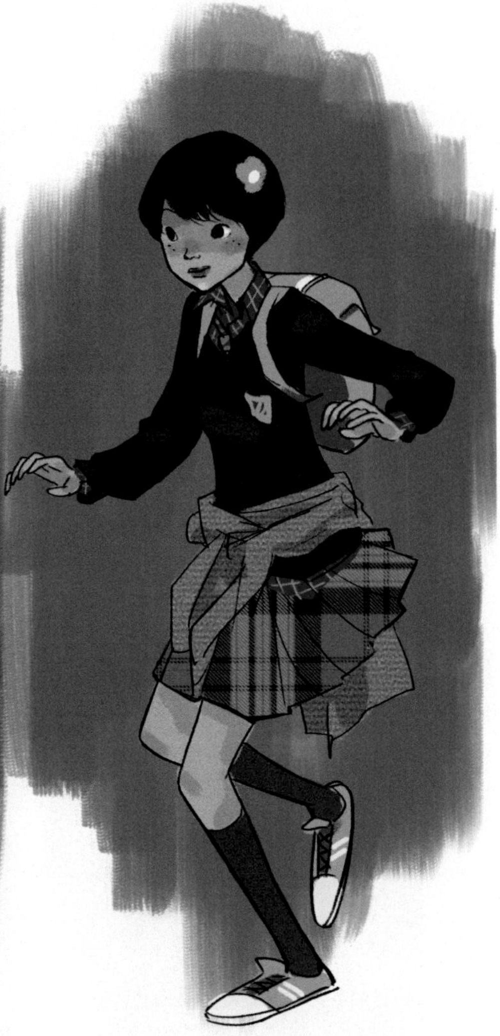

MAPS

Olive's design process was one of the longest of the cast. Because the story centers around her, I wanted her to look iconic and her hair ended up being white for that reason. Her face needed to be soft and round to project her sensitivity but I gave her red eyes to give her a formidable, otherworldly look. I kept the mole on her cheek from Becky's original design.

In contrast, Maps was the quickest design of the bunch. I pretty much had an exact image in my head from the moment I read the description of her — bob haircut, small in stature but huge in personality, and lots of black, yellow and gray (the same colors as a certain Gotham crime-fighter).

Kyle has the same color scheme as Maps because they're siblings. He sports a tennis visor almost all the time, and he's really into his shoes (that was in his character description!). He's basically designed to look like a K-Pop heartthrob.

Pomeline's wardrobe was referenced from a lot of goth fashion photography, though she still wears the Academy skirt and jacket (because those are the rules). Her jewelry is all based on real-world designs by our friend Elaine Ho. Pomeline's eyebrows are huge and severe and I love them.

I wasn't sure what to do with Heathcliff, design-wise. I went through a few different looks and then Brenden suggested that I reference Morrissey, so that's where his hairstyle and attitude came from.

–**KARL**

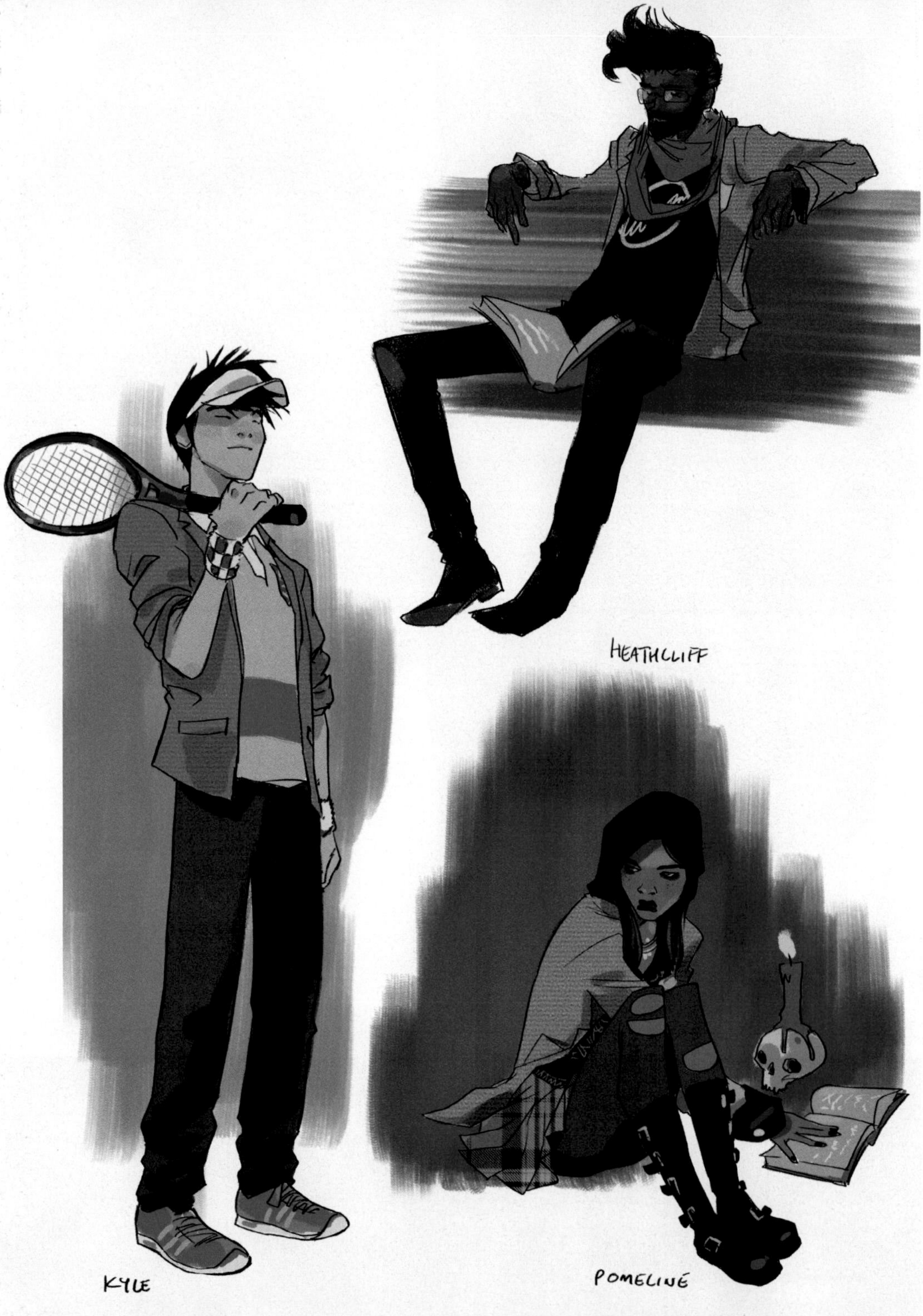
HEATHCLIFF
KYLE
POMELINÉ

COLTON

ERIC

Becky and I went back and forth a lot on Colton's design. She would leave little sketches on my desk of what she thought he should look like, and I would mostly ignore them. :) His final look is actually inspired by Israel Broussard in *The Bling Ring*.

Everything about Eric is awkward and ill-fitting. His pant hem is too high, his jacket is too big, his hair is greasy and unkempt, and he's just uncomfortable in his own skin. He also sweats a lot. I'm embarrassed to admit that his face is mostly just a rehash of the way I drew Aqualad in TEEN TITANS: YEAR ONE, because I think it's hilarious

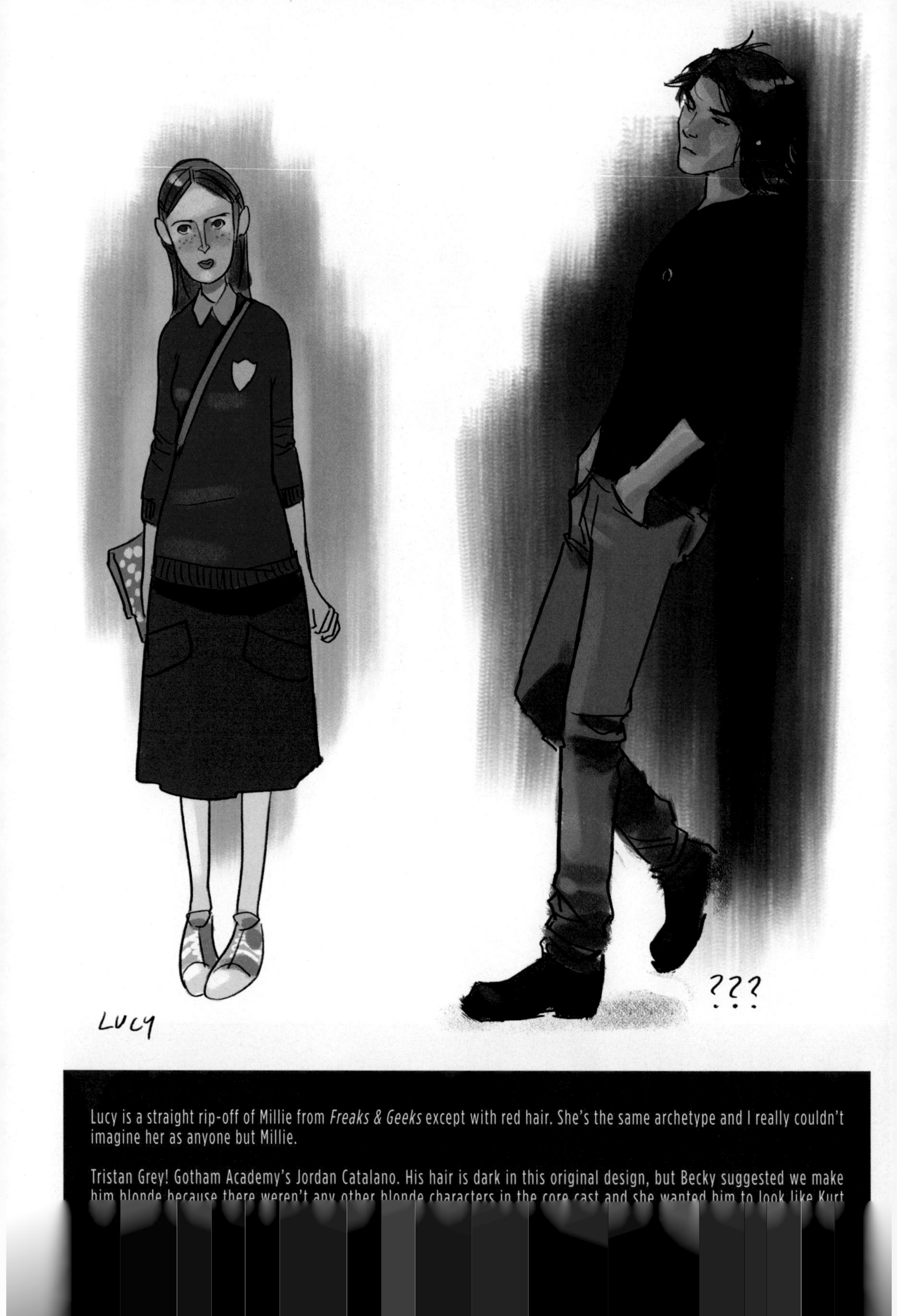
LUCY
???

Lucy is a straight rip-off of Millie from *Freaks & Geeks* except with red hair. She's the same archetype and I really couldn't imagine her as anyone but Millie.

Tristan Grey! Gotham Academy's Jordan Catalano. His hair is dark in this original design, but Becky suggested we make him blonde because there weren't any other blonde characters in the core cast and she wanted him to look like Kurt

Professor Macpherson started out as this Scottish redhead but she looked a little too much like Barbara Gordon, so I gave her dark, cropped hair with bangs. Now she looks less like a stuffy teacher and more like a confidant. I'm pretty sure she rides a motorcycle.

—KARL

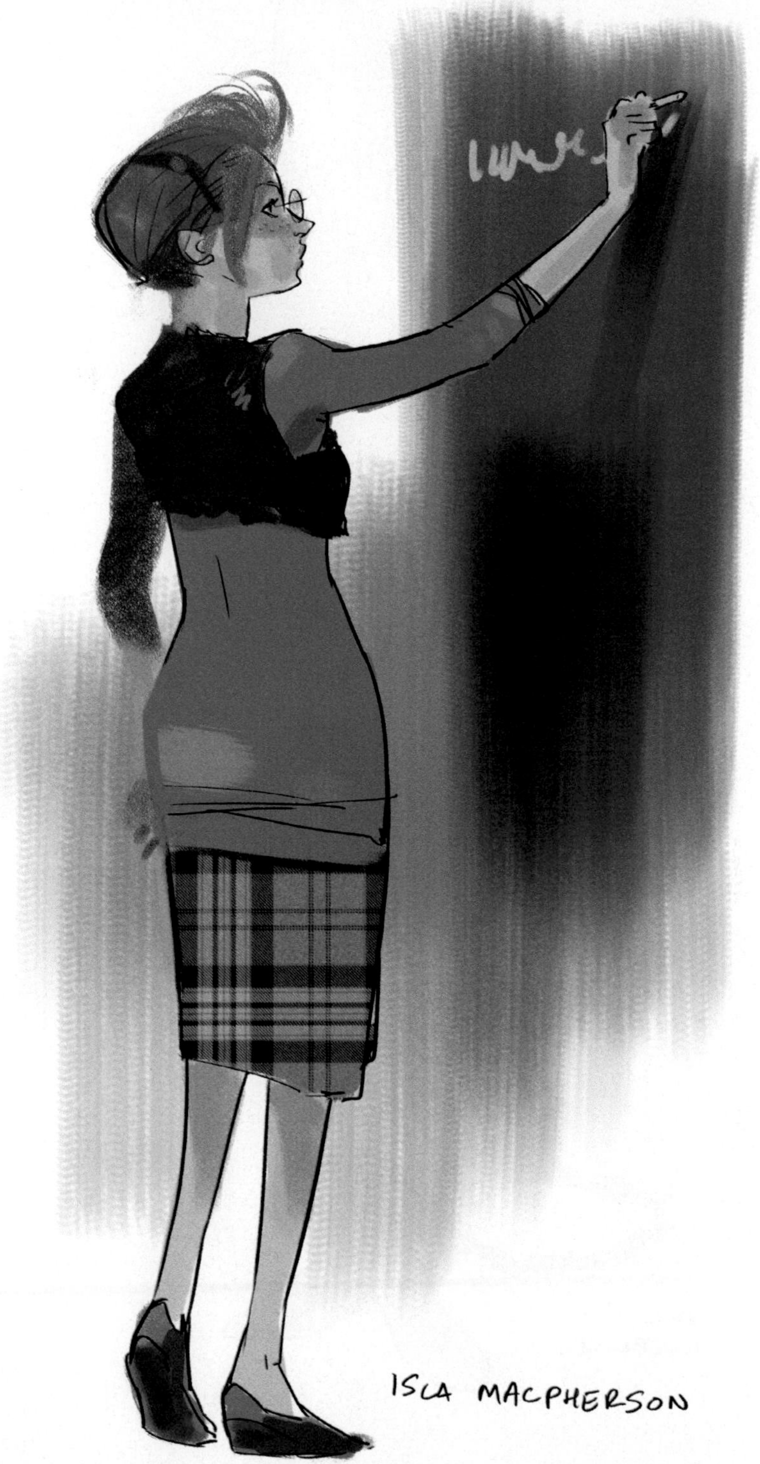
ISLA MACPHERSON

SYBIL
SILVERLOCK

## KARL KERSCHL SKETCH FOR AN UNUSED COVER CONCEPT FOR GOTHAM ACADEMY #6

I really love the idea of Olive & Croc together. Unfortunately, because of the way cover solicitations are released, this would have run before readers knew that Croc was the monster in the walls. Spoilers!!

—KARL

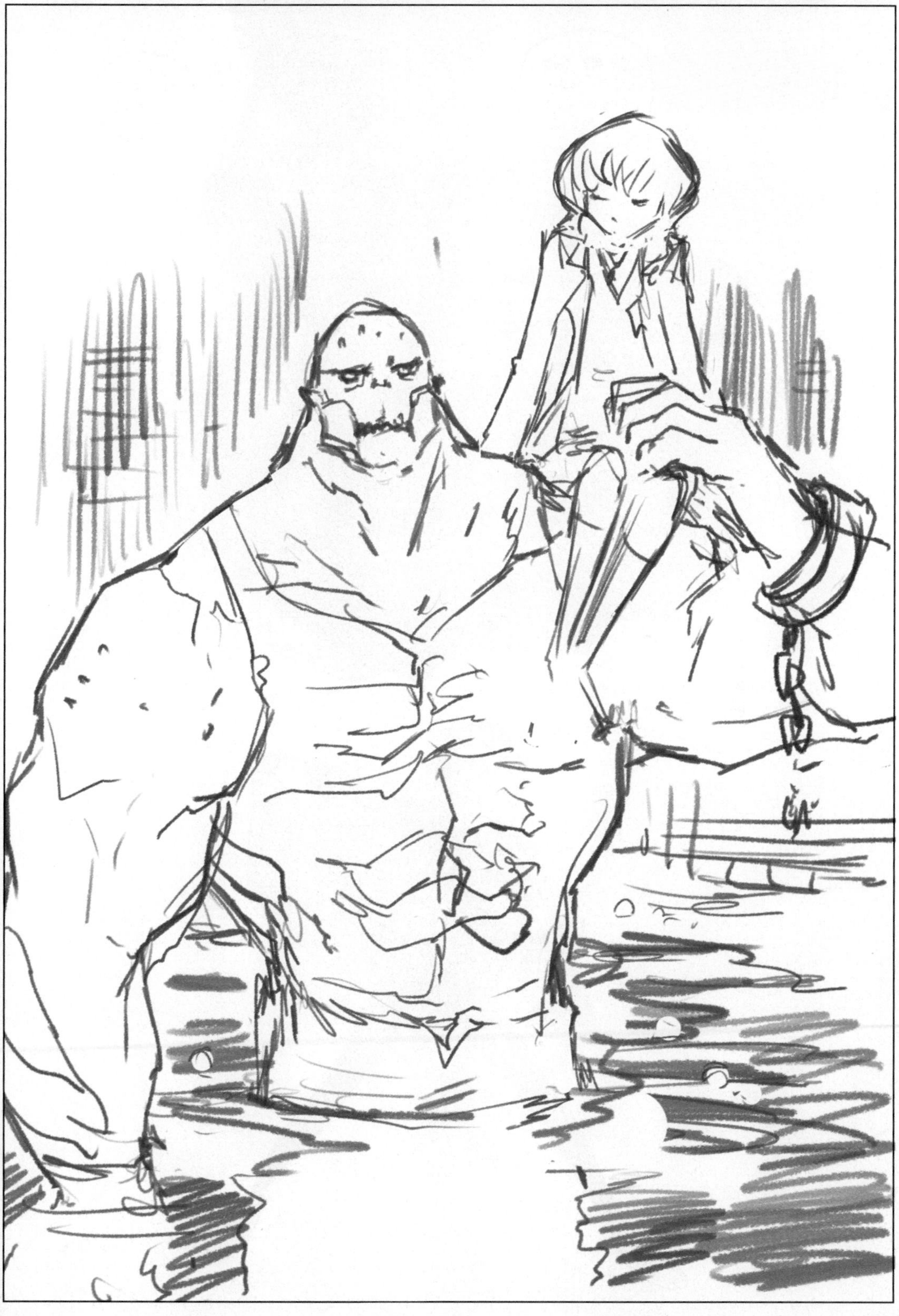

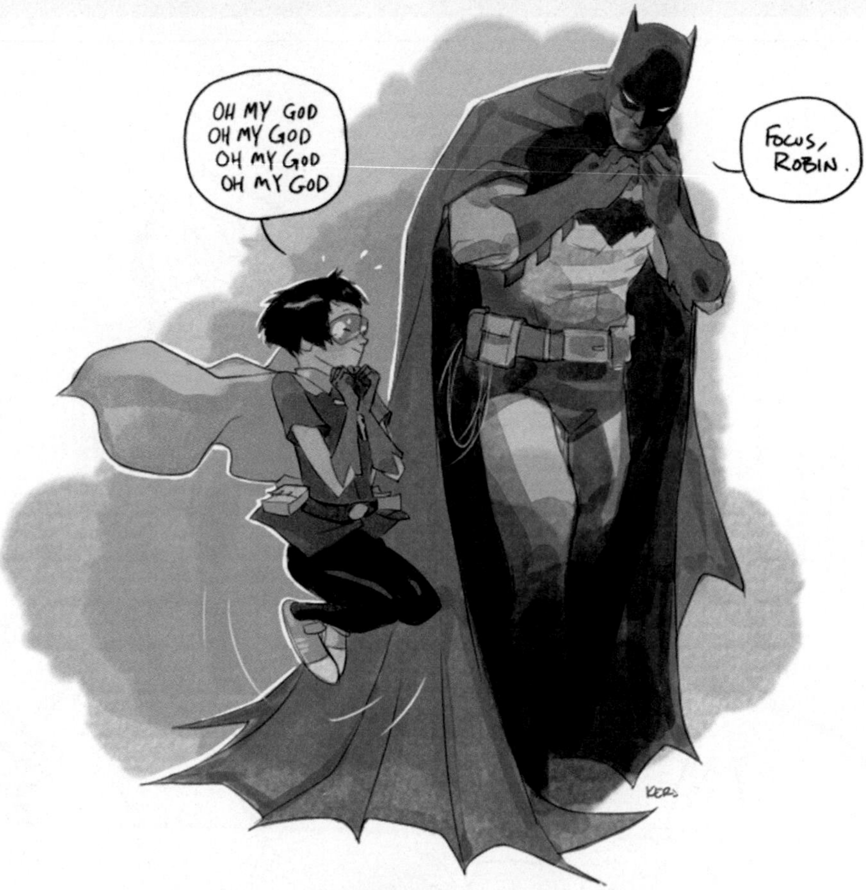
OH MY GOD
OH MY GOD
OH MY GOD
OH MY GOD
FOCUS, ROBIN.

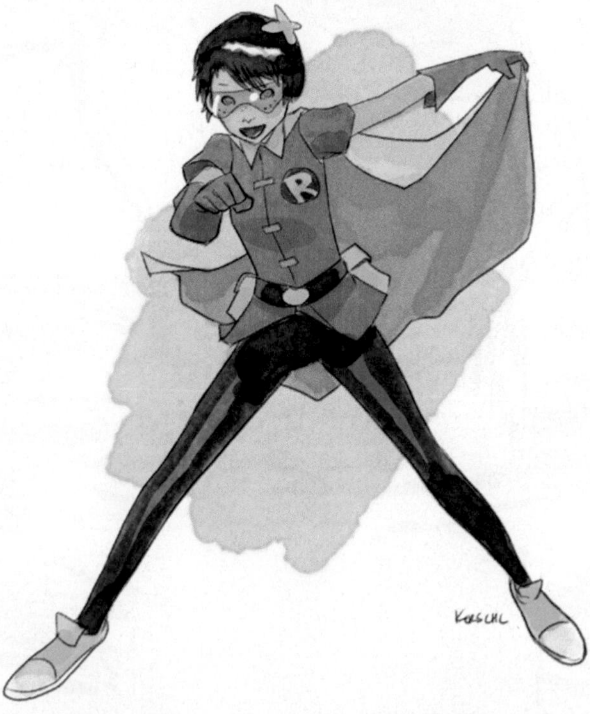

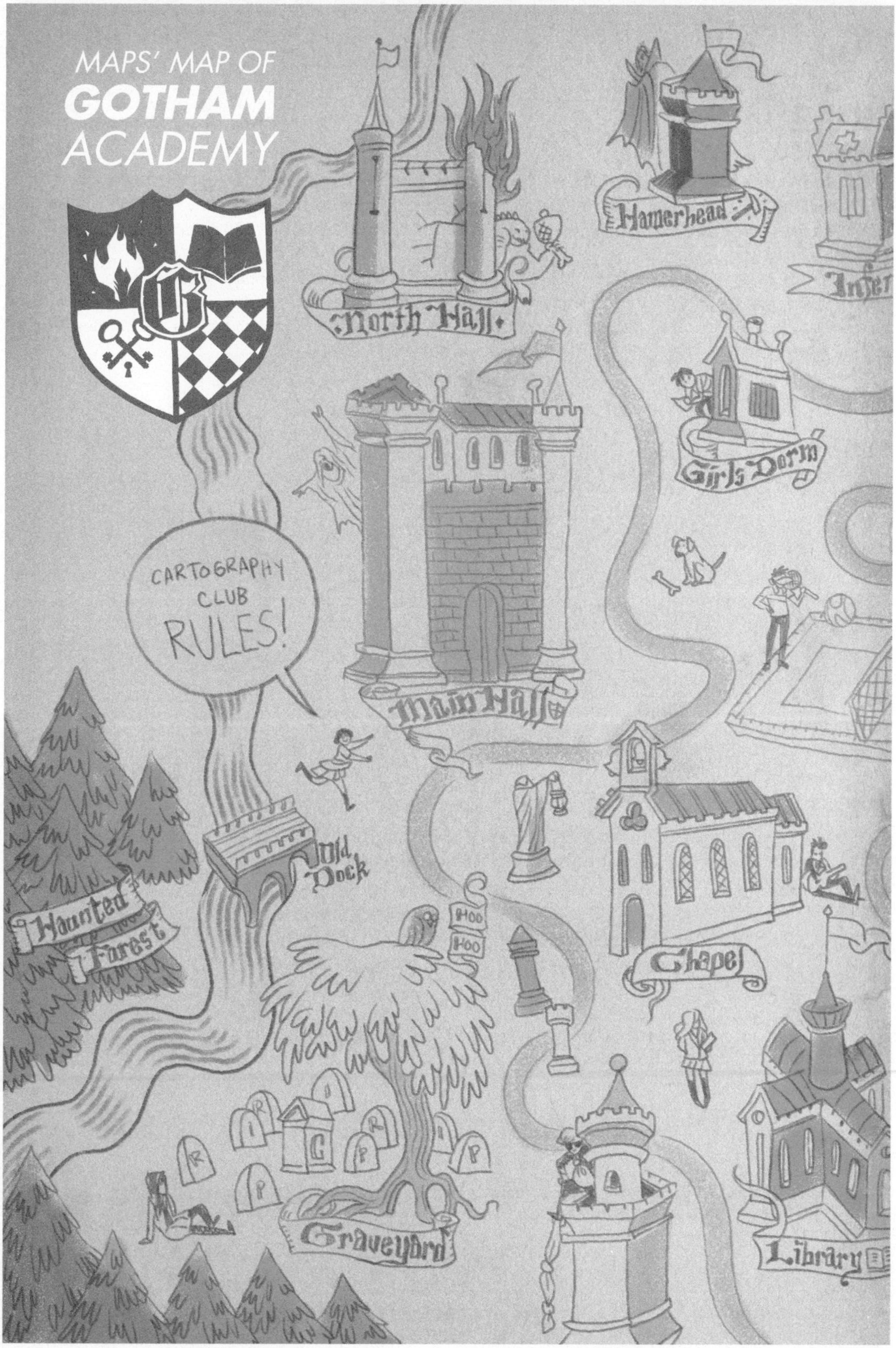

MAPS' MAP OF
GOTHAM
ACADEMY
North Hall
Hamerhead
Girls Dorm
CARTOGRAPHY CLUB RULES!
Main Hall
Old Dock
Haunted Forest
HOO
HOO
Chapel
Graveyard
Library

# PAGE 1
## PANEL 1
Splash page. Open on a creepy ext. shot of the main hall of Gotham Academy. It's early morning. The sky is dark. Lightning strikes. It's about to rain.

# PAGE 2
## PANEL 1
Int. Headmasters office. Olive and Maps sit like frightened rabbits, awaiting a punishment for a crime they're as yet unaware of. They're seated in massive, wooden chairs, clearly taken from the set of a horror film. The chairs are set quite a distance apart from one another, on either side of the doorway leading out of the office. There's a grand staircase on the opposite end of the room, which clearly leads up to some sort of torture chamber. A large, imposing desk sits at its foot. The room is illuminated by several small candelabras and a giant chandelier.

                         MAPS
              Olive!

## PANEL 2
Maps kneels in her chair, leaning over the arm, whisper-screaming at Olive.

                         MAPS
              OLIVE!!

                         OLIVE (annoyed)
              Shhh!

                         MAPS
              What?

                         OLIVE
              Just shush. You're just gonna' make it
              worse.

## PANEL 3
POV the landing atop the staircase, looking down on the girls. An old, veiny hand rests on the bannister. Maps creeps toward Olive.

                         MAPS
              What are you talking about? Worse than
              what? Hammer-Head loves you guys! He's
              always at Kyle's tennis games, right?

                         (Beat)

              Right? I've seen him there, when mum
              brings me out. Right?

                         OLIVE
              I... I don't know, Maps.

## PANEL 4
A creepy, dark figure descends the staircase, moving toward the girls, carrying a candle.

MAPS

Mum said to say "Hi", by the way. Told Kyle to invite you for dinner. Did he invite you? You haven't been over for a while.

## PANEL 5

OLIVE (downcast)

...

MAPS (to herself)

Hammer-head. Hammer-Head.

(Beat)

OMG. Hammer. Head. Duh! Way to go, Maps. I can't believe I just got it. You call him "Hammer Head" because he's…

HAMMER (O.P.)

…The *Headmaster* of this fine academic institution, young lady!

# PAGE 3

## PANEL 1

Headmaster Hammer looks pissed, underlit by his dripping candle. Then again, he always looks pissed.

HAMMER

And you would do well to address me in a respectful manner.

## PANEL 2

Two shot of the girls.

MAPS

Yes sir. Um. Headmaster Hammer. I'm sorry, sir.

## PANEL 3

Hammer puts his candle down on the desk and opens a large, old book.

HAMMER

Your brother is a fine student. I expect nothing less from you.

MAPS

Yes sir.

## PANEL 4

He sits before them, as if prepared to pass judgement.

HAMMER

Now, I'm sure you're both wondering why I summoned you. As you *missed* orientation, Miss Mizoguchi, you are likely not aware that all first year students are assigned a junior to "nanny" them. To get them accustomed to campus life. Miss Silverlock will be yours.

MAPS (whispers triumphantly)

Yes!

## PANEL 5

> **HAMMER**
> Get her settled in the dorm after classes
> today. Find time to show her around the
> grounds before tonight's assembly. But I
> warn you, Miss Silverlock, stay clear of
> the North Hall. There was… an *incident*.
> It has been deemed structurally unsound.
> There will be grave consequences for any
> student who disobeys. Do you understand?

> **OLIVE**
> Yes, headmaster.

> **MAPS**
> Mm hm! Yessir!

## PANEL 6

Close up of Hammer.

> **HAMMER**
> Very well then. Welcome to Gotham
> Academy.

## PAGE 4-5

DOUBLE PAGE SPLASH!! (don't kill me! perhaps *THIS* should be our 2-page map?!)

This is a Chris Ware style blow-out of the main section of the campus, with panels extruding from the buildings to reveal scenes of students, faculty and mysteries.

It's raining out and Olive and Maps run across the campus lawn to class. They don't need to be the focal point of the image but should be prominent.

> **OLIVE**
> Come on! We're already late!

> **MAPS**
> Ahhh! Wet shoes!

## PANEL 1

FONT FETISH PANEL! First of many (acting as mini-chapter markers) There's a sign outside the main building that changes on a weekly basis, providing updates on school events. Today it reads:

> **SIGN**
> Gotham Academy welcomes new and returning
> students. Fall semester begins now!

## PANELS 2a, 2b, 2c - from the Gym

Possibly a short series of panels. Kyle's gym locker is open. He's packing his tennis gear away, preparing to go to class. Focus in on the inside of his locker door. There's a pic of him and Olive in cheerier times.

## PANEL 3 - from the History classroom

Professor Macpherson is writing her lesson plan on the chalkboard of her classroom.

## PANELS 4a, 4b, 4c - from the Library

Eric sits in the library, drawing in his sketchbook, copying a symbol from a book. We move deeper, and deeper into the symbol until it's abstracted. (Perhaps we use "THE SYMBOL" and create a cyclical sequence where we move from his eye to the symbol which becomes his eye, etc…)

## PANEL 5 - from the Cafeteria

Heathcliff (Pomeline's BF) and his goth-y pals sit on a table in the cafeteria, swapping black metal tapes.

**PANELS 6a, 6b, 6c - from the Science Lab**

Professor Milo is in his chem lab, which is oddly decorated with taxidermy. He pours a formula into a beaker and smoke billows out, which we can see pouring out a window in the splash image.

# PAGE 6

## PANEL 1

Olive and Maps burst through the main doors of the hall, dripping wet from the rain. Olive's books and papers look soggy.

>               MAPS
> Soaker! I knew it! Why dost thou hate me
> so, Perkwunos, vile god of weather!

>               OLIVE
> She hates me more. I don't have a backpack
> for my books.

## PANEL 2

Olive leads Maps into the hallway. A few girls walk toward them.

>               MAPS
> Well she better calm the crap down by
> this afternoon because I've got a campus
> tour coming to me!

>               OLIVE (sideways glance at Maps)
> Mmm.

>               MAPS
> And anyway, what's the deal with that
> North Hall thing? Is it true that it was
> wrecked by the Ghost of Gotham Academy?
> That's what I heard.

## PANEL 3

Pomeline and her crew smash into Olive, sending her books flying.

>               MAPS
> Is that a thing? The Ghost?

>               OLIVE
> GUH!

## PANEL 4

Olive hits the floor, her books and papers scattered everywhere. Pomeline turns to look back at her.

>               POMELINE (snarky, sarcastic)
> Oooo, ouch! Sorry, Silverlock. That's
> gotta suck. Your garbage all over the
> hall and no BF to help. Hahaha!

## PANEL 5

Maps kneels down to help Olive gather her books.

>               POMELINE (walking off in the BG)
> Better not be late for Macpherson's class!

>               MAPS
> What's her problem? You *do so* have a BF!
> She obvs doesn't know that Kyle didn't
> graduate yet, right? What did she mean
> by…

**PANEL 6**

Olive barks at Maps, pointing toward her classroom down the hall.

OLIVE

MAPS! Leave it! Just get to class, okay?!

**PANEL 7**

Maps dashes off down the hallway, toward her class as Olive sits amongst her papers, dejected.

# PAGE 7

**PANEL 1**

Prof. Macpherson's lesson plan is on the chalk board.

CHALK BOARD (in cursive)

*Professor Macpherson*

*History of Gotham City - 201*

*Module 1 - The Civil War and the Cobblepots*

*Module 2 - Rebuilding and the Waynes*

*Module 3 - Architecture and the Arkhams*

**PANEL 2**

Prof. Macpherson stands before the board, book in hand, reading to the class.

MACPHERSON

...where they made their fortune. They seemed law-abiding to Gothamites back then but time has proven their riches came at the cost of soldiers' lives.

**PANEL 3**

Olive is lost in thought, staring out the rain-streaked window.

MACPHERSON (OP)

If I read this excerpt from the diary of young Millie-Jane Cobblepot, who was only twelve at the time, you'll see the children were already somewhat aware of their family's misdeeds.

**PANEL 4**

Olive hit in the face with a spitball.

SFX

THWAK!

OLIVE

Guh!

**PANEL 5**

Colton did it. Looks pleased with himself. Pomeline and her pals also seem quite pleased.

COLTON (whispers)

Morning, sunshine!

**PANEL 6**

Olive reaction shot.